"With THE DEEP SILENCE, the devotee of action at sea will feel the spray around his armchair!"
—***The New York Times***

"An edge-of-the-chair novel of a submarine in a cold war . . . in the tradition of *the best* of British naval fiction!"
—***Arkansas Gazette***

"Mr. Reeman steers through some stirring naval engagements, guaranteed to quicken the pulse!"
—***The New York Times Book Review***

THE DEEP SILENCE

Also by Douglas Reeman from Jove

THE DESTROYERS
DIVE IN THE SUN
THE GREATEST ENEMY
HIS MAJESTY'S U-BOAT
PATH OF THE STORM
A PRAYER FOR THE SHIP
THE PRIDE AND THE ANGUISH
RENDEZVOUS—SOUTH ATLANTIC
TO RISKS UNKNOWN
A SHIP MUST DIE
STRIKE FROM THE SEA
TORPEDO RUN
WINGED ESCORT

A JOVE BOOK PUBLISHED BY G.P. PUTNAM'S SONS
DISTRIBUTED BY JOVE PUBLICATIONS, INC.

This Jove book contains the complete
text of the original hardcover edition.
It has been completely reset in a typeface
designed for easy reading, and was printed
from new film.

THE DEEP SILENCE

A Jove Book / published by arrangement with
G.P. Putnam's Sons

PRINTING HISTORY
G.P. Putnam's Sons edition published 1967
G.P. Putnam / Berkley edition / January 1979
Jove edition / December 1982
Second Jove printing / May 1984

ISBN: 0-515-07637-6

Jove books are published by The Berkley Publishing Group,
200 Madison Avenue, New York, N.Y. 10016.
The words "A JOVE BOOK" and the "J" with sunburst
are trademarks belonging to Jove Publications, Inc.

PRINTED IN THE UNITED STATES OF AMERICA

Contents

1

The Black Pig

THE BLEAK waters of the Gareloch were speckled with countless tiny whitecaps as the stiff south-westerly wind bore up from the Firth of Clyde and flattened the gorse of the distant hills like wet fur. Firmly anchored at her usual moorings, the submarine depot ship caught the dancing reflections in her tall sides, which shone with spray and the drizzle which had been falling steadily since first light.

Yet, in spite of the wind and the damp air, it was warm, even humid, for early March, and the wide stateroom of the captain commanding the submarine squadron seemed still and lifeless, and the windows which overlooked the broad expanse of open water were misty with condensation.

The captain, a compact little man with sparse greying hair, sat watchfully behind his littered desk and studied his unexpected visitor with unrelaxed caution. Senior officers were not unusual aboard the depot ship, and with the growing importance of the submarine arm of the Navy they were almost a weekly disturbance to the intricate and dedicated routine. But Vice-Admiral Ronald Vane was not just another visitor on some fact-finding tour or other. As the prime organiser and guardian of the new nuclear arm to the submarine fleet he represented something special, whose word was worth full attention.

He was known to be an unpredictable man, and his sudden arrival from London by helicopter that morning, unheralded and without the normal ceremonial, had been a bad beginning to the day.

Even allowing for the eccentricities which were to be expected from any admiral, Vane was an unusual man. He was small and thin, and dressed in a grey pin-striped suit, the wide lapels and baggy trousers of which would not have been out of place in the twenties. It was still creased from the cramped flight in the helicopter, and the captain wondered what made a man of such power and importance dress in a manner which would be shunned by his own steward.

The admiral turned suddenly, his eyes bright in his pale, lined face. 'When did the *Temeraire* come alongside?'

The captain sighed and relaxed slightly. Perhaps it was a courtesy visit after all. It seemed as if every possible person had come to see the latest addition to the new nuclear force, from technical experts to hopeful newspaper correspondents, The *Temeraire* was, after all, something very special. One of the latest hunter-killer submarines, fully equipped with a fantastic range of homing torpedoes and ultrasensitive sonar detection gear, she was fully powered with a nuclear reactor which was at the head of its field.

'She came in at dawn, sir.' The captain pushed a thick folder across his desk. 'She's completed a full three months' trials and working up, and I'm sending her on to Rosyth for a final check-up for defects.'

The admiral ignored the folder. 'I'm afraid that's no longer possible. In my briefcase I have a new set of orders for the captain. He will be required to sail tomorrow at dawn.' His tone was flat and uncompromising. 'I suppose you can see to all his requirements?'

The captain stared at him with amazement. 'But it needs another month at least, sir! There are always teething troubles at this stage. We've ironed out a lot of them, of course, but the *Temeraire*'s brand new, and we can't afford to take chances!'

The admiral eyed him coldly. 'Fortunately, the choice is not yours, Captain.' He turned his back and wiped the haze from the window with his sleeve. He was looking straight down on to the vessel in question, and he found himself wondering what gave her the strange air of menace. Her rounded black hull was devoid of all the usual clutter of conventional submarines, and, apart from the tall, wafer-thin tower, there was nothing to break her smooth outline but for the hydroplanes which were folded on either side of her bows like two sharp ears.

There was silence in the cabin, and then the captain said, 'Where will she be sailing, if I may ask?'

The admiral stared fixedly at the black shape below him for several more seconds. In the far distance the tannoy squeaked and a metallic voice intoned, 'Up spirits! Up spirits!'

Then he said with sudden impatience, 'I'd like to go aboard at once. It will save time and repetitions.'

The captain controlled his irritation and picked up his cap. 'If you'll come with me, sir.'

The admiral followed the other officer out into the noise and bustle of the upper deck where oilskinned sailors moved busily beneath the swaying derricks as fresh stores were swung out to the waiting submarines. There was the sickly smell of rum in the air, and as the admiral passed the main galley he saw the cooks putting the finishing touches to the midday meal.

Then down a steep gangway and along a well-worn catwalk where a saluting sentry led the way across to the *Temeraire*. She began to look her size, the admiral thought. Her four and a half thousand tons made her almost four times as big as her conventionally powered contemporaries, but like an iceberg most of her bulk was concealed beneath the waters of the Gareloch.

He could see the scrapes and slime on her fat hull, the scratches on the black paint below the tower, or *fin* as it was now called, and it was hard to imagine her as being so completely new and untried.

A young, harassed lieutenant was supervising the loading of a large packing case, and he looked up startled as the captain snapped, 'I'm going below. I take it your C.O. is still aboard?'

The officer nodded, his eyes wandering to the admiral with the uncertainty of a man who has been told only part of the truth. 'Yes, sir.'

The admiral climbed through the screen door of the fin and peered down the oval hatch at his feet. He was a sceptical man, but even so was instantly impressed. The average submarine was constructed something like an underground train with one central passageway running from stem to stern. From his position above the hatch the admiral could see down and down as the ladders pointed the way through three decks and into another world. He followed his guide below and across the gleaming control room. Even without the watchkeepers at their stations it was somehow alert and exciting. Rows of shining dials and repeaters, the sheathed periscopes and radar scanners, all gave the impression of immense power and strength. He wondered what else apart from size made the *Temeraire* so different from the other boats which still made up the bulk of the fleet. He decided it must be the smell.

Normally a submarine was pervaded by the unchanging odour of diesel oil and machinery. Here there was nothing of the kind. It was more of a sweetly antiseptic smell, mixed with that of sweat and cooking, a strange, unreal essence like the steel shell which contained it.

A petty officer handed the admiral a small film badge without a word and another to the captain. The latter pinned his to his jacket and said without humour, 'The usual precaution, sir. Just to make sure you don't become radio-active without anybody noticing!'

They passed down a narrow, brightly lit passageway, the sides of which were covered by pastel-coloured plastic, and which again gave the air of unreality. Outside a door labelled *Captain* the admiral said flatly, 'David Jermain, isn't it?'

The other man nodded. 'He's had command right from the time the keel was laid, sir.' He tapped on the door. 'This'll be a shock for him. The whole crew is about worn-out by the trials. They should have been going on leave from Rosyth.'

The admiral merely blinked. 'The world is unfortunately full of surprises. Not all of them pleasant!'

• • •

Commander David Jermain waited until the admiral had seated himself in the small cabin and watched his hands busy with the lock of his briefcase. Once he glanced across the little admiral's head to catch the captain's eye, but the latter merely shrugged, as if the visit was a complete mystery to him also.

The admiral drew out a narrow folder and cleared his throat. Then surprisingly he glanced around the cabin and said crisply, 'You seem very comfortable here?'

Jermain smiled gently. 'I've not had a great time to get used to it yet, sir.'

The admiral studied him thoughtfully. Jermain was an impressive figure, a man who somehow suited the boat. He was over six feet in height, with a slight stoop to his broad shoulders, the mark of many months in submarines. The admiral knew that over half of Jermain's thirty-six years had been given to the Navy, and of that more than ten years had been in submarines. In spite of his high technical ability, which the admiral knew from his records, Jermain had a strange old-world appearance which made him instantly arresting. He had a thoughtful, grave face with deep lines on either side of his mouth. But his brown eyes were faintly humorous, and when he had smiled his whole countenance had become almost youthful. His dark hair was rather too long for the admiral's taste, but it seemed to suit him nevertheless. He recalled that Jermain was a Cornishman. That probably explained it, he decided. The bleak coasts of Cornwall had produced so many sailors, navymen and pirates alike that it was easy to visualise some of Jermain's heritage.

He realised that the others were watching him and he said rather sharply, 'I am afraid that I have new orders for you, Jermain.' He dropped the folder on the small desk. 'You must complete storing and take on a fresh outfit of torpedoes and proceed to sea tomorrow at dawn.'

Jermain's eyebrows lifted slightly. 'Destination, sir?' He was still on his feet, his tall frame loose and relaxed, yet giving the impression of vigilance, like a cat.

The admiral coughed. 'Singapore. The situation in the Far East has been deteriorating lately, as you are no doubt aware. The Americans, quite rightly, expect us to do our fair share in reinforcing the nuclear screen in the area, so for that reason I cannot afford to give you any more time to complete your final trials. *Temeraire* can get a fair amount of help from the Singapore base in the way of small repairs and so forth, does that suit you?'

Jermain stared at the folio. 'I don't have much choice, do I, sir?'

'No, you do not.' The admiral glanced at his watch. 'You'll be under the local control of Vice-Admiral Sir John Colquhoun when you get there. He is having a difficult time of his own without your adding to it!' He gave a brief smile. 'Our government is bent on cutting down the naval and military strength in the area, and I am afraid that Sir John's own command is an obvious choice for the axe! However, that does not concern you. The Chinese Communist government is making fresh infiltration and troubles which we think may endanger the peace of the Far East as a whole. The Americans are keen to contain this threat, but to do so they must have our backing. Anyway, it's all in your orders.'

'My numer one has left the boat, sir.' Jermain tried to read beyond the admiral's calm eyes. 'He has been appointed to take command of the *Phoenix*, this boat's sister ship.'

The admiral replied coolly, 'I know. I ordered it myself. I'm sending you Lieutenant-Commander Ian Wolfe as your new number one.' He paused. 'Your brother-in-law, I believe?'

Jermain dropped his eyes. 'He was, sir. Married my sister about three years ago. They're divorced now.' He continued quickly, 'I thought he was in line for a command of his own, too?'

The admiral looked down at his feet. 'A further cruise as your, er, understudy might well be to his advantage, Jermain.' He stood up. 'Anyway, I want this boat ready on time. Forget the little nagging problems and concentrate on getting her shaken down into a fully operational boat! If World War Three broke out this afternoon I suspect that you would be the first to badger me to be allowed to get into action! Well, this is an emergency. We don't want another Malaysia or another Viet Nam in the Far East, and if a show of real force in the right place and at the right time can prevent it, then I think your, er, temporary inconvenience will be well worth while!'

Jermain said, 'It is asking a lot of a brand-new boat, sir.'

'I believe in asking a lot, Jermain. It's the only way I get results!' He grinned unfeelingly. 'Send me a signal when you sail. I must get back to the Admiralty, or the Ministry of Defence as our political guardians now choose to call it.' He chuckled. 'Although what we are supposed to be defending is sometimes a complete puzzle to me!'

Jermain groped for his cap. 'I'll see you over the side, sir.'

'Please, no.' The admiral tucked his briefcase under his arm. 'I don't want any ceremony. There are too many starving defence correspondents slopping gin in the depot ship's wardroom by now. One sight of me and the whole thing will be on their front pages!' He paused momentarily by the door, his eyes searching. 'When you get to Singapore you'll be working with the Americans, something which is nothing new for you with the Holy Loch just over the hill. But Singapore itself is undergoing a reappraisal by our government, and the submarine section in the Far East will become less dependent on any base there.'

Jermain frowned. 'Vice-Admiral Colquhoun has always been fully responsible for our operations out there, sir.'

The admiral shrugged. 'Things change. God knows, I've seen enough during *my* service!'

He stepped over the coaming. 'I'll go now. There's a lot of do.'

Jermain listened to their footsteps fading along the passageway and then sat down to read the folio. After a while he picked up a telephone and said, 'This is the captain. I want all officers in the wardroom in fifteen minutes.'

• • •

The *Temeraire*'s wardroom ran almost the full width of the hull and was free of all the usual clutter to be found in the old-type submarines. The overhead pipes, the mass of complex wiring, in fact all but fittings essential for the comfort of the occupants, were discreetly covered by pleasantly coloured panels of bright plastic, and even the steel cupboards and bulkhead furniture were disguised in imitation graining to give the impression of well-polished woodwork. The lighting was concealed and carefully angled so that the whole wardroom was evenly lit, as if from an open sky. Only the gentle whirr of fans and the faint quiver of the toughened hull against its fenders reminded the silent officers of their other world.

Jermain dropped into a chair at the head of the table and laid the folio in front of him. He glanced around at the eight expectant faces. Apart from the missing second-in-command, there was still one absent. He cleared his throat. 'I see that the sub is adrift. But I shall have to carry on without our junior officer.'

There were a few laughs, and then Lieutenant Drew, the antisubmarine officer, said gruffly, 'I sent him ashore for some spares, sir.'

Jermain nodded. It was strange how he never got used to Drew's harsh Australian accent. He was a tough, restless man who seemed unable to relax at any time.

He continued, 'Any plans which you may have had must go by the board.' He saw Kitson, the electrical officer, glance quickly at his golf clubs propped in one corner. 'We have fresh sailing orders, and it will be up to each one of us to get the crew cracking in time.'

Jermain had their full attention now. When he had first entered the wardroom he had immediately noticed the air of relaxed ease, almost of gaiety after the three months of strain and hard work. In addition to the rigorous trials there had been the irritations of having a mass of passengers. Technicians and surveyors from the dockyard, experts from the base, and engine specialists from Rolls-Royce. Every inch of space had seemed to be full of men with notebooks and slide-rules, so that tempers had become frayed and even small problems had provoked open clashes.

Like his officers, Jermain had imagined that apart from putting right a few minor defects all these irritations had gone for good. The admiral had made it all sound so smooth, so easy. It was as if the *Temeraire* was a mere counter on a map, instead of being the most sophisticated and complicated weapon system ever to put to sea.

He said, 'We are going to Singapore, and we sail at first light tomorrow.' He looked at Lieutenant Mayo, the heavily bearded navigating officer. 'As soon as you've had lunch get straight over to the depot ship and collect everything you want.'

Mayo was as dark and brooding as his deep voice, but like the rest of the *Temeraire*'s team was hand-picked for his job. He grimaced and plucked at his beard. 'Singapore is it? God, that's a bit hard!'

Jermain looked next at Griffin, the doctor. 'Is everyone fit, Doc?'

Griffin was all arms and legs, so that he appeared to have difficulty in folding himself into his chair. He had round, liquid eyes, and seemed quite unmoved by the submarine's sudden orders. He smiled vaguely. 'I've not done a thing since I came aboard, sir. Apart from handing out a few pieces of Elastoplast and a couple of crates of contraceptives that is!'

Mayo scowled. 'The Black Pig is the best contraceptive ever invented! Christ, you never get ashore long enough to do any damage!'

Jermain smiled inwardly. When he had first conned the *Temeraire* into the Gareloch from the builders' yard a dockyard manager had said with awe, 'God, look at this black pig!' So the name had stuck.

It was indeed fortunate that the doctor had no outstanding cases. A relief crew was at Rosyth awaiting the submarine's arrival and would no doubt be on leave up to the exact time of takeover. The admiral's orders made it clear that no delays would be tolerated. They sailed on time, no matter what.

Lieutenant-Commander Ross, the engineer, rolled an empty glass in his strong hands and studied Jermain's features for several seconds. The oldest officer aboard, he looked even older than his forty-four years. His craggy face was lined and grey from his trade, and he spoke with a sharp staccato tone used to carrying above even the most violent piece of machinery. Not that he had to worry about noise in the *Temeraire*. On her trials she had exceeded all expectations, and when running deep had eluded two stalking frigates overhead, in spite of the fact that both commanders had been given the submarine's exact course and depth.

Ross said sharply, 'Bloody typical! Twenty million pounds of equipment and they want to throw it about like so much scrap!'

Jermain shrugged. 'I'd possibly agree with you, Chief, if I thought it would solve anything.'

Ross added stubbornly, 'I can just see it. We'll get to Singapore and the base will have damn all! Just a few spares off the steam submarines from the First World War!'

Jermain sighed and flicked over the pages of the folio. Ross was a good engineer. The best he had met. But he liked to have the last word.

Sub-Lieutenant Luard, the supply officer, leaned back and

closed his eyes as if to get a better understanding of what the orders would mean to him. Normally he was a cheerful, buoyant member of the wardroom, and was quite oblivious of the crew's friendly contempt. They had nicknamed him 'The Ace' because of his dashing, neatly cropped beard and his habit of wearing an obsolete submariner's sweater on every possible occasion. He was said to look more like the old wartime submarine commanders than those gentlemen in question.

He said wearily, 'Thank God I've nearly finished stocking up!' Luard was only recently risen from the lower deck, and in moments of stress displayed a distinct Cockney accent. At other times he managed to keep it well under control. In his mind's eye he could see every item of food required to sustain eleven officers and seventy-nine ratings across thousands of miles of unseen ocean. Only that forenoon he had checked in some five and a half tons of fresh meat, six hundred dozen eggs and, most important, one hundred gallons of good navy rum. A nuclear boat was always supposed to be ready for a long cruise at any time, but nobody ever took it seriously. Until now....

Jermain said, 'There'll be a new number one coming aboard shortly. Some of you may know Ian Wolfe. He's a first-class officer, and well able to take over at short notice.' He listened to his own voice, and wondered.

He had not seen Wolfe for over a year, and then only a brief moment. What was the real reason for his command being delayed? They had been friends for many years. At Fort Blockhouse, in the Mediterranean, wherever the Navy spread its influence, they were always bumping into each other.

Then Wolfe had married Sarah, his sister, and the knots had strengthened even more. Until they had started working on the nuclear boats with the Americans at the Holy Loch.

Looking back, it was hard to gauge the exact moment when things had started to go wrong. Jermain had returned from a long training cruise to find Wolfe beside himself with anxiety and despair. It had all seemed so confused and pointless. Sarah had left him, and it appeared that things had been bad for some time. When it became obvious that she had left him for another man, an American officer from the Holy Loch, Wolfe's bitterness had changed to an all-consuming anger. He had shut himself off from Jermain's friendship, and when the opportunity had arisen he had left for another course at the opposite end of the country. After that they had drifted apart. Sarah wrote an occasional brief letter, and when the divorce came and went without fuss or publicity, the letters became even less frequent. Jermain was still baffled. He and his sister had always been so close. When their father had died just after the war, their mother had married again, and somehow along the way the threads of family had been broken for good. Jermain's home was in Polruan, overlooking the old town of Fowey and the gentle, unchanging estuary. But now there was no home, and no link with the old life. Just the *Temeraire*. The Black Pig.

He looked slowly around the table. 'It seems likely that more pressure will be brought on the government to restrict the use of Singapore as a base in its fullest sense. Boats like ours which can go for a year without refuelling if so required are quite obviously the answer. The Americans have been working towards this ideal for some time.' He broke off and stared at Lieutenant Oxley, the sonar officer.

Oxley was a debonaire, outwardly casual man who made everything he did appear easy. It was an act, but as he avoided making mistakes it was a harmless enough affectation. He would certainly be earmarked for command, if he stayed out of trouble. He asked in his quiet drawl, 'But I still don't see the jolly old point of our dashing off to Singapore right now, sir. I mean, what about our people's leave and so forth? The lads aren't going to like it at all!'

Jermain showed his teeth. 'An understatement. However, it will be up to each of you to explain it to your own men. This is a picked crew. If you like, the cream of the Navy. They're not children who have to be pampered with promises! I will address the men later, but I shall want you to tell them the bones of this change right away. There'll be letters to write and various other arrangements they'll want to make before we sail.'

Ross said dourly, 'Bloody poor show! They never have any respect for how the lads feel!'

Jermain stood and picked up the folio. 'There'll be another briefing during the dog watches.'

Mayo, the navigating officer, plucked his beard and said dreamily, 'Sixteen thousand miles. I take it we'll be going round the Cape?'

Jermain nodded, satisfied that his bombshell had at last been accepted as unavoidable. 'That's so, Pilot. Should take about five weeks.'

The petty officer steward poked his head around the curtained doorway. 'Are we ready for the lunch now, gentlemen?'

Ross snorted. 'I just lost *my* appetite!'

Luard looked up from his notebook and scowled. 'That's typical! Rack your bloody brains to arrange a suitable and nutritious menu and *you* lose your bloody appetite!'

Jermain walked back to his cabin, their laughter hanging in the air behind him. It all seemed smooth enough. Perhaps the admiral was right about the way to handle matters after all.

He looked round the deserted control room and tried to think clearly about the days which lay ahead. He had told the others that the crew were the pick of the Navy. So they were. But they were also human, and like the boat had been under constant strain.

He bit his lip and walked back to his cabin. There was so much to plan and arrange. There would be time for suppositions later.

• • •

By early evening the drizzle had ceased and the wind had all but blown itself out. In the grey light the Gareloch shone dully like old pewter, its surface broken here and there by querulous little clusters of gulls which rode up and down on the gentle swell in search of scraps from the anchored ships.

Lieutenant-Commander Ian Wolfe paid off the taxi and stood for several minutes looking along the nearest wooden pier. But for a dockyard policeman near the barbed-wire gate at the far end the place seemed deserted, and beyond the gates and the low sheds of the wharves Wolfe could see the tall, stately hull of the depot ship, her ensign making a rare patch of colour at her stern.

He sighed and picked up his suitcases. His trim, athletic build made him appear taller than he was, and at first glance his open face and even, impassive features did little to mark him apart from any other naval officer of his age and rank. But closer inspection laid bare the unnatural tenseness in the set of his jaw, a certain controlled hardness in his grey eyes which might strike a stranger as being more unexpected than a physical deformity.

Wolfe felt tired and strained, and stared towards the distant town of Faslane with something like distaste. The long journey from the south of England had left him empty and irritable, and he had to quell the urge to speak his resentment aloud.

He strode towards the pier, his steps ringing hollowly on the wet timbers, his eyes fixed on the distant flag. He had been in Chatham when he had received his fresh orders for the *Temeraire.* He wondered why the change of events had not affected him more. Collins, the officer who had been given command of *Phoenix*, the new nuclear boat building at Barrow, had taken what should have been his. Not that there was any point in laying the blame at his doorstep. Their Lordships were quite oblivious to personal hopes and thwarted ambitions. Officers came and went, slotted and docketed like so many items of equipment.

It would be strange to serve with David Jermain again. He quickened his pace in time with his thoughts, his brain already exploring a new threat, a fresh change of fears. For months Wolfe had totally immersed himself in the study of his trade. He had ploughed fixedly through transistor theory, digital computing, Boolean logic and electronic circuitry, and the hundred and one other brain-wrenching problems he was required to master for his final command. And every hour of the day and night he was haunted by her face, the girl he had loved and lost to the American. Sarah, the strange, restless girl whose gipsy-style beauty had made him a slave at first sight when he had shared a leave with Jermain in the Cornish cottage.

He had imagined that a total involvement with his work would ease, if not actually banish, the misery from his mind. He never found theory easy to absorb, and he was more at home on an open bridge than in a classroom. He had been shocked to find that the reverse had happened.

The early warnings had shown themselves in lack of sleep. Then he had made stupid mistakes and omissions in his work, and twice he had lost his temper with the hard-pressed instructors.

But when he had found himself drinking just that bit more

heavily each night in his quarters he had seen the warnings for himself. Almost guiltily he had contacted a private psychologist in London, and while his classmates enjoyed their brief weekends with their families or friends, Wolfe made his secret visits to the quiet consulting room in London.

The thought of being discharged from the Navy had forced him to take this final step. He knew well enough that his career was the only thing holding him together.

Now he was joining Jermain as second-in-command. For a 'refresher' prior to actual command, as the admiral had so dryly indicated. Or was it merely to satisfy the Staff that he was only fit for second fiddle? Or nothing at all!

He stopped dead, the sweat like ice beneath his cap. He forced his nerves to return to normal with something like physical effort. It would be good to see David again, but for the nagging fear of his reminding him of Sarah.

Wolfe often wondered what Jermain really thought about him and his sister. Jermain had never married, had seemed strangely content with the almost monastic existence of a naval officer. Yet Wolfe knew that it was largely because of Sarah that Jermain had missed several promising chances. He had seemed determined that she would never be alone, and had sent for her to live near whatever base his ship was using. Wolfe guessed that because of this close tie Jermain would be feeling a sense of loss in his own way.

He noticed suddenly that there was a small group of figures huddled behind a hut at the side of the pier entrance. They were young teenagers in crumpled windcheaters and jeans, their bodies jammed together for warmth and comfort. Wolfe saw that two of them carried a rain-faded C.N.D. banner, and some of the others were listening to a raucous transistor radio.

He realised it was Sunday tomorrow. The usual invitation to ban-the-bomb enthusiasts to congregate around the Holy Loch or the Gareloch and chant their slogans to all and sundry.

Temeraire was probably the only British nuclear boat alongside at the moment, so this little gathering was no doubt for her benefit, he thought.

He felt the old anger moving again. Any little thing seemed to set it going. These long-haired teenagers, for instance. They would chant and protest like sheep until the *Temeraire* sailed.

Then it would be quite all right apparently for the other conventional submarines to stay in the Gareloch unmolested! As if being blasted to bloody fragments wasn't bad enough!

He swung round with a start as a young sub-lieutenant stepped from the group and saluted. He was a pale, almost delicate-looking youth, with the wide apprehensive eyes of a startled fawn. He said, 'Can I give you a hand with the bags, sir? I expect you'll be going aboard *Temeraire*?'

They fell in step as the policeman opened the gates and glanced at their passes. Wolfe had thought he would resent an early intrusion to his brooding, but the boy's casual acceptance seemed somehow soothing.

His name was apparently Max Colquhoun, the *Temeraire*'s most junior officer. He had been despatched ashore for some spares and was now returning to the ship.

Wolfe asked, 'Have you been aboard long?'

Colquhoun shrugged. 'Since she commissioned. My first real appointment actually.'

Wolfe smiled in spite of his tension. How the submarine service was changing, and changing fast. Gone were the days of oily hands, dirty sweaters and weeks-old beards. It was a clean, businesslike trade where young officers went in at the bottom and studied more like apprentices than junior watchkeepers of the old days. He asked, 'You knew I was coming then?'

Colquhoun sounded vaguely defensive. 'The gatekeeper just told me.'

'And those layabouts you were talking to. What the hell did you find to speak about?'

'Nothing really.' Colquhoun quickened his pace as a seaman ran down the brow from the depot ship to collect the bags.

His voice sounded sharper, Wolfe thought, like a little boy caught out. He sighed inwardly. What the hell! The sub-lieutenant could chat to Jesus Christ for all he cared!

On the other side of the big ship's main deck Wolfe stood looking down at the dull-painted submarine. Inside that fat hull was escape. A complete isolation which was more definite than distance or time. This was all he required. The London psychologist could go to hell from now on.

He clambered across the catwalk and returned the trot sentry's salute. A small group of men were mustered by the

Temeraire's ensign staff, and an officer watched the depot ship's yard, waiting for the official Sunset to be sounded and the flag lowered.

Wolfe swung round and found his hand gripped firmly by another.

Jermain said quietly, 'Good to have you aboard, Ian. The Pig will go like blazes now!'

Overhead from the depot ship's rail a bugle blared the Alert. But Wolfe did not hear it, nor did he trust himself to speak. He looked at Jermain's grave face and knew that he too was glad to be here. Not only that, he *needed* to be here.

• • •

Jermain paused in the forward torpedo space and watched as Wolfe ran his hand over one of the polished breeches. He had taken Wolfe on a quick conducted tour of the boat, down through the three decks, the crew spaces and storerooms, the galley and the control room. Approximately in the centre of the submarine was a massive bulkhead which separated the living and storage quarters from the vessel's driving power and the secret reactor room. The watertight door in the bulkhead was known jokingly as Checkpoint Charlie, and no unauthorised persons were ever allowed access to the engineer's private world beyond.

Now, in the very stem of the hull, behind the six torpedo tubes, he awaited Wolfe's first reactions.

Wolfe said suddenly, 'There's still a lot to get used to.'

Jermain studied him thoughtfully. His friend was changed even more than he had expected. It was nothing you could lay a name to. He seemed as alert as ever, and his keen interest was obvious. But there was something lacking. He seemed without his old dry humour, as if it had been forcibly removed.

He said, 'You'll soon catch on. It'll be a good chance to put your hard work into practice.'

They climbed up past the sick bay, where an attendant was polishing glass beakers, and back up another ladder towards the wardroom. Jermain glanced into each compartment as he passed and tried to gauge the reactions of his men to the sailing orders. It was always difficult to tell with men like these. An individual who was nursing some grievance or fear might be slow to display it before the rest.

The coxswain, a thickset giant of a man, padded from the chief petty officers' mess and called, 'All the men are off shore now, sir. Except for the postman, an' he's just taken the mail to the dock office.' He stared at Wolfe with a pair of bright, clear eyes. 'I hope you'll be happy aboard, sir.'

Jermain grinned. 'No doubt you'll look after him!'

The coxswain rocked back on his heels. 'That's right, sir. Twine's the name. Any time you want anything done aboard, just drop me the wink!'

They passed on, leaving the massive C.P.O. standing by his mess.

Wolfe remarked, 'They seem a happy lot.'

'They'll need to be, Ian. Cooped up aboard on trials is bad enough, but a further long cruise without even surfacing will test their will to survive!'

They entered the wardroom, where Baldwin, the petty officer steward, was busy refilling glasses for the assembled officers.

Jermain said quietly, 'If you want to drink, Ian, now's the time.' He did not see the quick hardness appear in the other's eyes. 'The ratings are all right for their rum when we're at sea, but for us it's almost a teetotal cruise. We're kept on the hop too much for a bout of mess life!'

Wolfe relaxed slightly and forced his mouth to smile as he was introduced to the other officers. They appeared to be a good bunch, he thought. The engineer officer looked a bit of a binder, and the navigating officer, Mayo, might well prove an irritating companion with his gloomy face and deep, husky voice.

Jermain took a glass and raised it to the light. 'A toast, gentlemen. To Singapore, and whatever lies beyond!'

They drank in silence, and then Colquhoun's voice broke into the pause, as if he was unable to control it. 'Sir, I understand we're sailing tomorrow morning?'

Lieutenant Oxley, the sonar officer, grinned. 'God, has the penny dropped?'

Colquhoun ignored him and kept his eyes fixed on the captain. His face was quite white, and Jermain could see the muscles twitching at the corners of his mouth. 'Could I ask for a transfer, sir?'

Jermain lifted his hand as several of the others started to speak. 'What's the matter, Sub? I'd have thought you'd have liked the idea, your father being the vice-admiral there?'

Colquhoun dropped his eyes and seemed to go limp. 'I—I'm sorry, sir. I just thought . . .'

Mayo banged down his glass. 'God Almighty! You should be proud of the chance to sail on this trip, Sub! I don't know what's got into you!'

Jermain stared at the sub-lieutenant. 'I'm afraid it's too late for second thoughts now, Sub. The mail is posted, the shore telephone disconnected.' He glanced at the bulkhead clock. 'And in four hours the Chief here will be pulling the first control rods in the reactor to start it "cooking". And then at 0600 we slip and proceed as ordered.' He picked up his cap. 'Now, if you'll excuse me I'm going to the depot ship to pay my respects to Captain S/M.'

Colquhoun looked at Jermain's broad shoulders, then with the others still staring at him gave a short gulp and ran from the wardroom.

Lieutenant-Commander Ross peered at his glass. 'I have a feeling that this trip'll separate the men from the boys,' he said dreamily.

2

An Ugly Word

JERMAIN STEPPED into the control room and glanced briefly at the clock. Ten minutes to go.

The brightly lit compartment seemed full of intent figures, each man busy with his own private checks and double checks as orders were passed back and forth through the boat's maze of telephones and radio handsets.

Jermain acknowledged the formal greetings and walked through into the chart-room where Mayo was stooping over the glasstopped table, a pair of dividers in his thick hand. He looked up and said, 'Wind's freshened during the night, Captain. Gone round to the south too.'

Jermain nodded and flicked over the pages of the log. He could feel the tension rising within him like a flood, his heart pounding in time to the relayed orders and muffled clatter of machinery. He never got used to it. Never felt quite sure that all would go exactly as the last time.

It was not just holding command, with all that it could mean to a man's nerves, it went far deeper. The power and meanings of the *Temeraire*, her stupendous cost and value, her very presence was always hanging over him like some untamed beast. Jermain often had the nagging feeling that if he once relaxed or turned his back, like the over-confident lion tamer in the cage, he would never get a second chance.

He looked at Mayo's bearded face and wondered if he ever had the same qualms.

A messenger peered in at them. 'Five minutes, sir!'

Jermain had already been right round the boat. There was nothing more he could do. Lieutenant-Commander Ross had reported that the sealed reactor had gone 'critical' and there was power to respond to all orders. On the deck above, Lieutenant Drew was supervising the wires which still held the boat to her parent ship, and was no doubt cursing the rain and cold in his rich Queensland vocabulary.

Jermain buttoned his oilskin around his throat and checked his glasses before slinging them on his chest. Through the door he could see the coxswain sitting by his wheel beside the planesman, the pair of them looking more like pilot and co-pilot of some weird aircraft than seamen.

Behind them, his face masklike in the overhead lights, Wolfe stood with his arms folded, his eyes fixed on some point above the helmsman's head. At his elbow, a messenger waited for any sudden change of orders or swift emergency.

Jermain took a last look round. Nothing had been overlooked, as far as he could tell. They were all trained men. They must be treated as such.

He walked to the foot of the long, shining ladder and began to climb. In passing he tried to catch Wolfe's eye, but the man seemed absorbed in his duties and did not turn his head.

Up and up. Through the surface navigation bridge, where a messenger and a communications rating stood shivering below the open hatch and the angry-looking sky above.

Jermain stepped from the ladder and into the tiny cockpit at the tip of the fin, the highest point in the boat. He waited a few seconds for his eyes to get accustomed to the gloom, and then he peered over the screen towards the forecasting where seamen moved restlessly around the wires, their caps making bright splashes of white against their shining oilskins and the black hull below them.

It was a bad morning, he thought. The low scudding clouds

and steady drizzle seemed to try to prevent the daylight from reaching the water, and only across the distant, craggy hills could he see any sort of detail.

The fin swayed lazily in the swell, and the starboard side squeaked against the depot ship's fenders. Jermain could see the usual cluster of figures atop the big ship's rail, including the white cap and gold leaf of Captain S/M, who was no doubt watching everything like an anxious mother.

Lieutenant Victor, the assistant torpedo anti-submarine officer, stood at his side, shifting from one foot to the other. Unlike any of the others, Victor found his rank and appointment hard to carry. He had come up the hard way from the lower deck only three years earlier, and at thirty-two was already deeply lined, and his hair was thin and greying. He had been happy as a rating, and had accepted each small promotion with satisfaction, if not actual surprise. Then with the growing technical requirements of the Service he had been recommended for a commission. At first he had been flattered, and his wife had been quick to urge him onwards, to take the one irrevocable step.

Gone was the coarse but good-humoured life of the petty officers' mess, the 'middle of the road' which had always seemed so clear and safe. The wardroom cult was harder to understand, the social divisions more difficult to overcome.

Victor was a good technical man, but his lack of imagination was a tremendous handicap for his new role. As a rating he had always understood that once a man was an officer he was in a world apart, a world so tight and unified that it faced outwards with calm dignity and constant self-control. Yet, in spite of similar uniforms and ranks, the officers were as unlike each other as chalk and cheese. At the top of the tree were the professional, Dartmouth-trained executive types, men like Jermain and Wolfe, and Oxley, the sonar expert. Then there were the indestructible and essential branch officers, engineers like Ross, and Griffin, the doctor. At the bottom of the ladder were the others. Victor knew he had over-simplified it all, but he could find no other explanation. Why else was it, for instance, that even now he was inwardly sweating as he stared at the captain's shoulders? As if expecting a reprimand, or some patronising comment. He knew he was being unfair to Jermain, but at the same time he did not want another letdown.

Once, when he had been first commissioned, Victor had been serving in a small patrol submarine at Gosport. He had just begun to feel at home, settled at last in his new uniform. The boat's captain had been a young lieutenant, a casual, self-assured officer who had apparently done all he could to make Victor welcome. Then one night there had been a wardroom party ashore and Victor had got very drunk. Happily he had stood on a table singing one old song after another while the other officers and their wives had watched him spellbound.

They had applauded him, and clapped his shoulder. For Victor the sun was truly at its zenith. When he had sailed on trials the following morning he had heard the captain speaking to the first lieutenant about the incident.

The latter had remarked casually, 'Our new Fourth Hand seemed to have a fund of songs, sir.'

The captain's reply had been icy and irritable. 'All the same, these bloody rankers! Give 'em an inch and they soon revert to type!'

Victor awoke from his brooding thoughts with a jerk as Jermain said, 'Let go springs!'

The wires grated across the steel hull, and from aft Petty Officer Jeffers, the second coxswain, yelled, 'Grab 'old of that wire, Archer! Stone me! You're like a bleedin' tart in a trance this mornin'!'

Jermain smiled briefly. 'Stand by!'

He lifted his glasses and swung them over the anchorage. Two dark frigates, still undisturbed at their moorings, and a small coastal minesweeper waiting to guide them down the channel.

There was a momentary break in the clouds, and a shaft of silver light played across the choppy water and lit up the *Temeraire*'s white number, S-191, on the side of her fin.

A few gulls circled overhead, and Jermain saw a scruffy drifter pushing down-channel towards Helensburgh.

He cupped his hands. 'Slack off the headrope!'

He saw Drew goading his small party in the bows, and watched as the dripping wire went slack and allowed the bows to swing slowly with the wind away from the depot ship's side.

Unlike older submarines, *Temeraire* had only one screw. It made her control and speed more silent at depth, but handling her on the surface was another matter.

The Captain S/M's voice floated from above. 'Good luck, David! Have one for me when you touch land again!'

Jermain lifted his hand but did not take his eyes from the widening gap of sloshing water. 'Slow ahead! Let go aft!'

The plating beneath his boots trembled only slightly, and he found that he was holding his breath. 'Port ten!'

With a gentle slop of spray around her bows the submarine began to circle away from the protection of the depot ship's side. Once clear, the wind and rain splattered into the small cockpit and rattled against the glass screen.

Jermain squinted at the gyro repeater, watching the minesweeper turn obediently as if on a string. 'Midships. Steer one five zero.' He half listened to his orders being repeated into the handset and wondered how Wolfe was coping below. He seemed collected enough. This trip, unwanted or not, might be the making of him.

The mooring wires had been lashed and stowed, and Drew clattered up the ladder and said breathlessly, 'All secure for sea, Skipper!' He peered across at his assistant. 'Christ, Jeff, you look like death this fine mornin'!' He grinned at Jermain. 'Still, he's not a bad bloke!'

Victor's thin mouth twisted into a smile. He wanted to reply with some cutting remark, something to whittle Drew down to size. Victor hated his brash familiarity before the captain, his earthy behavior with the men.

Jermain said calmly, 'Take over the con. I'm going to the control room.'

Drew rubbed his gloved hands. 'Aye, aye, Skipper. One five zero an' follow me leader!' He waited until Jermain had lowered himself through the hatch and then yelled down to Petty Officer Jeffers, 'Get those men fell in for leavin' harbour! This'll be the last fresh air they get for a bit!' To Victor he added, 'This is more like it, eh?'

The other man ducked as a curtain of spray lifted over the fin and soaked his face. 'If you say so.'

Drew winked at the signalman who swayed nearby with a small hand-lamp. 'That's what I like to hear, man! A real spirit of adventure! No wonder we've lost the bloody empire!'

Without either pipes or bugles to pay her respect the

Temeraire passed quietly down-channel, a black silhouette like some child's drawing, her wash hardly disturbing the moored yachts and still-sleeping warships.

• • •

Four hours had passed since the *Temeraire* had slipped her moorings, and with a stiffening wind pushing to meet her she thrust her round snout into each successive roller with something like anger.

Thirty feet above the deck in the open cockpit Jermain felt the spray and rain stinging his cheeks like wet sand, and he sensed the old exultation slowly replacing the strain, as alcohol will unwind a man's taut nerves.

Wedged by his side Wolfe stared into the weather and wiped the lenses of his glasses before training them across the screen. As the submarine pushed steadily down the Firth of Clyde he could see the unbroken line of the coast some four miles to port, whilst looming out of the spray like a grey smudge on the opposite beam he could just make out the lonely rock cluster of Ailsa Craig. A mile ahead of the yawing submarine the little minesweeper still manfully led the way, her frail wooden hull shining like glass as she rolled from one sickening arc to another.

Jermain shouted, 'When we dive it'll be as peaceful as a vault! You can pour a cup of coffee and hardly see a ripple!'

Wolfe nodded and swallowed a momentary pang of nausea. Too long in a classroom, he thought bitterly. Too long with memories and tortured hopes for company.

Jermain glanced sideways at his friend. 'How does it feel to be back?'

Wolfe considered the question. After the first tensions of getting under way, the unfamiliar feel of the control room, and the strange, alien faces of the men around him, he had slowly managed to find himself once more.

Once clear of the loch and butting into the open water he had handed over to the O.O.W. and joined the rest of the officers at a hasty breakfast. Hasty because the *Temeraire* was heading to sea, and there would be enough time later for looking inwards. Now the officers and men not required for immediate duty squeezed into the small surface navigation bridge below the cockpit, taking that last look at the land. By the ladder, smoking and hardly speaking, the next batch of men would wait their turn.

Wolfe replied, 'Good. It feels good.'

Jermain squinted over the bows, watching the dark-sided waves with their angry, curling crests. Submerged it would be peaceful, and there would be time to start work again. In her natural element the submarine looked clean and different, her rounded hull gleaming like the skin of a whale, with the surging water creaming back and over her sloping foredeck in an inverted horseshoe of frothing foam and spray.

He said, 'Increase revs for fifteen knots. Inform the escort, Bunts.'

The rating with the signal lamp nodded and cradled it in the crook of his arm. As the lamp clicked busily Jermain saw an answering stab of light from the minesweeper's swaying bridge. He said, 'I think if I had to go back to general service I'd spew my guts out!'

The rating intoned, 'Signal from escort, sir. "What is your diving position and time?"'

Jermain glanced at his watch and replied, 'We will be abeam of Portpatrick at 1230. Ten miles offshore we'll make the first test dive.' He added, 'Check with Lieutenant Mayo. With this damned wind in our teeth I may have to crack on speed a bit to make the correct area on time.'

Wolfe eyed him evenly. 'You always were a perfectionist. No wonder they gave you command!'

Jermain smiled quietly. 'I have my moments.'

After a few moments the light passed his signal to the escort. The he added, 'Once in Singapore, I shouldn't wonder if they fly you home for your own boat, Ian. You deserve it.'

'Maybe.' Wolfe watched a determined-looking gull circling above the corkscrewing periscopes. 'It's this trip or bust for me. I'll never take a shore job.' He forced a smile, but there were lines of strain around his eyes. 'Can you see me in gaiters and sword at Whale Island? Or lecturing to a lot of bloody recruits?'

One of the two bridge lookouts said sharply, 'There's a sail fine on the port bow, sir!'

A sail? Jermain swung his glasses. 'Out in this weather?'

The brown hills and a solitary church steeple swam

momentarily across the lenses, and then as the waves leapt into frightening size under the powerful glasses he saw the brief flash of dark red and a small flapping triangle of sail. It rose and dipped in the deep swell, but it was moving fast.

Jermain said, 'Damned fools! They'll have one hell of a time trying to beat back!'

A messenger at the intercom said, 'Turning on to new course, sir. Two one zero. Increasing revolutions for sixteen knots.'

'Very good.' Jermain seized the screen as a big wave broke across the bow and thundered against the foot of the fin. It was like a solid object, and he heard some of the men below laughing at each other's reactions.

Wolfe asked suddenly. 'Do you think there's more to our voyage than we've been told?' He shrugged. 'Or shouldn't I ask at this point?'

Jermain lifted his glasses again. The sail was fairly flying over the yellow-fanged waves. Like the fin of some giant shark. He felt vaguely uneasy, yet could not explain it.

He said slowly, 'As my Number One you have every right to know. But it's all pretty vague. Apart from a few routine details I've told you all I know. But the Chinese are getting restless. The Americans seem to think they'll try another push further north.'

Wolfe groaned. 'Not Formosa, surely?'

Jermain shook his head. 'Not this time. Something real is my guess. The games are over. The Chinese are getting tired of the cold war. They want to draw their little empire together with a piece of force.' Wolfe frowned. Jermain's obvious interest made him realise just how out of touch he had become. 'You mean Korea again?'

Jermain did not answer. He said sharply, 'That damned fool! He'll be across our bows in a moment!'

Wolfe followed his gaze. The dinghy was moving closer each minute, so that he could actually see the small varnished hull plunging like a polished walnut beneath the bright sail. He could see three, maybe four, figures aboard, their backs arched across the weather side to hold the boat on its careering course.

'He might pass ahead.' Wolfe looked at Jermain's face. It was then that he realised something of the strain and responsibility which lurked behind those calm features.

Wolfe asked quickly, 'Shall I signal the escort to head the boat off?'

'No chance now. It'd take some time to turn round in this. The poor bastard is rolling his guts out as it is!' He glared at the dripping compass repeater. 'Alter course two points to starboard. Maybe the fool hasn't seen us yet.' His eye fell on the signalman. 'Well, don't stand there gaping, man! Flash up the escort and tell them our new course!'

Jermain felt the tension growing around him. Below through the hatch he could hear the men whispering quietly. The captain was jumpy. The old man was losing the touch! He forced himself to grin. 'Not that I should care, I suppose. The old Black Pig would push that dinghy over like a matchbox!' The men laughed, but every eye rested on the red sail.

'Dinghy's going about, sir!' The lookout caught his breath. 'No it isn't, sir! The madman's coming straight for us!'

Wolfe watched spellbound. Through his glasses he could see the tense but determined faces below the sail, the way one of them was pointing at the submarine. It reminded him of an old painting of a whaleboat plunging on its quarry.

'Slow ahead!' Jermain ground his teeth as the eager wind pushed the sea heavily over the bows and swung the fin through one more sickening angle. He felt helpless, unable to control the four and a half thousand tons of steel below his skidding boots as it pushed on to some invisible meeting point on the sea ahead.

Wolfe said, 'Will you heave to, sir?'

Jermain shook his head. 'With this wind and sea running we'd slew right round.' He waved his arm through the rain. 'We'd be run aground in fifteen minutes hereabouts! It's shoal water out there!'

The bosun's mate asked, 'What orders, sir? Control room is asking for instructions.'

Overhead, the slim attack periscope squeaked slightly in its mounting, and Jermain guessed that the O.O.W. or Mayo was already watching the start of the inevitable.

Jermain said coldly. 'Close up the emergency deck party. And signal the escort to stand by to pick up survivors.' Wolfe watched Jermain's impassive face and felt strangely moved. What a rotten beginning, he thought. What a bloody senseless waste.

• • •

In the control room Lieutenant Oxley, the O.O.W., stooped down to peer through the partly raised periscope, his sleek head shining in the bright lights. He pursed his lips and murmured, 'Talk about David and Goliath!' He straightened up and glanced quickly at the gyro repeater. 'A collision course if I ever saw one!'

Max Colquhoun looked pale and tired as he watched Oxley's face beside the grease-smeared periscope. Apart from his general duties about the boat he was also assistant to Oxley in dealing with the complex sonar system which singled out *Temeraire* and her rare class. *Temeraire*'s function was to hunt and kill other submarines. To do this she had to be swift and silent, so silent that she remained undetected by her prey as well as by any possible hunter on the surface. Able to operate in great depths far below the isothermal barrier, she was virtually beyond the reach of any conventional sonar, yet could find and kill her enemies with calculated ease.

Oxley said, 'Come and take a look, Max.'

Colquhoun took the training handles of the periscope and peered through the spray-dappled lens. He saw the dinghy instantly, and felt his stomach contract as if from a blow.

The intercom barked, 'Emergency deck party close up at the double!'

Oxley grinned. 'That's you, Max! Watch you don't get your feet wet!'

Jeffers, the second coxswain, a squat, blue-jowled petty officer, was already climbing the ladder, his body deformed by his orange lifejacket, his cap tugged down over his eyes. He looked at Colquhoun and said, 'I'll lead the way, sir. It may be a bit dicky up top!'

The little party assembled in the lower part of the fin, four seamen and the petty officer, all jammed together and staring at each other like strangers.

Jeffers shrugged and knocked off the clips of the screen door. The wind was like ice after the swaying warmth of the control room, and Colquhoun stared out at the curved deck with something like shock. Below decks the submarine seemed vast and remote. Standing in the narrow doorway it was like standing on a partly submerged rock. He watched the hissing rollers breaking across the wet steel and the hostile sea beyond.

'Right then!' Jeffers stepped over the coaming and grasped the handrail which encircled the fin. 'Let's go and take a look at the silly bastards!'

The dinghy was less than fifty feet from the port bow, and appeared to be higher than the submarine's deck. As Colquhoun and his men appeared around the fin the boat's occupants gave a small cheer, their voices whipped across the water like the cries of sea birds.

Colquhoun could see the escort vessel plunging back along her course, her stern rising clear of the wavetops, while from her bridge came the metallic garble of a loud-hailer.

The dinghy's sail changed shape, and two of the occupants hoisted up a crude banner which whipped out stiffly like a sheet of metal in the wind.

Jeffers groaned and dashed the spray from his face. 'Bugger me! They're ban-the-bomb merchants!'

Rider, one of the seamen, yelled, 'Some of 'em have been hanging about the base for ages!'

Jeffers snapped, 'I don't give a pig's arse *who* they are! They're done for if they touch the Black Pig!'

The waving dinghy sailors froze as if they too had suddenly realised the depth and size of the great monster which pushed towards them. Arms waved and there was some attempt to retrim the sail. But it was too late. Like a leaf in a millrace the little boat began to tilt.

Jeffers snatched the grapnel and line from Rider. ''Ere! Let me 'ave a go!'

There was a sodden thump as the boat's drop-keel struck the curved bow, then it seemed to rush along the submarine's deck like a thing gone mad. The grapnel fastened into the gunwale and the seamen took the strain.

Colquhoun had a vague picture of staring faces and wet, shining oilskins as his little group struggled to pull the four figures clear of the stranded boat. From above he could hear the captain's voice, sharp yet controlled, as he swung the hull slightly off course to ease the strain of the wind and jubilant spray.

The four dinghy sailors stood dazedly against the fin, held in position by two of the seamen. Jeffers and the others manhandled the dinghy around the sheltered side of the swaying tower, the waves reaching at their skidding feet as they cursed and panted with their captive. More men appeared from the open door, and knives flashed in the dull light as they cut away the sail and rigging. Now that the immediate danger was over the seamen were even joking with each other and throwing pointed insults at the unexpected visitors.

Jermain swung down the bridge ladder and steadied himself against the safety rail. It had been a near thing. His relief was giving way to a cold and unreasonable anger, and he snapped, 'Signal the escort to come up astern! We can put these four aboard their dinghy and drop them back by line.'

Jeffers rubbed his hands. 'They're lucky to be alive, sir.'

Jermain ignored him and pulled himself around the fin to confront the dripping and exhausted figures who were still pinioned against the streaming steel. He stared at their faces. All young. All frightened but defiant. He started. One of them was a girl, her forehead bleeding from her hasty escape.

Jermain shouted above the wind, 'I hope you're satisfied? You damn nearly got killed!'

One of the youths said, 'It was worth it.' He grinned in spite of his discomfort. 'Thanks for being so decent about it.'

Jermain pointed towards the madly swinging escort. 'Save your excuses for him!' He turned his back and climbed up the ladder to rejoin Wolfe behind the screen.

Wolfe scowled. 'Little fools! I hope the authorities clap 'em in jail for a bit!'

Jermain fretted with impatience as the dinghy bobbed astern on a grass line towards the waiting escort. The little minesweeper had a scrambling net down. There would be another rough handling for the four youngsters before they were through. The dinghy would be a write-off. It was to be hoped that the brief demonstration would compensate the owner.

He replied slowly, 'Unlikely. It would be bound to get into the Press. I imagine that the admiral is unwilling for any extra publicity about our movements!'

He broke off as he saw the girl in the tossing dinghy turn to blow him an impudent kiss. In spite of his anxiety Jermain grinned. 'Well, they've got guts, whatever their motives!'

Wolfe turned away, masking his anger. He was worried, too. He had been leaning over the screen as Jermain had gone down to the deck after the rescue. Even with the wind whining over the bridge he had heard one of the young men from the dinghy say to his friends, 'Poor old Max! I thought he was going to have a fit when he saw us!'

Max. Max Colquhoun. Wolfe recalled with sudden clarity the young officer waiting by the pier in deep conversation with the small group of would-be demonstrators. The connection was obvious.

He wondered if he should mention it to Jermain. If an officer was stupid enough to blab about *Temeraire*'s movements he was a menace to everyone aboard. He thought of Jermain's other problems and decided against it. He watched Colquhoun pass below with the relieved deck party and nodded to himself.

I'll be watching you, my lad. Just one false move. Just one. . . .

• • •

Lieutenant Commander Colin Ross sauntered across the control room and paused outside the chart-room door. He was carrying a pair of disposable bootees which were worn by all persons required to pass through Checkpoint Charlie as a protection against possible contamination. He waited until Jermain looked up from the chart table and then gestured towards the bulkhead clock.

'Are we in position?'

Jermain smiled. In spite of the engineer's abrupt manner of speaking, he knew that Ross was a reserved, even shy, man. He was showing all the usual signs to be expected before the first dive.

'Coming up, Chief.' He tapped the chart. 'Portpatrick is ten miles abeam. Is your department ready?'

Ross sniffed. 'All checked and compensated. I'll be damn glad to get down. This motion is playing hell with my digestion!'

'Very well. Sound off diving stations.' Jermain picked up his glasses and walked briskly through the control room towards the ladder. The tannoy grated. 'Diving stations! Diving stations!' There was the usual flurry of padding feet, the click of equipment, and then the orderly shut down of all but essential traffic. Throughout the hull the various heads of departments reported their men closed up and standing by.

Wolfe was standing straddle-legged in the centre of the space, the trim book in his hands. 'Turn out the fore-planes!'

Jermain asked, 'All set, Number One?'

Wolfe licked his lips. 'I've just made another check, Captain. I've allowed for all extra stores and spares, as well as all other big items.'

'Good. It'll be different from the last time now that we've got rid of all the passengers.'

Wolfe allowed his brow to relax slightly. 'Ninety men aboard. That's ninety multipled by about one hundred and fifty pounds.' He closed the book. 'That should do it.'

Jermain began to climb. 'Very well. Rig for diving.' He reached the surface navigating bridge and stared through the salt-smeared glass. The upper cockpit was empty, and here only the lookouts and the signalmen still waited until the last moment.

The shoreline was almost hidden in a fresh squall, and Jermain wondered briefly if the dinghy sailors were being well looked after in the distant minesweeper.

Below he heard the snap of metal as the watertight doors were moved and tested. If anything went wrong in the dive they would be slammed shut in an instant, sealing the compartments into separate zones of safety, or individual tombs.

The intercom announced, 'Hydroplanes tested and correct!'

'Very good.' A pause. A quick look round with the glasses. A brief picture of a jumbled town, far away, like an aerial map. A few gulls, a streamer of smoke from the escort's short funnel.

'Signal escort, Bunts. Am commencing first dive. Depth sixty feet.'

The light clattered, then there was an answering flash across the tumbling water. Jermain wondered if anyone in the distant town would see the light and spare them a thought. He found that his throat was dry. He glanced sideways at the signalman, a competent, trusting face. No sign of doubt or uncertainty.

He snapped, 'Slow ahead. Open main vents. Take her down to sixty feet!'

He listened to his orders being repeated.

'Clear the bridge!' He stabbed the red button and heard the banshee klaxon echoing through his command. The lookouts vanished, and he pressed it a second time.

Jermain felt the deck tremble very slightly and begin to tilt. He followed the others and slammed the hatch with the locking wheel. Down to the foot of the fin and another hatch to be sealed.

In the control room all was quiet but for the gentle whirr of fans and the occasional creak of metal. It was hard to realise that the boat was diving but for the slight angle and the telltale needles on the gauges.

Side by side the helmsman and planesman sat at their control, their bodies hunched as if they were actually riding the Black Pig.

Down, down. Thirty feet. Forty-five. Fifty.

The planesman swung his controls and sighed, the sound very loud.

The orders were passed, voices hushed as if in church.

'Flood auxiliary tanks.'

'Engine room reports that shaft seals are one hundred per cent, sir.'

Jermain wiped his face with his hands. 'Very good.'

Although the hull was massively constructed to withstand the *pull* of eighty thousand pounds to the square inch, it had its weak points. The seals around the single shaft, for instance. But so far everything was fine.

'Steady at sixty feet, Captain.'

'Very well. Raise the radar mast and check on escort. Then make her a signal of our depth and speed.'

The dials flickered, the lights on the panels winked and obeyed each set move.

Jermain looked at his watch. 'Pressure in the boat.'

There was a mere hiss as air pressure was raised and measured.

The tannoy said, 'All compartments check!'

Wolfe listened to the rapid replies. 'No leaks, pressure constant, sir. All stations have checked.'

Jermain nodded and felt a nerve jumping at the corner of his eye. He looked across at Mayo's bearded face. 'Ready, Pilot?'

Mayo stretched and watched the helmsman. 'Yes, sir. Course one seven five. Revs for twenty-five knots.'

Oxley wrote rapidly in the log. It was somehow final.

Jermain waited a moment longer. Gone was the wind and

choppy sea. Here all was calm and ordered. He felt a sensation of inner pride in this machinery-crammed world.

He said, 'Make a signal to escort. Will proceed as scheduled. Thank you and goodbye.' He watched the signalman writing busily. 'No, scrub out that "goodbye". Better make it "until next time".'

The deck trembled suddenly as the power began to increase. The build-up of speed would carry them clear of the busy traffic lanes, down to the open sea of the Atlantic and still further south.

'Up periscope.' He leaned his forehead against the rubber pad and peered through the powerful lenses. He saw the little escort turning stoically through a black-sided roller. Her shape blurred even as he watched. By nightfall she would be tied up at her berth, her crew scattered through the bars and cinemas.

'Signal from escort, sir. "*Bon voyage* and keep clear of dinghies!"'

Jermain smiled wearily. 'Down periscope. Secure radar.' He looked across at Wolfe. 'Take her down to eighty feet and fall out diving stations. Commence passage routine.'

Fiske, the petty officer cook, raised his head through the hatch and blinked at the activity. In a stage whisper he asked, 'Is it all right to get the lamb chops goin'?'

Oxley stared at him and said, 'Plenty of gravy, Chef.'

The cook vanished. For him the business of diving was just a plain inconvenience.

• • •

Jermain finished writing his personal diary as Ross leaned inwards through the cabin door and said, 'Running like a dream. I just wondered if you were going to perform the usual rite?'

Jermain smiled and gestured to the cupboard. 'Help yourself, Chief. That was a pretty good dive.'

Ross poured two horses' necks and stood them on the deck. He pointed at them and exclaimed, 'Look at that! Not a quiver!'

'Cheers!' Jermain tilted the glass. Probably the last one before Singapore. 'We'd better go to lunch, Chief. There are a few points I want to discuss with you this afternoon about store space.' He looked up as Lieutenant Kitson, the electrical officer, hovered awkwardly in the entrance.

Kitson was a thickset, sad-looking man who appeared too clumsy for the task of controlling every electrical device and supervising many hundreds of miles of wiring which fed the boat like arteries. Yet he was as alert as he was busy, and even found the time to act as the *Temerarie*'s entertainments and sports officer. The latter duty was almost as demanding as the first. To keep the men fit and free from boredom the boat was equipped with films and taped music, as well as keep-fit devices and a whole cabinet of correspondence courses which covered just about everything from gardening to public speaking.

Jermain grinned. 'Not now. If one of your lads has broken the rowing machine it'll just have to wait till one of the artificers can fix it!'

Kitson did not smile. 'I'm sorry, sir. I *must* speak to you.'

Ross stood up and drained his glass. 'I'll be off.'

'No, Chief. This may concern you too.' Kitson shifted uncomfortably.

Jermain eyed him steadily. 'Well, what is it?'

'I've just finished my rounds, sir.' He held out his gloved hand across which there was a smear of fresh paint. 'I found this on the steering circuit, just forrard of the reactor control compartment.'

Ross scowled. 'So what? Christ, with all the dockyard mateys we've had aboard, I'm surprised there's any paint at all!'

Kitson swallowed hard. 'The paint was over the circuit wiring, sir.'

Jermain leaned forward. 'Just what are you telling me?'

'The paint was put there deliberately, sir.' He looked as if he was going to be sick. 'Underneath it the wires were half sawn through!'

Ross trembled. 'Do you know what you're saying, man?'

Kitson faced him stubbornly. 'The paint was still wet. There have been no strangers aboard for twenty-four hours.'

Jermain stared past him, his eyes empty of expression. 'Thank you. Carry on to your lunch now, will you? I don't have to tell you to keep quiet about this.'

When Kitson had gone Ross exploded, 'God Almighty, he's saying it's one of the crew! That would be sabotage!'

Jermain pushed away the half-empty glass. 'An ugly word, Chief. I'll have to think about it.'

3

Taking the Strain

LIEUTENANT-COMMANDER IAN WOLFE walked wearily into the deserted wardroom and stared for several seconds at the table. He had just completed the 1800 to 2000 watch in the control room, yet somehow the thought of food and rest seemed to jar on his nerves. The long table was laid for two only. For himself and his watchkeeping companion, Sub-Lieutenant Colquhoun. Every officer did two tours on watch and six off, working in pairs. Apart from the doctor, and Luard, the supply officer, no one was exempt, and even Ross and Kitson, the electrical officer, stood their watches in addition to their other duties. The latter seemed to enjoy the change, and kept their watches alive with questions and playful mistakes as they grappled with the mysteries of navigation and seamanship.

Wolfe slumped in a chair and heard Baldwin, the senior steward, stirring into action behind his pantry hatch. It was hard to get used to the wardroom's sudden emptiness after the close-knit world of conventional submarines. Here there were double cabins for the officers, places where they could hide their faces from their companions and find moments of peace.

Colquhoun entered the wardroom and sat at the other side of the table, an old magazine already open at his side. Wolfe watched him thoughtfully and pondered back over the last seven days. Seven days since leaving the Gareloch, many hours of silent running south and further south, while the daily routine went on, and the captain put the boat through one exercise and drill after another.

When Wolfe had handed over the watch to Lieutenant Oxley the *Temeraire*'s position had been off the West African coast, two hundred miles from Senegal, while to the east lay the Cape Verde Islands. Nearly three and a half thousand miles since they had last seen the Scottish hills, yet with little or nothing to show any change.

Every day of the voyage Jermain would bring the boat up to periscope depth, and only the brief glimpse through the powerful lenses would show any sort of difference. Gone were the short, steep waves of the Irish Sea, the great, sullen rollers of the Atlantic. Now the sea was bright blue and unbroken, with a sky which was so clear it seemed to mock at their stealthy passage.

At first there had always been a queue of seamen to peer through the periscopes on such occasions, but now there were hardly any who seemed interested. This was their world, and they were looking inwards, at each other, at themselves. Even now, in the lower crew space, there was a cinema show taking place, which accounted for the air of desertion. Jules Verne would never have visualised such an improbability, Wolfe thought. The big, whale-shaped submarine gliding through the dark water at some twenty knots while her crew whistled and jeered at the exploits of an escapist film show.

Baldwin pattered in the wardroom and placed some soup on the table. Wolfe sipped slowly and watched his silent companion. Nerves were getting tense already, and there had been several small outbreaks of temper. The captain never let up on the drills, and Wolfe guessed that it was partly to keep the men from getting bored, as well as his own way of carrying on with tests and trials left over from the curtailed working-up exercises.

Wolfe's thoughts kept returning to the unknown saboteur. The idea of such a man sharing his every hour aboard grated on his mind like a saw. And the more he thought about it, the more he found himself watching Colquhoun.

Ever since the young officer's first outburst when Jermain had confirmed the sailing orders Wolfe had watched him and worried. He had pondered on Colquhoun's friendship with the C.N.D. demonstrators, and added to it his belief that Colquhoun was in real fear of going to Singapore, where his father was a very senior officer.

Colquhoun looked tired and pale, and his eyes were only moving slowly across the open magazine, as if he was incapable of making the effort to read.

Jermain had approached the problem very carefully. He had spoken to each officer, and to all the senior ratings. It was to be kept quiet, a close watch was to be maintained and, above all, everything was to carry on as normal. It was unlikely that the culprit would strike again yet. His own life would be in danger, too. But once in Singapore anything might happen.

In spite of every precaution, however, Wolfe had sensed a difference in the boat. In the Navy the lower-deck telegraph was usually very active. Here, confined within the Black Pig's fat hull, the rumours moved quietly and uneasily, like an unseen gas.

Cruising on the surface it might have been different, Wolfe decided. A touch of spray, the sight of another ship, no matter how distant, would take the edge off the tension. But the *Temeraire* was not just a submersible boat, she was a submarine. She was built to stay under water, and her speed and manoeuverability depended on it.

He looked up at the brightly coloured reproduction of Turner's *Fighting Temeraire* which hung facing him on the opposite bulkhead. It depicted the old ship of the line being towed up the Thames to the breaker's yard in 1838. She was being towed by a steam tug, and Wolfe wondered if people shook their heads then over the change from sail to coal, as they did over nuclear power. It again reminded him of Colquhoun's quiet evasiveness that night on the pier, and he heard himself say sharply, 'I suppose you'll see your father when we reach Singapore?'

Colquhoun did not look up. 'I expect so, Number One.'

He could feel Wolfe watching him like a cat, and he had to

force himself to stare blindly at the open pages. Each swing of the *Temeraire*'s big screw was carrying him closer and closer. He had not seen his father for nearly a year, and even although he knew the separation could not last for ever, he had enjoyed every minute of it.

Colquhoun was the vice-admiral's only son. Like all his remembered ancestors it was expected that he too would enter the Navy as the only career. Colquhoun had fought his father right up to the last. He had never wanted to follow in his footsteps, and the conflict of wills leading up to his own final capitulation had broadened his resentment into hatred.

His father had been a submarine ace in the Second World War, yet it was hard to think of him as ever being young like Oxley, or Drew. It was equally difficult to compare him with Jermain's calm composure, or any of the other commanding officers he had met.

He glanced quickly across at Wolfe. He could well imagine his father being something like *him*, he thought bitterly.

Wolfe seemed to be two persons. Watchful and competent one minute, then giving way to short bursts of violent sarcasm, just like his father.

He thought about the dinghy escapade and the girl, Julie, who had nearly lost her life in the mad seconds before she was hauled aboard. He would just have to forget her now. Before, with the submarine going from the Gareloch or from Rosyth it had been easy to see her, to make the most of her exciting company. But she moved with a group, and Colquhoun tortured himself a little longer as he thought of her at this moment. Probably laughing and dancing with one of the others, while he might already be a faded memory.

They had met at the little club in Rosyth, a place frequented by students and others like Colquhoun who sought after their true identities. He had known it was wrong to tell them about the *Temeraire*'s sailing time, but how was he to know that her destination was Singapore and not Rosyth as originally planned?

He felt the cold resentment and hostility welling up as he saw Wolfe studying him with those grey, empty eyes. Perhaps he imagined that *he* had committed the sabotage! Colquhoun felt like laughing. It was probably a poor sailor who did not want to leave his wife, or some fool working off an old, vague grievance. It never failed to annoy him. The way that some people reacted to these small acts of wilful damage. It never seemed to occur to anyone that these clean and tidy ratings who said 'Aye, aye, sir' and saluted at their jobs, had any problems of their own. Only occasionally, when a man came to his particular officer and asked his advice about mortgages, an unfaithful wife, about promotion prospects or changing his religion did the hidden part of the iceberg show itself.

Colquhoun pushed the picture of the unknown culprit from his thoughts and considered how he would react when he again met his father.

Vice-Admiral Sir John Colquhoun, a compact, steely-eyed man who seemed so like the many framed paintings of past Colquhouns in the old Hampshire home which had been in the family for generations. Before Nelson had joined the Navy, before the Dutch had sailed insolently up the Thames, there had been a Colquhoun in the Service. Now, in his fifties, the admiral seemed as far off and unreal as one of those paintings.

Colquhoun could remember his father's rage when he had found him at home during his very first leave from Dartmouth. He had been reading a book about ballet, but if he had been studying a work of absolute filth and depravity his father could not have appeared more furious.

'My God! What sort of a son have I produced! You're too spineless for a son of mine!' And so on and so forth.

Colquhoun usually gave in, if only for his mother's sake. She was quiet and frail, unable any longer to withstand the admiral's sudden change of temperament.

He did not really know why he had entered the submarine service. Whether it was because or in spite of his father's past record was a point he could not decide. His mother had said, 'Your father will be proud of you, Max.' But the admiral had been strangely silent on the matter. Did he perhaps see his son's progress as some sort of challenge? It was indeed odd to realise that only within the same service had Colquhoun been able to show any sort of independence from his father.

He could well imagine what he would have thought of Julie. Like all his other girl friends, Colquhoun thought bitterly. The admiral used such words as *decadent* and *gutless*, and a *disgrace to their country*! He seemed to expect the whole country to be permanently under arms.

Colquhoun realised that Wolfe was saying, 'I thought your sonar department was a bit sloppy this morning, Sub. If we're called on to go into some sort of action you'll not get any second chances!'

Colquhoun kept his face non-committal. There had been another drill involving both the sonar and T.A.S. departments, and one of his men, a young seaman named Lightfoot, had made a complete hash of his settings. The result had been swift and disturbing. All the little pent-up tensions had flared and died like star shells, with voice-pipes and intercom snapping and barking complaints and reprimands until the error was sorted out and rectified.

He replied carefully, 'Lieutenant Oxley was in charge. He didn't seem too worried.'

'Covering up for you, I shouldn't wonder!' Wolfe seemed to control himself with an effort. 'Just keep an eye on your men in future. They don't respect softness.'

The first lieutenant stood up suddenly and walked from the wardroom.

Alone at the table Colquhoun stayed staring after him. When he gets a command of his own, that's one submarine I'll *not* join, he thought grimly.

• • •

Two decks below Colquhoun's lonely table the second crew space was equally quiet, and for a normally crowded compartment almost deserted.

It was crossed and lined by tiers of neat bunks and brightly enamelled lockers, and piped music insinuated itself from the tannoy loudspeakers at either end. Several seamen were sitting in their underwear around one of the tables intent on the serious game of uckers, and another solitary sailor was carving a model ship from a piece of wood.

Ordinary Seaman John Lightfoot lay in his bunk, his hands behind his head, and tried to make himself fall asleep. Through an open hatch in the deckhead he could hear the crack of gunfire and the muffled thunder of horses as the main body of the crew settled down to enjoy the Western in the main crew space.

Lightfoot was twenty years old, with wide eyes and a troubled mouth which added to his appearance of nervous expectancy. He tried to turn his mind away from his nagging, insistent apprehension, and he was almost inclined to leave the bunk and join the others at the table.

It was seven days since he had tried to cut through the wiring. Seven wretched and fearful days of waiting to be discovered and unmasked in front of the others. But although rumour passed upon rumour, nothing had happened. Sometimes he imagined that people were watching him, speaking about him behind his back and waiting for him to slip up. Innocent remarks became barbed and full of meaning. Casual comment could become immediately suspect. Nervously, like a badly injured man feeling the extent of his wounds, Lightfoot explored the terrible events which had driven him to an act of sabotage.

From the film show above he imagined he could hear a familiar laugh, and he felt the tears of anger and shame pricking his eyes like needles. Able Seaman Bruce, the tough, devil-may-care Scouse from the dock area of Liverpool who had started him on this nightmare train of events.

Unlike Bruce and the majority of the crew Lightfoot was a 'pressed' man. He had been happy in general service, but like many others of the sonar branch had been forced into the submarine fleet without consultation. The submarine service was growing too rapidly to depend on volunteers, and Lightfoot had found himself installed in the unnatural surroundings of submarine life for a period of five years.

His early misgivings had given way to awe and pride, and within a few weeks he had settled down completely. A Londoner, Lightfoot had rarely made the long journey south from the Gareloch when his brief leaves became due. He had been content to wander around the strange Scottish countryside, which in itself was as different to him as the submarine herself.

His home was in Battersea, that soot-encrusted area of decaying buildings which sprawled between the great railway yards of Clapham Junction and the Thames. The place was slow to change even in the face of the advancing blocks of soulless council flats, and the Lightfoot family had survived want and unemployment, wars and personal unrest in the same street for four generations. In his mind's eye he could see his mother, old before her time, in the peeling kitchen of the little terraced house. It was sandwiched between one of the many railway arches and a soap factory, and when the fast trains went through the junction every piece of furniture would rattle and a fine film of dust would defy even his mother's busy efforts.

He did not know to this day if his family were glad he had joined the Navy. They could do with the extra space he had left behind, but in some strange way seemed to resent his efforts to break away from the dreary surroundings which were their lot. When he had gone home with the new gold-wire tally on his cap, *H.M. Submarines*, for all to see, his mother had said flatly, 'Well, I suppose you know what you're doing.' His father, on strike from the bus depot, had remarked, 'Dead cushy from what it was in *my* day!'

Lightfoot had not understood this hostility. He wanted them to be pleased. To wish him luck. It was strange how the ties of family seemed to hold him still, in spite of the distance.

Bruce, or Porky as he was called because of his capacity to hold his beer, had come into his life during one of those rare fits of depression which occurred each time he saw the men reading their letters from home. There was never a letter from Battersea. Just a card at Christmas and one for his birthday. Yet Lightfoot dutifully posted a regular allowance to his mother and waited for recognition. Bruce had said on that first afternoon, 'Wot's eatin' you then?' He was hard-faced, with the belligerent look of a fighter. His Liverpool accent was as sharp as his eye, but he seemed genuinely interested in Lightfoot's problems.

Then he had said, 'Forget it, kid! I told my folks to get stuffed when I was thirteen!' He had shown his strong, uneven teeth. 'Jesus, the old man nearly threw a fit!' He had squatted on the bunk, his eyes dreamy. 'This regiment's a pushover if you keep out of trouble aboard ship. Then, once ashore, you do what the bloody hell you like! You come on a run ashore with me, kid. I'll show you!'

And he had, too. Lightfoot had got drunk for the first time, but true to his word, Porky Bruce had shepherded him back to the *Temeraire* and safely past the cold eye of the duty petty officer. He had undressed him and cleaned the vomit from his shoes with the calm indifference of an old campaigner.

They made a strange pair. Lightfoot, wide-eyed and desperately keen to prove himself; Bruce, brash and casual, with the hard-won knowledge of the lower deck to carry him through. Bruce seemed to have two faces. He worked on the sonar with Lightfoot and was extremely competent. Yet he made his skill appear like insolence, his brisk familiarity with his instruments seemed as if he was cocking a snook at his immediate superiors.

He had educated Lightfoot in his trade, and in the same manner had looked after him ashore. He had even laid low a marine outside a pub just to show his youthful companion how easy it was.

Only once on board the *Temeraire* had he shown the latent force to his mess mates. A seaman had jokingly remarked about Lightfoot's constant shoregoing habits with his unlikely friend. Bruce had seized the man and had shaken him gently like a rat, his face only inches away. 'Me an' the kid is oppos, see?' Shake. Shake. 'When I want your friggin' advice I'll ask for it, see?' Another shake. 'Any more squit from you an' I'll mark you for life!'

And that was that.

Then had come the night when things had changed. They had been together in a small pub outside Faslane. A dull place, full of sailors who were drinking because there seemed nothing else to do. Somehow or other they had got into conversation with a middle-aged civilian who told them he was a salesman. He had offered to drive them to his hotel where he had some bottles of better stuff than they were getting in the pub.

Several drinks later they had gone out to the man's car, and with a roar of noise had started down the open road away from the town. After a while Bruce had said thickly, 'Must get out. I'm burstin'!'

Lightfoot could remember every moment which followed. The car's sudden acceleration, a momentary glimpse of Bruce's startled face in the swinging headlights as he stood swaying at the side of the road.

Lightfoot had not grown up in the slums without learning that such men existed. In fact, when he was only ten his best friend had been picked up by some man and taken behind the hoardings off the Falcon Road.

Lightfoot remembered the man's hot, frantic hand, the noise of the engine and the weird moonscape within the powerful headlights. He had wriggled on the swaying seat, struggling first with anger then with fear as the car drove faster and faster in time with the man's voice.

It had only taken a few seconds, yet it had lasted a lifetime. When Bruce had come panting along the road he had found the car against a tree and Lightfoot standing motionless beside it.

The man lay a few feet away, his skull crushed against a piece of stone. In the headlights' reflected glare they could see the blood shining on the grass, the pebble-like stare in the man's dead eyes.

'I killed him!' Lightfoot had listened to his own voice like a stranger. 'He tried to . . .' He had staggered vomiting against the car. 'I pushed him hard and his door opened.'

The headlights had died at that instant and he remembered Bruce saying harshly, 'Serve the bastard right!' The next piece of the pattern was harder to remember.

Bruce stumbling in the darkness, making sure that they had left nothing in the car. Then the pair of them running like hunted animals beside the road, and ducking as an occasional car drove past. As they had reached the outskirts of the town a police car and ambulance had swept down the same road, sirens wailing and lights flashing.

They had returned to the submarine and climbed into their bunks. Bruce had merely paused to say in a fierce whisper, 'Take my word on it! The scuffers will never connect us with it!' That was all he seemed to care about it.

Looking back it was hard to understand what he had really hoped to gain by the sabotage. When the *Temeraire* had returned from her last batch of trials Lightfoot had waited for the police to board the boat and take him away. Nothing had happened at all. Everything seemed to be dwarfed by the news that the boat was sailing immediately for the Far East.

Lightfoot knew he would be unable to stand the waiting any longer. He had to delay the departure so that he could make his way to London and explain to his family before they heard the story from someone else.

Again he felt the tears welling up behind his eyes. He had even made a mess of that. He had dodged the trot sentry and found his way aft unseen. He had been at work with a hacksaw when Bruce had appeared at his side.

''Ere! Cut that out, you young twit!' He had spoken in a grating whisper. 'I saw you was missin' an' I guessed what you might try!' He had seized his wrist in a vise-like grip. '*I'm* in this too, remember! I told you before, the scuffers'll never latch on to us. An' anyway that bloody queer deserved what he got!' Briskly he had smeared paint across the half-cut wires. 'Now git forrard an' for Chrissake take a grip on yourself!'

The worst of it was, Bruce really did not care about it. He was up there in the film show hooting his head off as if he hadn't a care in the world.

Every time there was a pipe over the intercom or a petty officer called his name Lightfoot nearly fainted. He felt trapped and alone, with no one who could help but Bruce.

The leading hand of the mess, a tall Devonian named Haley, sauntered past the bunk. 'You okay, youngster?' He peered in at him. 'You look two-blocks to me!'

Lightfoot bit his lip. 'I'm all right, Hookey. Something I ate, I expect.'

Haley nodded sagely. 'That bloody Porky been feedin' you some of his rum again?' He grinned and walked over to join the others.

Lightfoot remained staring at the bunk above. He had to get a grip on himself. Had to.

The intercom broke into the music. 'D'you hear there! Ordinary Seaman Lightfoot muster outside the wardroom!'

Lightfoot shut his eyes and felt the nausea closing over him.

• • •

Colquhoun looked up from his thoughts as he heard the quiet knock on the wardroom door. 'Come in.'

Lightfoot paused uncertainly in the entrance, his cap held awkwardly in his hands, his eyes flickering around the deserted wardroom like, Colquhoun thought, a trapped animal.

'You sent for me, sir?' Lightfoot's voice was husky.

Colquhoun stared at him. Usually he saw the young seaman as a hunched figure over the sonar controls or another familiar face moving through the boat on some mission or other. Tonight he looked strange and quite different. His hair was dishevelled, as if he had just got out of bed, and there were dark shadows under his eyes.

'Just wanted a quiet word, Lightfoot.'

The young seaman waited, the well-lit wardroom spinning around him like some maddened whirlpool. Only the seated officer remained unmoving and still, like an inquisitor.

'I was a bit worried about the drill this morning.'

Lightfoot waited for Colquhoun to continue. Any second now. The accusation, the beginning of the end.

Colquhoun stood up. 'Are you feeling all right?' He saw the boy swallow hard. 'You look like death.'

'I'm fine, sir.' Lightfoot tried to bring the moisture back to his dry lips. 'Just a bit tired.'

'I'm sorry I dragged you up here then. It was just to say that we're having another drill tomorrow, and I thought it best to go over what went wrong this morning.'

'Is that all, sir?' Lightfoot stared at him as if mesmerised.

Colquhoun gave a small smile. He could remember the angry confusion and then Wolfe's 'They don't respect softness!' 'Some people take the view that it's quite important. I just wanted to make sure that nothing goes wrong in *our* section again.' He brushed his fair hair from his eyes. 'It makes for a quieter life that way!'

Lightfoot held himself upright with physical effort. He was safe for a while longer. In fact, the sub-lieutenant was trying to be friendly. It did not seem possible. He managed to reply, 'It was my fault, sir. I slipped up. The valve casing was loose and the vibration was getting on my nerves.' He faltered, looking for the right words. 'I'm sorry if I fouled up the exercise.'

He looked so miserable that Colquhoun felt vaguely sorry for him. As soon as he had ordered a messenger to pipe for Lightfoot he had relented. He was not even sure of the real reason. He saw the boy's eyes wandering about him as if marking the differences between his own way of life and those of Colquhoun.

'Have you settled down all right?'

Lightfoot nodded. 'I like it very much, sir. It's a bit different from what I'm used to.'

Colquhoun knew something of his background and said,

'Well, I expect even Battersea will seem good enough when you get back from this cruise!'

Lightfoot's chin lifted slightly. 'I didn't mean my home, sir. I was talking about leaving general service and coming to submarines!'

God, you bloody fool! Colquhoun felt a flush rising to his cheeks. He wanted so much to feel at home with these men, to understand them. If he had to be in the Navy he did not want to be just another officer, like so many he had met.

He said hurriedly, 'You must think I'm an idiot! I didn't mean to sound like that.'

Lightfoot studied him gravely. 'You don't have to worry, sir. I'm used to it.' He shrugged. 'Anyway, you're an officer.'

Colquhoun laughed in spite of his embarrassment. 'Well, I suppose that means something!'

There was an awkward silence. Then Colquhoun said, 'When we get to Singapore I expect there'll be a good deal of sport going on.' He made up his mind. 'Do you like sailing?'

It was Lightfoot's turn to smile. 'Never had much chance, sir. The Thames is pretty crowded off Nine Elms!'

'I asked for that.' Colquhoun tried to picture the seaman in the dismal surroundings which still seemed to haunt him. 'I'd be glad to have you in my dinghy crew if you like. Are you interested?'

Lightfoot thought briefly of Bruce and what he would say. Bloody officers! They're all bastards! Then he said quickly, 'Thanks. I'd like to have a go very much, sir!'

He looked closely at Colquhoun's pale face. It was difficult to spot where the difference lay. Perhaps in his easy, assured manner as much as in his accent. He thought that Colquhoun was not terribly good at his job, but then junior officers never seemed to be, anywhere. But he was different from the others. Not so sharp, not so quick with a reprimand when one was required and earned. He had heard Bruce say of him, ''E's as soft as 'addock-water! 'E wouldn't be where 'e was if 'is old man wasn't a bleedin' admiral!'

Lightfoot felt a nerve jump in his cheek as Colquhoun said casually, 'Let's hope we don't have any more wilful damage at Singapore. That might put the lid on everything!'

He shifted uneasily. 'This chap, sir. I—I mean, this one who did the damage.' He forced himself to meet Colquhoun's gaze. 'Do you reckon they'll find him?'

Colquhoun heard a buzz of noise through the door. The film must be ending. He glanced at his watch. 'Probably. We'll just have to keep our eyes open, won't we?'

'What would make a man do it, sir? Maybe he had a reason.'

Colquhoun watched him evenly. 'But no valid excuse, I expect.'

Lightfoot stepped back as Lieutenant Drew sauntered through the door and then said, 'Well, I'll check the gear tomorrow morning, sir. Before the drills start.'

Drew raised one eyebrow as the young seaman hurried away. 'One of your friends, Sub?' He grinned. 'Or are you just instilling a bit of discipline?'

Colquhoun did not reply. He was still staring at the open door, the picture of Lightfoot's face etched in his mind like a photograph. My God, he thought suddenly. It was Lightfoot! His guilt had been as naked on his face as if he had openly admitted to the sabotage attempt.

Colquhoun sat quite still, dazed with the shock of his unexpected knowledge.

• • •

The following morning, as soon as breakfast had been completed and the boat cleaned for another day, the drills started all over again.

Precisely at 0930 Jermain entered the control room and consulted the log. Then to Mayo, the O.O.W., he said, 'Bring her up to periscope depth, Pilot. It's time to take a look around.'

Jermain half-listened to the brisk pattern of commands behind him. Everything seemed to be running smoothly this time, he thought. And the sonar department had reported another ship some five miles away on the port bow. She would make a good mock target for the torpedo crew, something stronger than a figment of the imagination.

'Sixty feet, sir!'

'Very good. Up periscope.' He crouched down, his eye screwed against the slim monocular attack periscope. He blinked as a shaft of blinding sunlight lanced through the lens and then swung the handles towards the reported bearing.

There she was. A low-lying frighter with a long trail of greasy smoke hanging in her wake like a banner. She looked at peace with the world, no doubt making for Sierra Leone, he decided.

He turned the periscope through a full circle. The sea was flat and empty, a moving pattern of blue silk, glittering in a thousand hues in the reflected sunlight. He settled again on the lonely merchantman.

'Down periscope. Exercise Action Stations!' The alarm shrilled momentarily in the boat's still air, and he watched the clock as men hurried quietly to their positions.

'Steer one four zero. Reduce speed to twelve knots!'

Wolfe picked up his notebook and stood by his side, his eyes expressionless as he watched the coxswain easing the wheel over.

Jermain said, 'We'll attack with two tubes, and then run deep as if she had a destroyer escort, Number One.' He broke off as the reports began to come in.

'Target is bearing Red four five. Range ten thousand yards. Approximate course and speed zero five zero, six knots.'

Wolfe said sharply, 'I'd like to have a word with you after the drill, sir.'

Jermain broke into his train of thoughts and stared at him. 'Something wrong?'

'Young Colquhoun, sir. I think he's slack. I'll have to bear down on him for a while!'

Jermain felt a twinge of irritation but replied evenly, 'Has he done something stupid?'

Wolfe frowned. 'It's his whole attitude. Last night I saw him chatting to one of the men in the wardroom. I think he did it to spite *me.* I'd already told him not to try and curry favour with the men under him. But he's too damn clever for his own good!'

The petty officer at the plot said, 'Target holding course and speed, sir.'

Jermain snapped, 'Start the attack!' Then quietly to Wolfe, 'For God's sake, Ian, you can cope with that surely?'

'Well, I'm new aboard here. I thought it might come better from you!'

Mayo called, 'Ready, sir!' He was watching Wolfe's face with considerable interest.

'Up periscope!' Jermain tried to shut out Wolfe's set features and forget the ominous tension in his voice. He had sounded as if the matter was really important, not merely an everyday problem. Perhaps he was not yet ready for sea service again? Maybe the admiral had been trying to tell him just that when he had changed the orders.

The old freighter swam across the cross-wires and settled as if caught in a mesh.

'Stand by One and Two tubes!' He glanced quickly at a messenger. 'Check with the T.A.S. officer and tell him I want a complete timing of the attack. Down periscope!'

He expected to see that Wolfe had returned to his duties, but instead he stood facing him as stubbornly as before.

Jermain said evenly, 'Look, why not forget about it for a day or two? We've another three weeks yet before Singapore. You don't want to be too hard on a man, or an officer, until you've had time to test his metal!'

'If you think so, sir.' Wolfe sounded unconvinced. 'But if I was his commanding officer...'

The strain and responsibility of the past two weeks tore at Jermain's reserve like a steel barb. He stepped closer to the other man, his voice lowered to a whisper. 'Until that time, Number One, I suggest you try to keep a sense of proportion!'

He swung round as the messenger said breathlessly, 'Lieutenant Drew reports that the drill took fifteen seconds, sir!'

Jermain found that his hands were shaking from the sudden burst of anger, but he managed to control his reply. 'Good. Now we'll carry out the second part of the exercise.'

He strode to the intercom. 'Shut off for depth-charging! We will now carry out an emergency dive!' He heard the click of controls and the gentle hiss of compressed air, then he said, 'Right. Take her down to six hundred feet!'

Mayo said, 'Six hundred feet, sir! That's equal to our record dive on trials!'

The deck tilted very slightly, and with all the watertight doors and hatches slammed and clipped shut the air seemed suddenly flat and lifeless.

Jermain counted the seconds, his eyes fixed on the big depth gauges above the helmsman's head. Perhaps this extreme dive would help to drive out some of the stupid and petty irritations, he thought. Wolfe's sudden and unexpected outburst had been as unnerving as a mechanical failure, even more so because there was nothing in his face to show the reason for it. He seemed to have momentarily forgotten Colquhoun, he thought. Anyway, he was watching the diving operations and showed no sign of either anger or resentment. He had changed. *How* he had changed!

'Two hundred feet, sir!' The planesman's voice sounded taut.

Down, down, deeper into a sea which must have already lost sight of the sun and the calm sky above.

'Three hundred feet, sir!'

Jermain glanced at the clock. 'Increase to fifteen knots.'

In his mind's eye he could picture the *Termeraire*'s great bulk gliding down like a graceful whale, a shadow growing in the darkness. Gone would be her fat, even humorous surface outline. Down here she was in her true element. A hunter. A killer.

'Four hundred feet, sir!'

It was incredible to realise that only twenty years earlier, when men like Colquhoun's father had stalked enemy shipping, the diving depth had rarely gone beyond two hundred feet, and usually it had been half that amount. At this great depth their hulls would have been crushed, then burst apart by the mounting pressure. And the Black Pig could do better. Much better.

'Five hundred feet, sir!'

'Very good. Increase to twenty knots.' The greater thrust from the big screw would give the planesman an easier task as he guided the massive hull downwards.

Mayo coughed. 'It's a weird feeling! Apart from the dials we might be at periscope depth!'

The deck gave a slight quiver, and from beyond the chart-room came a dull, drawn-out groan of metal under pressure.

'Six hundred feet, sir!'

'Good.' Jermain could feel his shirt clinging to his back. 'Check all compartments!'

He looked across at Wolfe's stiff shoulders. 'After this we'll return to cruising depth and give the men a break.'

The messenger said, 'Chief Engineer on this telephone, sir.'

Jermain took it quickly, 'Well, what is it? And why don't you use the intercom and save time?'

Ross sounded far away. 'You'll not be wanting a full broadcast, sir. I've just finished my check down aft, sir. I'm not happy.'

Jermain felt the eyes of the others on his face, reading his lips like blind men.

Ross continued, 'Below the generator room there's a definite seepage. My lads are checking again now, but I'm pretty sure.'

Jermain stared at the handset. 'Do you mean a fracture in the hull itself, Chief?' He heard Mayo gasp and saw one of the seamen put his hand to his mouth.

Ross sounded firm. 'I can find no other reason, sir.'

Jermain bit his lip and tried to form a mental picture of the small, box-like compartment just aft of the reactor room. A small leak was to be expected at this stage and under these conditions. But a flaw in the hull! He felt his mouth go dry.

Even with every possible care such things could happen. Other nuclear boats like the *Dreadnought* and the *Resolution* had been docked with hairline cracks in their hull structures. But they had been in good hands, and their faults had been contained, if not completely cured, in dockyards equipped to deal in such matters. But out here, thousands of miles from any proper aid and attention, *Temeraire* had no such advantage.

Ross said suddenly, 'I suggest you reduce speed to twelve knots, to cut vibration, but keep at this depth for another twenty minutes or so. Then I'll come and tell you what I think.' A small pause. 'But if you want my advice you'll go up top and make a signal that you're returning to base!'

Jermain put down the handset and walked to the centre of the control room. He felt the content of Ross's report like a pain, as if the *Temeraire*'s very arteries had been injured and the extent of her damage was finding its way to him.

He looked at Wolfe. 'Open up the boat, Number One. I'm afraid those watertight doors will not keep this rumour under control!'

4

Sword and Medals

VICE-ADMIRAL SIR JOHN COLQUHOUN, Flag Officer Commanding the Far East Inshore Squadron, marched into the cool interior of his wide reception room and stood for a few moments to regain his breath. Normally he would have felt the old exhilaration of Sunday morning with the firm traditions of parades and divisions, but on this particular day he seemed unable to control his irritation and sense of annoyance.

Forrest, his elegant but harassed flag lieutenant, followed him into the room and made a quick gesture to a waiting steward who was hovering near the window which ran the full side of the far wall. The steward skillfully rolled up the blinds so that the glittering expanse of Singapore anchorage was displayed like a framed panorama, the moored warships and shimmering white buildings beyond pinned down by the sun's persistent glare, and made unreal by its intensity.

The admiral sighed and plucked quickly at his crisp white uniform. Beneath it his body felt dry and prickly from standing too long in the sun while the marine band went through its repertoire and the long ranks of sailors waited for inspection and the final ordeal at the mercy of the base chaplain. But Sunday was Sunday, and neither weather nor any of his other problems were allowed to alter the admiral's set routine.

He unbuckled his sword and threw it on to a chair. The steward was already pouring gin into an iced glass, and the flag lieutenant was shifting from one foot to the other as he waited for his master's next possible demand.

Sir John Colquhoun was a compact, impressive figure in his well-cut uniform, and the pale, steady eyes which gazed out over the harbour gave little indication of his uncertainty and anger. He stared steadily at the empty buoys directly opposite his new headquarters and thought back over the past months, so that without difficulty he could picture the old but impressive bulk of his flagship, the aircraft carrier which had sailed so recently on her last voyage to the breaker's yard.

Far away in London, a stroke of a pen, a unanimous decision at government level had changed life for him, and indeed for many others. The empty buoys seemed to symbolise his sense of isolation and loss as much as the sterile building over which his flag now flew. The thought of being tied to a desk, with all the clutter of charts and meaningless wall graphs made him feel his age and awoke the old bitterness like some nagging illness.

He snapped, 'Is the *Temeraire* alongside?'

The flag lieutenant read the signs and said carefully, 'She passed Beaulieu Point just before this morning's parade, sir. She picked up her moorings an hour ago.'

The admiral crossed to the open window and swung the giant telescope on its tripod until it settled on the squat, grey outline of the submarine depot ship. There was a sense of anticlimax in what he saw. The nuclear submarine was just another black shape. In the old but powerful lens he could see the slime on her hull, the signs of endurance of nearly five weeks underwater. All the same, it was an impressive achievement, he thought. The speed of her voyage from Scotland would have been thought impossible to a point of fantasy in the submarines of his day.

He said slowly, 'Did you tell the depot ship that I want the *Temeraire*'s captain over here?'

'Yes, sir. He has to pay his respects to Captain S/M and the Admiral Superintendent and so forth, but he should be here in a few minutes.'

'Good. We'll see if our important visitor is impressed!'

The flag lieutenant sighed and held the iced glass limply in his hand. He could not start his first drink of the day before the admiral, and the sight of the ice cubes already melting in the humid air filled him with gloom. The important visitor to whom the admiral referred with such open scorn was not the *Temeraire*'s captain, but the man who had been given the full honours only two hours previously.

James Conway, known in the popular Press as 'Big Jim', had been in Singapore for over a week. As a Member of Parliament and the government's trusted representative of the new Defense Commission, he seemed to symbolise, in the admiral's eyes at least, all the stupidity and irrational behaviour of a government solely interested in destroying its own power overseas for all time. The flag lieutenant had had to bear the weight of his superior's displeasure and was beginning to wonder if it would ever end.

The admiral closed the telescope and ran his finger over the worn engraving on its mounting. 'Presented to Lieutenant Michael Colquhoun, 1898'. He wondered briefly what his father would have thought about the new Navy. He glared at the flat, burnished water and tried to picture it as it had once been. Battleships and cruisers, trots of rakish destroyers and all the countless attendant craft.

Now, apart from two destroyers, the depot ship and her small brood of submarines, the anchorage seemed almost deserted. The main bulk of the Far East Fleet was made up in small patrol ships, minesweepers and the like. All excellent ships for hunting pirates and checking the flow of refugees and smugglers throughout the vast areas of the China Seas, but hardly suitable for showing the flag.

When his carrier had been at her moorings there had at least been something visible. A hint of what could be expected if one or more of the uneasy hotchpotch of small nations which lived off the admiral's command stepped out of line.

He touched his glass with his tongue. 'Where is our Defence expert at this moment?'

The young officer glanced at his watch. 'With the C.-in-C., sir. But he'll be joining you for lunch in an hour.'

The admiral groaned. 'I suppose he's bringing his bloody wife with him?'

The flag lieutenant hid a smile. 'I expect so, sir.'

'I don't know which of 'em is worse! Her with her good works, and her "My Jim works so hard, you know!", or that bloody husband of hers.' He glared at his glass. 'What *was* he in the last war?'

'I understand that he was a sergeant in the infantry, sir.'

'God Almighty! And to think that a man like that can come out here and tell us what to do!' He waved his hand vaguely across the window and the giant wall chart with its flags and coloured counters. 'To listen to him you'd think that our main work was to keep the local Chinese in employment in the ruddy dockyard, rather than patrol and protect one of the most difficult and dangerous sea areas in the world!'

The flag lieutenant said, 'I believe he won the Military Medal, sir.'

'So did thousands of others, Forrest! I hope you're not suggesting that makes all of *them* fit for running the Royal Navy!'

He warmed to his theme. 'Have you seen the way he panders to the locals? With his attendant photographers and whatnot. He deliberately takes off his jacket just to be seen talking in his braces to a lot of bloody dockyard workers! I think I'll have a stroke if he stays here much longer!'

An impeccable marine orderly stepped through the door. 'Beggin' yer pardon, sir. Commander Jermain is waitin' to pay 'is respects.'

The admiral's eyes glinted. 'Show him in!' He grinned at his flag lieutenant. 'We'll show these ruddy humbugs, eh?'

He wiped the smile from his face and stood quite still beneath one of the overhead fans as Jermain walked slowly into the room. In a quick appraisal the admiral noted the signs of strain and tiredness on his face, the white uniform which still showed traces of being too long in a metal case.

The admiral realised just as quickly that some of his own tension had been caused by this anticipated meeting. He felt something like relief and said, 'Good to have you here, Jermain!' He held out his hand. 'Now while we're having a drink I'll try and put you in the picture before my other guest arrives.'

The steward moved busily with the glasses, and the admiral continued evenly, 'As you know, Jermain, your arrival is quite an event. But it means more than you can possibly imagine.' He studied the other man's grave features, noticing the lines of tension around his eyes. He hurried on, 'I came out here to organise and control the Inshore Squadron.' He pointed at the chart. 'That covers about everything really. I've had patrol boats winkling out terrorists and gunrunners around Malaysia, and up north there are frigates and destroyers on the Japan run. There have been a few submarines, of course, but the Americans do most of the heavy work. They are, of course, better placed for the longer patrols.' His voice hardened. 'However, your *Temeraire* puts a different complexion on things. Even though you may work with the U.S. Fleet, you'll be under my control. It's absolutely essential that we can hold our end up, show the world that we are still capable out here!'

Jermain felt the tiredness pricking the back of his eyes and allowed the gin to move across his dry throat. The long cruise was over. The bright sunlight and heady salt air had made him feel drunk, like a man who has been too long away from natural living. From the very instant that the *Temeraire* had pushed her way into the anchorage, past the saluting warships, acknowledging the twittering pipes and lordly bugles, it seemed as if he had not found a second to stop and collect his thoughts.

Almost dazedly he had stepped ashore, the unfamiliar sword dangling at his side, to pay his respects to Singapore's chain of command. The Admiral Superintendent, the captain of the Submarine squadron, the captain of the base itself. The Commander-in-Chief had sent a brief but courteous welcome by messenger. He was known to be an understanding and competent admiral who no doubt was well aware that Jermain would be tired enough without adding to his ordeal by a long audience at this stage.

Jermain half listened to what the vice-admiral was saying. None of it counted, he thought bitterly. The sooner he put a stop to it the better it would be.

He said, 'I had hoped that the Captain S/M would have contacted you, sir.' He saw a glint of annoyance in the admiral's pale eyes. 'This has been a difficult trip, and, in my opinion, far too soon, before the *Temeraire* was ready for it.'

Sir John Colquhoun eyed him coldly. 'What do you mean?'

Jermain tried again. 'During a deep dive in the South Atlantic we found what may prove to be hull damage, sir. At six hundred feet there was a definite seepage.' He felt the ache of despair closing in on him. 'It's all in my report. I was under radio silence, otherwise I would have requested permission to return to the U.K.'

The admiral stared at him. 'Surely there must be some mistake?'

Jermain shrugged. 'We cannot be sure without proper docking facilities, sir. It would mean a complete infra-red analysis of the hull and dockyard services for this type of boat.'

The admiral rubbed his chin, his eyes unwinking and bright. 'But you only *think* it's a fracture, Captain?'

Jermain replied quietly, 'My engine-room staff have carried out a full check as far as they are able, sir. There is a seepage at extreme depths. Of course, it *could* be a faulty welding which may be concealed behind one of the frames. But it's far too risky to take chances.'

'Six hundred feet, you say?' The admiral walked to the chart. 'But on the trials there was no trouble, I take it?'

'Nothing you would not expect, sir.' Jermain tried to imagine how the admiral's mind was working. What did it matter about depth or what anyone else had seen? This was now, and vital.

'Well, that's a relief, Captain. You had me a bit worried there!' The admiral laughed shortly, but his eyes were cold. 'Six hundred feet in a brand-new boat must be expected to cause some teething troubles, after all! My God, when I commanded a little S-boat in the last war I sank over four thousand tons of enemy shipping without ever diving below *one* hundred feet!'

Jermain said sharply, 'This is different, sir. My command is too new for chances. I would suggest that I am ordered home immediately.'

The admiral's smile faded. 'If I choose to do so, you will be the first to know, I can assure you!' He calmed himself with an effort. 'Some of you young officers forget the meaning of your training. The *Temeraire* is not just a plum command, it's a responsibility, a means to an end!' He pointed at the chart. 'For months now the Chinese have been moving men and ships up to the north. To the Yellow Sea and beyond. Intelligence reports suggest more trouble in Korea, but whatever it is, we must keep every ship at first-degree readiness! My God, boy, a nuclear ship like yours is absolutely invaluable at the moment!'

The flag lieutenant said quietly, 'There have been Chinese submarines in the area too, Captain. We must be able to detect and track them, before they start to interfere with our own traffic.'

The admiral snapped, 'When I want your information service I'll ask for it, Forrest!' He turned to Jermain. 'These youngsters don't understand the submariner's mind, do they?'

Jermain swayed. All the weeks of worry and preparations, the strain of testing and gauging every small piece of equipment, had been bad enough. Then with the unexpected orders, the problems of welding a tired and resentful crew into a ready-made combat team, the burden had grown almost too heavy. He said stubbornly, 'It's not a question of over-caution on my part, sir.'

He did not get any further.

'I'm sure you're saying what you think is best, Captain. However, you must allow me to be the judge of that!' The admiral touched the array of medals on his tunic. 'We have to make a show of force in this area. The Chinese *and* the Americans understand that sort of thing! They have a saying out here. "An empty hand is never licked", well, I can assure you it's never been more true!'

Jermain took another drink from the flag lieutenant and saw the brief look of sympathy in the man's eyes. He heard the admiral say, 'After all, Jermain, it may only be a matter of a few weeks. It'll be a good training for your men. I'd have thought you'd have welcomed it?'

He made it sound so reasonable that Jermain found himself checking back along his thoughts, as he had been doing since that test dive. He could still hear the urgency in Ross's tone and feel the sick disappointment in his own heart.

As the admiral talked so it became more obvious what was making him so definite and insistent, Jermain decided. He was one of those admirals, thankfully rare, who could only measure strength and power by visible evidence. Big ships, massive formations. It was rumoured that the admiral had all but lost his appointment under the government's sweeping changes, the pruning of each and every branch of the Services. More and more responsibility for Far Eastern strategy was being left to the American Seventh Fleet, and Jermain could well imagine what *Temeraire*'s timely arrival could mean.

'I shall, of course, obey your instructions, sir.' Jermain saw a flicker of hostility in the admiral's eyes, but he continued doggedly, 'But my men are tired, and quite unprepared for this change of events. A lot of the crew are married. They'll be wondering about their families, getting them out here, and so forth.'

The admiral snorted. 'A lot of old women! This whole command is bogged down with bloody wives and children as it is! Heavens, Jermain, for every active officer or man there are about one hundred hangers-on! It's worse than a damned holiday camp!' He stared hard at the bright water beyond the building. 'The trouble is they're too soft today! Must have their wives and television sets just outside the dockyard gates! In my day we were grateful just to stay alive!'

Jermain said, 'But during the war...'

The admiral's face hardened. 'There's a war on *now*, damn it! Every hour of the day we're being hampered by terrorists, and our ships are stalked by Red warships! I would have imagined that the American's experience in Viet Nam was warning enough of what can happen!'

The flag lieutenant said hurriedly, 'The staff car has just arrived, sir.'

The admiral swallowed hard. 'That'll be our gallant Member of Parliament!' He fixed Jermain with a steady stare. 'Nothing you have said or heard must leak out, especially in front of *him*!'

Jermain replied stiffly, 'I am under your orders, sir.'

'Good. I was beginning to wonder!' The admiral added as an afterthought, 'I shan't ask you to do anything foolhardy, Captain. It is what you represent that counts!'

The flag lieutenant announced, 'Mr. James Conway, sir!'

The admiral switched on his smile. 'Delighted to have you here! I want you to meet the captain of the *Temeraire*!'

• • •

Ordinary Seaman John Lightfoot levelled his camera and squinted at the group of Chinese children who made up the sole audience of a giant Sikh street salesman. The man was holding several bottles of what appeared to be colourless medicine and his voice was as serious and confidential as if he had been addressing a crowd of hundreds.

Lightfoot sighed and rewound the camera before moving on with the slow, aimless throng in which he was carried like a leaf on a stream. He had been ashore for about an hour, but already his mind was pleasantly confused by the strange sounds and dialects, the bright colours and jumbled excitement of the stalls and open-fronted shops. It seemed as if all the world had gathered in this place. Above the narrow street he could see the bright blue sky, from which the afternoon sun blazed down on the drifting dust and defied the efforts of the small sea breeze to break through its power.

And everywhere there were British servicemen. Soldiers and airmen, and, of course, a generous sprinkling of white-clad sailors. It was strange to see British women in such quantities, Lightfoot thought. Against the background of oriental sounds it was odd to hear Yorkshire or Scottish dialects, and not a few from his own town.

Military and naval patrols stood quietly at street corners, swinging their sticks or fingering their pistols as they casually surveyed the passing crowds, and Lightfoot was reminded of the coxswain's short speech before the *Temeraire*'s libertymen had been allowed ashore.

The big chief petty officer had rocked back on his heels as he had run a critical eye over the assembled sailors. Apart from a few technical ratings and the duty officer, every man jack was being let ashore on this first day in Singapore.

Twine, the coxswain, had said, 'Now just remember, lads, this ain't Guzz or Pompey. This is Singapore, the main British base in these parts, and a place crawlin' with every kind of trouble an' temptation!' He had paused to allow the titters to die away. 'In addition it's full of pongos an' a whole heap of so-called sailors who ain't been to sea since they joined. These barrack-stanchions will more'n likely try to start a fight. If they do, it'll be up to you to sort it all out neat an' proper. Either move off at the sight of trouble or win! I don't want to see a lot of you skates bein' dragged aboard by the shore patrol an' bringin' disrespect on the Black Pig, got it?' His eyes had moved slowly along the ranks. 'The captain 'as made sure of full liberty. It's up to you to watch yourselves!'

Lieutenant Oxley, the duty officer, had added, 'Be on the watch for anyone trying to get information about you and the *Temeraire*. This may look like home, but it's terrorist country, and don't you forget it!'

Then the chattering, cheerful throng of men had surged ashore to the waiting trucks which would carry them the thirteen miles into town. Away from the work and strain, out of the steel which had become their world.

Lightfoot was surprised to find that he had at last started to relax. Shortly after the submarine had picked up her moorings alongside the depot ship he had nearly fainted with horror. Within minutes of the last line going over the side he had seen two grave-faced men in civilian clothes come down the bow with the Captain S/M. Then he had heard a petty officer say grimly, ''Ere they come. The bloody security boys!'

The men in question had gone to the wardroom, but after enduring an agony of suspense Lightfoot had heard nothing more. He had mentioned their arrival to Bruce who had made investigations of his own. Later Bruce had said calmly, 'Just routine. They're here to make sure you don't cut any more wires!' He had still been laughing when they had found their way ashore together.

But within fifteen minutes of de-bussing in the town Bruce had got involved with a dark-eyed Malay girl who had beckoned invitingly from a window above the street. Bruce had said huskily, 'Just the job! I bin waitin' weeks for this!'

He had told Lightfoot to follow his example, but when he had stammered out excuses the big seaman had just grunted, 'Suit yourself! But even if you catch a dose off one of 'em it only means a couple of needles in yer arse!' He had gone off chuckling with plans for a rendezvous later in the day.

Lightfoot wished he had had the nerve to follow his friend. If only to see what it was like. He grinned at the thought and realised it was the first time anything had made him smile since before the night of the car smash and the man lying dead beside the road.

Anyway, it was good to be alone for a bit. At first the sun and strange air had made him feel sick, but now as he sauntered along the street with his camera at the ready he felt a real sense of peace.

He thought momentarily of Colquhoun and wondered why he had shown such an interest in him. Admittedly he had not mentioned the dinghy-sailing again, but then he was no doubt too busy. Especially as his old man was a vice-admiral right here in Singapore.

He heard someone call his name, and a seaman called Archer panted up beside him. 'Here! Hold on, mate!' He fell in step with him. 'I missed you when you got off the bus. I've been trying like hell to catch you up.'

Lightfoot watched him cautiously. There was no need for such a display of friendship, he thought. Archer, known as Gipsy because of his swarthy skin and slicked-back hair, had never bothered to speak to him before, even when cooped up in the boat for five weeks underwater! He said, 'I'm going to meet Porky Bruce.' It sounded defensive and he blushed angrily.

Archer eyed him lazily. 'It was you I wanted.'

They had reached a narrow sidestreet and without warning Archer piloted him down it, brushing aside a whining carpet salesman as if he had been a piece of cardboard.

Archer seemed strangely excited. 'Look, I won't beat about the bush, mate.' He gestured crudely. 'I got a nice bit of crumpet stowed away, just whimpering for it!' He grinned. 'But I'm a bit short of the ready, see?'

Lightfoot stared at him. Archer was a senior seaman with far more pay than he ever earned. 'I can let you have a bit...'

Archer cut him short. 'I want the lot, mate.' He eyed him with mock surprise. 'You don't get it, do you?' He leaned forward. 'I was there, mate. Don't you understand, I was *there*!'

Lightfoot shook his head, but his madly pumping heart made him sway on his feet. 'I don't know what you're talking about!' But his voice was broken and defeated.

Archer's eyes were unwinking and completely devoid of pity. 'I was in the pub when you went off with that bloody queer. I suppose you robbed the bastard before you done him in?' He lifted his hand. 'Don't bother to explain, mate! Just so long as you understand how we stand!' He winked. 'With them two security blokes aboard it would be too damn easy to drop a hint in the right place, an' we don't want *that*, do we?'

The grinning seaman seemed to be standing behind a mist, and Lightfoot blindly pulled out his frayed wallet, his ears still ringing with Archer's casual threat. 'This is all I've got.' He watched wretchedly as the man pulled the notes out. 'I was going to buy a present for my mother.'

It sounded so strange on the face of what had happened that Archer said, 'In that case, have ten bob on me, mate!'

Leaving Lightfoot staring at the empty wallet, Archer strolled back towards the sunshine. He paused and called, 'Don't lose that nice camera! I might take a fancy to it later on!'

So there was no escape after all. If he had gone straight to the authorities at the time things might have been different. After all, it *was* an accident! He remembered the man's clawing fingers and felt the helpless anger rising to mock him once more.

If it hadn't been for Bruce he would have turned himself in.

Lightfoot walked blindly through the crowd, but this time there was no pleasure in his heart.

• • •

The reception for the *Temeraire*'s officers was held that same evening at Vice-Admiral Colquhoun's headquarters. The guests filled the big reception room and flowed out over the wide terrace beyond. In the evening's purple light the water below the balustrade looked cool and inviting, and the brightly lit warships across the anchorage shimmered above their own reflections.

In a slightly self-conscious group the submarine's officers in their white uniforms stood out against the women's coloured dresses and the gently perspiring marine orchestra.

Jermain felt as if his smile was welded to his mouth as the flag lieutenant made one introduction after another. Even the friendly reception and the soothing effect of cool champagne did little to ease the nagging concern for his command.

He glanced at his officers. They at least seemed to be enjoying themselves, he thought. Even Wolfe appeared relaxed and calm, and was in deep conversation with the Member of Parliament he had met earlier. The latter was a heavily built man with a shining red face and a laugh which came regularly and without effort, as if it was switched on for the occasion.

Sir John Colquhoun, resplendent in full mess dress and a chest of miniature decorations, beamed across at him and said, 'A good turn out, eh, Jermain?'

He nodded, 'Yes, sir.' He thought of Lieutenant Victor, the duty officer, imprisoned in the cool safety of the *Temeraire*'s wardroom. Whereas the others pitied him his lonely vigil, Jermain would willingly have traded duties with him.

Conway, the M.P., was saying loudly, 'I'll be having a look at your ship as soon as I can squeeze it in.'

Wolfe replied, 'There's quite a bit to see.'

Conway shook his head and sighed. 'I'm afraid I don't get much time for luxuries, old chap.'

An anxious little woman in an expensive scarlet dress said quickly, 'Jim's so busy these days, you know! The P.M. is always giving him such hard jobs!'

Jermain smiled in spite of his tense nerves. That must be Mrs. Conway. He saw the vice-admiral's eyes harden and heard him say, 'We're not exactly relaxing here ourselves!'

Conway wagged a finger. 'Now then, Sir John! We've been over all that! There have to be cuts in our expenses, and let's face it, the Navy has never been one for economising!'

Sir John Colquhoun was about to make a sharp retort when his eye fell on his son, who until this moment had been hidden by the others. 'Well, hello, Max.' He held out his hand. 'How are you shaping up?'

Jermain only half caught the young officer's mumbled reply. He studied them thoughtfully. The slim uncertainty of the sub-lieutenant against his father's bluff, almost belligerent, confidence. Yet there was some small likeness, Jermain decided. The same pale eyes, the same tilt of the head.

The admiral looked across at him and said offhandedly, 'I hope you can make a man of him, Jermain! Although I expect it'll be an uphill task!'

Jermain said calmly, 'I have no complaints, sir. We're all learning aboard the *Temeraire*!'

For one brief instant Jermain saw the doubt in the admiral's eyes, then he said, 'We shall see.'

Jermain realised that the M.P. was speaking to him.

'I'm very interested in your ship, Captain. I like to keep in touch. Mind you, I'm still to be convinced of the worth of such a vessel!'

Wolfe interrupted sharply, 'I suppose that if war broke out tomorrow the government would expect a graph made of tonnage sunk against man-hours and rum consumed!'

Conway grinned. 'You should be in Parliament!'

Oxley plucked at his tunic and drawled, 'Well, I didn't get into my ice-cream suit just to listen to my betters arguing.' He looked at the admiral. 'With your permission, sir, I'd like to go and try my prowess on the dance floor?'

Conway's grin broadened. 'Another one ripe for politics, eh?'

Oxley eyed him coolly. 'Actually, I hope to follow my father into the House of Lords!'

Jermain caught Wolfe's eye and said quickly, 'I think we had all better circulate, Number One. Before any eggs get broken!'

But the admiral said testily, 'You stay and talk, Jermain. Time enough for that sort of thing later!'

Conway became serious. 'Are you satisfied with the *Temeraire*?'

Jermain saw the admiral stiffen. He replied, 'She's a magnificent submarine. Still ripe from trials, of course, but a major step forward in every way.' From the corner of his eye he saw the admiral relax slightly.

What the hell did words matter anyway? The admiral was doing what he thought was best for public relations, and so presumably was the M.P.

Conway took another glass of champagne. 'You hear all this talk of safety and radiation leakage, it's all a bit confusing for the layman.'

'There's no danger on that score.' Jermain watched Lieutenant Drew guiding a laughing girl around the floor. Against his white tunic her tanned skin looked like silk.

He said absently, 'The nuclear submarine used to be a freak. Now it's a fact of life. We have to live with it.'

Conway frowned. 'And what will you be doing here?'

Jermain waited for the admiral to say something, but he appeared to be in deep conversation with Conway's wife. He said at length, 'Certain exercises with the Americans. I've not had my final instructions yet.'

The big man nodded. 'Good. We must show the Americans we can be relied on, militarily speaking!'

A colonel of marines with an upturned, ginger moustache paused to say a word with the admiral, and Jermain saw Conway stiffen as if in defence. For a moment Jermain saw through the big man's guard and felt strangely affected. Conway was not finding his work as easy as the admiral thought. At heart he might still be a sergeant, and his apparent ease with men like Sir John Colquhoun and the unknown colonel was a hard-won battle.

Conway saw Jermain's quiet scrutiny and laughed shortly. 'That young officer of yours. Is his father really a lord?'

Jermain smiled. 'I believe so. I'd never really thought about it.'

'I agree with the admiral about one thing, Captain. You are an unusual man.' Conway laughed again to hide his sudden embarrassment. 'I think the *Temerarie* is in very safe hands!'

Just as quickly the guard dropped back into place. 'Well, I must be off. I've a lot to do before tomorrow!'

The admiral looked round. 'Thank goodness *he's* gone!' Then he turned as his flag lieutenant appeared at his elbow. 'Well?'

'The signal, sir.' The flag lieutenant held out a pad and glanced meaningly at Jermain.

Jermain watched the admiral scanning the signal pad and wondered. The lieutenant had said *the* signal. It was too pat, too coincidental with the M.P.'s exit.

The admiral cleared his throat. 'It's from London, Jermain. Your orders are to sail tomorrow for an exercise with the Americans.' He skimmed quickly over the preliminaries. '*Temeraire* will proceed to U.S. Fleet area Romeo Tango Five for Exercise Flashpoint.' He gave a small smile. 'I hope you put on a good show!'

Jermain took the single copy of the signal and read it slowly. 'Did you confirm this with London, sir? Are they aware of my report?'

The admiral snapped, 'Of course I did. You are supposed to

be fully operational for this sort of thing. Anyway, it's confirmed under my responsibility!'

'I see.' Jermain felt the anger boiling inside him like fire. The words, the careful deceit, made him reckless. 'My own responsibility is to my command, sir. There may be flaws in the hull, as I know you are aware.'

'I am more interested in possible flaws in the crew, Jermain. In any case you'll be better off at sea. The Singapore government is worried about your being here in the harbour. Rumours about contamination and all that rot. That fool Conway wouldn't like any trouble with the local government at this stage of his work. He said as much earlier.'

'Very well, sir. But my decision must be upheld should I have to break off the exercise.'

'I don't think that will be necessary, Jermain.' The admiral's tone was final. 'The sooner you get this job done, the quicker I can arrange your passage home.'

Jermain walked through the laughing guests and leaned against the cool balustrade. The anchorage was quite dark now, but against the floodlit hull of the depot ship he could clearly see the *Temeraire*'s black whaleback and the number on her fin.

Only aboard her did he feel in control of things. Here nothing was certain, and little seemed to go below face value.

But the orders were definite enough. The area referred to was three day's sailing to the north east off Hainan Island and close to the coast of North Viet Nam. The Americans were used to this sort of exercise, and as the admiral had remarked, the sooner it was completed, the earlier they could leave.

But Jermain knew from past experience that nothing was ever that simple.

5

Romeo Tango Five

JERMAIN ROLLED over in his bunk and groped wearily for the telephone. He had been in a deep sleep so that he was not even sure if the insistent buzz had been part of some disordered dream. 'Captain speaking.' He peered at the luminous face of his watch and tried again to clear his brain.

From the control room he heard Oxley's calm voice. 'Five-thirty, sir. We'll be coming up to the rendezvous in fifteen minutes.'

Jermain switched on the bunkside light and stared emptily at his small cabin. The charts and open logbooks were still as he had left them only four hours earlier. One hundred and fifty feet above his bunk the early sun would be feeling its way across the water. There might still be the vicious little squall which had blown up when they had left Singapore nearly three days ago, and which had greeted the probing periscope each time they had planed upwards to take a look at the outside world.

He realised that Oxley was still waiting at the other end of the line. 'Very good. Were the hands called early?'

'Yes, sir.' Oxley sounded a bit peeved. 'Shall I have some breakfast sent along to you, too?'

'No.' Jermain dropped the handset and swung his long legs over the side of the bunk. The canned air of his cabin felt cold to his skin, and he shivered slightly as he pulled on his shirt. He had been sweating in his exhausted sleep, and as he groped for the rest of his clothing his mind reluctantly returned to the nagging problems which waited for every awakening like playful tormentors.

To go to sea immediately after the enforced voyage from Scotland had been bad enough. There were faults to rectify, spare fittings to be installed, and the thousand and one other items which always dogged the captain of a new vessel.

But Vice-Admiral Colquhoun's bombshell had been almost too much to bear. Fleet manoeuvres were a nightmare at the best of times, with every senior officer breathing down the neck of his next subordinate. For the admiral to throw the *Temeraire* into some pressurised Anglo-American exercise with neither preparation nor discussion was asking for trouble of the worst kind.

The admiral had saved his worst act until the very moment of departure. As the submarine had tugged at her moorings and men had scampered along the casing in readiness for letting go, he had presented himself at the brow with the calm statement that he intended to accompany *Temeraire* to the exercise area.

Jermain took two of the little tablets which Griffin had given him to help him keep going. He washed them down with a glass of water and grimaced at himself in the bulkhead mirror.

Sir John Colquhoun had been like a child with a new toy. As the boat had moved free from her moorings and the tense business of conning the great black hull safely through the harbour traffic had begun, he had wandered happily through the boat, stopping every so often to peer into a compartment at a startled rating or to watch an officer at his controls, usually with a 'Don't mind me, boy! Just act as if I wasn't here!' As if the sight of a flag officer wasn't bad enough, he had changed into a roll-necked sweater, commenting, 'Can't get used to all this clincial stuff! When I was in submarines we had to *dress* the part!'

He seemed to be enjoying himself well enough, Jermain

thought. He had refused to accept or even share one of the cabins, but insisted on using one of the wardroom spare bunks which were kept for excess passengers of more lowly state.

Consequently, it was impossible to enter the wardroom, even during the night watches, without Sir John's face popping out from between the bunk curtains with some comment or jocular criticism.

It was getting on everyone's nerves. Jermain knew that the admiral's son hardly ever entered the wardroom and had been seen snatching a quick meal during his watch. Ross too avoided the admiral, but for different reasons. Whenever the admiral was able to corner the chief engineer he would ask some question about the complex machinery or some detail concerning the reactor, and after the chief's lengthy explanations Sir John would wave his hand and say cheerfully, 'I'm afraid it's all new to me! Completely new!'

Jermain had even heard Lieutenant Drew taking advantage of the admiral's impossible questions. The T.A.S. officer had answered two questions in Jermain's presence with such sincerity and eloquence that the admiral had been deeply impressed. Only Jermain knew that the Australian's answers had been so much gibberish. After the last occasion he had reprimanded Drew, and the latter had said gloomily, 'It's just that he gets on my wick, sir!'

And then of course there were the two security officers. Usually seated in the ship's office or at the wardroom table, they never seemed to separate. They had checked the men's service records and questioned the heads of departments. They had even insisted that Lieutenant Kitson should show them the actual place where the wiring had been tampered with. Naturally they had not found the culprit. Like the admiral, they had only succeeded in getting on everybody's nerves.

The previous afternoon Jermain had approached the admiral about the matter. The latter had been standing in the small chartroom making his own calculations of the course and speed.

After a while he had said playfully, 'I'm just a passenger, Jermain. You mustn't ask me things like that!'

Jermain had replied coldly, 'The security officers are aboard at your insistence, sir. I only wanted them to make a check when we entered Singapore.'

The admiral had stared at him for several seconds. 'They know their job, Jermain. While this boat is under my control I want it free of trouble, see?' There the matter had ended.

Jermain picked up his cap and walked through the passageway to the control room. It would soon be time to go to periscope depth and the control-room lighting was dimmed to a warm orange glow to ease the strain on the eyes of the watchkeeping officers.

Oxley said formally, 'Course zero one zero, sir. Speed twenty knots.'

Jermain nodded and walked slowly through the control room. The men looked clean and fresh-faced, but their expressions were tense and strained, and he knew that they were all thinking about the exercise and about showing their paces in front of the Americans.

In the chart-room he found Wolfe and Mayo leaning over the table. He felt them watching him as he checked the course and the *Temeraire*'s position, as he had done every day since her keel had first felt salt water.

It was still hard to realise that the world outside the hull had changed yet again. He stared at the pencilled lines, the neat crosses which marked each interval of their most recent journey. Out of Singapore, and in silence across the South China Sea. Northward up the coast of unhappy Viet Nam, and then eastwards towards the mass of the Chinese mainland, where Hainan Island hung like an ulcer from the parent body.

On the exercise chart this area was marked as Romeo Tango Five. In such areas the Americans searched and probed continuously, like wrestlers circling for openings in their opponents' guard. Along three thousand miles of little-known coastline their nuclear submarines patrolled and watched, tested their weapons and waited for that one dreaded day when their terrible power would be flung against China and any other potential enemy.

Temeraire's part in Exercise Flashpoint was small but vital. She had been ordered to shadow one such Polaris submarine to a proposed firing position one hundred miles south of Hainan Island. While the bigger and more cumbersome American submarine manoeuvred into her pinpointed firing zone, *Temeraire* would cover her with a protective sonar screen so that she could do her deadly work undisturbed.

A day after leaving Singapore Jermain had made his first rendezvous with a small task force of the U.S. Seventh Fleet. At the prescribed time he had surfaced between two parallel lines of sleek warships while helicopters hovered like giant locusts overhead and on the deck of a nearby cruiser a naval band played 'Rule Britannia'. It was a bizarre and slightly unnerving experience.

The admiral in charge of the force had been dropped neatly on the swaying fin from one of the helicopters, and after a brief but searching inspection had given Jermain his instructions. He had been more than surprised to meet Sir John Colquhoun. To Jermain he had said quietly, 'Don't they trust you alone, Captain?' Then with a grin he had added, 'I'll be happy to take him off your hands if he's willing to leave!'

But Sir John had not been willing. He had queried several points in the American Plan, not least the selection of the exercise area.

The American admiral had studied him gravely. 'It's like this, Sir John. By 1970 there will be one hundred and seventy-two nuclear submarines in the world. In thirty years maybe double that figure. And now, this very day, the Red Chinese are the fourth largest submarine power! We have to be ready for anything. We have to learn to use what we have at our disposal right now!' He had let his eyes move across the chart as if to see more clearly the sleeping mass of China. 'You never know what the Reds'll try next. But the only thing they respect is power, and plenty of it! So just to keep 'em in line we must lean on them once in a while!'

After he had been hoisted back to his helicopter Jermain had thought about his last words. But Sir John had said stiffly. 'Bloody Americans! You'd think they owned the world!'

Jermain sighed and picked up the intercom handset. 'This is the captain speaking.' He heard his voice echoing through the compartments of the hull and could imagine his men watching and listening. 'In a few moments we will make contact with the American Polaris boat which some of you saw two days ago.'

The big, rocket-firing submarine had been at the rear of the fast-moving formation, and repeatedly Jermain had found his eyes drawn to her with cold fascination. Larger than the

Temeraire she showed little outward sign of her devastating power. Jermain knew from past experience that beneath her rounded hull were two erect lines of Polaris missiles. Sixteen rockets, each with a range of over two and a half thousand miles. Such a craft could reach inland and destroy anything and everything. Yet in the harsh sunlight she looked dangerously normal, with her high-mounted planes shining on either side of her fin like two scythes.

He continued, 'We will patrol an area to the north of her and south of Hainan Island. A conventional submarine will carry out an attack through our screen. It will be up to us to find and destroy the attack before it makes a successful contact with the Polaris boat.' He glanced at his watch. 'You will now go to action stations. I will keep you informed at each stage of the operation.' He wanted to wish them luck, to tell them he was relying on them. But they were all experts at their own jobs. It would seem superfluous, even apprehensive of trouble.

He nodded toward Wolfe, who pressed the emergency buzzer.

Chief Petty Officer Harris, the radio supervisor, stood up from his control panel and wiped his hands on his thighs. 'All checked, sir.' He stared suspiciously at a small loudspeaker at his side, the ear of the acoustic radio through which they could talk with or listen to the other submerged boat.

'Boat at action station, sir.'

'Very good.' Jermain glanced at Wolfe. 'It's a damned eerie feeling, isn't it? Two great submarines making a rendezvous in the middle of nowhere!'

The acoustic radio crackled and Jermain stared at it as the voice said slowly, 'NEMESIS calling BLUEBOY. Do you read me? Over.'

Harris cleared his throat. 'BLUEBOY to NEMESIS. Read you loud and clear. Over.'

Mayo called from the chart-room. 'Right on course, sir!'

From the sonar compartment Oxley's voice came calmly through the intercom. 'We have the Polaris boat, sir. Range ten thousand yards. Course zero nine zero. Speed twenty plus.'

Harris repeated the information and Jermain heard the American say, 'Right on the button! Nice to have you around, pal!'

Then a new voice, clipped and precise. Even the weird distortion caused by five miles of water could not hide the tension in his speech. 'Hallo, BLUEBOY. This is the captain. We will carry out phase one at two zero zero feet. Over and out.'

Jermain stood beside the sheathed periscope, his eyes watchful. 'Take her down, Number One. Two hundred feet. Steer zero four five and reduce to twelve knots.' The dials flickered and the deck tilted very slightly.

The admiral's voice broke into his thoughts. 'What's happening, Jermain?'

'We're cutting across the American's stern. Then I will turn on a parallel course between him and the mainland.'

The admiral sounded excited. 'How close inshore will you go?'

Jermain had to force his mind away from the tactical problems to concentration on the admiral's question. 'Seventy-five miles at the nearest, sir. We're right over the start of the Continental Shelf hereabouts.' He gestured towards the depth recorder. 'We've got a thousand fathoms under the keel. Just five miles further inshore and the shelf rises to less than fifty fathoms.' He watched the admiral's pale eyes, but in his thoughts he could see the great undersea cliff rising in a green wall, against which a submarine would be like so much tin.

Oxley's voice again. 'Starting the sweep, sir. No contact.'

The admiral remarked. 'Bloody tame after all this waiting! When you think back to the war, Jermain, what a difference! The stalking and listening. The days of misery while the depth-charges rattled the teeth in your head!' He rubbed his hands. 'But at the end of it all, the ship in your cross-wires! That was the moment.'

Mayo called, 'Altering course, sir. Zero nine zero.'

Twine at his wheel intoned. 'Course zero nine zero, sir.'

Jermain peered at his watch. 'Any contact yet?' He bit his lip. The admiral's constant muttering was getting him rattled. Oxley would rightly resent any unnecessary questioning. He snapped, 'Belay that!'

The intercom came to life. 'Nemesis has changed course for second run, sir.' Oxley sounded tired. 'Bearing two two five, twelve thousand yards.'

Jermain glanced at the petty officer by the plot. 'Got that?'

'Yes, sir.' He ran his rule carefully across the glass-topped table. 'She'll be exercising her missile crews now, sir.'

Jermain tried not to look at the clock. Minutes dragged past and still nothing happened. Six miles away the Polaris submarine was going about her business, her crew of over a hundred men no doubt absorbed in the intricate drill of preparing the missiles for a mock launching. But where was the attacker?

He checked the chart and tried to think it out step by step. The *enemy* was a conventionally-powered killer submarine with a maximum speed of perhaps eighteen knots. Her skipper would be well aware of the practice area and could guess to within a few miles their approximate position. Whereas his position was a complete mystery. He had a dozen choices, and he only needed one break in the screen to make a quick attack.

Jermain bit his lip. Where would *I* go?'

He made a decision. 'Take her up to one hundred feet, Number One.' He heard the slight hiss of pressurised air and saw the slender needles begin to swing back.

The admiral said, 'Aren't we expected to stay at two hundred feet?'

'This is supposed to be the real thing, sir. The enemy won't stick to the rules.'

Jermain forgot the admiral as Wolfe reported. 'One hundred feet, sir!'

Jermain crossed to his side and said quietly. 'The crafty bastard will probably keep close to the surface as he makes his run in.'

Wolfe nodded. 'More than likely. He'll take his time so that his screws and motors make as little sound as possible.'

'Suppose he closes from Hainan Island?' Jermain was thinking aloud. 'He would stand a much better chance. He'll know that we're unlikely to cross the Continental Shelf into shallow water. But *he* could do it very easily.'

Wolfe's eyes glowed. 'It's a thought. Sonar echoes would be distorted anyway by the shelving bottom. He'd be up to us with his own detection gear and we'd be on equal footing!'

Jermain smiled. 'I agree. That's what I would do.' He peered down at the chart. 'Alter course to zero one zero. We'll close in a bit.'

The sounding recorder began to swing as if caught by a magnet.

Mayo said doubtfully. 'Fifty fathoms, sir.'

Jermain picked up the engine-room handset. 'Is everything all right, Chief?'

Ross answered immediately, as if he had been sitting with the phone in his hand. 'Running like a clock, sir.'

'We're turning towards the land and into shallow water, Chief. If we draw blank or the sonar gets a strong echo in the original area I'll turn back and go to maximum speed. So be prepared!'

He heard Ross chuckle and felt slightly relieved. Ross said, 'Like looking for a nigger in a coal-hole, sir!'

Oxley's voice caught his attention. 'Getting distorted echoes, sir. Could be a throwback. But definitely not another vessel.'

'Keeping searching. I shall make another sweep to the westward in ten minutes.'

The admiral had sat on a stool as if the suspense was getting him down. He remarked. 'The Americans will have something to crow about if they break through your screen, Jermain.'

So it's *my* screen now, is it? Jermain said aloud, 'I don't suppose the *target* will be too pleased, sir!'

The admiral ignored him. 'I can just hear that idiot Conway if the *Temeraire* makes a hash of this! He'll probably withdraw every blasted British warship from the Far East!' He glared at the round-eyed control-room messenger, the only man present who was not employed and therefore listening. 'What do these mildew-minded little shop stewards know about this sort of thing, eh?'

With her searching sonar swinging around her like an invisible shield the submarine prowled nearer and nearer to the shoreline. No one spoke any more, and men became conscious of the silence, of heart-beats, and the endless, dragging minutes.

• • •

Right forward, in the *Temeraire*'s underbelly, Max Colquhoun sat stiffly in his steel chair, his eyes moving restlessly across the shoulders of the sonar operators. By his side Oxley lounged with his chin on his chest, his fingers drumming a little tattoo on his microphone. On the tall panels the lights flickered and the operators' headsets squeaked and muttered with all the noises from the sea around them. It was a strange world, Colquhoun thought. As if the whole crushing force of the sea was filled with unknown chattering creatures.

Petty Officer Irons, the senior sonar rating, readjusted his dials and said briefly, 'There it goes again, air.' The microphone at his elbow relayed the strange bleeping sound which had earlier aroused Oxley's attention.

It reminded Colquhoun of a disturbed bird in a hedgerow. Chirping irritably before dropping once more into a doze.

Oxley said, 'I still can't make it out.' He glanced at the sounding gauge. 'God, we're in forty fathoms now!' He yawned and stretched his legs. 'Why didn't I stay in *ordinary* boats? What could be better than a rainy day in Gosport, sipping beer in the old Anglesey?'

Irons said sharply, 'There it goes again, sir.' He paused and then added, 'I think it came from a slightly different bearing.' His fingers readjusted the red dial. 'Three five five degrees or thereabouts.' He twisted round to look at Oxley's frowning face. 'I'm sorry, sir, but it only makes a sound for a few seconds!'

Colquhoun said, 'Well, there's nothing on the surface. We'd have heard it long ago.'

Oxley stared at him. 'Sub, you can be very helpful at times.' He ignored Colquhoun's expression of surprise and switched on his intercom. 'Captain, sir? I think I've found out what the strange echoes are.' He winked at Colquhoun. 'I think there are fishing boats overhead. Maybe several over a wide area. Small boats without their engines running would be almost impossible to detect at this stage.'

Jermain's tone was patient. 'So what did you hear?'

'I read some months ago that the Russians have been using some sort of underwater fishing gear. It makes a *fish sound* and helps to attract any nearby shoals to the area.' He scowled at Irons, who was openly grinning at him. 'Well, that's what I read, sir.'

Jermain did not laugh. 'You could be right. I should have thought of that. There are no Russian trawlers in this area, but no doubt the Chinese have this gadget, too.'

Another pattern of bleeps rattled in the microphones, and

Irons rubbed his ears angrily. 'Hell, that was close!' He glared at the panel. 'I hope the bastards catch a bloody whale!'

Without warning the gauge on the centre of the panel gave a sharp jerk and then settled firmly at an angle. Irons crouched low and began to move his dials with set concentration. Through his teeth he said, 'Strong echo, sir! Bearing Green one zero zero! Extreme range but *definite*!'

Oxley came to life. 'Continue tracking!' In the intercom he said sharply, 'Definite contact, sir! Extreme range, bearing Green one zero zero!'

As if in reply the intercom crackled, 'Start the attack!'

Oxley grinned. 'Soon be over now!'

• • •

Jermain listened to the brisk passing of orders as the helm went over and like a circling aircraft the *Temeraire* swam round in a tight turn on to the new bearing. Half aloud he said, 'Just as I thought. The enemy must have known about the fishing boats and has been sculling about behind them all day. Just waiting his chance!'

'Course one one zero, sir.'

'Very good. Increase to twenty knots!' He looked at Wolfe. 'As soon as we cross into deep water I'll dive to three hundred feet!'

Wolfe nodded and tapped the planesman's shoulder.

The admiral was on his feet. 'Can you head him off?'

'Should be easy, sir. He's taken too long to make his attack. Nemesis will be making her next turn in five minutes, so he'll have to crack on speed. I shall close the range as for two homing torpedoes and then loose a grenade.' He smiled in spite of his earlier uncertainty. 'All parties will hear the grenade and know that the hunter has been hunted!'

He watched the gyro repeater as the admiral said, 'That'll make 'em sit up! You see now why I wanted your boat on this exercise? To me it's more than a show of force, Jermain, it's the only way to prove our worth out here!' He rubbed his hands. 'I might get a couple more nuclear boats under my command in the near future. That'll stop any possible chance of our authority being undermined!'

Mayo called, 'Crossing the Shelf now, sir! Eight hundred fathoms in five minutes!'

Jermain heard Drew's harsh voice on the intercom as he goaded his torpedo party into the final part of the attack drill. He did not really care what the admiral saw in the exercise. The important thing was that the crew had behaved extremely well, and at no time had a single defect been reported. Now perhaps they could get on with the business of training undisturbed.

The sounding recorder began to swing slowly and then more steeply as the sea bed fell away. Maybe at their present depth of one hundred feet they would make a slight shadow across the treacherous cliff edge as they swam into safer waters.

Without warning there was an insane screech of metal, like a handsaw across solid steel, and as the deck gave a warning tilt to port the nerve-searing sound was followed by a violent, shuddering lurch which threw some of the men from their feet.

Jermain reeled against the periscopes, his ribs aching from a blow against the greased metal, his mind momentarily stunned as the hull received a full jolt as if from a solid object. For an instant he imagined that they had collided with another submarine. Already the depth gauge was rotating wildly, and he heard Wolfe yelling hoarsely at the coxswain.

Jermain forced his mind to hold steady. 'Slow ahead! Watch your gauges!'

Jeffers, the second coxswain, sounded breathless. 'Can't hold her, sir! The planes is jammed!'

'Diving, sir!' Wolfe was gripping the planesman's seat, his eyes glued to the dials.

Jermain felt the deck corkscrewing beneath him and heard Wolfe say tightly, 'One hundred and fifty feet, sir! One hundred and seventy-five feet!'

As if to emphasize the danger, the hull shuddered again and more violently. It was like hearing an oil drum being beaten with a giant hammer. And in between each boom there was a screech of metal, grating at the hull like steel tentacles.

'Emergency surfacing drill, Number One!' Jermain listened to his own voice and found time to wonder. It sounded calm and unemotional, yet he could feel his nerves screaming in time to the *Temeraire*'s struggles with the thing which was trying to destroy her. 'Close all watertight doors!' The control room seemed to become smaller as the oval doors were clipped shut.

Wolfe added, 'Still diving, sir. Two hundred and seventy-five feet!'

Jeffers gasped as his control wheel slackened for a few seconds and then locked again. Every eye was fixed on the dials, and each ear was numbed by the regular booming impacts against the tough steel.

Jermain said, 'Must be one of those fish-buoys! We've got it wrapped round the fin and the after hydroplane!'

He could feel the sweat pouring between his shoulders like ice water, could sense the horror around him which already fringed on the edge of panic. The young messenger was gripping a petty officer's sleeve, his eyes filled his face like mirrors of terror, and in the chart-room entrance Mayo stood with his arms wide against the tilting hull as if he had been crucified.

Ross's voice came on the intercom. 'I'm blowing everything, sir! Can you try and free the aft-planes?'

Jermain said, 'Try opposite helm, Coxswain! See if you can shake it off!'

Twine swung the wheel, his eyes steady as he watched the gyro repeater. Twisting and turning like a snared fish the submarine thrashed wildly from one side to the other.

Only the admiral appeared unmoved, Jermain noticed. He stood against the plot table, his pale eyes empty of expression, like a man already dead.

'Four hundred feet, sir!' The man's voice sounded fractured.

Jermain dashed the sweat from his eyes and listened to the banshee screech against the hull. Down and down. Nearly five thousand feet to the bottom. No one had ever lived from a last dive. Friends of those lost in early disasters spoke glibly of a 'quick death', but who could tell? Jermain saw a seaman staring at the curved side as if expecting to see it cave in at any second.

'Four hundred and fifty feet, sir!'

There was a long-drawn-out rattle and then a violent jerk which nearly threw Jermain to the deck.

Jeffers yelled, 'It's free, sir! She's answerin'!'

The sounds were changing again. Now it seemed as if a giant piece of metal was being bounced along the casing, its trailing cable rattling jubilantly behind it.

Jermain said flatly, 'Hold her, Number One. I don't want to pop up like a cork!' He saw the needle begin to turn in their favour, and heard a seaman sobbing quietly behind him. He added, 'Keep her at periscope depth.' Over his shoulder he snapped, 'All sections report damage and injuries!'

Voices crackled and hummed through the intercom system, voices unrecognisable in strain and relief.

'Open up the boat. Stand by emergency deck party!'

Jeffers did not turn. 'Shall I be relieved, sir?'

Jermain shook his head. 'No, I want you there at the planes. We're not out of the woods yet!'

Wolfe said, 'No apparent damage, sir. Two torpedomen slightly injured in the fore-ends.'

'Very well. Pass the word for the doctor.'

Oxley's voice sounded loud over the speaker. 'Lost contact, sir. The submarine must have turned away.'

Twine said between his teeth, 'Not bleedin' well surprised, with all this row goin' on!'

Jermain met Wolfe's eye and wondered if he too had been struck by Oxley's behaviour. With the boat diving headlong for the bottom Oxley could still retain an interest in his hard-won target.

The deck party were already mustering below the bridge ladder, their expressions mixed between shock and surprise at being alive.

Sub-Lieutenant Colquhoun slung his leg over the coaming of the control-room door, his fingers fumbling with his lifejacket. He did not seem to see either Jermain or his father, but stared blindly at his waiting men.

The admiral broke his silence and said tightly, 'Well, Jermain, I hope you're satisfied!'

Jermain tore his eyes from the depth gauge. 'About what, sir?' He saw the anger flickering in the admiral's eyes, like reflections in the side of an ice floe.

'By your pig-headed stupidity you've not only lost the submarine contact, you also damn nearly sunk this boat!' He waved his hands around him. 'You should have stuck to the instructions!'

'We would have made no contact, sir.' Jermain eyed him

angrily, 'At least, it would have been too late to intercept.'

Sir John Colquhoun turned away. 'We don't know for sure that Oxley did make a true contact. It might be just one more piece of damned incompetence!' He seemed to be talking to himself now. 'The humiliation! Your excuses'll cut no ice with me, I can assure you!'

'Sixty feet, sir!' Wolfe was watching the admiral, his features grim.

'Up periscope.' Jermain staggered, and for a moment he thought the steering had jammed. But as the periscope hissed from its well he saw that the weather had worsened, and in spite of the watery sunlight the lenses seemed to be shrouded in heavy mist. But it was rain, steady, torrential rain, which was beating the sea's surface into froth and fine spray.

He straightened his shoulders. 'Can't see a thing. Surface!'

He brushed past the admiral and stopped beside the deck party. 'You will have to get out on the hull. It'll not be easy, and speed will be essential.' He looked at Colquhoun's pale face. 'But no risks, understand?' He saw him nod, but there was little understanding in his eyes.

Mayo yelled, 'I'm sending up an additional rating to replace Jeffers, sir!'

The hull staggered, and Jermain swarmed up the ladder, knocking off the first set of clips and opening the hatch in automatic movements. Up the ladder with the deck party panting at his feet and then through the second hatch and on to the surface navigation bridge. The water was still draining away, and the fin's fiberglass covering was thick with crusted salt and trailers of weed.

With the rain beating savagely at his head and shoulders Jermain pulled himself the last few feet into the open cockpit at the top of the fin. The rain was as deafening as it was heavy, and the masked sunlight shimmered around the wallowing hull and made the sea seem like steam. As if the sea was angry to lose its victim and its rage had been transformed into heat.

Jermain clambered over the edge of the screen, his eyes straining astern. He saw the raw welts on the black whaleback where the trapped cable had scored through the paintwork to the metal itself. And then bobbing astern like a sea-anchor he saw the dull-coloured buoy and the last coil of wire which appeared to be holding it to the boat's vertical rudder.

He shouted above the hissing rain, 'Pass the word to the control room! We must retain this speed the whole time. If we stop the buoy may sink and wrap itself around the screw, then we are done for! Not that the Communists would mind towing us into port!' The joke had no effect, and he heard his instructions being relayed tonelessly through the intercom.

Lieutenant Victor squeezed into the cockpit. 'Number One sent me up to lend a hand, sir.' He blinked at the sea and added, 'God, what a mess!'

Jermain turned to Colquhoun. 'Are you ready?'

Colquhoun nodded dumbly.

'Right then. Take your men down to the rear of the fin, just like you did when the dinghy came aboard. I suggest you rig a tackle to the handrail and pay out two men towards the vertical rudder. Once there they should be able to hack that wire free without too much difficulty.' He gripped the boy's arm. 'I'll trim the boat as high as I can, but the men who do the job will be swimming for part of the time, so hold on to their lifelines like hell!'

'Yes, sir. I'll go myself.'

Jermain watched the little group climb down to the partly submerged deck and waited as they rigged the lifeline and huddled together for a last conference.

During all the confusion no one had reported hearing the end of the excercise, which was hardly surprising. The attacking submarine was to detonate two grenades to signify a successful strike, and no doubt at this very moment her captain was congratulating himself at this unexpected result.

Jermain gritted his teeth and plucked his sodden shirt away from his chest. All it needed now was for the unseen fishing boats to arrive and demand damages!

6

Human Error

MAX COLQUHOUN shouted above the noise of the dinning rain, 'Right then! Pay out the lifelines and make sure there's no slack!' He looked directly at the seaman who was to accompany him along the wave-washed deck. 'We'll take one hacksaw each and work in relays!'

The man, Gipsy Archer, bared his teeth and wiped the water from his black hair. 'Should get a tot of neaters for this, sir!'

Colquhoun tore off his streaming clothes and stood swaying on the steel casing. Under his bare feet it felt like ice. Then he tightened his underpants around his waist and tied one of the lifelines hard against his hips. He had to work fast, and not give himself time to waver in front of the watching men.

At first he had thought his legs would not even carry him down to this treacherous place, and his offer to do the job himself had seemed all the more a cruel mockery. He missed the tough competence of Petty Officer Jeffers, whose seamanship appeared to come as much from instinct as from any set drill.

He blinked the spray from his eyes and handed Archer the end of a loose rope bridle. Like lumberjacks on a giant log they would walk down the side of the hull, held apart by the bridle and steadied by the slender lifelines.

He tried to grin. 'Right, Gipsy! Let's see how good a seaman you are!'

Archer shrugged and moved the hacksaw on to one hip. Against his tanned and tattooed body Colquhoun seemed frail and delicate. He had volunteered to accompany the officer not out of loyalty but for the sheer guts of the thing. He was proud of his strength, and was always ready to match it against the other seamen.

Slipping and sliding they moved away from the swaying fin, each step taking them nearer the deeply shelving whaleback towards the stern where the angry water boiled across the steel like a millrace.

Colquhoun winced as the backwash surged around his legs. It was very cold in comparison to the rain, and he could feel his breath wheezing in his lungs with each precarious movement. Once when he looked back he saw Able Seaman Rider taking charge of the line party and, above him, silhouetted against the sheeting rain and washed-out sky, the watchful figure of the captain.

Just this once they were depending on him, he thought desperately. Perhaps it was that thought alone which was making him keep going. Yet his father had not said a word, not even wished him luck. The memory of the admiral's angry face in the control room made him suddenly bitter. But why should it matter? He had known their meeting would be just as it was.

A wave curled lazily over the hull and pushed him kicking againt the *Temeraire*'s rough flank. For an instant he saw the sea right below him and felt his shins grate cruelly on the metal.

Archer pulled on the bridle and yelled, 'You takin' a dip then?' He was actually grinning.

With sudden determination Colquhoun fought his way along the casing, ignoring the cuts and bruises on his hands and feet and concentrating on the tall rudder blade which seemed to cruise quite independently from the rest of the boat. He was quite frozen now, yet his senses seemed sharper instead of dulled by his constant pounding. He could see the score marks left by the snared cable and even small patterns of rust around the horizontal rudder.

He paused, sobbing for breath. Without looking at his companion he gasped, 'We'll jump together! For God's sake don't slip or we'll miss the rudder and fall into the screw!'

Archer scowled, 'I ain't stupid, *sir*!'

Momentarily blinded by the criss-cross of surging water Colquhoun leapt towards the upright sheet of steel with its mocking halter of wire cable. For a brief instant he thought he had missed his direction and fell kicking into the maelstrom, his mouth filling with salt as he screamed meaningless words and curses into the sea itself. The bridle pulled him against the rudder fin with a savage jerk, and he saw his own blood running freely into the creamy froth around the bar-taut line. But they had made it.

Working at top speed they freed themselves from the bridle and clung on either side of the rudder, blind to everything but the cable and the job in hand.

Colquhoun sawed at the wire for a full minute and then croaked, 'You take over!' As Archer carried on with the muscle-wrenching work Colquhoun found his eyes drawn down and behind his perch to where the distorted sunlight cast an occasional glow on the great whirling propeller blades. One slip . . . He shuddered.

Back below the fin, Rider tested the lifelines and shouted, 'Play 'em like fish, lads! Don't jerk 'em off!' He looked round startled as two more figures emerged from the screen door.

Lightfoot and Bruce stood staring at the drama, and then the latter growled, 'We come up to lend a hand!'

Rider nodded, his panting making him bend over. 'Good! It's about time you bloody sonar people did somethin'!"

Bruce spat on his hands and seized one of the lines. To Lightfoot he said, 'Looks like they're nearly through.'

Lightfoot took his place behind him and braced his legs against the hull's uneasy roll. He was almost blinded by the rain, and he stumbled awkwardly as the churned waves swept up and over the casing, trying to push the men from their hold.

He had almost lost his head when the *Temeraire* had tilted crazily towards the bottom. The men in the sonar compartment had stared at each other without recognition, their faces like masks of terror, too shocked to comprehend what was really happening.

There was always the risk, of course. It was mentioned in the training depots in a matter-of-fact, clinical fashion, as if it only happened on very rare occasions, and then only to others.

All Lightfoot's past anguish, his terror of the seaman, Archer, had vanished as the boat had plummeted down. His world had been confined to the small steel room with its glittering, mocking equipment and the men who sat like caged waxworks.

Over the intercom, from another part of the sealed hull, he had heard sharp, brittle orders being passed and snatches of meaningless conversation. Then every so often the captain's voice would penetrate his whirling mind, so that he waited for it, like the word of God.

When eventually the wire cable had slipped free from its first hold and the deck had swung slowly upwards he had felt a hand on his shoulder and heard Colquhoun say, 'It'll be all right now. You see!'

Perhaps he did not know what he was saying, and maybe he was not even aware he had spoken. But the quiet encouragement in his tone had made all the difference to Lightfoot.

The events were like dream sequences. Short, vivid pictures. Fierce, inexplicable sounds. And now they were out in the air, being lashed from all sides by rain and blown spray.

He wondered vaguely what Bruce was thinking as he cradled the line in his big hands. Had he been shocked out of what had gone before?

When Lightfoot had told him about Archer's threats Bruce had been unusually quiet and calm. They had spoken in whispers and the submerged submarine had sped northwards from Singapore and the men around them slept in their bunks. Lightfoot had tried to explain his own feelings and what he ought to have done.

Bruce had said sharply, 'Makes no difference now, wack. What's done is done.' Then with a flare of his old belligerence he had added, 'Leave him to me!'

But again, nothing had happened. If anything, Bruce had appeared to make a point of avoiding Gipsy Archer. Perhaps Bruce never intended to say anything, Lightfoot thought bitterly. After all, Archer had said nothing about him at all. So if he did not know Bruce was connected with the accident and the man's death, why should Bruce take any action at all?

A freak gust of wind cleared the rain and spray from the rudder, and Lightfoot felt a cold hand tightening around his heart. Gipsy Archer was the man on the rudder beside Colquhoun. Even through the downpour there was no mistaking his dark features and the arrogant tilt of his head. And he was tied to the line which Bruce held with such earnest concentration.

He opened his mouth to attract Bruce's attention, but at that moment he felt the line go slack as Bruce pulled violently, the full power of his shoulders against it.

Archer was just about to slide down the rudder blade as his last thrust with the hacksaw severed the wire. There was a loud twang and the bobbing fish-buoy curtsied free and sank in the submarine's wake. But Archer seemed to lose his hold, and as the rest watched with fascinated horror he slithered down the blade, his legs and arms kicking madly, his skin bleeding from a dozen places as he fought to save himself.

Bruce muttered hoarsely, 'The wire must have cut him down!' But when he glanced round Lightfoot saw that his eyes were cold and indifferent.

Another series of shouts made him turn again, and Rider yelled, 'Gipsy's caught hold of the sub!'

Archer made one final effort. Reaching up he seized Colquhoun's ankle and with all his strength pulled himself clear of the water.

Colquhoun was already weakened by the effort of holding on, and this last strain was more than enough. Lightfoot saw him struggle to reach down as if to assist the big seaman, but Archer pushed his hand aside, and using the officer like a ladder he dragged himself to safety.

Whether the strain on the lifeline was too much, or whether it had got frayed by the friction with the rudder, no one could be sure. Just before another fierce squall swept the watching men Lightfoot saw Colquhoun's hand begin to slip, and watched sickened as his legs disappeared into the creaming water below him.

He heard Jermain shout, 'Stop engine! Stand by with heaving lines!'

But even Lightfoot knew that would not be enough. In this

weather, and allowing for the way already on the submarine, it would be some time before the captain could go about and find a single, drowning man.

Looking neither right nor left, Lightfoot ran back along the casing, and when his legs could no longer cope with the sluicing water he took a deep breath and dived clear of the hull.

Colquhoun was held afloat by his lifejacket, but limp and only half conscious he allowed his head to loll as the water washed over him. He opened his eyes and stared at Lightfoot, and tried to speak as the boy turned him on his back and trod water.

The latter said hoarsely, 'S'all right, sir! I'm a good swimmer!'

Colquhoun retched. 'You might have been killed!' Then as the memory crowded his mind. 'Is Archer safe?'

Lightfoot paddled round to peer at the submarine's misty shape as it moved slowly out of the squall. 'He's okay.' So he should be too, he thought with sudden fury. He had knocked Colquhoun off the rudder in his efforts to save himself.

A yellow liferaft splashed alongside and bobbed obediently on its line. Hands were reaching down, and familiar faces moved vaguely around the two sodden figures as they were hauled up on to the casing.

Bruce hissed at him, 'You young *fool*!' But Lightfoot could not look at him. It needed time and it needed thinking about. But whichever way you looked at it, Bruce had tried to murder Archer.

Colquhoun found himself wrapped in a blanket and sitting in the wardroom while Griffin, the doctor, poured something fiery between his lips. He became aware that he was surrounded by a quiet watching group of figures. Baldwin, the steward, grinning all over his freckled face. Lieutenant Drew giving him an admiring smile, and Griffin watching like a hen with a day-old chick.

Drew said, 'You did a good job, Max! I thought that goddamn wire was with us for ever!'

Griffin frowned severely. 'You'll have to rest. Too much excitement in one day for anyone!'

Then Colquhoun saw his father. The admiral was standing in the wardroom entrance, his hand gripping the curtain as if for support. He looked suddenly old, Colquhoun thought.

The admiral said, 'I'm glad you're all right, my boy.'

Colquhoun tried to define his feelings but could sense nothing. He replied, 'It was damn cold, sir.'

The admiral saw the others watching him and seemed to pull himself together. 'You should never have gone. The men could have managed it on their own!'

Colquhoun lay back and closed his eyes. That was more like it, he thought. Even now his father appeared unable to find a single word of warmth or pleasure.

The sudden realisation that it no longer seemed to matter filled Colquhoun with astonishment. It was as if his ordeal had been a test, a last chance to prove his individuality. The ideas became vague and distorted, and he heard the doctor say, 'I'll take him to the sick bay. I think he's had enough!'

But Colquhoun's eyes were shut, so he did not realise that the last remark was directed at his father.

• • •

Jermain wedged himself in the corner of the cockpit and tried to peer through the hissing curtain of rain. Through the hatch at his feet he could hear the clatter of orders, the questions and answers being passed back and forth over the intercom, but his mind still rebelled against the necessary routine and he was unable to free himself from a feeling of uncertainty.

A messenger called above the downpour, 'Steering and hydroplane tested and answering correctly, sir!'

'Very good!' Jermain stared at the rain and marvelled at the way it seemed to enclose the slow-moving hull like a steel fence. It should have been a bright clear morning, yet from his perch at the tip of the swaying fin it might have been any time, on any sea.

He snapped, 'Tell the first lieutenant to speed up the checks. I want a quick report from all sections on damage.'

The man ducked out of sight and Jermain returned to his thoughts. It was like some inner sense of danger. Something uncertain yet real.

He could feel Lieutenant Victor shifting his feet behind him and wondered what he was thinking about the *Temeraire*'s failure during their first real exercise.

He sighed and rested his arms on the wet steel and stared directly ahead. It was like being aloft on a small, isolated lighthouse or on some forgotten rock, he thought. There was no sense of belonging to the hull which was all but hidden by the seething water.

Victor whispered loudly, 'The admiral's coming up, sir!'

Jermain tightened his jaw and waited in silence as Sir John Colquhoun hoisted himself through the hatch to stand beside him. The admiral looked angry. As if he was only controlling himself with real effort.

Jermain said, 'I understand your son is all right, sir.'

'So it would appear.' The admiral glared at the strange mirage of rain and spray without any sort of recognition in his pale eyes. 'What the hell are you waiting about for?'

'I'm checking for damage, sir. In addition, I'd like to get a look at those fishing boats.'

The admiral did not seem to hear. 'What a bloody mess!'

'I thought our people behaved very well, sir. And your son made a fine display of courage.' Jermain's face was impassive.

'He was lucky!' The admiral ignored the hardness which had crept into Jermain's eyes. 'Right now I'm more worried about this exercise! All I've got to offer the Americans is your brief sonar report. At best it will prove that we could have destroyed the attacker but for this unfortunate bit of mishandling.'

The messenger reported, 'No damage, sir!'

The admiral snorted. 'I hate to think what would happen on active service!'

The radio supervisor scrambled through the hatch and stood stiffly in the rain in the crowded cockpit. He seemed afraid of touching the admiral with his own body, Jermain thought.

Jermain asked flatly, 'Well, Harris, what is it?'

The chief petty officer tried to shield his signal pad from the rain. 'Signal from Nemesis, sir. Exercise cancelled.'

Jermain frowned. Cancelled? Surely it should have been *completed*?

The radio supervisor glanced quickly at the admiral's face. 'The attacking submarine was diverted back to base with engine trouble, sir.' Harris gulped. 'All units to clear exercise area.'

The admiral snatched the pad and read through it searchingly. He exploded, 'This is the last straw, Jermain! First you disobey instructions only to get tangled in a lot of wire which a first-year subbie could have avoided!' He waved the pad. 'Now *this*! And to think I might have believed your findings! Damn it, man, there was no submarine at all!'

Jermain said, 'My sonar department is very efficient, sir. Every officer and rating is hand-picked.'

'I don't care if they are all university graduates!' The admiral seemed unaware of the silent men around him. 'I was prepared to overlook your efforts with an inexperienced crew and a new boat, even to the point of making some suitable signal to the Americans in the way of an apology!' He glared at Jermain's grave features. 'And what a bloody fool I would have looked, eh? Telling 'em about your wonderful sonar report when there *was* no submarine!'

The messenger's voice was hushed. 'Control room request instructions, sir.'

The admiral took a grip of himself. 'I suggest you submerge and return to base post-haste, Jermain! At least nobody outside the Service will know of your escapade!'

Jermain looked across his shoulder and said calmly, 'Retain course and speed. We will remain at Action Stations.' He returned the admiral's look of open amazement. 'I am not satisfied, sir. If Lieutenant Oxley obtained a contact, then there must be an explanation.' His mouth tightened. 'As you reminded me earlier when I asked for your assistance, sir, you are a passenger in this boat. I take full responsibility.'

The admiral could only stare at him for several seconds. Then he said, 'You'll be sorry for this, Jermain. You will pay an expensive price for your show of independence!'

Jermain allowed his stomach muscles to relax slightly as the admiral ducked through the hatch. For a full minute he allowed the rain to wash over his face and chest, like an athlete after some test of endurance. Then he said, 'I think the squall is moving over. Be ready to dive.' He heard Victor mumble an assent and half smiled to himself. It was as if Victor was afraid to speak too openly with him now, in case some of the shame rubbed off on him, too.

Maybe it had been a bit of useless defiance. The admiral was right about one thing at least. The Navy would have no time at all for a captain who had blotted his copybook so openly!

He watched the rain moving diagonally away from the hull. The fin and the small length of exposed casing began to steam immediately as the sun felt its way through the spray and windblown salt, and Jermain noticed for the first time that he had been standing in the downpour in his shirt and shorts. He felt the warmth soaking his body, and with it came another pang of uneasiness. There was something wrong with the pattern in his mind, yet he still could not explain it.

Perhaps if he had tried to describe his feelings to the admiral an open clash might have been avoided. But he recalled the man's stony expression when his son had led his small party to cut free the treacherous wire, and knew it was pointless to continue that line of thought.

Sir John Colquhoun had been prepared to be his friend on his own set conditions. The *Temeraire* was not important as a weapon, or even part of a new strategy. To the admiral it had represented only the chance of holding on to an obsolete command and the opportunity of displaying its potential in the face of the Americans, who challenged his control in the area. Not even the near death of his only son had been able to move him from the apparent realisation that his position and authority might be damaged rather than heightened by this most unfortunate of circumstances.

He saw the rain moving slowly away, and as if at a signal the wind too began to diminish. The sea's surface smoothed itself under the gathering sunlight, so that it glimmered like milk beneath a low but impenetrable haze.

The radar would have saved any further search, but to use it would certainly be asking for real trouble. Radar transmissions could be detected immediately, and any unfriendly warship in the vicinity would be quick to take an interest.

Jermain tugged his cap over his eyes. There I go again. Was it caution or imagination?

Victor spoke quickly, 'There's one of them, sir! Fine on the port bow!'

Jermain rested his elbows on the screen and levelled his glasses. At first he thought it was a slow-moving aircraft. But as the haze twisted and danced across the lenses he saw that he was looking at the mast and upper yard of a small ship. Far beyond it was a second one, cut off and lost like part of a mirage.

Jermain glanced briefly at the gyro repeater. 'Steer one one zero.' He stared hard at the floating masthead. Probably one of the trawlers. Yet it was apparently stationary and quite unmoved by the loss of a buoy and a few hundred feet of wire cable. Aloud he said, 'I'd have thought there'd be a bit of excitement! After all, the Black Pig is no lightweight. It must have given them a bit of a jolt, too!'

Victor said uneasily, 'We're getting a bit close, sir.'

Poor bastard thinks I'm round the bend. Jermain turned and smiled. 'Not quite what I expected, I must admit!'

At that moment the haze seemed to fall apart like a transparent curtain and there, rocking gently above its own reflection, was the other ship.

At first Jermain imagined that it was some sort of modern trawler. But even as he moved his glasses along her high, raked stem and over the compact bridge he saw the sudden flurry of foam beneath her stern and the telltale surge of power from the hidden screws.

Abaft her squat funnel was a long, white-painted deckhouse, and as the ship gathered way Jermain saw the sides of the structure fall away to reveal the gun mounting which even now was swinging towards him.

He shouted, 'Diving alarm! Clear the bridge!' He heard the lookouts stumbling down the ladder and Victor's heavy breathing as he groped for the button.

'AOOGAH! AOOGAH!' The klaxon screamed its warning just as the sea lit up with a bright orange flash. The shell passed directly above the fin with the sound of tearing silk, and Jermain felt the shockwave slashing at his shoulders as he tried to keep his glasses trained on the other ship.

He yelled, 'Hard a-starboard! Full ahead!'

As Victor repeated his orders Jermain turned to watch the slender waterspout as it fell slowly on to the calm sea across the other beam. A few feet lower and the shell would have cut through the fin like a knife through butter.

The water around the hull was already boiling in torment as the tanks were flooded, and the hydroplanes took control and thrust the submarine's bows down.

Another bright flash, and the whole hull shook like a mad thing as the shell exploded within twenty feet of the side. All at once the air was full of screaming splinters and the stench of salt and cordite. Water seemed to be falling everywhere, and Jermain almost fell as the deck tilted forward and down.

He took a last quick look at the other vessel. She was moving fast and was barely a quarter of a mile away now. Just one hit was all she needed. Just one!

Jermain jumped for the hatch and then stopped in his tracks, his eyes fixed on Victor's upturned face and the long pattern of blood which poured from beneath his spread-eagled body. Victor was staring at him, his eyes filled with shocked horror and disbelief. He was opening and shutting his mouth, but no words came, and when he tried to move his legs toward the hatch the stream of blood became a torrent. It was then that he began to scream.

Jermain forced his mind under control and with steady, deliberate movements lifted the other man's legs over the coaming, shutting his ears to the terrible screams which went on and on and which seemed to exclude every other sound. And all the time Victor's unblinking eyes were fixed on him, hating, pleading and despairing with each passing second.

Hands reached up through the hatch, and with one final scream Victor was dragged down the tilting ladder. Jermain jumped after him, his shocked eyes only half taking in the water as it cascaded over the lip of the cockpit to shred away the bright scarlet stain from the steel plates.

Behind him the two hatches slammed shut, muffled and final as the boat continued in her steep dive.

In the control room the men at the controls worked their wheels and instruments as if detached entirely from the huddled group around the foot of the bridge ladder. Two seamen trying to hold Victor's thrashing body, Griffin, tense and controlled as he searched for the wounds, and the men who had carried the officer down the ladder, their clothes streaked with blood, their faces shocked and drained of colour.

Jermain said tightly, 'Three hundred feet, Number One. Alter course to one seven zero. Maximum revolutions!'

He saw Wolfe studying his face and heard the confident clicks from the diving panel. He forced himself to watch the gauges, to listen to the efforts of his command to obey him.

Like a far-off diesel train he heard the ship's thrashing screws as she passed somewhere overhead. For an instant he felt something like madness sweeping through his mind, the urge to hit back, and kill and keep on killing until the sea was empty.

'Three hundred feet, sir.' He caught Wolfe's eye and added flatly, 'Tell the sonar to track the other ship. He might try and detect our position.'

He saw Griffin stand up from the silent men by the ladder and knew that Victor was dead.

The doctor said slowly, 'Three splinters in his back, sir.' He stared down at the dead man. 'I don't know how he survived as long as he did.'

Jermain looked at Victor's face. It was like a stranger's. Not like a human being at all. Just an effigy. A thing.

He replied, 'Take him to the sick bay, Doc. I'll be along later.'

What was there to say? Jermain stared at the waiting men. They seemed shocked, dulled by the savage turn of events.

Wolfe said quietly, 'That was close, sir.'

Jermain eyed him emptily. 'They were waiting for us.' He looked across towards the wardroom entrance where he could see the admiral silhouetted against the light. 'It was no imagination. Neither was that submarine.'

'Would you like me to take over?' Wolfe sounded strained. 'Poor old Victor.'

Jermain felt the anger returning like a flood. 'Just carry on with your watch, Number One.' He did not recognise the harshness in his voice. 'And get that blood mopped up. There'll be time enough for grief and recriminations later on!'

He forced himself to walk unhurriedly to the chart-room. Once there he leaned on the table and stared fixedly at the chart. He tried to focus his eyes, to visualise how and why such a trap had been sprung. Only *Temeraire*'s unexpected arrival and her tangling in the fish-buoy had averted what might have been much worse. Where better to destroy a loaded Polaris submarine than in the middle of a set exercise?

Jermain found neither consolation nor pride in what had happened. His training, even his old instinct, did not allow for Victor's sudden death. In his mind he could still picture those wild, desperate eyes, and in the silence of the chart-room he imagined he could hear the echoes of far-off screams.

• • •

Lieutenant Commander Ian Wolfe walked slowly into the wardroom and then paused uncertainly. The admiral was seated at the head of the empty table, a small book open in front of him. It was just after one o'clock in the morning, and the boat seemed silent and subdued as it cruised steadily towards Singapore. Wolfe was to take over his watch at two o'clock, yet for some reason felt unable to sleep. Ever since the previous morning when he had parcelled up Victor's few belongings he had been feeling restless and vaguely apprehensive. He was not sure he knew the full reasons for this, but he was unwilling to take the risk of facing his innermost thoughts in the small world of his cabin.

The admiral looked up and nodded towards a chair. 'Take a seat, Number One.' His eyes looked bright in the single reading light beside the table. 'It seems too quiet to sleep.'

Wolfe slumped in a chair and took a cigarette from a tin on the table. The last thing he wanted was to speak with the admiral, to take sides, to offer any sort of opinion on what had happened.

Perhaps it was his lack of feeling over Victor's death which troubled him most, he thought moodily. Over the whole boat there was an air of dejection rather than sadness. The swift horror of Victor's fate hung over officers and men alike, yet there appeared to be more than sorrow. It was like watching guilty men, Wolfe decided.

Victor had not been very popular in the wardroom. He had been withdrawn and defensive, and quick to show resentment if even a casual comment was challenged. Wolfe knew that some of the officers were now very conscious of his isolation amongst them, and were troubled because of it.

Wolfe, on the other hand, had made little effort to increase his own personal contact with any of them. It was enough to perform his duty, to use the passing time to prepare himself for the real challenge which still eluded him. A command of his own. There was no room for stupid and empty arguments, no point in allowing himself to become involved.

The admiral was watching him. 'I suppose you're wondering what will happen when we reach base?' He raised one eyebrow and smiled. 'I don't think you have anything to reproach yourself for. You handled the diving of the boat very well indeed. I shall certainly mention the fact at the enquiry.'

Wolfe pricked up his ears. So there was to be an enquiry now? He kept his voice non-committal. 'I believe the captain has made a full report, sir. I can't think of anything to add.'

The admiral smiled. 'Now then, Number One! You don't have to prove your loyalty to me, you know! I admire you for it, but we must face the facts.'

Wolfe stared at him. 'Victor was killed by some sort of Chinese patrol boat, sir. It might just as easily have killed the captain, too.'

'Quite so.' The smile was clamped on the admiral's face. 'But I was referring to the whole affair.' He waved his hands. 'In my position you get to see the whole picture of operations like a panorama!'

Wolfe tried to relax his stiff muscles. His headache had returned and he wanted to massage his forehead, but the other man's unwinking gaze made him resist it.

He said slowly, 'I understand the Chinese were on some sort of operational patrol. When we surfaced and moved amongst them they opened fire. It's not the first time there's been such a clash, sir. The Americans are always running foul of those bloody scavengers!'

'Maybe. But only the captain and poor Victor know for sure what really happened. And Victor is dead.'

Wolfe stirred uneasily. You bastard. You dirty-minded little bastard! He tried to see beyond the admiral's cold eyes, to be one jump ahead.

The admiral said calmly. 'I shall, of course, put in a good word for Jermain. There is no point in being vindictive. No point at all. But *Temeraire* is far too valuable to be used like a battering ram, don't you agree?'

The question came out with a snap and Wolfe felt pinned down by the admiral's relentless stare. 'But the other submarine, sir? The one Oxley detected.' Wolfe tried to avoid the point-blank question. It was an open challenge, to test which way his loyalty would go. He thought quickly of Jermain's impassive face after Victor had died, of the sharpness in his tone. Perhaps he was rattled, even unprepared for his massive weight of responsibility. He tried to halt his line of reasoning, to blot out the picture of Jermain's masklike features. He had been like a stranger, a man apart.

The headache was getting worse, throbbing at his skull like insistent hammers.

'The submarine?' The admiral shrugged. 'Underwater echoes are unreliable at the best of times, Number One. I can remember when I took my little S-boat off the Dogger Bank after a Jerry destroyer. I thought I was being tagged by an enemy submarine but at the same time I used my head and acted with the right spirit!' His face was flushed. 'Got him with a full salvo! A copybook attack!' He became serious again. 'I admire any man who tries to uphold the honour of the Service in front of a foreign power. But any man who *invents* a situation to cover his own mistakes is far more likely to bring discredit rather than praise!'

Wolfe cleared his throat. 'Do you mean the captain, sir?' He regretted the question immediately. He saw the shutters drop behind the admiral's eyes and cursed himself for his stupidity. He could not afford to take sides. There was neither time nor valid reason for it. Jermain had been a friend, a *real* friend. But that was long ago, when the Navy and all that went with it had been another, more enjoyable way of life.

The picture grew in his racing thoughts like a spectre. After all, what had Jermain *really* done when Sarah had left him? Maybe he was bound to take his sister's side. He could even be corresponding with her, sharing her other life just as he had once done. Did anyone know anyone any more? Jermain was a stranger like the others, a man out for himself.

Wolfe felt the sweat gathering on his brow and said harsly, 'I am not really in a position to say anything, sir!'

The admiral gave a thin smile. 'Of course not. You have your own future to contemplate. That is enough for any aspiring officer, eh?'

Wolfe nodded, feeling sick. 'I suppose so.'

Sir John Colquhoun eyed him thoughtfully. 'Have you seen much action, Number One?'

'The usual, sir.' The headache tightened its grip. 'I took part in the Suez campaign, and I was in Malaysia for a while.' He shrugged heavily. 'Yet one is never really expecting trouble until it happens.'

'Perhaps.' The admiral closed his book with a snap. 'But when these incidents occur, even in the Cold War, we must be ready. Instantly prepared for the unexpected! The country is too soft, too indifferent to care about what we are doing. It is a lonely, uphill struggle.' He gave an elaborate sigh. 'But we must accept our responsibilities and face them!'

Wolfe tightened his hands into fists under the table. If he told the admiral about his son's mixing with the C.N.D., *that* might wipe some of the smugness from his words! But he knew he was only deluding himself. Men like the admiral left no room for manoeuvre.

He glanced at his watch. 'I think I'll get ready to take over my duty, sir.' He noticed with surprise that the admiral's book was a cheap thriller from the *Temeraire*'s library. He added hastily, 'I'll look in the sick bay and see that your son is all right.'

The admiral opened his book. 'Very well if you think it necessary.'

Wolfe stared at the admiral's lowered head and marvelled. He was even jealous of Jermain because of his own son, he thought. Suddenly Wolfe felt disgust for himself and the way he had failed to stand up to the admiral's thinly veiled attack on Jermain.

He walked quickly into the passageway and half paused beside the captain's door. There was still a light in the cabin, and he could picture Jermain sitting at his little desk, his calm face intent on the never-ending stream of affairs which awaited his attention.

Command of the *Temeraire* had been a culmination of hard work and dedicated concentration on Jermain's part. Now, in the twinkling of an eye, everything had changed. A clash with the admiral, wilful damage and an officer killed. The list seemed endless, yet it was, Wolfe knew, only a beginning.

He wondered if he would have behaved as Jermain had done under the same circumstances. It would be so easy to save face, to admit a sonar fault and promise better for the future. Curiously enough, Victor's death was the least important of the problems. The authorities would say it was unfortunate but unavoidable. A sad loss incurred in the path of duty.

Wolfe remembered the empty cabin with its frayed bathrobe behind the door. The small bundle of personal effects which represented a man's hopes and fears. A few well-thumbed photographs of a wife and children. All wrapped and sealed along with an official letter of grief.

Wolfe rested his head on the cool metal and breathed out hard. It was stupid to think of it. It was nothing to do with him. He still allowed his mind to torture him a little longer. The animal-like screams ringing around the tower, the blood-splattered seamen on the ladder.

He had thought it was Jermain who had been hit. But even now he was afraid to face what his reeling mind knew to be a fact. In some inexplicable way he had been sorry when he had seen that it was Victor and not Jermain who lay twisting on the deckplates.

With a sob he hurried into his cabin and threw himself full length across his bunk.

7

Welcome Back

JERMAIN RETURNED the salutes of the marine policemen and walked briskly through the wide gates. Beyond the neat barriers of anti-terrorist sandbags he could see the tall white buildings and the painted sign. 'Commander-in-Chief, Far East'. An admiral's flag hung limp in the harsh sunlight above a circle of dried grass, and sailors walked to and fro with messages and folios on errands of varying importance.

Jermain glanced at his watch and grimaced. He was five minutes late already, although he had left the *Temeraire* at her moorings with plenty of time in hand. He had not been to Singapore for several years, and he was stunned by the density of traffic in the jammed streets and the mad abandon of drivers and pedestrians alike. He had sat sweating in his taxi while an accident between another car and a rusty trishaw had been sorted out by an impassive policeman and the two gesticulating culprits. Above him, the hands of the Memorial Hall clock had moved slowly towards eleven o'clock, the time set for the preliminary enquiry at naval headquarters.

Temeraire had docked in the eary dawn, this time with

neither fuss nor ceremony, and Jermain had been thrown into a full measure of work until the very last moment. Nobody aboard even pretended any more that the submarine would be returning home in the foreseeable future. The ratings received the waiting wads of home mail and retired to their messes in silence, aware perhaps for the first time that there was little hope of a quick reunion with that other, domestic, life.

Jermain saw Lieutenant Oxley and his senior sonar rating, Petty Officer Irons, walking towards him, the latter carrying the leather case of the exercise reports. Oxley was wearing sunglasses but his down-turned mouth showed his irritation and resentment only too clearly.

He saluted in his usual casual manner. 'They've finished with me, sir.' He gestured towards the main building. 'I've been in Sleepy Hollow for two hours with the brains of the operations staff, and now I feel as dim as they are!' He forced a grin. 'I still don't know if they accept my report.'

Irons said respectfully, 'They ran the rule over me an' all, sir.'

Jermain felt the pent-up strain changing to bitter indignation as he listened. It was like being at school again. Like a mischievous, over-imaginative child.

He said, 'I'm going in myself now.'

Oxley shrugged. 'Good luck, sir. I'll be at the Tang-Lin Club for a bit if you'd like to meet me later on? Perhaps I could help to smooth away the wrinkles of pique?'

Jermain smiled tightly. 'I'll see. And thanks.' He walked on, and when he turned the corner he saw they were still staring after him.

What did Oxley really think? he wondered. Did he blame him for this damned enquiry? It might prove to be a slur on him as much as himself.

He slammed angrily through a swing door and into the glacier chill of the air-conditioning before an orderly could open it for him. More stairs, following the neat signs and attentive orderlies. Everyone seemed to be watching him, yet avoiding his eye, and the realisation only added to his mounting anger.

A cool Wren officer stood up from her desk and meaningly glanced at her watch, 'This way, sir.' She smoothed down her jacket. 'The admiral is waiting for you.'

Jermain stared at her slim shoulders. Go on, you bitch! Just tell me I'm late! But she opened the double doors and said evenly, 'Commander Jermain, sir.'

The room was very wide and very quiet. Even the overhead fans seemed muted, and the distant sound of traffic was a discreet murmur.

Sir John Colquhoun was perched on the corner of one of the big map tables, and a stout captain whom Jermain recognised as the C.-in-C.'s Chief of Staff sat behind a littered desk. The Captain S/M was also there and gave Jermain a quick smile of encouragement.

The admiral looked more relaxed and much calmer than he had appeared aboard the submarine. His white uniform was perfect and his face shone as if from a cold shower. He nodded briskly. 'As you can see, Jermain, the C.-in-C.'s not aboard. He's up country on tour as it happens, but I think I can deal with this unfortunate affair.'

Jermain relaxed slightly. So this was how it was to be.

He said formally, 'I apologise for being late, sir. I was delayed by . . .'

Sir John shook his head. 'Late? I hadn't noticed. Ah well, I suppose it takes time to get used to a place.'

The Chief of Staff sighed. 'I've been over your report, Jermain. Very interesting indeed.' He tapped the open folio. 'I am with it until the moment of surfacing, and then I think we're all in the dark. But of course it's not new for a warship of any kind to be fired on. The Chinese like playing at pirates!' He frowned. 'However, I am a bit worried about the sonar contact. I understand that your sonar department is a bit green and could quite likely have got ruffled.' He glanced briefly at the admiral. 'I know myself what it's like in a new boat, and with half the Americans watching for a cock-up!'

The admiral snapped, 'Yes, I think we can discount the contact entirely.'

Jermain swayed back slightly on his heels. 'I disagree, sir. The contact was positive. It *was* a submarine.'

The captain looked down at his desk. 'I see.'

Jermain hurried on. 'Which means in my view one of two things. Either the Chinese were on an exercise and using the Polaris boat as a target, or,' he looked directly at the admiral, 'they were in deadly earnest!'

The admiral began to swing one leg quickly across the other. 'Are you trying to suggest that the Red Chinese would *attack* a Polaris boat, Jermain?'

The Captain S/M shook his head very imperceptibly but Jermain ignored him. It was too late now. It was all or nothing.

'That's about the strength of it, sir.'

The Chief of Staff spread his hands and said, 'But don't you think the Americans were aware of all these risks when they selected this area for an exercise?' He looked up, scowling. 'They're not fools, you know!'

'I know, sir.' Jermain saw the disbelief in the man's eyes and added stubbornly, 'In my opinion the Americans were only on an exercise up to a point. I think that the Polaris submarine was on her normal combat station and that we were the ones *on exercise*!'

The Chief of Staff stood up and began to pace in front of the wall maps. 'So it all hinges on your contact. Out of that assumption you make this statement that the Reds were likely to have a crack at a Polaris boat, and in addition the Americans are deliberately keeping *us* in the dark, right?'

'That's about it, sir.' Jermain felt the anger giving way to despair. They did not want to believe him, and on the face of it he could hardly blame them.

The Captain S/M said quietly, 'Boats from my squadron have sometimes been in that area, I must admit that this idea of yours is new to me.' He looked unhappy and added, 'After all, Jermain, your boat is equipped with the best sonar in the world, and the attacking submarine you say you detected was an ordinary conventional boat. Now how could such a boat hope to get near a nuclear one without being discovered long before she got in range? Even supposing the *Temeraire* had not been there at all, the American boat would surely have pipped her and made off at full speed?' He forced a smile. 'I know I'm old-fashioned, Jermain, but just give me one good explanation.'

Jermain felt tired. 'I can't, sir. I can only give you the facts as I have been taught to translate them.'

The admiral closed his eyes and rocked gently on the table. 'I don't like to say this, Jermain, but it has to be said. There is a great difference between the tactics table and real life. Only experience and time can give you that definite eye for the chance, the possibility. Until that time you must rely only on your present reserve of ability and training.'

The Chief of Staff glanced at his clock. 'This is what I propose to do. The *Temeraire* will re-provision and make good any damage and defects during the next few days. Lieutenant Victor's remains can be flown back to U.K. on the next available plane, as we don't want a lot of unnecessary publicity out here.' He knitted his brow in concentration. 'Mr. Conway and his party are still on the base, and this sort of thing won't help him to placate the Singapore government when he's trying to put his case. As you know, Jermain, Conway intends to pare down this command both from the point of view of forces as well as commitments. The Malaysian set-up has changed fast, and although they want our protection they won't want us to provoke their neighbors, the Red Chinese.' He closed the folio with a snap. 'I must say, I agree with them.'

Jermain heard himself ask, 'And what about the emergency? I was sent here because of it.'

The admiral yawned. 'Well, of course that is another matter. The Chinese are moving ships and men into North Korea, or at least the Americans seem to think so. That's really their problem at the moment.' He waved a hand across the charts. 'We have to show our strength in a different way. We must indicate that we are with the Americans, but not *of* them. Our image must be stability.' He smiled. 'I *like* that.' He repeated it half to himself and then added sharply, 'So that covers it, I think. *Temeraire* will await fresh orders. In the meantime I will draft my own report for the pundits of Whitehall, and one for the U.S. Navy. I shall state firmly that your boat did all that was expected, but that whilst surfacing to clear away a fouled fishing cable you were fired on by some unknown vessel and incurred the death of an officer. They are the facts. There is nothing else to add.' He paused and frowned meaningly. 'At *this* stage!'

They were all watching him. Jermain kept his face calm in spite of his inner feelings. 'Is that all, sir?'

'For the present.' The Chief of Staff ruffled his papers. 'In the meantime you will pay special attention to internal security and make sure your men behave themselves ashore. Singapore is crawling with spies and informers as well as ordinary trouble-makers. As soon as you are ready for sea again I will draft some new orders. You will no doubt be going north to work with the

Americans for a bit. But all that is confidential.'

The Captain S/M added swiftly, 'My men will do all they can to help, Jermain.'

Jermain thought of his silent crew and the hasty leave-taking from Scotland. And all for this! To be used as a status symbol. He recalled too with sudden clarity the senior American officer under whom he had studied when he had first started his training for nuclear submarines.

The officer had rasped. 'You'll be awed and goddamned afraid when you start. Then one day you'll command a boat of your own. When that happens you might think you've made it, that you're one of God's disciples!' He had leaned on his desk and glared at the class. 'The nuclear submarine is a weapon, not a possession or a mark of your own damn prowess! Learn to use it as a weapon! Ride it, and take charge of it! By the time you take control you should be ready to throw it about like a goddamn rifle!'

He answered flatly, 'And my own report, sir. What will happen to that?'

The admiral stood up, his face expressionless. 'I cannot say how it will be received. No doubt Their Lordships will treat the matter with fairness in view of your record and your, er, comparative inexperience in these waters.'

It was over. Jermain turned on his heel and walked back through the doors.

The Wren officer said, 'There's a message for you, Commander. Mr. Conway would like to see you at his house this evening.' She held out a scrap of paper. 'It's all on there.'

Jermain stared unseeingly at the neat writing. Now Conway would want to stick his oar in. Well, if he asks me what I think, I shall tell him!

The Wren said, 'Was it rough, Commander?'

Jermain turned angrily and then checked himself. The Wren was quite pretty, and she sounded as if she cared. He replied, 'I was impressed.'

She smiled and turned away as the telephone began to ring. Over her shoulder she remarked quietly, 'But not, I suspect, *convinced*!'

• • •

Jermain signed the last of the official letters and leaned back in his chair. At the other side of the small cabin Wolfe sat in silence, his eyes moving restlessly across the pile of signals on the desk.

The *Temeraire* felt deserted and dead, and only the purring fans gave any hint of activity outside the cabin. The libertymen were ashore along with most of the officers, and with the reactor cool and run down only the minimum of machinery was kept running.

Jermain said wearily, 'That's the lot for the moment. I've made a signal to Flag Officer Submarines requesting a replacement for Victor, though God knows when he'll arrive, or where we'll be when he does!' He waited for some sort of response but Wolfe remained silent and watchful. He seemed too relaxed, too controlled, Jermain thought. It was as if he had lost or deliberately erased all his old personality and only his outward appearance remained the same. He added, 'You feeling all right, Number One?'

Wolfe stirred himself. 'Good enough.'

'I'm sorry I can't take you with me on this visit to Conway's place. I could do with a friendly face.' He straightened his fresh drill uniform and dragged his eyes from the neat bunk. He would far rather spend a few hours on his back, he thought.

Wolfe said flatly, 'I may take a run ashore later, when it's cooler.' He sounded indifferent. 'I don't suppose I'll get much further than the Officers' Club.'

Jermain toyed with his pen. 'I haven't mentioned it before, Ian, but are you still brooding about Sarah?' He saw the caution creep into Wolfe's eyes. 'You should try and make a new start. I think I would.'

'Would you?' Wolfe eyed him emptily. 'It's all right for you. You've never married. It's different when you know what there is to lose.'

Baldwin, the steward, peered through the door. 'Captain, sir? There's a car alongside the depot ship for you.'

Jermain stood up and reached for his cap. He continued slowly, 'I've thought about you and Sarah a lot. Much more than I thought I would. There must have been something to break you up. You were so right for each other, I thought.' He smiled gently. 'Maybe you should have waited a bit instead of rushing madly for a divorce. I mean, it may not have been as black as you imagined?'

Wolfe lurched to his feet. 'Imagined? Coming from you that's pretty damn good!'

Jermain said, 'Hold on, Ian! I only meant...'

'I don't care what you meant! I'm sick to bloody death of being lectured! I know what happened. She got tired of waiting about for me, and like all bloody women she thought she'd go and enjoy herself with the first pretty Yank who whistled to her!'

'I think that's ridiculous!' Jermain studied Wolfe with concern. 'She was never like that.'

Wolfe swallowed hard. 'Well, it's my affair. I'd be glad if you'd keep out of it in future!'

Jermain shrugged. 'Suit yourself. But I hate to see you tearing yourself apart over what's over and done with.'

'It'll never be over for me.' Wolfe was staring past him. 'Never in a thousand bloody years!'

By the time Jermain had climbed to the upper deck to where Kitson, the O.O.D., and the trot sentry were waiting to see him over the side, Wolfe seemed to have returned to normal.

Jermain turned by the gangway. 'All the same, Ian, I don't want you to get the idea you're on your own. It's unhealthy, and in our present circumstances potentially dangerous.'

Wolfe lifted his hand in salute and said quietly, 'I think I can hold down my job, sir!'

Jermain felt the sun playing across his neck and with it the old nagging feeling of irritation. It had been a mistake to have Wolfe aboard. He would have been better off in a boat full of strangers, where he could feel his own way in his own time. He hurried across the depot ship's wide deck and down the brow towards the jetty.

The sun was already low in the sky, but a total absence of wind did little to clear away the humidity of the day. Flags hung limp on their masts, and two large junks hovered motionless on the still water of the harbour like timeless reminders of the East and all its problems.

There was an open sports car standing beside a tall gantry and a small group of white-clad sailors were hanging around it as if in hopes of getting a lift into town. The group seemed to melt into the dusty jetty itself as Jermain approached the car, the oak leaves on his cap apparently being enough to dispel any such beliefs.

Jermain pulled up with a start. The driver of the car was a girl, who was leaning against the passenger seat and watching him from behind a pair of dark glasses. She was wearing a plain, sleeveless dress and her skin was evenly tanned and looked very smooth.

She said, 'I've come to collect you.' She pushed open the door and revved the engine noisily. 'I thought you'd prefer this to an official car.'

He slid in beside her and pulled his cap tighter on his head as she rammed the car into gear and drove bumpily across the jetty railway tracks. As she drove through the maze of sheds and parked cranes Jermain watched her from the corner of his eye. It seemed an age since he had been with a girl of any sort, let alone as attractive as this one. In her middle twenties, he thought. Probably one of the girls from the Defence Commission. The short brown hair which framed her face was bleached by the sun and her bare legs were strong and well formed.

She drove past the security guards with a casual wave and gathered speed across the causeway. She said suddenly, 'Are you looking forward to this evening?'

'I'm prepared for it, if that's the same thing.' Jermain tensed in his seat as the car sped past a ramshackle taxi with inches to spare.

She laughed. 'You're not a bit what I expected!'

Jermain frowned. 'How do you mean?'

'I was just talking with some of your men back there. They're as scared as hell of you!'

'Rubbish!' Jermain felt vaguely pleased. 'They've no cause to be!'

The girl turned to look at him, her eyes hidden by the glasses. Her mouth was turned down in a mock grimace. 'They like you. That's the main thing. Pretty rare out here.'

'And how long have you been here?' Jermain was getting out of his depth.

'Oh, about six months. I've been helping to pave the way for the Commission and all that.' She laughed at some inner joke. 'It's a bit of a hoot really!'

I can imagine, Jermain thought. She would have the pick of every eligible officer on the base.

She said after a few moments, 'I understand you've already met everyone who matters here?'

'If you are referring to your boss, Mr. Conway, well yes, I have.'

She looked sideways at him. 'What's the matter, Commander? Don't you like him?' She grinned. 'He's waiting for you right now. He'll have his "Man of the People" suit on, I expect, all creased in the right places!'

Jermain said dryly, 'You don't sound very loyal.'

'Oh, he's sweet really! You should get on well together.'

She jammed down the clutch and changed gear, her skirt riding carelessly around her thighs. Jermain noticed that her skin was the same even tan all over, and he had a tantalising picture of her stretched out on some beach, the clean limbs naked to the sun.

He said quickly, 'Do you like your job, whatever it is?'

'At times.' She touched her lower lip with one finger. 'It's all very secret, of course. Even the tape-recorders have to be blindfolded!'

Jermain realised with a jerk that the car had covered several miles without his noticing the distance. Houses and open shops flashed past, and the car's low bonnet seemed to cleave its way through a mad maelstrom of scurrying Chinese, loaded handcarts and the white and khaki of off-duty servicemen.

He said, 'Will you be there this evening?'

'For a bit. But I have a date tonight.' She glanced at him. 'But don't worry, you'll get a car to take you back to the base.'

Jermain lapsed into silence. She reminded him of the girl in the dinghy which had crashed into the *Temeraire*'s bows. There was something so fresh and natural about her, and he felt strangely unnerved. It was, of course, ridiculous even to think along these lines. He had been too long under strain, too long at sea. That was all there was to it.

She said, 'I was sorry to hear about the officer who was killed.'

Jermain stiffened. 'There's not much security around here!'

'I thought I might go and see his widow when I get back to

U.K., to see if there's anything I can do to help.'

She sounded so completely genuine in her concern that Jermain felt confused. 'I'm sorry.' He turned to stare at her. 'I didn't mean to yell at you.'

Her lips parted across her even teeth. 'Like your men said. You really are a *pig* when you want to be!' But she was smiling.

Jermain grinned in spite of his embarrassment. 'I must say, I'd rather have you as a companion than some idiotic Member of Parliament!'

The car screeched sideways between two open gates where a dozing native constable leaned against a tree, and ground to a violent halt outside a square, shuttered house. She said, 'We've arrived, Commander!'

Jermain stood beside the car as she climbed from the driving seat and pushed the hair from her forehead. She was taller than he had imagined, and beneath the crumpled dress he could see the smooth lines of her body, the firmness of her breasts.

She stood looking at him. 'Now tell me, Commander, do you really *like* what you see?'

He coughed. 'Was I staring?'

She nodded gravely. 'A trifle.' She turned as Conway appeared at the top of the entrance stairway. 'Well, I must be off. Need a shower.' She gave Jermain a mock salute. 'May see you later, then?'

Jermain stared at Conway. He was indeed wearing a creased suit and his tie was hanging loosely around his shoulders.

Conway held out his hand. 'Come into the house, Commander.' He guided Jermain into the cool passageway. 'I see you got the car all right.'

Jermain asked carefully. 'Who was that girl?'

Conway grimaced. 'That was Jill. My daughter!'

• • •

Max Colquhoun wandered thoughtfully through the deserted control room and shone his torch across the gleaming panels. It was unnaturally peaceful in the boat and he found himself wondering why he had offered to relieve Kitson as officer-of-the-day. The latter had hurried ashore immediately, loaded down with golf clubs and a tennis racquet. It was too late in the evening to play anything, Colquhoun thought, but no doubt Kitson was eager to arrange a full programme of games while the submarine was in port.

The ensign had been lowered, and he felt that he might easily be the only soul aboard. From the direction of the chief and petty officers' mess he caught the distant strain of dance music and then he heard a man whistling in time with the radio. He felt vaguely comforted and paused to massage his back. He could feel the angry bruises and the dressing which Griffin had pasted across the cuts he had sustained on the rudder. It was odd how the others looked on him as some sort of hero. He had not even been able to save Archer when the lifeline had parted. He conjured up a stark picture of the water rising to meet him and the suffocating crush of salt in his lungs. It had been a near thing all right. Maybe that was why he did not want to join the others ashore. He needed to reassemble himself. To sort out his confused thoughts.

He climbed down a ladder and stood for a few moments looking along the full length of the upper crew space. The lines of empty bunks seemed to be waiting expectantly for their drunken owners when the libertymen came off shore. Perhaps they would feel the benefit of a good 'booze-up'. Some of the gloom and apprehension left by Victor's death and the boat's near disaster might be lost in a bout of drunkenness and all that went with it. Then only the married men would still be affected, Colquhoun thought. They always seemed to be more worried with mortgages and children's schooling than anything that occurred within the Service.

He was about to carry on with his rounds when he saw a solitary figure squatting beside one of the mess tables. It was Lightfoot. He was leaning on his elbows, his eyes unseeing as he stared down at a crumpled sheet of notepaper. Beside it, neatly arranged like part of a pattern, was an equally grubby envelope.

Colquhoun felt a sudden pang of guilt. Apart from the usual tongue-tied words he had hardly found a suitable opportunity to thank the boy for saving his life. That was one of the troubles with the Navy. Outstanding acts of kindness or bravery were hardly mentioned. It was simply not done. Small gripes and irritations, on the other hand, found plenty of outlets in wardroom and lower deck alike.

He tucked his cap under his arm and coughed quietly. 'Hello, Lightfoot. I'd have thought you'd be ashore with your mates?' He smiled. 'You're not duty, are you?'

Lightfoot looked up startled and half rose to his feet.

Colquhoun slung one leg over a bench seat and tossed his cap on the table. 'Don't get up for me. This is *your* home!'

Lightfoot sat down with a jerk, like a puppet, the strings of which have been severed. He said, 'I didn't hear you, sir.'

He stuffed the letter inside his shirt. 'I stood in for another bloke. I didn't feel like a run ashore.'

Colquhoun nodded. 'Like me.' He had another disconnected picture of his father sitting in state in his spacious headquarters. Maybe that was why he had taken Kitson's duty. To avoid meeting his father. Not that he need have bothered, he thought bitterly. The admiral had sent neither invitation nor greeting since he had left the boat.

Lightfoot said suddenly, 'Are you feeling all right now, sir?'

'Not too bad, thanks.' Colquhoun saw with a start that the young seaman's eyes were red-rimmed. As if tears were not far away. He added quietly, 'Nothing wrong, is there?'

'It's me mum, sir.' Lightfoot tapped his pocket. 'She's dead.' He stared wretchedly at the table. 'The first letter I've ever had from me father and it's to tell me that she's dead!' He sounded stunned.

Colquhoun leaned forward. 'I'm terribly sorry.' He saw the boy's eyes studying him emptily. 'Really. I mean it.'

Lightfoot said, 'She worked her guts out for us. For *him* in particular.' He closed his eyes and two bright tears showed on his lashes. 'The lousy, stinking bastard!'

'I don't quite understand? Do you mean your father?'

'That's who I mean all right!' Lightfoot brushed his eyes with the back of his hand. 'Never given her nothing! Just moan, moan, moan! Pub every night, even when we were kids. Even when he was on strike or laid off he always had his fags and beer. Never mind about Mum!' He shook with an inner convulsion. 'Now *this*! On top of everything else!'

Colquhoun swallowed. 'I was going to write to her, too.' It had been a lie but he found that he meant it. 'To tell her what you did.'

'D'you mean it, sir?' The washed-out eyes were staring at him.

'You saved my life, and don't forget it.' He forced a smile. 'I know *I* won't.' He became serious. 'I'll tell you what I'll do. I'll get the captain to make a signal and have you flown home. He's bound to release you.'

Lightfoot's head dropped. 'You don't understand, sir. This letter is asking for more money. Mum's been buried already!' He stared hard at the table. 'Dead and buried, and I never knew!'

Colquhoun did not know what to say to him. The boy's father could have contacted the authorities. A signal would have been flashed to *Temeraire*. Perhaps too late for him to be flown back in time for the funeral. But it would have been a worthwhile try.

'He says he can't afford all the expenses for the burial, sir.' He gritted his teeth. 'The bastard! I'll bet he was at the Falcon for his pint just as usual!'

There was a thump overhead and the sound of a door slamming. The first of the returning libertymen no doubt, Colquhoun thought. The duty P.O. could deal with them on his own. In fact, he was better suited for the job. A quick thump on the chin would not be taken amiss from a petty officer by an unruly sailor on the rampage. But Lightfoot was in no state to be here when his messmates returned. Understanding or not, their fogged questions and commiserations would turn into a nightmare.

He said quickly, 'I suggest you come with me. You can sit in my cabin for a bit until things quieten down.' He picked up his cap. 'Sub-Lieutenant Luard won't be aboard for hours yet. He's dated a little nurse from the hospital.' The remark seemed to fall flat, but Lightfoot was already on his feet, his face suddenly defenceless.

'Thank you, sir. I'd like that.'

Colquhoun led the way past the empty galley with its gleaming stove and regimented pots. 'It's time we had a yarn about that dinghy sailing, too,' he said easily. 'You need time to think. To get your system clear.'

He switched on his cabin light and gestured towards a chair. 'Help yourself.' Another switch connected the cabin with the boat's piped music. 'As you can see, your officers are not as tidy as you chaps!'

Lightfoot perched on the edge of his chair, his eyes

wandering around the chaos of discarded uniforms, magazines and the usual junior officer's clutter.

Colquhoun pulled open a drawer. 'This is strictly against regulations, but I think you can do with a drink.' He poured two measures of gin. 'It's on its own, I'm afraid, but Mr. Luard has scoffed all the tonic!'

Lightfoot took the glass and turned it in his hands as if it was some delicate crucible.

Colquhoun said, 'Well, here's to us. Thanks to you, I'm able to say this. And I'll not forget what you did for me!'

He felt himself knocked sideways as the door burst open behind him. The pain was all the more intense because the door's edge had struck his bruised back, and with a gasp he found himself on top of Lightfoot, his hands and face soaked with gin.

He staggered to his feet and turned round. 'What the hell d'you think you're doing?' He paused as he saw that it was the first lieutenant's square shoulders which were framed in the rectangle of light from the passageway. Behind him, his face bobbing anxiously from one side to the other, was Mason, the duty petty officer.

Wolfe was wearing a lightweight shoregoing suit and seemed to be breathing very heavily. For several seconds he stood in the doorway, his hands on his hips, his hair falling across his forehead.

He said at length. 'So this is where you are!' He put his head on one side but the passage light threw a shadow across his face. 'I might have bloody well guessed it!'

Colquhoun felt the blood rising to his face. 'Now just a minute, Number One!'

Wolfe threw back his head and roared, 'Say *sir* when you address me, *Mister* Colquhoun!' He walked stiffly into the cabin, his eyes moving round the place like a dog searching for clues. 'I have just come aboard in time it seems!' He peered down at Lightfoot who was standing stockstill as if mesmerised. 'Who are you staring at?'

'I was just discussing a personal matter with . . .'

'Keep *silence*!' Wolfe stood inches away from Colquhoun, his chest heaving with anger. 'I came aboard to find the trot sentry swilling tea in the radio room and the duty P.O. sculling about the crew space like a first-year recruit!' His voice dropped so that he sounded almost reasonable. 'And where was the duty officer?' He took a half-pace forward and Colquhoun could feel the man's fury, could almost taste the drink in his throat. Wolfe yelled, '*Where was he*?' He did not wait for an answer. 'He was in his bloody cabin with his young friend!' He glared round at the wretched Mason.

The petty officer said thickly, 'But, sir, I was just explainin'.'

Wolfe thundered, 'Save it, Mason!' He swung round. 'And as for you, Sub-Lieutenant Colquhoun, I can only say it is *exactly* what I expected! Not content with balling up your duties and sheltering behind your father's rank, you apparently think you can get away with this sort of thing!'

Colquhoun tried to control the tremor in his voice. 'Are you implying that we, that I...'

Wolfe prodded him in the chest. 'Yes, you bloody little ponce, that's exactly what I *am* suggesting!'

Colquhoun thought of his father's cold eyes, of Lightfoot's pathetic gratitude, of all the other tormenting acts and incidents which had dogged him for so long. His first fear was slowly giving way to anger. Not a reasonable reaction to Wolfe's insinuation, but something worse, like madness.

In a surprisingly clear voice he said. 'As officer-of-the-day, I am placing you under arrest, sir! In my opinion you are under the influence of drink and therefore in an unfit state to perform your duties.'

Mason stared at Lightfoot and muttered, 'My Gawd!'

Wolfe swayed against the bunk. 'You're doing *what*?'

Colquhoun felt the strength leaving his legs but continued quickly, 'I would advise you to go to your quarters and await the commanding officer's return.'

Wolfe looked as if he was going to hit him. Then, to Colquhoun's shocked surprise, he said quite calmly, 'Suit yourself. It'll all be the same in a hundred years!'

He left the cabin, and Petty Officer Mason said shakily, 'I 'ave a feelin' that this is goin' to be one of them nights, sir!'

8

And Goodbye

THE MALAY houseboy cleared away the plates and then placed a large silver coffee-pot on the table.

Conway, whose wife had quietly left the room a few moments earlier, loosened his tie which he had previously knotted for her benefit, and grinned across at Jermain. 'That feels better! I like to unwind when I'm out of the public eye!'

Jermain allowed his body to relax slightly. It had been a simple but excellent meal and not a bit as he had imagined it would be.

When he had first arrived at the house he had expected Conway to brush aside the preliminaries with his usual outspoken forcefulness and then continue along much the same lines as the admiral. But it was not to be. Both Conway and his rather frail wife had been more than pleasant. The big M.P. had questioned him about the *Temeraire* and her crew, and his wife had rambled vaguely through her memories of Cornwall when she heard that it was Jermain's home.

It seemed that Mrs. Conway was not very strong and Singapore's harsh climate, coupled with her husband's whirl of activities, left her little in reserve. She apparently retired to bed early, no doubt to wonder at Big Jim's widening horizons.

Conway pushed a cigar-box along the dark table-top. 'Try one of these if you like. I'm not a cigar man myself.' He pulled an old pipe from his breast pocket. 'I make the most of this at these moments. If I smoke it in public my lass says it's just to impress the voters!' He grinned to himself. 'She's a cheeky one!'

Jermain dropped his eyes. Jill Conway had joined them for pre-dinner drinks and then after a brief explanation to her father had driven back into town. To her date. She had been wearing a short dress of black silk, against which her tanned skin and supple arms had shown to perfection. Without the sunglasses her eyes were large and candid, and Jermain had observed that they were a strange grey-green, like light shining through clear water.

He realised that he too had pulled out his own pipe and he smiled awkwardly. 'Me too. I enjoy my old pipe.'

The coffee and brandy warmed Jermain's stomach like soothing fire. He said, 'I'm very glad I came. The first time I've relaxed for some time.'

Conway swilled the brandy around his glass and frowned. 'I asked you here because I was impressed when we last met.' He looked directly across the table. 'I'm not being pompous. It's a fact. You and I have a lot in common, you know. We're both doing something we like, but neither of us has all that much co-operation, right?'

Jermain eyed him steadily. 'I'm not sure I follow you.'

'That's all right. I'm not trying to trap you. You're too smart for that.' He leaned on one elbow and watched the smoke drifting from his pipe and vanishing into the fans. 'It's very hard to make some of the old stagers out here understand what the government is trying to do. Any sort of change is suspect. Any kind of reorganisation is shunned. You can't reason with men like them. Sir John Colquhoun, f'rinstance. Thinks he's only second to God. And that's just due to seniority!' He grinned openly. 'Don't worry! I'm not asking you to take sides. You've had enough of that since you came out here!' He became serious. 'I read your report. A lot of it was complete mumbo-jumbo to me, but I have my own experts to worry over that!'

Jermain sat very still. Conway was not so empty as he had first appeared. As he had *made* himself appear.

As if reading his mind Conway continued, 'I came up the hard way, Jermain. Hard and rough. Before the war I was a truck driver up in Manchester. I got a reputation for looking after the lads when there was a strike in the offing or when the bosses got a bit mean. It just seemed to happen to me. Then there was the war.' His eyes were glazed as he stared into the smoke. 'Dunkirk taught me a lot of things. That was where I learned to love the Navy, when there was only the bloody sea at my back! It also taught me a lot more. About government stupidity, and the crass negligence which had got us all in that unholy mess!'

He paused to pour some more brandy. 'There was a young subaltern in charge of my lot. No more than a kid. Rather like your young Colquhoun, in point of fact. I was just a lance-corporal at the time. Green as grass, and sick of the whole business. We had one empty Bren and half a dozen rifles between the lot of us. And coming smack down the road was a great Jerry tank! I nearly wet my pants, I can tell you! We'd been fighting and running for six days, and I was all in. We still had half a mile to go to the sea where the Navy was waiting to lift us off. Half a bloody mile, and this tank squatting there like a great iron toad. I knew we'd never make it. We'd be like the others. Just dusty corpses on that ruddy road!' He drank fiercely. 'I looked at this kid, the poor, terrified subaltern who'd hardly got his boots dirty since leaving Sandhurst, and I asked him what we should do. He just looked at me. I can see him now. Just looking at me as if I should have known what to do.'

Jermain waited. 'What happened?'

Conway shrugged. 'He ran up the road and threw himself across the tracks of the tank. He was carrying our last grenades. Just before they blew the tracks off the tank he was smashed to pulp. Ground down like a beetle!' He shook his head. 'I'll never forget him. Never.'

'He must have been a brave fellow.' Jermain was reluctant to speak. To break the spell.

Conway snorted. 'Maybe. But it was a damn stupid waste! When the war was over I was full up to here! I wanted to try and put things right. To make sure it couldn't happen again! I pushed my way into politics. You have to push in our party. Of course, my old mates despised me for it. Thought I was "ratting" on them. But I pressed on. And I made it.' He peered at Jermain's grave features. 'The country can't afford hundreds of useless bases just for the personal importance of a few brasshats! So what we have must be good. It must be better than anyone else's!' He smiled awkwardly. 'Like your submarine. It's probably worth more than all the other ships in the Far East Fleet at this moment!'

He continued in his thick voice, 'But we must not think of the Far East merely in terms of power and conflict. That's where *we* come in, we're not too involved as yet. The Americans and the Chinese *are* involved, and both are resigned to confrontation at the best, and at worst,' he shrugged, 'World War Three, is my guess.'

Jermain said slowly, 'And you read my report?'

'I did. It worried me. It still does.' He leaned back in his chair and plucked his shirt away from his ribs. 'I get all my reports direct from Whitehall. I like it that way. I don't have to crawl to Sir John for scraps of information which will probably be useless anyway! I like to cut through the red tape.' He winked. 'Or is it *blue* tape in the Navy?'

Jermain smiled. 'I know what you mean.'

Conway wagged his pipe. ''Course, they're not all like that. A contact of mine, a Vice-Admiral Vane, he's a sharp one if you like!'

Jermain pictured the little admiral standing in his cabin aboard *Temeraire* with the Gareloch swilling against the moored hull. It seemed so long ago. So remote.

'Vane has seen your report. He thinks as I do. That the Chinese are up to something.' He laughed shortly. 'If your guess is wrong, then we're none the worse off, as I see it.'

'And if I'm right?' Jermain found he was leaning forward.

'One of my jobs out here is to put out feelers. Not a direct peace offensive, but a kind of neutralising probe, as the newspapers would say.'

Jermain could feel the excitement rising within him. 'Let me guess. You're talking about Korea?'

'Right first time. If we could find some way to bring the

North and South together after all this time it would be a major step towards peace out here. It would be like uniting Berlin, or clearing up the mess in Viet Nam.' His eyes gleamed. 'That's why our Defense Commission has to show first that we are willing to pare down military strength to basic requirements.' He grinned widely. 'This is all top secret, of course!'

Jermain returned his smile. 'So is the *Temeraire*!'

'Just so. That was why I wanted to see you. You'll be getting fresh orders soon, as you know. You'll be going up north for a bit to work with the Americans again.'

'You know more than I do.' Jermain stared at him.

'Have to, in my job. I can tell you too that I'll be up there myself. I'll be contacting a few people from the other side. All very cloak-and-dagger!'

'A bit risky, isn't it?'

'I don't think so. I'd not be taking my daughter otherwise, would I?'

Jermain persisted, 'You think that the Chinese would try something to break up any sort of interchange?'

'Wouldn't you, for God's sake? They're bound to suspect our motives. But we'll take it step at a time. Nice an' easy!'

'Where do I come in?' Jermain watched the other man's mind at work behind his dreamy eyes.

'Maybe nowhere. But you might be our only real link. You'll get more orders and counter-orders I expect. The Americans will be told about your sonar contact. They might take it as a hint to clear their Polaris submarines out of any area where they might be detected. If the Chinese could provoke an incident on Korea's doorstep during our peace feelers, it would be a disaster.' He tapped out his pipe. 'They've been moving troops into North Korea for weeks. It's not just for the hell of it!'

A car screeched to a halt outside the house and Conway grinned. 'Jill's back. The date can't have been up to much!' He eyed Jermain thoughtfully. 'Not much like her dad, is she? I've done my best for her, but she's earned all that she's got.' He cocked his head on one side. 'When I was driving a truck I never thought my kid would go to university and get an honours degree and all the rest of it. It was just a pipe dream then.'

'Does she help you a good deal?' Jermain heard a telephone ringing and the girl's voice answering it.

Conway frowned. 'She does a hell of a lot. She tackles the welfare side of the job. You know, all the clutter about rehousing and re-employing local families who lose their jobs when we close down a base here and there.'

The door opened and the girl stood framed in the entrance. She spoke to her father, but her eyes were on Jermain. 'That was the *Temeraire* on the phone. They want Commander Jermain back aboard right away.' Jermain was halfway to his feet as her continued, 'Something about an argument.' She raised her eyebrows. 'Is that serious?'

Conway led the way to the door. 'Depends who is doing the arguing, my girl!'

He turned to Jermain. 'Sorry about this. I was enjoying our talk. I'll send for the car.'

The girl was already down the steps. 'I'll drive him, Dad. It'll be quicker.' She looked at Jermain. 'The fresh air will help to clear your mind for the fray!'

• • •

Jermain sat with his fingers interlaced on his desk blotter and stared steadily at Wolfe. The first lieutenant was standing directly in front of him, his cap under his arm, his eyes fixed on some point above Jermain's right shoulder.

It was morning and beyond the closed door Jermain could hear the muffled sounds of normality and purpose. The squeak of a hoist, the casual mutter of conversation from the men at work. Up on deck, their bodies bared to the early sunshine, more men would be busy with paint-brushes restoring the fat hull to its old dull lustre and removing the telltale scars of shell splinters. But down in the cabin it was still and quiet, with only the fans and their own breathing to break the spell.

Jermain said evenly, 'I've just seen young Colquhoun and heard all that he had to say. Now what is your story?'

'I'm not a bit surprised at his attitude.' Wolfe seemed very calm. 'I've been riding him pretty hard since I joined the boat because of his general slackness. As you know, he thinks the Navy owes him a living!'

'I'm afraid I don't know.' Jermain felt tired. He had driven back from Conway's house in almost complete silence. Wrapped in his own thoughts, yet all the time conscious of the girl beside him. Only when the car had jolted to a halt on the jetty had she interrupted his ruminations.

'You know, Commander, you really care about your men, don't you?'

Jermain had dragged his eyes from the depot ship's pale side where the quartermaster watched them in silence. 'Does that surprise you?'

She smiled. 'With most of the men I've met, it's just show. Only for the record!'

He had seen her eyes shining in the reflected headlamps, had wanted to stay and be alone with her. He had replied slowly, 'I'm sorry to drag you out here like this. I had hoped we might talk some more.' He had felt foolish under the calm scrutiny. 'But then I expect you're pretty hard to pin down?'

She had switched on the engine, her face in deep thought, as if weighing his words. 'Perhaps I'll see you around, Commander. It's a small town, for all its noise!'

Jermain had watched her drive back towards the gates and had climbed up the steep brow to the depot ship.

An apprehensive group had been waiting for him in the *Temeraire*'s wardroom. Colquhoun, flushed but defiant. Griffin, the doctor, still dressed in mess kit and smelling of someone's perfume, and Oxley, who seemed to have taken charge of the situation.

Jermain had listened to each and all of them, his first fears giving way to disappointment and then anger. He had made no judgement at that moment. Tempers were too frayed, opinions too vague for real assessment. But alone for a moment with Griffin he had asked sharply, 'Well, was he drunk?'

Surgeon Lieutenant Toby Griffin often appeared offhand and easy-going, but when it came to his own trade he was very exact. 'I examined Number One as soon as I came aboard, sir. In my opinion he had not had very much to drink.'

Jermain's mind had moved quickly to the next point. 'So all this about the O.O.D. putting him under arrest might have been to cover up something else?' It was an unfair question, but to avoid this matter getting beyond the *Temeraire*'s hull speed and clarity were essential.

Griffin had repeated, 'He was not, in my opinion, too drunk

to know what he was doing. But I do think he was suffering a form of intoxication.' He had hurried on as Jermain's face had become grimmer. 'Maybe he had been taking drugs, for a headache perhaps? Anything like that added to a few normal drinks could produce the same result. I know for a fact he had eaten nothing all day. He seemed to be worried about something.'

Now, in the calm of the morning it was hard to imagine anything abnormal had ever occurred. If anything, Wolfe seemed more amused than angry.

Jermain started again. 'Tell me in your own words what happened.'

Wolfe shrugged. 'I went ashore. When I returned aboard the boat was a shambles. No trot sentry, and the duty petty officer out of the rig-of-the-day lounging about the mess decks. Then I found Colquhoun in his cabin.' He breathed out hard. 'Drinking, if you please, with a junior rating!' He shifted his glance momentarily to Jermain's face. 'Now, if that's normal, just say so!'

Jermain said, 'Colquhoun states that you were insulting and made certain allegations. In other words, you were drunk.'

Wolfe sighed. 'He must be off his head. I was angry right enough, and with good reason. He just lost his head, that's all.'

'I see.' He tapped his desk. 'Well, I've told Colquhoun what *I* think about it.' Jermain watched for some sign of uncertainty, but Wolfe's gaze was steady. 'He was upset, over-anxious, and in his position it seemed quite reasonable. The rating, Lightfoot, had had some bad news from home. Colquhoun thought he was doing the right thing.'

Wolfe said stiffly, 'So you're taking his side?' He shrugged. 'I spoke my mind to him, and he took the easy way out, or so he thought.'

Jermain eyes him coldly. 'Don't be such a bloody fool! You know it's not as simple as that. I know he acted hastily, but he hasn't your experience. This is a new crew, untried, and unsettled by all the trouble we've been having. I expect you to set them an example and not add to their problems!'

Wolfe nodded. 'I know it's hard for you. I'm sorry. It can't be easy to have to back an incompetent officer just because his father is your admiral.' He sounded quite reasonable.

Jermain stood up, his eyes blazing. 'You know damn well there's nothing like that about it!'

'I'm sorry, sir. I must have misunderstood.' Wolfe studied him flatly.

'If this thing goes any further it might mean a court martial. I intend to see that it does not!' Jermain made himself sit down again. 'For one thing, I have already spoken sharply to Colquhoun and explained in no uncertain terms that there are required ways of behaving. That it is not his lot to entertain ratings in his cabin, no matter how deserving it might appear to be.' He added harshly, 'And I am not convinced that your attitude was blameless either!'

Wolfe drew himself up very stiffly. 'Then there is to be an enquiry, sir?'

'No.' Jermain got a brief picture of Colquhoun's pale face, his mouth set in a stubborn line as he had listened to his words that morning. He continued, 'To behave as you did in front of two ratings is far more damaging. And at this stage of events I would have expected you to act differently.'

'So I suppose it's all over the boat now.' Wolfe gave a small sigh. 'Well, I suppose I might have guessed that would happen. I underestimated Colquhoun, it seems.'

Jermain ignored him. 'Mason, the duty P.O., is slow, but one hundred per cent reliable. It won't go beyond him. As for Lightfoot. We shall just have to hope that he has too much on his mind to complicate matters.'

'And you're doing this for me? Because of our friendship?'

Jermain leaned back in his chair. 'Partly, perhaps. I want you to get over your old troubles, and I need you to help me run this boat. In the next few weeks, maybe even days, we shall be required to act as a combat-ready submarine, and all that it entails. If I lost interest it would mean a court martial, and that would do more than damage reputations, it would injure the efficiency of the *Temeraire*.' His tone hardened. 'And that I will not tolerate, do you understand?'

'Perfectly, sir.'

'In any case, if there was an enquiry outside this boat it might wreck your chances of a command at any time.'

'You are implying that they might doubt my sanity, sir?' Wolfe's eyes were very bright. 'I consider that I acted as any responsible officer would under the same circumstances. I may have made a joke to Colquhoun, but if he implied that I said more, then I shall deny it.'

'Colquhoun has merely stated that he thought you were too drunk to know what you were doing. We've all been under strain, so let's leave it at that!' Jermain dropped his voice. 'But I will not destroy everything we've worked for just because of a few petty jealousies and hatreds! I have lost an officer killed. I am not losing more officers in a legal tangle to suit you, Colquhoun or anybody else, is that understood?'

Wolfe nodded. 'Yes, sir.'

'Very well.' Jermain softened his voice slightly, hating the barrier between them. 'And try not to let your domestic affairs interfere with your life now.'

He stared hard at Wolfe's impassive face and wondered. He wanted to ask him about the pills Griffin had said he was taking. To break through and find the man he had known so well in the past. But he could not bring himself to do it. Not here and now. Wolfe had enough on his mind for a bit.

Colquhoun had acted hastily and without thought. In submarines discipline was often at variance with the rest of the Service, but, nevertheless, he obviously felt he had no alternative. If they could get to sea again things might be different.

Of one thing he was certain. If Wolfe left the *Temeraire* under a cloud he was finished. Finally and for good. The Navy looked after its own in so many ways but was equally ruthless with those who betrayed its code and ritualistic management.

Jermain was equally certain that if Wolfe let his emotions betray himself in the open once more, it would be the *Temeraire*'s captain whose sword would lie on the court martial table. The same rules covered all men.

He added, 'I saw Conway last night. I gather we might be used in something big pretty soon. When it comes we must be ready.'

Wolfe replied calmly, 'Yes, sir. I heard that you had come back with his daughter.' There was no emotion in his voice yet Jermain felt a sting in his brief comment.

He said wearily, 'Very well, Number One. You can return to your duties. I hope this incident will be forgotten, and quickly!'

Wolfe paused with his hand on the door handle. 'About my wife, sir. Your sister, that is.' He watched Jermain dispassionately. 'I realise you think she was a blameless angel. Even taking into consideration that she nearly left me on two previous occasions and that she eventually went off with her Yank, I still believe she was talked into it. But I was left out of the matter. Shut off like a damned schoolboy!' He continued in the same flat voice, 'So you see, I've had a lot to consider.'

'I know. And I'm sorry.'

Wolfe opened the door, then said dryly, 'Good. That makes me feel a lot better.'

When the door had closed Jermain dropped his head on to his hands. It was no good. Wolfe was sick with bitterness and self-pity. He might even be a danger to others if pressed too much.

He found his eyes drawn towards his personal signal pad, but instantly dismissed the sudden impulse. He remembered Wolfe's face as he had stepped aboard in Scotland. The look of need and reprieve.

Like the *Temeraire* herself, he had to be given his chance.

• • •

The battered sports car wound its way through the press of traffic and somehow managed to filter into a narrow side street. Jermain sat fascinated as a yelling trishaw driver appeared beside his door, and wondered what would happen if the car actually came to a halt. He imagined that the surging mass of people and vehicles would pile up and up into an immovable tangle until the street was filled.

His mind was still confused with the speed of events which had taken him from the busy activity of the *Temeraire*'s clinical atmosphere to this open car and the girl who sat seemingly relaxed behind the wheel.

He had received a brief telephone call whilst working through a mass of reports at his desk. She had sounded casual, and her invitation to 'take a look round' had been matter of fact, as if she did not really care one way or the other.

Jermain had paid a hasty visit to a Chinese tailor and was already beginning to regret his choice in clothing. The lightweight suit was pretty good for length, but across the shoulders it left nothing to spare, and once when he had leaned forward to fill his pipe he had felt an ominous split beneath his arm. But he was happy in spite of his uncertainty. Pleased that she had remembered him at all.

She said suddenly, 'There's a place down here where we can eat. Nothing fancy. But it's fairly quiet.' She did not wait for a reply but swung the wheel towards an even narrower street where the overhanging houses made as if to touch each other.

Above the shaded walls the evening sky was still bright and clear, like a strip of blue silk, and the narrowness of the street seemed to hold all the smells and sounds of the East, to tempt them from every direction at once.

Jermain stood beside the car and stared at the low-windowed foodstalls and the small shops which crouched in total darkness away from the harsh light of the main road. There was a strong scent of fish and spices, and the fragrant odours of cooking meat and charcoal burners. It was all just about as far as you could get from the ordered life of the submarine, Jermain thought.

A grey-bearded Chinese in a white smock bowed politely as the girl led the way into one of the small restaurants. It consisted of half a dozen booths, all but one of which were empty.

Jill Conway sat opposite him, her eyes grave as she watched his face. 'Will this suit you, Commander?'

'The name is David.' He smiled awkwardly. 'The other is a bit formal!'

She nodded. 'David. It suits you.' She looked up at the old proprietor. 'The usual, please.' She added for Jermain's benefit. 'It saves time this way. You can ponder over a Chinese menu for years and you nearly always end up with the same.'

Unaccountably, Jermain felt a pang of jealousy. She was known here. Her casual confidence made him picture her with someone else, sitting just as he was. He said, 'This is fine. I was going to take you to the club. All the trimmings, but this is much better.'

She smiled. 'I guessed that. I also guessed that you would hate going to the club as much as I would!' She seemed to notice his suit for the first time. 'Out of uniform it would be hard to guess what you do for a living.' She placed her head on one side. 'But there's definitely something about the sea in you.' Her mouth quivered in a grin. 'A sort of homespun charm!'

The meal when it came was good and served with all the usual ceremony. It was *satay*, the neatly skewered meat all the more succulent when dipped in the hot peanut sauce. Jermain found that he was very hungry, and once when he met the girl's eyes he saw that she was watching him with open amusement.

She said, 'You look as if you've not eaten for days!'

He dabbed his mouth carefully. 'Like everything else aboard ship, eating becomes routine.' He added slowly, 'Besides which, the company is not so attractive.'

'Thank you.' She toyed with her plate. 'I've enjoyed being with you. But then I knew I would. I always know.'

Once more the pang. Jermain kept his voice noncommittal. 'I imagine you get a lot of entertaining?'

'What a delightful way of putting it! Actually it's pretty much of a bore. All talk. Not much else.'

The little Chinese had placed a pot of tea on the table yet Jermain had hardly noticed. He was suddenly aware of the darkening shadows outside the window. Of the relentless passing of time.

She said, 'I guess I'll have to be getting back soon.'

Jermain controlled his disappointment. 'Well, thanks for everything. I must have bored you sick with all my talk about the *Temeraire*.' He forced a grin. 'It was good of you to listen!'

She shook her head. 'I'd have told you if I was bored. I was surprised that I was so interested.' Impulsively she laid her hand on his. 'But I'm leaving with my father tomorrow morning. I have to make a few calls.'

Jermain stared at her hand. 'I know. I'm only sorry we didn't have more time.'

'I know. I am too. You meet someone. For some reason you seem to click.' She shrugged. 'Then you move on.' Her eyes moved over his face. 'I'm not just saying this. I mean it.'

'I knew you would be leaving soon. I just hoped . . .'

She smiled gently. 'What did you hope?'

Jermain dropped his eyes. What was the point of going on? She belonged to another world. Another kind of generation. He answered, 'It was nothing. I was just being stupid!'

She pulled her hand away and began to rummage through her handbag. Without looking up she said quietly, 'What would you think of a girl who was conceited enough to expect a man to wait for her after she'd been out enjoying herself late at night?'

Jermain felt a surge of excitement, but replied carefully, 'It all depends. If she was important to the man I think he'd be only too happy.'

She looked up quickly, her face serious. 'I don't want it to end like this. Not just here and now.'

He smiled. 'Just give me the address. I'll wait for you if it takes until dawn!'

Her guard was down and she seemed confused but strangely pleased. 'I have to go to the United Nations place outside the town.' She looked uncertain. 'It's a long way, David.'

'I'll find it.' They were both staring at each other as if surprised at their own voices. 'Don't you worry about me.'

She swallowed hard. 'Well, that's settled then. But I won't blame you if you change your mind. I've got a damned cheek really!'

Jermain stood up and paid the watching proprietor. 'What time shall I come?'

'I'll make some excuse and leave the party about ten. You can wait in the old car if you like.' She touched his arm impulsively. 'It's crazy, isn't it?'

'Not to me.' He guided her to the car. 'You go and get to your party, Jill. I'll take a taxi back to the boat. I'll pass the time with a bit of work!'

She studied him seriously. 'It must be the heat, but I wish I was coming with you!'

Jermain watched her drive back into the traffic, her hair rippling against her face, then after a moment he walked in the opposite direction.

• • •

The taxi sped along the tree-lined road, its headlights reflecting on the overhanging branches and the tangle of thick brush which seemed to be only temporarily held at bay by the strip of tarmac. The turbaned Sikh behind the wheel drove extremely fast, his massive head bowed slightly towards a small radio which swung from the driving mirror, his shoulders twitching in time to the discordant music.

In the back seat Jermain clung to a side strap and tried to think clearly about the immediate future. When he had returned to the *Temeraire* he had found the new orders waiting for him as if to curb his small moment of freedom and pleasure.

The *Temeraire* was to proceed to sea the following day. The destination was Taiwan, where she would join up with units of the American Seventh Fleet.

He had called his senior officers together and told them the news. Wolfe had accepted it with something like relief, Jermain thought. No questions or regrets. Just a few bald comments of duty and nothing more.

Ross, the engineer officer, on the other hand, had been openly pessimistic. 'It's not that I wish to criticise the motives behind these orders, sir.' He had stared woodenly at Jermain. 'It's just that I'm not happy about the condition of the hull. We've had no real check-up since that leak. On real sea duty anything might come to light!'

Jermain had known it was an unspoken criticism of himself. Only he as captain could have stood out for the submarine's immediate return home for docking and inspection. But on the face of it there was neither opportunity nor real evidence. It might well be as the admiral had said. Just a fluke. A settling down of a new boat. Either way, there was no time left for manoeuvre. The Americans expected British co-operation. Any sign of prevarication would certainly be taken as unwillingness to help in the delicate situation which threatened the peace and security of the Far East.

Bleakly Jermain had stated what he expected of each and every man aboard. He had made each point clearly so that there should be no argument later as to where the blame would lie. He knew that he had driven a wedge between himself and the others, but there was no other way. Weakness led to slackness, which in turn could destroy all of them.

It seemed a far cry from the excitement and adulation of the early days in *Temeraire*, he thought grimly. Then just to be aboard the new boat had been enough. The actual purpose of her role had seemed too remote to contemplate.

The taxi squealed up a steep drive towards a brightly lit house. There appeared to be a light in every window and the wide forecourt was crammed with cars. Jermain paid off the driver and walked slowly towards the familiar silhouette of the old sports car. Already he was feeling foolish and began to wish he had not let the taxi leave without him.

He ran his hand over the car seat. Tomorrow it would belong to someone else. And, like himself, would be forgotten. He eased himself behind the wheel and stared towards the stars.

It had been easy to forget his real responsibilities. But there was no escape from any one of them.

He tried to think about Taiwan and the voyage which lay ahead. It would be strange to work with the Americans again. To be committed to a course of action instead of merely contemplating a vague possibility.

He heard the muffled beat of dance music and imagined Jill Conway in someone's arms. It would be better to leave now, he decided. There was no point in hoping for the impossible. Just his being here could only cause her embarrassment and humiliation.

'So you came, David!' Her voice came out of the darkness and jolted him from his brooding thoughts.

She was wearing a long dress of some dark colour so that her face and arms seemed to shine in the dim light. Jermain could smell her perfume, the same that she had worn that afternoon.

He started to climb from the car but she said quickly, '*You* drive. For some unaccountable reason I think I may have had a bit too much to drink!'

Jermain started the engine and drove carefully through the gates. Beside him the girl lay back in her seat, her face upturned towards the night sky. He said, 'You should wear a coat. It's cool now.'

She laughed. 'I don't care about anything. You came. You said you would come and you did!' She swayed against him as the car took the first curve, and Jermain felt her head rest momentarily on his shoulder. She added, 'I thought that party would never end!'

When they reached the outskirts of the town she sat upright and peered through the screen. 'Take the next road on the right.' She sounded tense. 'Just along here.'

Jermain followed the line of buildings and said, 'This isn't the way to your house.'

'I know. Before my father came out here I shared a flat with two other girls. I told you.'

Jermain felt her staring at him. 'Yes, you did.'

'Well, that's where we're going.' She lapsed into silence.

They passed a parked police Land Rover with its occupants smoking quietly beside the road and then swung into a small cluster of low buildings. It was very quiet. As if there was nobody else alive.

Without speaking Jermain followed the girl up some stone steps and then waited as she switched on a light and flooded the small apartment with personality.

She waved vaguely. 'They're away. Now we can find a bit of peace.'

Jermain stood uncertainly in the centre of the room and watched her as she moved round him. He saw that the dress was deep blue and that she looked both beautiful and unreachable.

She stopped in front of him and then gave him a push. 'For God's sake sit down!'

Jermain fell on to a sofa and felt his jacket give in to the unexpected treatment. He peeled it off and held it up. 'I had a feeling it was a bad bargain!'

She did not reply. She was still standing in the middle of the room, her arms hanging quite limp at her sides.

Jermain stood up and walked towards her. Her eyes were fixed on his face, her expression a mixture of concern and excitement. She did not move or resist as he cupped his hands around her bare shoulders and pulled her to him.

Then, suddenly, she pressed her face against his chest, her voice muffled and unsteady. 'It has to be now, David. There might never be another time!'

He could feel her shaking, just as he could sense his own longing. It was like pain. Like finality.

'Are you sure?' He no longer recognised his voice and the words seemed drowned by his heart-beats.

She pushed herself away but would not look at him. She nodded violently. 'Now. It must be!'

Then she walked quickly from the room, so that for a brief instant Jermain thought he had imagined it all. The seconds dragged into minutes, then something made him follow her, as if at some kind of signal.

The blue dress lay discarded on the floor, her shoes where she had kicked them in one corner of the room.

Her eyes were wide and unblinking as she studied his face. She said, 'Don't say anything, David. Just come to me!'

He crossed to the bed and ran his hand gently across her throat and breasts. He felt her shudder, felt his own longing roaring in his brain like unquenchable fire. Then his ready-made suit lay beside her dress and his body against hers.

As if from a long way off he heard her say, 'Hold me!' Her arms were about his neck, pulling him down, and she quivered as if from pain as he found her mouth and felt her tongue against his own.

Long after the first desperate passion had passed they lay quite still, their bodies together, their limbs entwined like part of the whole.

Jermain touched her spine and she moved her face against his shoulder. He knew that she was asleep but for a long time he held her against him, watching her, feeling the warmth and perfection of her body.

He knew that this could never be the end of it. Not now. Not ever.

9

'If You Can't Take a Joke...'

THE TANNOY speaker on the control-room bulkhead hummed into life. 'During the dog watches there will be a talk on astronomy given by Lieutenant Mayo. The film show tonight will be a Western, called *Waggons West*.'

The men on watch glanced at each other and grinned. It was back to normal. The private, regulated life of a small town.

Max Colquhoun shifted his weight to the other foot and peered at the clock. Another hour of the watch still to run. Through the open hatch at the end of the control room came the heady aroma of rum as Sub-Lieutenant Luard supervised the forenoon issue, and above the faint hum of machinery Colquhoun could hear the distant clatter of dishes from the galley. He looked down at the chart. Two days out from Singapore, with the submarine's silent power pushing them swiftly north-eastwards across the vast open waters of the South China Sea. Some two hundred miles away on the port beam was Hainan Island, which before had been just a name on a map. Now Colquhoun could never think of it without remembering Victor's sudden death and the nightmare struggle with the wire on the rudder. Yet he was able to think of it more objectively, even calmly. He felt stronger within himself, and perhaps for the first time sensed a feeling of belonging to the *Temeraire* as a vital member of her community.

Right now he was in sole command of the control room. The boat was running smoothly at a depth of one hundred and fifty feet, and the men at the controls were relaxed and easy with the now familiar instruments around them.

Colquhoun still shared his watch with the first lieutenant, but Wolfe had made a curt excuse and had gone to the sick bay to see Griffin.

That was another strange thing, Colquhoun thought. He had expected the captain to keep them apart, to avoid another clash like the night Wolfe had come aboard in such a dangerous mood. But it seemed that Jermain intended to ignore the affair. To kill it and keep it in its right perspective. The more Colquhoun thought about it, the more he felt doubts about his own behaviour. He had heard that Wolfe was going through some personal misery which had been at the root of his sudden rage. Colquhoun still did not know how else he could have coped with the situation, but he knew deep down that it was not yet over completely.

He had tried to make contact with Wolfe. To clear the air once and for all. The day the submarine had sailed from Singapore he had found the first lieutenant alone in the chart-room. He had said quickly, 'I'm sorry about the row, sir. I expect you think I acted stupidly. Looking back, I guess we both got a bit worked up!'

Wolfe had glanced from the chart, his brows wrinkled slightly as if to grasp what he was talking about. Then he had given a mere shrug. 'Oh that. Well, we live and learn, I suppose.' He had tapped the chart. 'It'll be strange to work with the Americans again.' His face had hardened. 'Like old times for me.'

And that was all. No recriminations. No further comment. But on the other hand he had stayed aloof and detached during all watches, and in the wardroom. Colquhoun had observed that he rarely seemed to speak to anyone, but went about his work with the quiet concentration of a man completely absorbed in his own personal sphere.

Then there was Lightfoot. It was odd the way he kept crowding into Colquhoun's thoughts. On the last day in Singapore Colquhoun had kept his word and taken the boy sailing in a borrowed dinghy. The latter had said nothing at all about Wolfe's insinuations, but if anything it seemed to have drawn them closer together. In his cabin later Luard had said awkwardly, 'I saw you out with that chap Lightfoot, Max. Taking a bit of a chance, aren't you?'

Colquhoun had stared at him with surprise. It was rarely that Luard ever spoke of anything in such a serious tone. 'What of it?'

Luard had tried to pass it off. 'You know how it is. People talk. You should know. It *happens*!'

Colquhoun walked thoughtfully across the deck and peered over the helmsman's shoulder. It happens. What did it mean?

He tried to analyse his own feelings and motives towards Lightfoot. It seemed ridiculous that he should feel so close to him, to someone so removed from his own way of life. Yet it was true. In the dinghy Lightfoot had patiently followed his instructions, yet once he had grasped the problems of sailing the boat he acted more as an equal than a subordinate being offered a favour. He had a quick, alien wit and a surprising interest in all that went on around him, and was quite unlike any other rating Colquhoun had met.

They had grounded the boat on a sandbar and lounged in their swimming trunks, basking in the hot sun. Often Colquhoun found himself wondering about the clumsy attempt to sabotage the submarine's steering and tried to imagine Lightfoot as the culprit. It surprised him to find that it no longer seemed to matter. The boy had had some desperate reason, probably connected with his family. Right or wrong in his line of reasoning, Colquhoun knew that he would keep it to himself. Lightfoot had saved his life. And in some inexplicable way he seemed to need Colquhoun's friendship, just as he knew his own feelings were reaching out in the same direction. It made him feel guilty and yet elated. It was like some inner challenge which set him apart from the others.

The planesman whispered between his teeth, 'Captain's comin' up, sir!'

Colquhoun pulled himself from his rambling thoughts and glanced quickly towards the watertight door.

Jermain ducked his head down as he stepped through the oval frame and seemed quietly surprised as Colquhoun reported, 'Course zero four zero, sir. One hundred and fifty feet at twenty-five knots.'

'Where's Number One?'

Colquhoun said, 'Sick bay, sir. Just slipped away for a minute or two.'

Jermain smiled. 'Can you manage her on your own, Sub?'

'Just about.' Colquhoun relaxed slightly. There was something very reassuring about Jermain. He was never sarcastic or overbearing. In fact, he did not seem to fit any mould at all. Even his interview after the clash with Wolfe had been patient and devoid of threats. Rather like a schoolmaster with a promising but tactless pupil, Colquhoun decided.

Jermain walked through to the chart-room and checked the log. 'We'll go to periscope depth in half an hour, Sub. We'll raise the radio mast and get ready to receive our first American signals.' He seemed more preoccupied than usual, as if his mind was only half on his duties.

Colquhoun watched his face with close interest. It was like being allowed to share something private. Jermain rarely showed anything but complete dedication to his daily routine, and this trace of uncertainty seemed to add to rather than detract from his stature.

Jermain ran his finger down the neat line of pencilled figures and calculations left by the navigating officer and tried to relate them to what might lie ahead. In a day and a half they should reach the American operational base at Taiwan, and from there almost anything might come their way. He made an effort to build some enthusiasm out of the new destination as he had always been able to do in the past. It ought to be a great experience to use his new submarine alongside a fully trained and operational force. It should be a challenge, a rightful culmination to the months of training. Even Taiwan itself would be entirely new for all of them. The island which guarded the Formosa Strait and the main approaches to Communist China. Its ancient and feared General Chiang Kai-shek, whose gaunt shadow seemed to hang over the scene like some grotesque cardboard cut-out, supported by American money and materials of war, was a predominant factor in the undeclared battle between East and West. Yet as Jermain stared at the chart and the calculations he could feel neither excitement nor pride.

He had slept badly, tossing and turning in his bunk, and jerking awake at the most normal shipboard sounds. Time and time again he had pictured the girl in his mind, had almost sensed her touch and the warm softness of her body.

An hour before the *Temeraire* had sailed Jermain had gone aboard the depot ship for his final briefing, but after leaving the operations-room he had come face to face with Conway. The meeting had been so unexpected that Jermain had been conscious of a sudden feeling of guilt. It was entirely new to him, and for a few moments he had been almost unnerved.

Conway had been carrying his briefcase and was dressed for his flight to the north. He had said, 'I had to come and see you before I pushed off, Commander. There was a lot I wanted to say to you, but it seems we're bound for separate points of the compass.' He had given his lopsided grin. 'Very nautical, eh?'

Together they had leaned on the rail and stared down at the black submarine. A blue haze had hung around the diesel generator outlet, and men had been moving purposefully about the upper deck loosening the mooring wires and stowing away the final stores for the journey.

Conway had said suddenly, 'I hear you had a good time with Jill. She hasn't said much, but I think she was sorry she couldn't spend more time with you.'

Jermain had tensed at the mention of her name. It was obvious that Conway knew nothing of his daughter's later meeting with him. Of the fact that they had slept together.

Conway had hurried on, 'Yes, I wish you could have seen a bit more of her. She needs someone a bit mature. Someone who's not just another young hanger-on.' He had glanced sideways at Jermain. 'I'm not suggesting that you're an old man, it's just that she's had a bad time in the past. Her mother and I have had a few worried moments, I can tell you.'

'In what way?' Jermain could not meet the other man's gaze. He had wanted to change the subject or to end the conversation altogether.

'When she was at university she met this man. He was much older than she was, and, worse still, he was married. He was a tutor of some sort, but I didn't hear about it until the whole thing blew up. Well, of course it had to end, but I don't think she ever really got over it. She went completely off the rails for months. Drank too much, mixed with all the wrong people, you know the sort of thing.' He had seemed unable to stop talking, and Jermain had guessed Conway had bottled it all up within himself for a long time.

'Somehow I managed to get her fixed up with my department. It's got a pretty wide range of work, and above all it keeps her busy and occupied most of the time. But every so often I see the signs, and I get worried as hell all over again. She's all I've got. I just want her settled.'

At that moment Oxley had called up from the casing, 'Fifteen minutes to go, sir!'

Conway had added, 'I hope I've not embarrassed you, Commander? I thought you might understand.'

'I think I do.' Jermain had tried not to think of the girl's body naked on the bed like a pale crucifix. He had known he was doing wrong, and Conway's confidence had added to his sense of guilt.

Perhaps she had been using him as another 'experience', and he had remembered with sudden clarity that once during the night she had clung to his shoulder and called 'John'. At the time he had put it down to the excitement, the all-devouring elation which had left them weak and at peace together. But Conway's words had changed all that. She must have been thinking back to that other man, to those precious days which Jermain could never share. A passing substitute, the momentary recapture of a dream. He had felt sick.

Conway had held out his hand. 'Good luck, Commander. I hope we meet again with more time to spare.' By the time Jermain had climbed down to the submarine's casing Conway had vanished.

Jermain had tried more than ever to push himself harder into his work, but even that evaded him. The boat was running like silk, there seemed little to do but think and brood over what had happened.

If only he could have seen her just once more. In the dawn light he had dressed quickly beside the bed while the girl watched him through half-closed eyes. They hardly spoke, but once when he stooped over her she gripped his hand so fiercely that her nails broke the skin.

She had shown no regrets. Neither did she seem to care what he might have thought of her willingness to sleep with him. Each was wrapped in his and her private thoughts, and when the actual moment of departure came there was no longer any time for words.

She had held his hand under her breast and watched the emotions crossing his face. 'I won't get up till you've gone.' Her voice had been low and husky. 'There's no point in adding to the pain.'

'I have to see you again.' His voice had sounded as hopeless as he had felt. The waiting submarine, the remorseless passing of time, added to his feeling of inevitability and loss. 'I have to!'

She had kissed him quickly and hard, and then pulled the sheet up to her chin so that in the half-light she looked defenceless, like a child. 'You might forget me by tomorrow.' She had shivered beneath the sheet. 'It might all be different then.'

'What about you, Jill? How will you feel?'

Her words still stayed with him, awake or in his restless sleep. 'At this very moment I cannot bear the thought of your leaving this room. I cannot pretend to know how I will feel tomorrow.' She had turned her face on to the pillow so that her hair had hidden her eyes. 'Now go quickly, David. I'm not strong enough for farewells!'

Jermain realised that Colquhoun was speaking again.

'I saw the two security men go ashore, sir. Does that mean they're satisfied with everything?' Colquhoun was watching him closely.

Jermain shrugged. 'Maybe. Anyway. I'm glad to be shot of them. To get the boat welded into some sort of order again.'

Colquhoun gave a quick grin. 'No admiral either, sir!'

Some of the tension drained out of Jermain's face and he smiled. 'Did you see your father before we sailed?'

'I saw the *admiral*, sir.' Colquhoun looked away. 'I took a present up to the house to be posted back to my mother. My father was having a conference but condescended to come out for a few minutes.' His voice became bitter. 'He said I was wasting my time in submarines and that I should go back to general service.'

Jermain said gently, 'He means well, I expect. He probably expects big things from you.'

Colquhoun sighed. 'I find his reasoning beyond me.'

Jermained turned away. Don't look to me for guidance, he thought. I imagined that I knew myself. Now I am not sure of anything!

• • •

Wolfe returned to the control room and glanced quickly at the clock. A few minutes to go and then the boat would be gliding upwards to listen to the far-off world of command and naval strategy. He felt depressed and uneasy, and his converstion with Griffin, the doctor, had gone entirely the wrong way.

He had found Griffin seated at a table in the sick bay, apparently absorbed in studying a small carved figurine. He had said cheerfully, 'Picked it up in the market in Singapore, Number One. Only cost a few bob. Marvellous piece of work.'

Wolfe had said, 'Probably made in Birmingham! They're all bloody sham!'

Griffin had sighed and placed the figurine carefully in a drawer. 'It's like that, is it?' He had studied Wolfe carefully. 'What can I do for you?'

'I have a headache. I want a few tablets for it.' Wolfe had felt angry beneath Griffin's cool scrutiny. 'For God's sake, it's only a headache!'

'Did I suggest otherwise?' Griffin had pulled out his keys. 'I'll fix you up certainly. But have you had any sort of treatment recently? Are you sure it's nothing worse?'

'Look, if you don't want to give me a simple remedy then say so! I can manage without a lecture!'

Griffin did not seem to hear him. 'Serving in submarines affects different people different ways. It can produce the same effect as, say, alcohol. A man can show his real character, just as he will do under the influence of drink or drugs. What he can cover up under normal conditions can overpower his usual control and become all-important and outsize, so that he can think of little else.'

Wolfe remembered his angry sarcasm. 'And how long have *you* been in submarines, Doctor?'

"Two years, on and off.' Griffin had eyes him calmly. 'But you don't have to be able to dig holes in the ground to learn about architecture!' He had given him the tablets. 'These should do the trick, but if they don't I'll give you a going over.'

Wolfe had snapped, 'Should I rely on your judgement?'

'It seems that I must rely on *you*, Number One, so why not?'

The petty officer of the watch said, 'Time, sir!'

Wolfe started. 'Very well. Take her up to periscope depth.' He felt easier in his mind when something was happening. He watched the gauges and listened to the gentle hiss of pressurised air.

'Sixty feet, sir.'

Wolfe grunted. 'Up periscope!' For several seconds he swung the big periscope in a slow circle, his eyes squinting against the glare. The sea was flat and glittering with a million bright mirrors. Like the pale sky it was empty. Not a gull or even a piece of flotsam marred the probing lenses.

He said, 'Raise the radio mast and inform the W/T room.'

He heard Jermain's voice at his side. 'All quiet, Number One?'

'Yes, sir. It's a pity we can't raise the radar mast, too. It would save all this scratching around for information.'

'I agree.' Jermain seemed distant. 'But our orders do not change on that point. Any radar transmissions could easily be detected.' He added suddenly, 'I hear you were in the sick bay?'

Wolfe caught sight of Colquhoun across the captain's shoulder. 'Just for a moment. Did he say I have been adrift for the whole watch?' Even as he said it, Wolfe cursed himself. There I go again. What the hell is the matter with me? A matter-of-fact question becomes a major issue. Perhaps Griffin is right after all.

Jermain replied calmly, 'He made his report, nothing more.'

Wolfe said, 'Just a headache. What with one thing and another . . .'

The radio supervisor interrupted by poking his head through

the radio-room hatch. 'Signal coming in now, Captain! From American Group Ten.'

Jermain pursed his lips. 'It feels strange.'

'I'll bet the Yanks have been waiting for this.' Wolfe scowled as he listened to the muted stammer of Morse. 'They'll just love to throw *us* around!'

Jermain said, 'I'd have thought they'd be more occupied in other directions.' He broke off as the radio supervisor called, 'We'll have it all in another minute, sir.'

Jermain said, 'Right. Let's have the code book and all the combat material in the chart-room. I have a feeling this is more than a social call!'

• • •

Able Seaman Bruce spooned down the last of his tinned pineapple and wiped his thick fingers on the front of his shirt. He looked around the mess table and continued with the story. 'Yeh, as I was sayin'. I gets this tart back to her place and we starts bargainin' for a fair price. Now, I bin out East afore, an' I know the form...'

Haley, the leading hand of the mess, reached for his pipe and said dryly, 'I can imagine!'

Bruce scowled. 'These Chinese toms who hang about the dockyard don't bargain unless it's for a purpose.' He winked across at Lightfoot. 'When they've got a fair idea of the wad you're carrying' they gives a signal, an' out comes a hairy great wog from behind the bleedin' bed! Afore you can say "kiss my arse" he's clobbered you, an' when you awakes in the arms of a shore patrol you got no money, and no enjoyment!'

Dale, another seaman, asked wearily, 'So what happened *this* time?'

Bruce smiled knowingly. 'I dived for the back of the bed, and sure enough there's this tart's bloke hidin' behind the screen. I kicks him once, and hard, then jumps on top of this bird.' He threw back his head and roared. 'I guess if I'd been a bleedin' marine I'd 'ave done the bloke as well!'

Lightfoot eyed him distantly. He had heard much the same story before. The Place varied, but the situation was always the same. He stiffened as he heard Archer's familiar voice behind him.

'Anyone got a fag to keep me goin' till the canteen opens?'

Someone threw a tin across the table but Archer seemed reluctant to return to his own mess. He said, 'I heard a buzz that we're staying with the Yanks for six months.'

Dale choked on his cigarette. 'Jesus! I was due for leave. It's not damn well fair!'

Bruce eyed him scornfully. 'Pipe down, *Mrs.* Dale! You shouldn't have joined if you can't take a joke!' He turned his gaze back to Archer, who was now standing directly behind Lightfoot. 'So what else did you hear?'

'That Jimmy the One caught some officer in his bunk with one of the lads.' He laughed harshly. 'I'll bet it's true an' all.'

Lightfoot tensed. He could almost feel the man's breath across his neck. He kept his eyes fixed on Bruce's face and wondered how he could appear so casual. There was absolutely no sign of tension or caution. No sign that he was chatting with a man he had tried to kill.

Bruce continued, 'That's a load of squit! Do you think they could keep it quiet?'

Archer sounded angry. ''Course they could! Bloody officers stick together like dung on a blanket! I'll find out who it was before long, you see!'

Lightfoot stared down at his plate. Once again things seemed to be moving too fast for him to regain control. After the incident in Colquhoun's cabin his inner sense had told him to stay away from the officer, to withdraw completely into himself. It had always been his method of keeping straight in the past. But Colquhoun's kindness over his mother's death, his genuine willingness to help, had been difficult obstacles to overcome. Furthermore, he had wanted to accept Colquhoun's invitation to go sailing. He had really wanted to go. It had been a kind of challenge, like when he was a kid, answering a dare to run across the railway track only seconds before a passing train.

At first he had imagined that he was using this unexpected relationship with the young officer as a possible shield against Archer, but deep down he knew it was not so. After all, if anything else went wrong it was obvious that Colquhoun had much more to lose.

The realisation made him feel uneasy and sick. It was as if Archer's crude rumour had been a picture of truth. Suppose Colquhoun felt that way about him? He screwed up his mind with unusual concentration. It was unnerving even to think of it. And he knew that it was not because Colquhoun would appear like the groping man in the car. He realised, even before he had time to think further about it, that he would have made no protest.

Vaguely he heard Archer say, 'The security blokes 'ave gone. That's somethin'!'

Leading Seaman Haley looked up and smiled. 'I suppose they were on the game, too, eh?'

Archer slammed back, 'You mark my words, this is going to be a rough commission. What with the old man bustin' a gut to show how marvelous the Black Pig is, an' half the crew goin' round the bend, I'm glad I'm a bloody A.B.'

Haley said coldly, 'Bloody marvellous. Like the time you fell off the rudder! A real nice piece of seamanship that was!'

Archer was about to make a retort when the tannoy speaker came alive overhead.

'Stand by for an announcement.'

Archer said excitedly, 'See? What did I tell you?'

Haley growled, 'Stow it!'

Jermain's voice came over the speaker, bringing silence to the crowded mess tables. 'This is the Captain speaking. I have to tell you that I have just received a signal from the American Task Force to which we are now attached.' He paused, and those nearest the speaker could hear the faint rustle of paper. 'We are to proceed at maximum speed to a rendezvous point one hundred miles off the west coast of Korea in the Yellow Sea.' His voice became less formal. 'For the benefit of those who have not been reading the daily reports on the notice boards, it means we have to steam another two thousand miles to the north, without breaking the journey at Taiwan as expected.'

A chorus of groans came from the listening seamen. Bruce muttered, 'Strike me blind! It's gettin' like a flamin' round-the-world cruise!'

Jermain continued, 'The object of this assignment is to patrol and, if necessary, intercept shipping which is reported as being used to ferry guerrillas and political agitators from the Chinese mainland to South Korea.' He cleared his throat. 'It means, of course, that the *Temerarie* will be on a full and active duty, with a possibility of action. This is a picked crew, and I expect nothing but the best from all of you. This is not the sort of work we had been expecting, but as you saw very clearly on our last patrol, when Lieutenant Victor lost his life, it is as real and deadly as any publicised emergency.'

Another voice came on the speaker, and Lightfoot was again reminded of that night in Colquhoun's cabin.

Wolfe sounded unruffled and confident. 'With regard to the captain's announcement. General drill will commence at 1400, and all sections will test and exercise equipment. Damage control and fire-fighting parties will muster in the main crewspace at 1415.' Some of the old sharpness returned to his tone. 'Any defects in either equipment *or* personnel will be promptly dealt with. That is all!'

Bruce said, 'I should think it's a bleedin-nough! Roll on my bloody twelve!'

Lightfoot stayed silent. It was going on and on, with one crisis blending into another. It was like the 'Flying Dutchman' he had been forced to read at school. Only worse.

Archer turned to go but added casually, 'Well, mates, this will give us all a real good chance to get to know each other!' As he passed he brushed against Lightfoot's arm. The latter knew it was no accident, just as he knew that his own danger was still with him.

• • •

Jermain rolled up his chart and looked around the wardroom table at his silent officers. 'Well, I think we've gone over all the known possibilities, gentlemen. Any questions?'

Ross shook his head. 'I still think this is more than ridiculous!' He was speaking directly to Jermain, excluding the others. 'If we had gone to Taiwan direct as originally planned we could maybe have used some of the Ameican infra-red gear to check over the hull. I would have felt much happier.'

Jermain nodded. 'Our last patrol seemed to rule out any real danger of hull flaws, Chief. We threw the boat around a good deal. If anything was about to come adrift it would surely have happened then?' He saw his words were having no effect. And why should they? He alone was taking the full weight of responsibility. Was it pride in the boat or personal conceit? He dragged his mind back to the lengthy coded signal. One part of it seemed to overshadow all the rest. But again, was it his own strain, his imagination which was giving it too much emphasis?

Inserted in the patrol orders had been the phrase, 'In response to the request of your Flag Officer Inshore Squadron you will proceed, etc., etc.' It might merely have been a typical piece of American courtesy to a lonely unit of another navy. Or it might have been their way of pointing out that Sir John Colquhoun had insisted on this early venture into well-tried and dangerous territory.

He tried to put himself in Sir John's state of mind. The admiral knew of Conway's secret mission to meet envoys from North Korea at a time when East/West relations were strained to breaking point. He knew too that any success on Conway's part would be a sign for further cuts in the Royal Navy's strength and importance in this and adjacent areas. His own command would be reduced to almost nothing. Yet it seemed impossible that the admiral could use his authority to put the *Temeraire* in a position where she would be implicated in any sort of open clash. A man of his experience and undoubted skill must surely take the long view, with the country's security as his first concern.

He said slowly, 'We will go to patrol routine and bring the men up to a first degree of readiness. I don't imagine the Americans will give us much to do at first, but out here we must be prepared for anything.'

Oxley drawled, 'It seems that their main reason for wanting us is to use a protective screen of long-range sonar. We pick up the ships, and they move in surface craft to investigate and board if necessary, right?'

Jermain smiled. 'That just about sums it up.' It was easy to picture Oxley in later life as an admiral. In spite of his apparent casual atittude to Service life he had a mind which he used to grasp at and use the bare essentials. The rest he discarded as no part of an officer's requirements.

That is how *I* should act and think, Jermain decided. I above all, with this valuable ship and trained complement should be able to ignore vague possibilities and personal standards. It is no part of my work. I am merely a part of a whole. A section of an over-all plan.

Wolfe said suddenly, 'Do you really believe the American Intelligence reports, sir? They see a Communist plot in everything!'

'They've had a lot to put up with, Number One.' Jermain found time to marvel at the way Wolfe appeared to have dismissed completely the near disaster over Colquhoun. He seemed almost at ease, and while Jermain had been running through the orders he had been writing busily in his notebook. There was no sign of uncertainty or of his earlier strain. That at least was a good omen, he thought.

Wolfe said flatly, 'I'll bet the top brass back in Whitehall are congratulating themselves over us. I can just see all the little flags being stuck in maps and memos being passed from desk to desk!' He gave a tight smile. 'When the Navy has been cut down to the *Victory* in Portsmouth Dockyard, Whitehall will still have its full quota of admirals and civil servants!'

Lieutenant Kitson glanced uncomfortably at Ross and then blurted out, 'Of course, if there is some sort of flaw in the hull it would be serious for the electrical department, sir.'

Jermain guessed that Kitson and Ross had been having a private conference of their own. 'I am aware of that. We'll cross our bridges when we come to them.' His tone was final. 'Now, I shall lay off the new course and then inform the engine room of the calculated speed. My immediate guess is around thirty knots.'

Jermain sighed. They were all writing in their notebooks again, the grim possibilities and doubts momentarily held at bay.

Sub-Lieutenant Luard remarked vaguely, 'I suppose I'll have to check through all the menus again. If it's not one thing it's another.'

The others stared at him, and then Lieutenant Drew said dryly, 'Fair makes you sweat, doesn't it? Here we are about to embark on a great campaign, and all you can think about is how many tinned sausages you've got to last the voyage!'

They laughed, and Jermain decided it was time to end the conference. If Drew, whose assistant had been killed, could still make jokes, things could not be too bleak.

• • •

For another two days the *Temeraire* thrust further northwards. Like a black shadow, her smooth whaleshape hastening through the depths at a speed which would leave most of her surface contemporaries astern, she moved through the Formosa Strait and up into the East China Sea. Only once a day did she swim upwards to periscope depth, when after a quick look round through her powerful eye the radio mast was raised and for brief moments she was once more in contact with the outside world. But again she was only listening. Like her nuclear power, her voice was silent.

The privileged few who saw the periscope's view of the outer world looked around with mixed feelings. Envy and suspicion, fear and excitement. As the submarine moved further north and away from the remaining shipping lanes each sighting report became a small event. The occasional patrolling frigate or destroyer, the dilapidated freighter and the ghostly silhouettes of junks, each became a need, a certain reminder that there was another life beyond the confines of the *Temeraire*'s hull.

The submarine seemed to have become smaller, and the past air of casual acceptance had given way to a watchful tension. Men rarely bothered to discuss the possibility of returning home in some near future, and the general atmosphere had become brittle, even apprehensive.

Jermain watched the change moving through his command and tried to block each problem before it got out of hand. Arguments flared over small things, and discipline tightened accordingly.

Above all, waiting was the worst part. It gave men too long to wonder and distrust, it helped to break down the established pattern of routine.

It was with something like relief that Jermain received the awaited signal even as he took one of his rare looks through the raised periscope. It was brief. The clipped brevity from that unseen chain of command seemed to add to the impression of tension and urgency.

Temeraire would take up a patrol area between the jutting peninsula of Shantung Province in Red China and the twisting coastline of Korea. Less than two hundred miles separated the two countries at this point, so that the *Temeraire*'s patrol line would correspond almost exactly with the thirty-eighth parallel which cut Korea in half, and which had decided that men on one side of it would fear and hate their countrymen on the other.

Eight hours after receiving the signal Jermain conned the submarine on to the first leg of the patrol, and like the remainder of his mind, settled down to wait.

10

Decision

JERMAIN LEANED against the chart table and stared through the open door into the control room. From the back of his neck to the soles of his feet he felt as if every muscle was aching in unison, yet he knew that if he returned to his cabin sleep would still elude him.

For five endless days the *Temeraire* had carried out her slow search of the patrol area. Back and forth. Up and down. If the sea remained empty, the radio frequency did not. Each time the submarine raised her radio mast the signals came thick and fast. It was as if the whole Yellow Sea was packed with invisible ships and impatient commanders. Unfamiliar routines and complicated code names became almost commonplace, and even the American voices on the acoustic radio had welded themselves into the daily pattern.

As the coded signals poured in Jermain and his officers plodded through the intelligence reports and conflicting information without rest. Only the submarine herself stayed immune, and her smooth-running complacency helped to add to the frustration and strain of her crew.

The *Temeraire* remained at periscope depth for most of the time now. There was not much point in exercising diving anyway. The Yellow Sea was mostly shallow, and even now there were less than twenty fathoms beneath the ballast keel.

The narrowest point between the Korean coast and the Chinese mainland had been selected as the most likely area for infiltration. It would be quick and hard to detect. Along the Korean shoreline Jermain knew there was a waiting company of American warships, added to which there was a sprinkling of South Korean vessels. Then southwards there was a well-stretched chain of patrol ships, including several American submarines. But the plum piece of the line was the *Temeraire*'s. Alone at the northern end, she swept back and forth in complete silence, her long-range sonar probing and listening, while her periscope kept a regular watch for less formidable vessels.

The next immediate link with the rest of the task force was a South Korean frigate. They had seen her only twice since the beginning of the patrol, and then only as a shadow or a smudge of smoke. She carried an American naval officer for liaison duties, and when the two craft were within range of the acoustic radio it was his voice which entered the submarine's hull, like that of an old friend.

As soon as Jermain contacted any suspicious vessels, all he had to do was whistle up the frigate and allow her to board and search it. It sounded simple.

Only the previous day when they made a brief contact the American officer had said, 'For God's sake sight something soon, so that we can get the hell out of here! If I eat much more rice aboard this bucket I'll be getting slant eyes!' It was not exactly a correct form of signaling, but it showed the listening submariners that they were not the only ones dying of boredom.

Oxley was the officer-of-the-watch and stood in the centre of the control room, his hands deep in his pockets. His eyes looked dark with strain, and Jermain wondered if he was beginning to doubt the efficiency of his sonar devices.

Jermain heard a petty officer report, 'Coming up to twenty-one thirty, sir.' The end of another sweep. Time to make a turn on to a new course. The submarine was now at her nearest point to the Chinese mainland. The first time it had happened there had been an edge of excitement in the boat. Now there was nothing. It was just a fact and little more.

Oxley grunted, 'Very well.' He glanced at the captain.

Jermain walked stiffly into the control room, the sudden movement making his legs throb with pain. 'Up periscope.' He waited as the greased tube slid from its well and then pressed his forehead against the pad. The sea looked like deep purple satin, above which the sky seemed pale by comparison. He switched the periscope to full power and swung it gently in a slow arc. The darker line below the sky was not the horizon. It was the land. Nothing solid or distinct, but just a hint of the vast, endless country beyond. He murmured, 'Carry on.'

Oxley said wearily, 'Starboard fifteen. Steer two two five.'

Jermain moved the periscope in rhythm with the boat's gentle turn and wondered how long this uneasy peace would last. His hand slipped on the handle as the intercome suddenly barked, 'Surface contact, sir! Bearing green one one five! Range twenty thousand yards!'

Jermain swung round and met Oxley's astonished stare. 'Down periscope!' Jermain had to lick his lips to clear their sudden dryness. 'Close up action stations!'

He stood for a few more seconds, his ears deaf to the yammer of alarm bells as he forced his mind to work like a slide-rule. Around and below him doors slammed shut and the narrow passageways were alive with running figures. The telephones and voice pipes crackled to life, and as Oxley vanished towards the sonar compartment Wolfe appeared in the control room, his face crumpled from sleep but his eyes alert and calm.

Jermain said, 'Contact the frigate at once. It may be another scare, Number One. But I have a feeling about this one.'

Oxley's voice came over the intercom. 'Captain, sir. It's a firm contact. Distorted but regular. Maybe three or four small vessels. Moving fast but parallel with us.'

Jermain frowned. Moving fast. That would explain the sudden flurry of echoes hitherto undetected. Probably fast patrol boats. Just the craft for a swift crossing to the other side. And what better time to choose? With darkness closing down and the sea like a millpond.

A messenger opened the radio-room door and scurried away with a signal pad. Before the door closed again Jermain heard the distorted garble from the acoustic radio. The American sounded as if he was speaking through a heavy rainstorm.

'Hello BLUEBOY, this is VIGILANT. Your message received and understood. Suggest you close contact and shadow. Listening out.'

Jermain walked slowly to the chart table. The frigate would be turning away now to contact and alert the rest of the waiting force.

He watched Mayo's hands moving across the chart like busy crabs. 'Alter course, Pilot. We'll move to the west to intercept.'

Mayo did not even look up. After a few more minutes he scribbled on his pad and called, 'Steer two seven zero.'

Jermain found that he could not stay still, and it took real effort to make his movements slow and controlled. 'Increase to twenty-five knots. And tell the chief to be ready for maximum revolutions!' He could imagine Ross sitting in his gleaming domain of steel and brass and wondered if he would appreciate what was happening. At least he would not have to worry about a deep dive. In these waters it was an impossibility.

Oxley again. 'Contact appears to be retaining same course and speed. Bearing now green nine zero.'

Mayo said, 'Contact's moving ahead, sir.'

Jermain nodded. 'Increase to thirty knots.' He felt the smallest tremble run through the deck plates and then nothing. The boat was responding like a thoroughbred.

This brief excitement might make all the difference, he thought. A success, no matter how small, would bind the crew together and make all the other irritations fade away for good.

'Range now fifteen thousand yards.'

Jermain thrust his hands into his pockets and balled his fingers into tight fists. He watched the attack team bending over the plot table as the ranges and bearings poured through the headphones and intercom. The ultimate would be to close and challenge the other ships and, if necessary, to attack. But that was impossible, and the *Temeraire*'s men would have to be content to know that the rest of the plan had worked successfully on their work. Even now the far-off American ships would be wheeling into position to spring their trap. Jermain found himself wondering what Conway would think when he was given definite proof that the Chinese were far from eager to accept a peaceful solution to an undeclared war which they believed they were winning.

He made up his mind. 'Slow ahead. Stand by to raise the search periscope.' He waited as the hull shuddered slightly and the racing screw slowed its pace. He looked at the flickering lights above the plot table and tried to imagine how the other ships would appear in the powerful lenses. Just over seven miles. But with the light fading it might be very difficult.

'Up periscope.' He ducked down and came up with the periscope lenses already to his eyes. He found himself holding his breath, his forehead moist against the pad.

The sea was much darker now. Almost black, its surface heaving like polished ebony. There were a few pale stars in the sky, and around the raised periscope Jermain could see the green glow of dancing phosphorescence. It would have to be a quick look.

He caught his lower lip in his teeth and blinked to clear the film from his eyes. There they were. He counted the bright triangular bow waves which stood out against the darkening sea like tiny breakers. There were eight at least. Very small and extremely fast.

He snapped, 'Down periscope.' Then to Wolfe, 'PT boats, I would guess. An arrowhead formation and well grouped.'

Wolfe shrugged. 'Could be a sort of exercise.' Some of his earlier intolerance crept into his tone. 'The Americans aren't the only navy in these waters!'

Oxley's voice said, 'Contact altering course, sir. Swinging round to the south and still turning!'

Jermain nodded. 'Very well. Increase to twenty-five knots again.' He stared hard at the chart. 'It's my guess the PT boats are going to make a complete turn and head out away from the mainland.' He waited a few more seconds. 'Ask sonar what the hell is going on?'

Oxley sounded unruffled. 'Contact still turning, sir. Present course estimated at one one zero degrees.'

Jermain smiled. 'Reduce speed to fifteen knots. They'll pass clear astern of us now.'

Mayo leaned his elbows on the chart and grimaced. 'And that's all there is to it. The little Chinks will steam happily into an ambush and get a dose of gunfire. Then there'll be a few diplomatic notes exchanged and it'll be all quiet until they think of another way of getting their agents and equipment across!'

Jermain eyed him with amusement. 'You're a cynic, Pilot!'

Wolfe said, 'What now, sir?'

'As Pilot has just remarked, we just applaud from the sidelines. As soon as the PT boats are well away we'll flash a further sighting report and resume patrol. I don't imagine we'll be there much longer.'

The intercom interrupted their speculations. 'Another contact, sir. Faint propeller noises and a good deal of throwback from the shallows, but definite enough.' Oxley sounded entirely absorbed. 'I would think that there is another ship or ships keeping along the coast, close inshore.'

Jermain felt vaguely uneasy as the bearings and tracking information began to form a picture on the plot table. The Chinese coastline at this point was desolate and little used. For five days they had sighted nothing, and the nearest port of any consequence was a hundred and fifty miles to the south west.

He said sharply, 'Take the con, Number One. I'm going forrard to talk with Oxley.' Without waiting for a reply he ducked his head through the door and hurried along the passageway. He caught vague glimpses of his men sitting or standing quietly at their stations, their eyes expectant as he passed. He found Oxley and his operators hunched over their equipment, their faces flickering in the lights thrown back from the dials and gauges.

Even Oxley showed some surprise at Jermain's entrance. He pushed the headset from his ears and said, 'There's no change, sir.'

Jermain glanced round the crowded compartment, the dark figures suddenly taking on personality and meaning. There was Colquhoun, and in front of him, in the operator's seat, young Lightfoot. There was Petty Officer Irons, and another operator, their eyes unblinking as they watched and listened.

Oxley added, 'We'd have to get much closer inshore, sir. The echoes are very distorted at this range. Now, if we were tracking another submarine it'd be different!'

Jermain studied the gauges. The *Temeraire* was cruising in barely ten fathoms of water. And in any case, what explanation could he give for his actions?

He asked, 'Can you make any sort of guess about these ships?'

Oxley shrugged. 'I would say two ships. Both twin screw and doing about fifteen knots. From the rhythm and power I would definitely say that they are warships.' He shook his head. 'No doubt about that, in my view.'

Irons looked over his shoulder and squinted at the captain. 'That's right, sir. Too powerful for coasters or the clapped-out freighters the Chinks use hereabouts!'

Jermain rubbed his chin. It felt rough under his palm but he did not notice it. He said, 'Keep tracking. I'll move in a bit closer, but you'll have to keep contact as best you can.'

Oxley asked, 'What do you have in mind, sir?'

Jermain studied him calmly. 'I wish I knew. But there's far too much activity for mere coincidence. We'll run down the coast, but keep about ten miles offshore. If we stay on roughly a parallel course you should be able to detect any sort of sudden manoeuvre on their part.'

He returned to the control room and waited impatiently until Mayo had transformed his ideas into a working plan.

The helmsman listened to the new orders and leaned forward over the wheel. 'Course two four zero, sir.'

Thinking aloud Jermain said, 'We can't raise the fleet without giving our own position away. In this shallow water it's too risky. The Chinese would feel more than justified in lobbing a few depthcharges down on us, on their own back door so to speak!'

Somebody laughed but Wolfe said doggedly, 'Why not let the Yanks handle it from their end?'

'Our last instructions were to track shipping, Number One. So let's do that, shall we?' He smiled at Wolfe's pensive expression. 'It'll do no harm.'

Wolfe said, 'You're really saying that the PT boats were a decoy. That the Yanks will be so busy chasing after them they'll not expect the Reds to try a crossing further south over the wider distance?' He eyed Jermain fixedly. 'Is that it?'

Jermain nodded. 'I could be wrong.'

Surprisingly Wolfe replied, 'I agree with your idea. That's exactly what they would do.' He paused. 'What *I* would do.'

Jermain watched him thoughtfully. Now that he had stopped

thinking about himself Wolfe was dropping into his proper role. The realisation made him feel strangely satisfied.

'We'll just have to wait and see,' Jermain replied.

He turned abruptly as the radio supervisor entered the control room. 'What is it, Harris?'

'Just received the fleet broadcast, sir. Usual shipping movements for the most part.'

Jermain looked at the clock. 'God, is it that late already?' It seemed incredible that the normal signals traffic could still be flooding the networks in spite of their own personal tensions.

Harris added doubtfully, 'There's just one thing, sir. The American Intelligence report that a single ship will be passing through the southern grid between midnight and 0200. The S.S. *Malange*, outward bound from Taiwan to Inch'on in South Korea.'

Wolfe said irritably, 'Well, what of it?'

Harris kept his eyes on the captain. 'There's a Top Secret signal about her, sir. She's carrying a V.I.P., Conway.'

Jermain felt a slight chill in his spine. It would be just like Conway to make his way to South Korea in some unconventional freighter. He had obviously flown north from Singapore and picked up the ship in Taiwan only days ago.

He peered down at the chart and snapped, 'Check these figures, Pilot, and plot the *Malange's* approximate course, using the American grid reference. You'll have to start with her intended midnight position and work backwards.' To Wolfe he added, 'Finish checking those signals. I want a complete build-up of ship movements in this area.'

Wolfe opened his mouth and then changed his mind and went to the radio room with Harris.

Oxley again. 'Contact still retaining course and speed, sir.'

The petty officer at the plot reported, 'We're getting a good picture, sir.' He peered at his vibrating table. 'The two ships seem to be keeping about three miles offshore. Our range is fourteen thousand yards.'

'Very well.' Jermain watched Mayo's face as he stepped out of the chart-room. 'Well?'

Mayo regarded him calmly. 'The *Malange* will have crossed latitude thirty-five about one hundred and thirty miles west of the Korean coast at midnight, sir. So assuming she's doing between ten and fifteen knots, and not many of her type of scow do much more...'

Jermain snapped, 'Cut out the dialogue, Pilot. Just give me the facts!'

Mayo plucked his beard and said coldly, 'So right now she should be about one hundred and seventy miles south east of us.' He coughed noisily and then added, 'Of course, it's all largely guesswork, but give or take twenty miles it's fair enough.'

Jermain brushed past him and walked to the chart table. For a long moment he stood staring down at the pencilled lines, and in his mind's eye he seemed to see the isolated freighter plodding unconcernedly across an empty sea.

But just suppose he had been right about the two mysterious ships which even now were cruising just a few miles abeam? If they turned as suddenly as the others and made a dash into open water they would almost certainly make contact with the *Malange*.

He kept thinking about Conway's quiet optimism, of his hope for some sort of peaceful solution to the East/West conflict. When Jermain had voiced his fears Conway had said, 'I'd not be taking my daughter otherwise....' He had been so sure of his safety and of the value of his mission.

The realisation of his own helplessness made Jermain suddenly angry. If he used his radio he would foul up the whole planned operation, with nothing to offer in return but his own imagination. If he stayed silent and remained on station he would be equally guilty if the Chinese decided to break out from another point.

Mayo had moved to the entrance, his shadow across the chart like a cloud. 'We're in Chinese territorial waters now, sir. In fifteen minutes we shall have to alter course to the seaward.' He studied Jermain's grim features. 'It's already shoaling, and the maximum depth will be less than seven fathoms.'

Jermain was aware of the silence inside the boat. It seemed to be pressing on his eardrums, as if he was submerged in water. It was one problem after another, like a series of maniacal tests.

He replied, 'Very well. But we must try to retain contact with these ships. In open water the detection devices would be doubly effective, but inshore we could be fobbed off by false echoes.'

Mayo sounded cautious. 'The ships may be heading south to Tsingtao, sir.'

Jermain stared at him. 'They've chosen an odd time for it.' He called through the door, 'Try and get the frigate on the acoustic radio. We might still be able to raise her.'

Harris bit his lip. 'Unlikely, sir. The change of water temperature and density inshore won't help, and the distance alone will kill any clear transmission.'

Jermain said sharply, 'Just do as I say.'

Harris glanced at the plot petty officer and gave a brief shrug before returning to the radio room. Through the open door came the usual stammer of Morse and the gentle purr of power from the sets, and Jermain heard Harris speaking quietly to one of the operators. They think I'm going round the bend, he thought bitterly. He watched the clock, mentally counting each dragging second.

Mayo walked to the control room and gave his instructions for alteration. 'Port fifteen. Steady. Steer two one zero.'

Harris reported carefully, 'No response from VIGILANT, sir. Just static.' He waited and then added, 'We could make a quick signal on W/T. It might pass undetected.' He did not sound too hopeful.

Jermain shook his head. 'We'll keep shadowing.'

Wolfe walked across to him. 'The Yanks must have made contact with the PT boats by now. I shouldn't wonder if we get a recall at any moment.'

Jermain nodded. 'Do you think I'm making a mountain out of this?'

Wolfe glanced around the control room before answering. '*Temeraire*'s not really suitable for this sort of caper, sir. It's either the whole works or nothing for us. We've no deck gun like the conventional subs, so we either use the torpedoes or keep clear and listen.' He smiled dryly. 'The top brass hardly had this kind of operation in mind for us!'

The minutes dragged past so that Jermain had the wild impression that every man aboard was waiting for his conviction to crack, for the boat to go about and return to the original patrol area.

Harris reappeared. 'We're getting a lot of garbled signals, sir.

The Americans have made some sort of contact to the north. It sounds as if they're having a running skirmish along the coast.'

Jermain walked to the chart. The American patrols were at least doing something. Whatever the outcome of the small clash, it was unlikely that it would make the world headlines. It was amazing how this form of brinkmanship had become personal and accepted by individual commanders instead of being the tool of major statesmen.

In the days of the British Raj the Army had used much the same system on India's north-west frontier for training infantrymen in the real arts of war. The live bullets from lurking Afghan tribesmen had put many a sweating soldier in his grave with never a mention in the British Press. Today the world powers played the same game, but with more far reaching weapons. One stupid miscalculation might plunge both sides into war, yet the game went on. Viet Nam, Malaysia, and now back to Korea; the deadly moves went on. Test and thrust. Kill and run away. With neither side making either complaint or asking for quarter.

As Wolfe had remarked, *Temeraire* was unsuitable for this work. She was designed for killing submarines and not for local skirmishes. She either used the big stick, or stayed as helpless as a toothless shark.

Oxley's voice came over the intercom. 'Ships seem to be turning, sir. Heading out to sea.'

Jermain banged his hands together. It seemed he had been right.

Oxley added, 'Range closing to about twelve thousand yards, sir.'

'Right, Pilot. Alter course to intercept again. We will keep to the south of these ships and close the range to three miles.' Jermain saw Wolfe's face watching him over Mayo's shoulder. 'It looks as if they're making a dash for it.'

Wolfe waited until Mayo had gone to his chart and then said flatly, 'Will you follow them all the way across, sir?'

'I think not, Number One. Once they're a hundred miles out we can make a W/T sighting report. The Americans have a carrier to the south. Her planes can track the ships and home any surface craft right on to the escape line.' He sighed. 'Then it's up to them what they do.'

The submarine turned in a wide arc and nosed closer to the two fast-moving ships. As each man strained his ears and tried to still the noise of his own heart the distant thrashing of powerful propellers became more apparent.

Mayo stood with his head cocked and muttered, 'Reminds me of the last time, sir. Poor old Victor.'

Jermain did not answer. It was true. The same sound. The steady beat, beat, beat. In his mind he could picture Victor's bloody limbs, the helpless desperation as he had screamed on the ladder. He clenched his fists and forced himself to think.

An hour dragged by, and then another. The cook and his assistants moved quietly through the boat with tea and thick sandwiches which the waiting men took and consumed without pausing in their listening.

Three miles on the *Temeraire*'s port bow the invisible ships retained a steady twenty knots, the sound waves from their screws sweeping over the submarine's hull like hail on a metal roof.

Twice Jermain raised the slender attack periscope, his eye straining to pierce the darkness. If there had been even a hint of a moon he might have seen them, but only the spray from the periscope broke the impenetrable blackness.

Mayo lounged by the chart table, his jaws champing on a sandwich. Between bites he remarked, 'They are staying on our course, sir. They'll pass well to the north of the *Malange*.'

Wolfe said harshly, 'Bloody merchant ships should be forbidden to use these waters! Some of the bastards will trade with anyone. They carried guns to the Indonesians when we were fighting them. They'll hump ammunition and stores for the Reds if the price is right!' He glared at the gyro compass. 'If Conway wants to show how brave he is, and how immune his pink politics will keep him, he wants to go on like he is now!'

Jermain turned away. It was difficult to know if Wolfe's comment was directed at him or just hitting out at large.

Oxley's voice once more. 'Slight alteration, sir. Closing the range.' He cleared his throat. 'Nearest ship closing to five thousand yards.' Another long pause, then, 'Steady on new course, sir.'

Mayo scribbled busily on his pad and passed his findings to Wolfe. 'Bring her round to one one zero, Number One. We'll be in a parallel course again.' He watched his words affecting Jermain's expression. 'They're turning to the south, sir. It's no accident. They both wheeled like bloody soldiers!'

Jermain stared at the plot table. 'Calculate the *Malange*'s present position, Pilot.' He found that his mouth was quite dry, as if he already knew the answer.

Mayo's fingers worked busily, his beard only inches above the chart. He said, 'We're on a converging course, unless *Malange*'s altered hers.' Mayo brushed a crumb from his lips. 'We'll be within twenty miles of her in two and a half hours.'

Wolfe said, 'She may have turned inshore, sir. Just to be on the safe side.'

Jermain shook his head. 'If her captain has heard of this skirmish he's bound to think he's safe. The PT boats will be two or three hundred miles from his passage route by now. Anyway, he's probably used to it. The Reds don't interfere with local shipping much. It's too useful to them, as you remarked.'

Wolfe grimaced. 'Except that this one has a V.I.P. aboard.'

Jermain eyed him searchingly. Behind Wolfe's controlled features there was something more. Almost as if he was enjoying the situation.

There were no further alterations of course, and apart from a sudden increase of speed, which *Temeraire* matched without effort, the other vessels seemed settled on their objective.

Jermain listened to the quiet reports and watched their combined progress translated into pencilled lines across the chart. Suppose Wolfe's casual remark was right? Would the Chinese really risk an open battle to search out and destroy the *Malange*? Or was their operation merely planned as a complementary one to the PT boats in the north?

If they attacked the freighter it might take all of an hour for help to arrive. An hour in pitch darkness was a lifetime. And if *Temeraire* flashed a radio signal too soon everything would be lost. The two darkened ships might even turn on the submarine with depthcharges. In these shallow waters there was not much Jermain could do then. Except turn tail and run.

He stared hard at the silent figures around him, and knew what he must do.

'We may have to surface later on, Number One.' He was speaking fast, as if he were afraid he might change his mind. 'I shall require a full boarding party to be ready for a sudden emergency. None of the usual gear will be necessary. I want each man armed with a Stirling, and each man to be a volunteer.' He saw the incredulity brighten and then fade in Wolfe's eyes.

Wolfe said, 'Can I say something, sir?'

For an instant Jermain could imagine Wolfe just as he remembered him so long ago. There was concern in his voice. 'Go ahead.'

Wolfe looked away. 'This boat is all that you hoped for. What I hoped for, too. Do you realise what might happen if you are openly challenged by these bastards?' He did not pause. 'You can't fight them with Stirlings. You can't even ask your men to die for nothing! If it comes to an open confrontation what have you left?'

Jermain tightened his jaw. 'I cannot stand by and allow a British merchant ship to be challenged and interfered with, no matter *who* is on board. If these ships attack the *Temeraire* I shall hit back and hard.' His eyes flashed dangerously. 'The tubes are loaded, and I have no doubt that Lieutenant Drew is only too willing to use them after what happened to Victor!'

Wolfe studied him as if for the first time. At length he said softly, 'If you make a mess of this you'll never clear your yardarm! The brass will crucify you!'

Jermain tried to smile. 'That'll be the least of my worries, Number One!'

He stared at the clock. 'We should make contact with the *Malange* at four o'clock. I shall then make a signal and report what we are doing. After that we're on our own for a while.'

He walked away, and Mayo said quietly to Wolfe, 'Does he mean it?'

Wolfe nodded slowly. 'It's become something personal for him.'

He ignored the mystified expression on Mayo's face and walked slowly towards the diving panel. He had seen the momentary flash of anxiety in Jermain's eyes when Harris had reported Conway's presence aboard the *Malange*. Conway *and* his daughter, no doubt.

Wolfe looked sideways at Jermain's shoulders stooped across the chart table and felt the old wildness returning to his mind. Now *you* know what it feels like!

With a start he realised he was grinning and that a rating was watching him with fixed fascination. Angrily he barked, 'Tell Lieutenant Drew to report to the control room at once!'

He ran his hand across his face and felt the sweat on his fingers like warm blood.

11

Rank and File

'DOWN PERISCOPE!' Jermain wiped the palms of his hands on his thighs and peered quickly at the control-room clock. The time was twenty minutes to four. He walked the three steps to the plot table and stood frowning for a few seconds. Around him in the weird orange glow of the action lights the men on watch looked unreal and ghost like.

'The *Malange* is early.' He spoke what was uppermost in his mind. Minutes earlier Oxley's delicate listening devices had reported the heavy, thrashing beat of a single screw almost dead ahead of the submerged submarine. Moving slowly from right to left. It could be no other ship, but even allowing for miscalculation on Mayo's part she seemed well ahead of time.

Wolfe said, 'I make her present course three two zero, sir.'

Jermain tried not to listen to the other ship's muffled beat. 'That would account for her crossing our course at this point.' He stared at Wolfe's shadowed features. 'But it would mean that she's hopelessly off her proper route!'

Mayo said, 'She is, sir. According to my reckoning she's steering almost north west.' He did not sound as if he believed himself. 'It's ridiculous, sir! She's heading *away* from Korea!'

Jermain swallowed hard. 'Keep checking, Pilot. And let me have any information you can about the other ships.'

Oxley called over the intercom, 'Both other vessels have turned away to the north, sir. Range about six hundred yards.'

Jermain stared hard at the plot table. Like counters on a staff officer's map the ships were moving inexorably in a strange and meaningless formation. He said, 'Alter course, Pilot. We'll close the *Malange* from astern but keep on her starboard quarter.' He walked to the periscope. 'I want to get a better look at her.'

The boat began to swing on her new track as the periscope broke the surface. Jermain screwed his eye tight against the pad and stared for several seconds at the hard black shape of the other ship. He could see the high white froth at her stern and the paler rectangle of her upperworks framed against the sky. The stars were still there, but even now the sky seemed to be brightening.

'Course two two zero, sir.' Twine sounded tense.

Through the hatch at the end of the control room came the faint click of equipment and the subdued mutter of voices as the boarding party assembled. Volunteers had been taken from each part of the boat and included stokers and signalmen as well as a small handful of seamen.

Jermain snapped, 'Keep those men quiet, Number One! There'll be time for letting off steam later on!' He saw a momentary flash of surprise on Wolfe's face and cursed himself inwardly.

He was getting rattled, and worse, he was showing it to the others. In a steadier tone he added, 'We will raise the periscope every thirty seconds, Number One. In the meantime you can tell the boarding party to finish checking their gear and muster up here below the fin.'

Wolfe replied flatly, 'Do you think you should be sending Colquhoun, sir?'

'Who else is there?' Jermain tore his mind from the nagging problem of the *Malange*'s alteration of course. 'With ten ratings and a good petty officer he should be all right.' He added coldly, 'I can only send those who can be spared.'

Mayo, who had been looking through the periscope, called, 'I think we're running towards a fishing fleet again, sir.'

Jermain took his place and peered at the tiny pinpricks of light which reflected across the lens like fireflies. It was another part of the same nightmare, he thought. All it needed now was for Oxley to pick up those nerve-racking sounds from the fish-buoys.

He stepped clear as the periscope hissed down. 'It will make our approach better this time. The *Malange*'s screw is making enough racket as it is, but the additonal craft will help, too.' He forced a smile. 'Maybe the other ships were put off by the freighter's appearance.'

Oxley called, 'The freighter is fine on the port bow now, sir. Range down to one thousand yards.'

Jermain brushed the hair from his forehead. Nothing was making sense. The *Malange* must have slowed down to cut the range in such a short time.

He saw Colquhoun standing with his men by the bulkhead door and noted the tight set of his mouth. He was carrying a Stirling with both hands, as if his life depended on it.

Jermain called, 'Just take it easy, Sub. When it gets a bit lighter up top I may want you to go across to the *Malange* to bolster morale. You could stop anyone from boarding her with your party, and I will deal with the other opposition until help arrives.'

He saw Jeffers, the second coxswain, tighten his webbing belt and grin broadly. 'Like old times, sir! I ain't shot anyone since I was in Borneo!'

Some of the men tittered and Jermain was thankful. 'Well, I hope that won't be necessary this time.'

Mayo sounded excited. 'Sir! I saw a flash on board the freighter!' He was clinging to the periscope, his beard smeared with grease.

Jermain asked sharply, 'Some sort of signal?'

Mayo swallowed. 'It looked like a shot to me, sir!'

Jermain pushed him aside, his body already stooped over the lens. There was the freighter again. He blinked the sweat from his eye. She looked huge in the crosswires and distorted above her encircling wake of churned spray. He stiffened. There was no mistaking the sudden ripple of orange flashes from her maindeck. They lit up the tall, spindly funnel and the black, eyeless windows of the bridge beyond.

'Down periscope!' He swung round, his mind suddenly ice cool. Either there was already a boarding party aboard the *Malange*, or some sort of mutiny had broken out. Most solitary merchant ships went with fear and caution of pirates and terrorists alike. Their bridges were usually protected with barbed wire and steel gates, behind which their officers were expected to hold out until help was available. But the freighter's absence of distress signals showed that this was no clumsy attack. This was well organised and well planned.

He barked, 'Stand by to surface, Number One. I will want the boarders up on the casing abaft the fin as we go alongside. There won't be much time, so two ladders and grapnels will have to suffice.' He stared at Colquhoun's glistening face. 'You take one ladder and Petty Officer Jeffers the second one, right?' He saw Colquhoun nod dazedly. 'My guess is that the sight of the Black Pig right alongside will do the trick.' He wished he felt as calm as he sounded. 'Keep listening to the other two ships and watch the nearest fishing boats. I don't want to foul any nets if I can help it!'

Mayo jumped to obey him and he saw the lights flicking obediently above the diving panel.

'Take the con, Number One. As soon as we surface I shall go to the upper bridge and supervise the boarding from there.'

He climbed up the ladder and knocked off the clips of the lower hatch. Behind him the boarding party milled around uncertainly, fingering their weapons and staring around the control room as if appreciating what awaited them above.

Jermain peered at his watch. 'Surface!' He was already at the upper hatch as the deck tilted sharply, and with a thunder of cascading water the submarine heaved herself bodily through a maelstrom of surging water and bursting air bubbles and broke surface.

Everything was running with water and ice-cold to the touch, but gasping and stumbling the men moved like automatons as they opened the fin door and staggered into the night's clammy embrace.

Even as he reached the open cockpit above the fin, Jermain's ear became attuned to the outside world. The sigh of spray, the rumble of water alongside the submarine's shining flank, and then, sharply insistent, the brittle clatter of small-arms fire.

He wiped his sleeve across the gyro repeater and shouted, 'Port ten! Steer three one five!' The old freighter seemed to hang over him like a cliff and for a heart-stopping moment he imagined that he had misjudged the distance. The lifeboats in their davits, the single line of scuttles, even the sagging guardrail were visible in the stabbing light and the faint brightening from the sky.

He ground his jaws together with concentration. If the freighter had been a larger ship he would never have managed it. But she was barely ten feet higher than the *Temeraire*'s casing. Even so, the boarders would have to watch out. One false step and a man could fall and be ground between the two hulls.

A lookout at his side nudged him excitedly and levelled a Stirling over the screen. Jermain gauged the final distance and marvelled that no one had noticed the submarine's approach.

'Starboard ten! Stop engine!' He felt the deck quiver and watched narrowly as the black bows began to swing slightly to cut across the freighter's sluggish backwash. The momentum carried the *Temeraire* up and past the high poop, and from the casing he heard Jeffers yell, 'Stand by with them lines!'

Jermain saw the trapped spray leaping like a pack of phantoms right alongisde as the two hulls idled together. It was now or never. . . . He shouted, 'Boarders away!' From the corner of his eye he saw the gleaming hooks soaring over the rusting rail, heard the clatter and scrape of weapons as his men waited and then leapt for the twin ladders. The deck quivered again, and with a dull boom the rounded hull grated against the freighter's plates.

Jermain realised that he was shaking, and he had to grip the screen with both hands to control it. It seemed crazy and impossible to realise that this was happening. That only feet away were men dedicated to open murder, to whose mercy he had just sent a mere handful of his crew. And Jill, too. He tore his mind away.

'Midships! Slow astern!' The boat began to slide free, her fin almost brushing the overhanging lifeboats.

A messenger at the intercom yelled. 'The two ships is turnin', sir! Swinging' around the fishin' fleet!' He made an effort to control the break in his voice. 'Bearin' red four five! Range six thousand!'

Jermain watched the *Malange*'s wallowing shape swinging

across the bows and nodded. 'We will remain surfaced. Tell the first lieutenant to prepare tubes One and Two for firing!'

He had a brief, impossible picture of Sir John Colquhoun's watchful expression when they had taken part in that last exercise. Jermain felt the anger washing away his pent-up anxiety like a cold shower. Perhaps now he would be satisfied, he thought savagely.

He had wanted the *Temeraire* to be baptised, and it looked as if his wish was about to be granted.

The intercom muttered, 'Tubes One and Two ready!'

• • •

Colquhoun's limbs felt like lead as he pulled himself the last few feet up and over the freighter's bulwark. Below him the taut ladder quivered and then swung heavily against the ship's side as the last of his five men kicked himself clear of the *Temeraire*'s hull and allowed the struggling cluster of dangling figures to pound painfully on the pitted plates.

Colquhoun stumbled down on to the unfamiliar deck and was instantly aware of the sudden and eerie silence. There was a brief, subdued swish of water behind him as the submarine idled astern, and then as the men on the other ladder pounded over the tail he was also conscious of a terrible feeling of loneliness. After nearly a week sealed within the tight world of the submarine the sudden rush of events left him panic-stricken and naked.

Petty Officer Jeffers pushed him unceremoniously to the deck and dropped on his knees beside him. He was already cocking his gun and peering forward towards the bridge. Between sharp breaths he gasped, 'What now, sir? Shall we split up?'

'I—I suppose so!' Colquhoun tried to project his tumbling thoughts beyond the small dark patch of deck below the tall derricks, but he could find nothing but a void of uncertainty and fear.

Jeffers snapped, 'Right! Rider, you take the port side with Stone and Lancing. Cover the bridge and shoot if anything moves this way.'

Colquhoun managed to say, 'But what about the officers up there?'

Jeffers snorted. 'Too late to worry about them, sir. Anyway, I reckon the other bastards are in charge up there. Otherwise the ship'd be on course!'

They both ducked as a sudden burst of automatic fire swept down from a small catwalk abaft the bridge, the flying bullets striking sparks from the hold coamings.

Jeffers yelled, 'See what I mean?' Then to the crouching seamen, 'For Chrissakes open fire! This is no frigging garden party!'

The Stirlings opened up nervously and then joined as one in a dancing pattern of fire across and around the shadowed bridge structure.

Colquhoun rested his head against the cool of a hold coaming and tried to control his fierce breathing. It was a nightmare. It could not be happening. He saw the savage fusilade finding and holding the rear of the bridge and heard the clatter of glass as the fast-firing Stirlings swept away the windows. His lungs seemed full of cordite fumes and he had to hold himself physically from hiding his head below the protective steel.

Jeffers roared, 'Move up, lads! We'll cover you from this side!' In a savage whisper he added, 'Come on, sir! Get a grip of yerself!' He shook Colquhoun's arm. 'The lads will be lookin' to you.' Then he rose to his feet, the Stirling jumping in his hands as he poured a blind volley across the exposed deck. 'Take that, you bastards!' His voice was wild and unreal. Like a madman's, Colquhoun thought. Then he found that he too was on his feet, running with the others, his voice mocking him in its own insane excitement.

They reached the final hold between themselves and the bridge ladders. Jeffers looked up and jammed another magazine into his smoking gun. He said in an almost matter-of-fact tone, 'We've got 'em foxed for a bit, sir. They can't fire down on us without showin' their 'eads against the white paint up there. Right now we've got to decide what to do next.' He stared sideways at Colquhoun.

The latter looked momentarily over his shoulder as if he still expected to see the *Temeraire*'s fin looming alongside.

Jeffers said calmly, 'It's no use, sir. The skipper'll be too busy to care about us.'

Colquhoun made another effort. In a strangled voice he said,

'I'm sorry. I won't let you down.'

''Course you won't.' Jeffers was grinning. 'Just keep with me. I've killed more of these bastards than you've 'ad 'ot dinners, sir!'

Colquhoun shook his head dazedly. These bastards? They did not know they were fighting yet. But Jeffers' tough confidence was acting like raw alcohol.

He said quickly, 'They must all be up there. There's been no firing from anywhere else.'

Jeffers gripped his wrist like a steel claw and swung his Stirling across the coaming. '*Still!* Not a bloody word, sir!'

The men around them froze and waited, each man fingering his gun and trying to pierce the darkness with his eyes.

Colquhoun heard the slow, scraping movement on the other side of the deck below the bulwark, but as Able Seaman Rider jumped forward with his Stirling raised, Jeffers snarled, 'Get back, you twit! It's one of our lot!'

They pulled the crawling man to safety and turned him over on his back. He was a sturdy, square-faced man in officer's uniform, his head swathed in a rough bandage, the front of which was soaked in blood. In the strange light from the sky overhead the blood glinted on the bandage like black paint.

The man stared up at them, his eyes wide and unblinking. For a second Colquhoun's reeling mind imagined that he was already dead, then he muttered, 'The Navy! For Sweet Jesus' sake, the *Navy*!' He sounded as if he doubted his own reason.

Jeffers shook him gently. 'Take it easy. Just tell us what 'appened!'

The man winced as a shot whined down from the bridge and ricocheted out over the sea. It was met by a savage volley from the watching sailors.

He said slowly, 'I'm Duncan, first mate. We were jumped a day ago just after we had made our signal to the port of destination.' Even dazed and in pain he seemed unable to free his mind from normal, routine phrases. 'There are about twenty of them. Most of 'em were included in the crew.' He grimaced. 'One of the bastards was the steward. He was the only one allowed on the bridge at sea, and he lobbed a grenade right amongst the watch! Killed the old man and most of the others, too!'

Jeffers asked, 'Are you the only one left?'

The mate shook his head. 'The bosun is just below the bridge back there, and I've got seven more lads up forrard behind the winch.' He pulled a big, obsolete Webley from his belt. 'Like me they're down to their last few rounds!' He tried to grin. 'But I've fixed 'em!'

Colquhoun stared over the man's body and tried to see some small movement on the bridge. He heard the mate continue with sudden venom. 'This is a coal-fired ship, y'know. I just happened to be down aft when they rushed the bridge, so I was able to organise a few of the crew myself. Not that they're much use. The usual sweepings. Chinks mostly.' He shuddered. 'I heard them pull the second mate from his bunk. He was screaming like a pig. It sounded as if they were hacking him to death with an axe!'

Jeffers persisted. 'You said you'd fixed them?'

The mate relaxed slightly. 'I closed all the engine-room vents. The bastards will suffocate or blow the bloody boilers now! Either way they can't keep up steam!'

Jeffers nodded. 'So that's it. That explains the loss of speed.'

'What of the passengers? Conway?' Colquhoun felt sick.

The mate shrugged. 'They are in no-man's-land. Their cabins are up there below the radio room. So long as you can keep the bridge isolated they're reasonably safe.' He added grimly, 'Unless they're already butchered!'

A huge Malay in a torn singlet and shorts wriggled around a ventilator and rolled his eyes in the gloom like two marbles. 'Lawd be praised!' He peered at the armed sailors. 'My prayers is answered!'

The mate grinned ruefully. 'This is my bosun.'

Jeffers said urgently, 'The sky's gettin' bright, sir. It'll be dawn shortly. They'll pin us down in the daylight and knock us off like bleedin' flies!' He peered at Colquhoun warily. 'What about it, sir? Shall we make heroes of ourselves?'

Colquhoun fought for time. For just a few seconds to clear his brain and make the nightmare recognisable. 'Who are these people? *What* are they?'

The mate shrugged. 'God knows. Pirates maybe. But they're well organised.'

The bosun nodded. 'We killed a few of 'em, sir. Just a few.' He groped behind him and pulled a sacklike object around the coaming. In the dim light Colquhoun could see the thing's teeth bared in a savage grin, could smell the sweet stench of death. He retched.

Jeffers pushed the corpse away with his foot. 'Well, this one's got a few friends waitin' out there.' He gestured towards the hidden sea. 'So we ain't got much time.'

Colquhoun said in a small voice, 'What do you think is best, Jeffers?'

The petty officer smiled in the gloom. 'Like I said, sir. It's not easy.' He peered up at the dark bridge windows and was immediately met by two swift shots. He ducked and cursed as the bullets screamed past his head and slammed into the deck. 'Nasty,' he said.

Rider wriggled across on his stomach, his Stirling like a toy in his big hands. 'They don't have any more grenades, else we'd have got 'em by now!'

Jeffers' voice was biting. 'That's a bloody big help!'

The seaman laughed quietly. 'No good sittin' like a blue-arsed fly, P.O. We gotta do somethin'!' They both looked at Colquhoun.

The wounded mate said, 'On the starboard side there's a ladder. I had it lashed up the side of the bridge two days ago ready for a bit of red-leading.' He sounded doubtful. 'If you could get a man up there . . .'

Jeffers rubbed his chin. 'Just the job, mate. We'll 'ave a go!'

Colquhoun said desperately, 'I'll go.'

Jeffers eyed him quietly. 'Beggin' yer pardon, sir, but I think not.' He chuckled. 'Well, let's face it, sir, officers is officers. They gives orders, they don't go dashing about like bloody marines!' Without waiting for a reply he added in a sharper tone, 'I'll be goin' for the ladder, got it? Rider and 'is mob will rush the port side as soon as I open fire. Porky Bruce can cover me and bring up in the rear.'

Bruce bared his teeth. 'Mind I don't blow your manhood off with me gun, P.O.!'

Colquhoun wiped his face and shuddered. They were joking. Actually joking about almost certain death. He felt Jeffers touch his arm.

'You keep with Bill Rider, sir. 'E's only an A.B., but 'e's more used to this sort of thing. Out in Alex I saw 'im clobber three coppers with a bottle an' go on to smash up a Wog café single 'anded!' He grinned. ''E's a good bloke in a rough 'ouse!' Then he was gone, and Rider yelled, 'Open fire, you canteen sailors!'

The Stirlings started their maniac chatter once more and the bullets ripped and whined across the bridge like hornets, bringing down shattered woodwork and broken glass like rain on their heads.

Rider gasped, 'Don't forget, sir! This is for real! Don't stop to argue with 'em! Kick their bleedin' faces in!'

Colquhoun nodded numbly. He could picture the little petty officer climbing over the rail and up the flimsy paint ladder beside the bridge. If he was wounded, or even slipped, he would fall straight down into the sea below.

I should have been there! I should be showing these men what to do!

It was not like that other time with the trapped wire on the rudder. Then he had been more afraid of showing fear than of fear itself. This horror was altogether different.

There was a burst of automatic fire from a high angle and Rider yelled, 'The Casing King has made it! Come on, lads! Up them bleedin' stairs!' Then they were all running and screaming like maniacs, their guns firing with neither aim nor care as they tore up the ladder and plunged across the wing of the bridge.

Colquhoun was knocked sideways as his whooping men poured into the crowded wheelhouse. In the growing light he saw several crouching figures outlined against the shattered windows and more sprawled across the littered deck. The air was filled with banging guns and the gasping cries of terror and fury as the two sides came to grips. Here a knife flashed home, cutting short an animal scream of agony. In another corner Colquhoun saw a tall seaman kicking a cowering man in the chest before pouring a full volley into his writhing body. There was blood everywhere, like some ghastly mural, and Colquhoun almost fell as he skidded on a mutilated corpse wearing a captain's uniform.

Through the other side of the bridge Jeffers peered across his smoking Stirling. 'Anyone hurt?'

Rider turned over a body with his foot. 'Nah. Just O'Toole. 'Is guts is playin' up by the smell of it!'

The sailors laughed wildly. As if they were drunk. As if it was all one huge joke.

Jeffers nodded and swung himself through the gap. 'Right

then. Mop up the other ones aft. They'll be poppin' out of the engine room soon, I should think!'

Duncan, the mate, stood silently surveying the carnage. 'Thanks, lads.' He did not seem able to speak.

Jeffers said easily, 'Hold on, chum. We'll get yer ship back for you!'

Colquhoun swallowed the bile in his throat and pushed his way through the wheelhouse door. Outside the air felt cool and damp, and he was startled to see how light it had become in those short, terrifying minutes. Already the sea had lost its deep shadows and the gentle, undulating surface had changed to a pale milky green with a clinging haze hanging lazily above it. In his shocked eyes it seemed too remote, too beautiful and settled for reality. It was like some Japanese water-colour, and even the vague shapes of the motionless fishing boats hung in the distant haze with no more substance than the artist's casual brush strokes.

Jeffers said, 'The mate's put his bosun on the wheel, sir, but there's hardly any steerage way on the ship now. The engine-room mob will be up directly to get a breath of air.' He checked his magazine. 'They'll come shooting!'

Colquhoun took a deep breath. 'Put some men to cover the hatches.' He stared round the deserted decks. 'But we must find Conway and the others!'

Jeffers barked off a string of orders which to Colquhoun's ears sounded like so much gibberish. But the men seemed to come out of their state of crazed elation and pattered away in twos and threes on both sides of the *Malange*'s deck. The petty officer added, 'You check the cabins, sir. I've given you two good lads to help you.' He strode away, his cap tilted over his eyes like a visor.

Able Seaman Bruce watched Colquhoun's strained face and then said, 'The cabins are in one block, as I see it. There's one of our blokes on the far side by the lifeboats.' He gestured with his Stirling. 'You an' me could go right through the central passageway and flush any stragglers out at the other end.' He squinted at the sea. 'How does that suit?'

Colquhoun took a grip on himself. 'Good idea, Bruce.'

Bruce showed his teeth. 'I'll just nip round and warn the other chap.'

He shuffled away, and once more Colquhoun was aware of

the terrible silence. There was no sign of the submarine. The ship was alone but for the fishing boats. The latter too could have been deserted and forgotten by their lack of movement.

Bruce came back, breathing hard. 'Okay, sir.'

Colquhoun entered the open door and walked slowly between the cabins which flanked the passageway. There was a deserted pantry, the dishes smashed and scattered on the deck. There was a smear of blood on the handrail, and some empty cartridge cases. Silent witnesses of the horror which had swept through the ship.

Bruce spoke between his teeth. 'Call out, sir! It can't do no 'arm!'

Colquhoun's voice echoed around the passage and seemed to mock back at him. He imagined that each cabin contained either a corpse or a waiting terrorist, that every second invited a new disaster.

Then from the far end of the passage he heard Conway's voice. 'Who is that? Speak up or I'll shoot!'

Colquhoun opened his mouth to call, but as he passed another cabin his eye fell on the mutilated body of the second mate. It was hard to imagine that it had once been human. With a sob he fell against the door, retching uncontrollably.

Bruce yelled, 'It's the Navy! Hold your fire!' Ignoring Colquhoun, he ran forward as the door was pulled open, his small eyes darting from side to side and his gun at the ready.

Colquhoun staggered after him and then halted, staring in the cabin entrance. The wooden panels on the far side were riddled with bullet holes and gun smoke hung trapped in the stale and unmoving air. Conway half lay against the lower bunk, a pistol cradled on his knee. A crumpled form in torn dungarees was lying under the table in a pool of drying blood, an axe still gripped in one clawlike hand.

Colquhoun realised that Conway was wounded, but as he moved forward the big man gasped, 'Help my wife, for God's sake! I can last out!'

The girl, who until now had been standing with her back to a splintered scuttle, stooped down beside her father. She was wearing a short nightdress which had been all but ripped from her body. Across one shoulder Colquhoun saw three deep scratches, like the imprint of an animal's claws. She looked up at him, her eyes shocked but determined.

'No! Leave her alone! She's safe in the next cabin!' But behind her father's back she shook her head sharply, her eyes clouding with tears.

Colquhoun said, 'Let me have a look at you, sir. I think your wife is better left alone for a while.' He tried to lift Conway's hands from his lap, but felt the man shudder as a stream of bright blood spilled through his shirt and cascaded on to the deck.

His mind tried to keep all the other horror at bay as he concentrated on what he had to do. Conway was badly wounded. Possibly in the lower stomach. His wife was obviously dead in the other cabin, and the girl must be near hysteria. He must get a signal to the *Temeraire*. Griffin would know what to do. If there was still any time left for Conway.

Conway looked ashen. 'Burst into the cabins during the night. Lucky I had a gun. God, I thought we were done for . . .' He moaned 'Shooting all night long! Twice they tried to break in here. Lucky I woke up in time!' He stared fixedly at Colquhoun. 'My God! You're one of David Jermain's officers! I remember you!' He broke into a fit of coughing and then muttered, 'I'm so damned hot, boy!' But his hands were like ice.

The girl said, 'The *Temeraire*? Is it really?' The effect of her father's words seemed to have shocked her more than her experience. 'Tell me!'

Colquhoun nodded. 'Yes. The skipper sent me across to help.'

Conway sighed. 'I said to David when I saw him. You are like that young subaltern at Dunkirk.' He leaned his head against his daughter's breast and closed his eyes, all his reserves of strength used up. 'A good boy. But not to be wasted.'

Bruce leaned forward and dug his fingers into Colquhoun's shoulder. 'Sir! The door 'andle! It *moved*!'

They all stared at the small door which apparently connected the cabin with the bathroom. The handle was of bright brass, and as Colquhoun concentrated his stare it seemed to swell and glisten like the sun itself.

Then Bruce said thickly, 'My Gawd! My magazine's empty!' He gestured wildly. 'Shoot! *Shoot*, sir! Before the bastard does for us!'

Then tension and terror broke in Colquhoun's mind like a fractured dam. He felt the gun jumping in his hands, saw the girl holding her fingers over her ears as the staccato rattle filled the cabin with noise and smoke. The unaimed volley cut away the wooden door like paper and burst the lock and handle into flying splinters.

Then the gun fell silent, and mesmerised Colquhoun watched the shattered door as it opened slowly towards him.

There was distant shouting and the sound of feet on the ladder, then Jeffers panted through the other door, his Stirling across his chest. 'Heard the shootin'! Have you got one of the . . .' His voice trailed away as the door swung inwards with a final jerk and the riddled corpse pitched forward at his feet.

The bullets had torn across the chest and stomach like hideous stitching, almost cutting the man in half. The face was unmarked, and seemed almost peaceful compared with the horror below it.

Jeffers wiped his face with the back of his hand and said harshly, 'I think you'd better lit me take the gun, Mr. Colquhoun.' He tucked the Stirling under his arm, his face expressionless as another seaman called:

'I can see the *Temeraire*, P.O.!'

Jeffers said, 'That was the only time you fired, sir.'

Colquhoun did not answer. He was still staring with shocked disbelief at the man on floor. Able Seaman Archer.

• • •

Jermain ducked his head beneath the glass screen and wiped the lenses of his glasses as a tall curtain of spray lifted lazily from the bows and spattered across the front of the fin. The *Temeraire* was trimmed high in the water, and each thrust from the powerful screw pushed the stem harder into the calm sea and patterned the hull and fin with glistening diamonds of blown salt.

As each dragging minute stripped away the darkness Jermain was conscious of the submarine's vulnerability. On the pale green water, her whale shape outlined in bursting spray, she seemed huge and defenceless. Nevertheless, he allowed his mind to accept that his crude bluff had worked. The two warships which they had dogged all the way from the Chinese coast had swung away to the north, beyond the vague shapes of the fishing boats, as if startled by the unexpected arrival of the giant undersea craft.

A lookout reported, 'Freighter, sir. Bearing green four five!'

He levelled his glasses again. There she was. The old *Malange*, apparently drifting, with hardly a ripple beneath her high bows.

'Starboard ten. Steer zero nine zero.' He shifted the glasses along the freighter's length, noting with cold relief the occasional figure of one of his boarding party and that of a uniformed officer on the bridge. But had he been completely in time?

The radio mast squeaked in its mounting above his head and he imagined Harris and his staff waiting to send off his first signal. He snapped, 'Flash a signal to *Malange*, Bunts. Ask her what is happening.' He saw the hand lamp begin to stammer his message across the narrowing strip of water, and he took time to reassemble his thoughts. Everything had happened so quickly. It was still hard to imagine that it was not just another drill or exercise. He drummed his fingers on the screen. If only both sides would make peace or declare war openly. Then they would know where they stood.

The bridge messenger said, 'Fishing boats have started their engines, sir. Lieutenant Oxley reports continuous and confused propeller noises.'

Jermain nodded. The fishermen would no doubt be unwilling to be involved in anything which might jeopardise their future freedom. Life was difficult enough for them. Preyed upon by the Chinese and Allies alike, they still managed to drag a meagre harvest from the sea to keep themselves and their village intact in a world gone mad. It would pay them to see nothing.

The freighter was much nearer now. Less than half a mile away. Already her gaunt upperworks were haloed in weak sunlight, her upper yards shining like ungainly crucifixes.

He watched the slow stabbing light from her bridge and wondered how Colquhoun was making out.

'Slow ahead. Close up deck party.'

The signalman said, 'All resistance has been overcome. Request medical assistance immediately.' He paused. 'One seaman dead.'

Below on the submarine's casing he could hear the clatter of feet and the subdued mutter of orders as the two vessels drew close together.

The signalman continued, 'The passenger, Conway, is badly wounded. Can doctor be sent across?' The man watched Jermain's face curiously.

Jermain kept his voice calm. 'Tell them we will . . .' He broke off as the light began to flicker like a mad thing.

With disbelief the signalman shouted, 'They are reporting a submarine, sir! Bearing zero four five!'

Every pair of glasses was blocked by the freighter's motionless bulk, and Jermain felt the sudden threat of that brief signal like the stab of a knife.

The bridge messenger called, 'Sonar reports contact at red four five, sir! Range six thousand yards!'

Almost before the words had dropped from the man's lips the intercom barked, 'Torpedo running on same bearing, sir!'

Jermain pushed past the startled lookouts. 'Signal the *Malange* to abandon ship!' He punched the signalman's arm. 'Immediate!'

But even as the light began to stammer the *Malange* seemed to lift painfully as if on a steep roller. The roar of the exploding torpedo rolled across the water like the clang of a giant anvil, and as Jermain watched he saw the telltale column of spray and brown smoke rising from the far side of the ship even as the shockwave fanned his face with its hot breath.

The intercom was chattering without a break. 'Submarine is still surfaced, sir. Has altered course away. Now steering three four zero!'

All at once Wolfe was in the cockpit at his side, his eyes fixed on the listing ship. 'We could get that sub, sir. With a homing torpedo we could still catch the bastard!'

Jermain dragged his eyes from the freighter and the rising death cloud of smoke. 'The submarine is making for the fishing fleet, Number One. We can't afford the risk of hitting one of those boats. Stand by with a contact torpedo.'

Wolfe stared at him. 'For God's sake, you're not going to let him get away? We could dive now and outdistance him within half an hour!'

Jermain's voice was cold. 'We shall stand by the *Malange* to pick up survivors. Now get below and stand by to fire!'

He could picture the scene below as his orders were relayed to Drew in the torpedo compartment. One torpedo to explode on contact. It was an unlikely chance.

A lookout said thickly, 'She's beginnin' to roll over, sir!'

The freighter was sagging badly, her bows already rising slowly as if in protest. She had bared her bilge keel, and Jermain could see the running figures along the upper deck and the spurting syphons of escaping steam. In a few minutes the sea would reach her boilers. He pounded the screen with his fist as two liferafts splashed over the ship's side, followed by a small handful of leaping figures.

It took physical effort to drag his mind clear of the pitiful scene as the freighter began to capsize. 'Port fifteen. Steer zero one zero.' He crouched over the gyro repeater. 'Report when ready!'

The messenger said, 'Three tube ready, sir!' Another pause. 'Echoes distorted by fishing fleet, sir, but submarine still surfaced and increasing speed. Bearing now green two zero. Range six thousand five hundred.'

Jermain levelled his glasses and stared helplessly at the drifting haze. He could imagine the fishing boats scattering before the escaping submarine, just as he could picture the *Temeraire*'s complex firing controls plotting and estimating the range and bearings. 'Fire when ready, Number One.'

Still the seconds dragged past. Then through the bridge microphone he heard Wolfe's voice, angry and terse. 'Fire Three!'

The hull gave a slight jerk as the single torpedo left the tube. Nothing more. Not a hint of the murderous charge or the small powerful screws behind it.

'Starboard ten. Steer one one zero. Stand by to pick up survivors!'

The minutes passed and eventually the messenger reported, 'No contact, sir.' The torpedo had missed. A homing torpedo would have found and destroyed the other boat whatever her manoeuvre, and Jermain was still not sure of his real reason for not firing one.

Almost gently the big submarine nosed its way between the pieces of nodding flotsam and the widening patch of oil and coal dust. The *Malange* had vanished as if it had never been, and the bobbing heads in the water seemed painfully few. Heaving lines were already being thrown, and some of the sailors were lowering themselves into the sea to help the weak and the injured aboard.

Wolfe appeared again on the bridge. He did not look at Jermain but watched intently as the girl was hauled half naked from one of the liferafts.

His voice shook with anger as he said, 'I hope she was worth coming back for! You've thrown everything else away!'

12

Play It Cool

JERMAIN CLIMBED briskly up the varnished accommodation ladder which hung down the side of the American submarine depot ship. Beneath the soles of his shoes he could feel the rubber treads of the ladder soft and clinging in the blazing afternoon sun, but he made himself run up the last few steps, knowing that otherwise the weariness in his legs would drag him to a halt.

He reached the top and paused on the polished grating, his hand to his cap as the formal salute was given by the waiting side-party of white uniformed seamen and stiff-backed marines. A large, corpulent captain in neatly starched khakis stepped forward and thrust out his hand.

'Welcome to Taiwan, Commander.' He studied Jermain's tired face. 'Sorry we couldn't let you have time to get settled, but the boss wants to see you.'

Jermain looked back over the rail towards the sheltered anchorage where the pale grey warships sweltered in neat ranks beneath their awnings and limp flags. The Nanlien Inlet, on the north-east coast of Taiwan, but his tired eyes it could amost be

Cornwall. On either side of the inlet the lush green trees swept right down to the water, leaving neither beach nor reef to identify it with the Far East. Take away the warships, and ignore the pointed roof-tops of a distant town which showed briefly between the banks of trees, and he might have been back in his childhood.

Jermain said, 'Thank you for your help, sir.' It sounded inadequate.

The *Temeraire* had come alongside the depot ship that forenoon after speeding for two days from that place where the *Malange* had been sent to the bottom with neither warning nor reason. Two days of strain and tension, as each man within the hull waited and wondered what the next landfall would bring.

By some sort of miracle Conway was still alive. During the voyage he had lain in a drugged coma, watched over continuously by Griffin and Jill Conway. To Jermain it seemed incredible that he had carried the girl with him in the same submarine which now lay resting below the depot ship's shadow. Incredible, for he had seen her for barely minutes, and spoken even less.

Once he had torn himself from the inrush of signals and fresh instructions and the urgent business of preparing his reports and had visited the silent group in the sick bay. Conway had looked smaller and older inside the cot and had stared at Jermain's features without recognition.

The girl had said quietly, 'He keeps saying they must have misunderstood him. It's uppermost in his mind.' She had been wearing a sailor's shirt and trousers, her hair still dishevelled with salt water.

Griffin had told him later that he had deliberately kept Conway under strong drugs. The shock of learning of his wife's death would destroy any remaining chance of survival.

Jermain had spoken directly to the girl across the cot. 'I tried, Jill. I tried to get to the ship in time.' How stupid the words had sounded. Like an excuse. Like an epitaph.

She had stared at him gravely. 'I don't want to talk about it, David. Not now. Not here.' She had looked around the sick bay like a trapped and helpless animal. 'If I start to think about what happened I shall break! And he needs me. I *know* he needs me!' She had turned away, her eyes clouding.

Griffin had given a brief shake of the head. 'Later, sir. Maybe later.'

But that time had not come. All too soon they had come into the orbit of the American command and another opportunity had not arrived.

Within minutes the submarine had been swamped by Americans. The *Malange*'s few survivors had been ushered away with swift but gentle efficiency. Jermain had been faced by two American liaison officers, one of whom carried the usual bag of waiting information and instructions. When he had finally torn himself away the girl had gone. One of the Americans had patted his arm. 'It'll be okay, Commander. Every goddamn thing will be taken care of!'

After all, what else had he expected? Even his own men seemed to be avoiding his eye. As if they anticipated his fate and wanted no share of his failure.

The captain said abruptly, 'I guess we'd better go right on up.' He led the way past the saluting sailors and through a wide screen door. There was a smell of fresh polish. An air of practised efficiency which Jermain had noticed as he had conned his boat alongside. To the Americans this was no manoeuvre, no show-the-flag mission. This was as near to real war as made no difference.

The captain said over his shoulder, 'Don't pay too much heed to the admiral. He's a great guy in his way, but he likes to act a little!' He chuckled. 'Don't underestimate him either!'

A marine clicked his heels together outside a door with four stars above it. The captain became more formal and said, 'I'll go on in.' He smiled. 'Take it easy, Commander, you're an ally, not a prisoner of war!'

Jermain tried to relax. The captain's words had hit home. He felt alien and unsure of himself. The American flags, the strange accents, even the ship seemed to have a different feel to it. It was stranger still to realise that it was only two months ago he had left that other depot ship in the bleak Gareloch. Two months, and thousands of miles. High hopes and sudden death. The hopeless love of a girl, already lost in a memory.

Beneath the visor of his cap the marine stared at him unwinkingly. Jermain looked down at his own creased white uniform which he had dragged hastily from his metal trunk.

Hardly a fitting representative of the Royal Navy, the commander of the *Temeraire*.

The captain walked from the door. 'Okay. You can go in.' He strolled away whistling to himself, and Jermain found himself in the big cabin alone with the American admiral.

Admiral Arnold J. McKelway was a very small man. He was dressed in neat khakis and was chewing thoughtfully on a fat cigar. But his face commanded instant attention. It was tanned and wrinkled like tooled leather, and the eyes which watched Jermain's approach across the claret-coloured carpet were like bright pieces of washed glass.

McKelway said brusquely, 'Welcome to my command, Jermain. Take a seat before the sweat cuts you down to my size!' He flicked open his shirt across a scrawny chest and directed a portable electric fan across it.

He continued in the same irritable tone, 'I've read your report, Jermain. Quite a potful!' The cigar rolled to the opposite side of his mouth. 'Pity about the M.P. But I guess if you feel strongly enough about an ideal you can expect to risk your life once in a while.' He turned over some papers on a table. 'Our boys knocked off a couple of those PT boats you were shadowing. But nothing much else happened. There'll be other times though.'

Jermain clutched the arms of his chair and wondered if he was dreaming. No mention of the way he had left the patrol line. Hardly a regret about the torpedoing of an unarmed freighter.

He said, 'I don't quite understand, sir. Did you read my report about the submarine?'

McKelway's eyebrows lifted slightly. 'Ah yes. The submarine. I read about it.' He shrugged. 'It's a pity you couldn't have got a tinfish into him.'

Jermain rose to his feet. 'Look, sir. I want to make myself clear. The submarine attacked without provocation. But I had to attend to the survivors.'

'So you say, Commander.' McKelway's face was masklike. 'You did what you thought right, so what?' The cigar bobbed up and down in time to his words.

'Well, isn't something going to be done about it?' Jermain's despair was putting an edge in his voice.

'As I see it, Jermain, you were the only one who could have

done anything, as you put it.' He shrugged. 'But you put your clean, humanitarian principles first.'

'Conway was on an important mission...'

McKelway laughed quietly. 'You British kill me, Jermain! You really do! You talk as if we were at peace, or something. Don't you ever read the papers? Hell, where is all that Churchillian stuff about blood and fire?'

Jermain said hotly, 'I am under your orders, sir. But I don't have to accept that kind of reasoning!'

McKelway's face hardened. 'You are under my control only in part, Commander. If you were one of my boys I'd have kicked your ass for you!' He threw the cigar into a waste-basket. 'I have never heard such sanctimonious crap in all my life! Just try to see further than your goddamn British pride, will you?' He stood up and walked to his wall map. 'You say there's no war on? Since the Second World War the United States has lost nearly a quarter of a million boys killed and maimed to defend freedom.' He glared. 'To defend America *and* Britain!' He waved a small hand. 'Hell, I know your country has its own problems, too, but I don't hear your government standing for any outside criticism either!'

Jermain sat down. 'What will happen now?'

'Now?' He rubbed his thigh. 'There will be the usual communiqué.' He tapped a signal pad. 'It's right here.' He skimmed briefly through the typed sentences. 'The S.S. *Malange* was seized by unknown terrorists and was intercepted by Her Majesty's Submarine *Temeraire*. The ship sank after an internal explosion and the survivors were landed at a Taiwan port.' He stared at Jermain's frowning face. 'That about winds it up.'

Jermain felt the walls closing in on him. It was mad. Unreal. No mention of the two shadowing warships. Not a word about the torpedo attack.

He heard himself say flatly, 'I understood you to say that we are fighting a war, sir. This communiqué hardly bears that out!'

The admiral ignored the sarcasm. 'You say this submarine fired a torpedo, Commander?' He spread his hands. 'Well, so did you. But whereas you got no hit, the other skipper managed to sink the freighter.' His face became intent. 'I am trying to get you to see it through the Red's eyes! If I release this story to the world press, you'll be crucified! The Reds will deny they had a submarine in the area. They'll say that they *wanted* to meet Conway. That their ships were going to welcome the *Malange*, or some such crap.' He stared hard at Jermain. 'And they'll say that *you* torpedoed the *Malange*!"

Jermain's face felt tight with anger. 'But that's ridiculous!'

'Is it?' McKelway sighed. 'You returned with one fish fired. There's no evidence but your word that a Red submarine ever existed.' He waved down Jermain's angry retort. '*I* believe you. But that doesn't count for much outside the fleet. Who gave the sighting report, anyway?'

'My boarding officer. Colquhoun.' He had a brief picture of Colquhoun's anguished face as he had been pulled from the water. But for Oxley's report he might have disbelieved Colquhoun himself. The young officer seemed completely crushed and broken by Archer's death. He could have been mistaken. No one else in the boarding party seemed sure of anything.

McKelway grunted. 'You also reported a submarine when you were on the exercise with my task force.' He drummed his fingers. 'It's all very strange. And very dangerous.' He seemed to be thinking aloud. 'Your boat is fully equipped with the best detection gear in the world. The Commies have nothing like it; *yet*. But they still got near enough to hit and run. Very strange!'

'Are you saying that I'm mistaken, sir?'

McKelway gave a cold grin. 'I made you mad, Jermain. It's a habit of mine. I can't stand yes-men, and you certainly don't come in that category.' He frowned. 'If there is a submarine on the loose, I *want* it. Otherwise,' he shrugged, 'they'll get cocky and go after big game. A carrier maybe.'

'Or a Polaris submarine!' Jermain felt the sweat running over his chest. The admiral's unruffled manner defeated his own anger.

'Could be.' McKelway glanced at his watch. 'So you see, it's better to play it cool. No need to tell the Reds what we think we know. Let 'em make one more move, and then we'll be ready!'

McKelway walked to a scuttle. 'We're learning, Jermain. But it takes time. We've got to make ourselves fight with *their* weapons.' He looked at the waiting communiqué. 'You failed to fire a homing torpedo because you were afraid of killing a few fisherman. Yet the Reds fired a torpedo smack into the

Malange, knowing it would kill a lot of their *own* men aboard!' He grinned. 'They weren't to know you were there. A Limey sub right on the doorstep. By putting it in the communiqué it will kill their little plan stone dead. I'll bet they intended to kill Conway if they couldn't take him alive and blame it on the Americans, and so drive another wedge between us!' He stared fixedly at Jermain's eyes. 'There's no rift between *us*, is there, Commander?'

Jermain smiled wearily. 'When you put it like that, sir...'

'I do put it like that. We can't afford personal misunderstandings any more.' He waved towards the map. 'There's one hell of a lot of people depending on us now.'

McKelway held out his hand. 'Believe me, Jermain, it's best this way. An acceptable solution.'

• • •

Everything about the American shore base gave the impression of temporary occupation. Buildings and store sheds were either prefabricated or merely wooden sections bolted to metal frameworks, as if the whole base could be packed up overnight and set down elsewhere at an hour's notice.

A large portion of the *Temeraire*'s crew soon found itself comfortably ensconced in a vast, air-conditioned shack, more like an aircraft hangar than a canteen, and had split into noisy groups amongst their American opposite numbers.

Lightfoot sat quietly sipping a can of ice-cold beer, his eyes moving restlessly around the packed tables with their unfamiliar occupants. A giant jukebox blared jazz continuously so that everyone seemed to be shouting above the din, their faces sweating in spite of the refrigerated air. Chinese girls in PX uniforms ladled out beer and soft drinks, hamburgers and ice cream with stoical calm, apparently immune to the barrage of orders and demands from the waiting men.

A gangling American gunner's mate sat at Lightfoot's table, his jaw working busily on a wad of gum as he acted the part of host and general guide. On his shirt his name-tag read Smirner, but to all and sundry within earshot he was known as Jake.

He said, 'Yeah, we got a good deal here. It's more of a rest camp between trips than a proper base. The ole depot ship deals with the repairs and so forth.' He pushed another can across to Bruce whose face had changed to a mottled scarlet. 'Get it down you, pal. There's plenty more where that came from!'

Leading Seaman Haley tamped down his pipe and sighed deeply. 'You're off the Polaris boats then?'

Jake grinned. 'Thank Gawd! Each boat's got two crews. As she puts into the inlet one crew comes ashore for a coupl'a months and the relief boys take her out for the next patrol. Real sweet.'

Bruce belched. 'Trust the Yanks! We've been swanning about the bleedin' 'oggin for ages without *any* bloody relief!'

Jake stared. 'What sort of goddamned accent is that, man?'

Haley grinned. 'Liverpool. Where the Beatles come from!'

The American shook his head. 'What d'you know!'

The tannoy doused the jukebox with a metallic roar. 'Now hear this! All enlisted men of the Blue Watch will muster at 1830! Local liberty will cease at 1800.'

The music came back with a triumphant bellow of noise. Jake shrugged. 'That's how it goes! That's our crew. We go aboard this evening an' take over.'

Lightfoot felt the beer rasping in his empty stomach. It had taken less than he had imagined to affect him, but instead of numbing his troubled mind it seemed to bring each item alive with stark and outsize clarity. Through the haze of tobacco smoke Bruce's face hung like a red balloon, his eyes and mouth, even the individual hairs which poked from beneath his tilted cap standing out from the crowded figures around him as if superimposed.

Lightfoot remembered suddenly the nerve-wrenching explosion as the unseen torpedo had struck the freighter. The shockwave had shaken the hull from stem to stern, like a madman tugging at a well-tuned instrument. He had tried to piece together what had occurred by listening to the staccato comments through the intercom, and gauge the danger from the tight faces around him.

The boarding party had been hauled dripping and coughing down the control-room ladder along with a few Chinese seamen and a man so badly wounded that he looked already dead. There had been a girl, too, and one of the watching men had said, 'Christ! This is more like it! The comforts of home!' But no one laughed.

Then he had seen Colquhoun, white-faced and shaking as if from cold, his uniform torn and bloodstained, his eyes staring around the boat as if he had never seen it before.

Later the boat had dived and increased speed away from the scene, and Lightfoot had found Bruce sitting wrapped in a grubby towel in the crew space, a cigarette in the centre of his mouth.

Lightfoot had asked, 'What happened to Archer?'

He could see Bruce as he had been then, less than half an hour after jumping from the capsizing freighter. Bruce had drawn deeply on the cigarette as if considering the matter.

''E's kaput! Dead as a bleedin' sardine!' It seemed to amuse him. 'So you see, wack, there's no need to worry any more. We're in the clear for once!'

'How did it happen?' His voice had been unsteady. Looking back, he knew it was because of the uncontrollable relief Bruce's words had brought him. It made him feel unclean and guilty at the same time.

Then Bruce had said coolly, 'Your pal, Mister bloody Colquhoun, done for him!' He had chuckled. 'Cut 'im fair in 'alf with a full magazine!'

Lightfoot had left the crew space, and Bruce had returned calmly to the business of completing his toilet. He had met Petty Officer Jeffers outside the galley, a mug of tea in his hands. But when he had tried to question him Jeffers had answered sharply, 'It's not for me to say, lad. Archer's dead. That's the one thing I do know!' He had wiped his oil-smeared hands on his shirt. 'Now leave me be. I've had a bellyful of questions for one day!'

Rumours sped around the boat like fanned flames, each more positive than the one before. Colquhoun had lost his head and shot Archer by accident. He would be court-martialled. He had reported sighting a submarine on the surface, but Bruce had said it was unlikely, as *he* was with Colquhoun at the time, and the officer was too scared to see anything clearly!

Even the captain did not escape. He had failed to save the freighter. He would be relieved of his command and so forth....

Jake stood up and stared through the smoke. 'Right, you blue-blooded Limeys! Let's see how you make out at bowling. It'll do me good to beat the hell out of you before I sail!' The group broke up noisily and moved towards the end of the canteen.

Bruce tried to follow but collapsed in his chair. His early humour rapidly giving way in a haze of beer.

Lightfoot stood uncertainly beside the table. 'Aren't you going, too?'

Bruce stared up at him morosely. 'Nah, I'll have a few more cans an' then get my head down.' He gave a lopsided grin. 'You still mopin' about Gipsy Archer?' His eyes were red-rimmed and he seemed unable to focus them properly.

Lightfoot watched him cautiously. Bruce was hiding something. His very manner showed that he was bursting apart with some new secret. He sat down and deliberately opened a fresh can and pushed it across.

Bruce lifted it to his lips and allowed the beer to run down his thick chest. Then he started to laugh. There was no sound, but his whole body shook as if he was having some sort of fit.

Between shakes he gasped, 'Your face! Oh, my lovely Jesus, your *face*!' Tears ran down his cheeks and mingled with the beer. 'I wish you could'a been there! Poor old Gipsy. 'E never knew it was comin'!'

Lightfoot opened another can without taking his eyes from the other man. 'What happened?'

''Appened? You may well ask, my old son!' He was half sliding from his chair now. 'I clobbered 'im with the butt of my Stirling and then *leaned* 'im against that bleedin' door! Then all I 'ad to do was tell Colquhoun that there was a bogeyman behind the door an' that my own gun was empty!' He rocked from side to side. ''E was so bloody scared by that time, 'e'd 'ave believed me if I said the 'Oly Ghost was there!' He crossed himself and chuckled again. ''E let rip and blasted Gipsy to bits! Gawd, I nearly peed myself laughin' when I saw Colquhoun's mush after 'e'd done! I don't know 'ow I kept a straight face, I really don't!'

Lightfoot staggered away from the table, his face ashen. 'You're lying! You're just saying that to...'

Bruce stared at him glassily. 'Like bloody 'ell I am!'

Lightfoot knew that Bruce was in deadly earnest. Any sort of cunning or restraint had gone with the empty beer cans which filled the table. His mind was a complete maelstrom of confusion and horror. He could remember Colquhoun's stricken face, the way the other men had watched him in silence. They were destroying him because of what Bruce had done.

What they had both done. He tried to speak but nothing came.

Bruce propped himself on one elbow and muttered, 'Don't you worry about *Mister* Colquhoun, mate. 'E can go to 'ell f'all I care.' Some of his old manner returned momentarily. ''Course, if someone told 'im what really 'appened, it wouldn't do no good. It would only drop *you* in the cart. Anyway, I should 'ave to deny it.' He tried to wink. 'We wouldn't want that now, would we?'

Lightfoot walked blinkly away from the table and blundered out into the waiting sunlight. Two American shore-patrolmen watched him pass, lazily swinging their sticks and chewing their gum, but he did not even see them.

He walked fast but without direction, his breath gasping in his lungs as the furnace heat pressed down on his head and shoulders. He had to find a way to explain to Colquhoun. There had to be a way.

Back in the canteen, Bruce slept amidst the chaos of beer cans, his head pillowed on his arm. His face was relaxed and smiling, as if he had not a care in the world.

• • •

The car jerked to a halt and the sailor behind the wheel turned in his seat to stare at Jermain through his dark glasses. 'Here it is, Commander. Bungalow Number Thirty. There don't seem to be much sign of life.'

Jermain climbed out of the car and felt the late afternoon sun on his neck. 'Thank you for the ride,' he said.

The American grinned. 'A real pleasure.' The car rolled away in a double-banked cloud of yellow dust, and Jermain was left alone on the road.

The road was very new and as straight as a ruler, with neither tree nor any difference in construction in the neat bungalows to break the harsh, unfinished monotony. But here, during their rest spells ashore, the American officers lived their strange lives in something which seemed a pseudo representation of a piece of America.

Jermain sighed and walked up the path towards the front of the wide bungalow. He pushed through a hanging screen which protected the deep veranda from the dust and flies and found himself in a spacious hallway beyond. Every door was open, and he could feel a stream of fanned air cooling the sweat on his face and hands.

He moved uncertainly into a large living room which looked over the rear of the building and the green hills beyond. Peeping over a line of trees was the newly constructed wall of a canning factory with a brightly painted sign which read: 'Presented by the people of Michigan, U.S.A., as a mark of friendship.' Jermain turned away and found himself staring down at a canopied cot in which a small, round-faced baby was fast asleep. In spite of the surroundings everything was very normal, and very quiet.

Somewhere on the other side of the building a door slammed and he heard a man's voice speaking in a slow, unhurried drawl. 'Now quit fussing, honey. I've packed everything I need for the trip. I'm not leaving you for good, you know!'

A shadow fell across the doorway and Jermain said awkwardly, 'The door was open. I just came in.'

The American was about the same age as himself, and the collar pins in his neat khaki uniform showed him to be the same rank. Oddly enough, his hair was completely grey but cut very short, so that if anything it added to his general appearance of youthful vigour.

'I was kinda expecting you.' He seemed vaguely uncomfortable. 'You must be David Jermain.' His handclasp was firm. 'Jill Conway is in our spare room.' He walked to a table and touched a line of bottles. 'She's asleep right now. The doc gave her a couple of pills.'

Jermain asked, 'Is she all right?'

The American shot him a quick glance. 'It's hard to say. I guess you'd know better than I would.' He poured two large whiskies. 'She came back from the airstrip about an hour ago after seeing her father flown out.'

Jermain dropped his eyes. He still could not understand what had made the girl stay behind in Taiwan when her father was being flown back to England for further treatment. Nothing seemed to make sense any more. Even his journey up here had been in vain. And now this American was acting so strangely. He was obviously a very competent and self-assured officer, yet Jermain's inner senses told him that he was unsure of himself, even rattled. Could it be because Jill had confided in him? Had told him that she did not in fact wish to see Jermain again?

The American thrust a glass into his hand and said abruptly, 'Look, I don't have much time. I'm skipper of the *Pyramus* and we're due to sail in an hour.'

Jermain watched him closely. 'A Polaris boat. The one by the depot ship?'

The man nodded. 'That's the one.' He gulped down the drink in one swallow and refilled his glass. 'I guess I owe you an apology, Commander. I wangled it so that Jill Conway could be sent here. I thought she would be company for my wife while I'm away.' He bit his lip. 'Also, I guessed you would come sooner or later.'

Jermain sipped his drink and waited.

The American banged down his glass. 'Hell! I'm one of the guys who is supposed to be capable of handling the most deadly weapon ever invented and I can't even speak my piece.' He called out, 'Come in, darling, I can't cope with this situation!'

The door opened again and he added, 'Meet the wife, Commander.'

Jermain stared, the American and the rest of the room fading into shadows around him. He said quietly, 'Sarah! For God's sake, it's really you?'

Then she was in his arms, her face pressed to his shoulder, the same dark hair hanging rebelliously across her neck.

She stood back and studied him, her face torn between laughing and crying. 'Oh, David! I hated to do this to you! But when I heard your boat had docked here I had to get you to come.' She caught her husband's hand and pulled him towards her. 'This is John.' She looked from one to the other. 'I was so afraid you wouldn't come if you had time to think about it. I did so want everything to be right again.'

Jermain sat down heavily and then looked towards the cot.

His sister nodded. 'Yes, he belongs to us. He's three months old.'

Her husband said, 'His name's David, too.' He grinned with sudden relief. 'For obvious reasons, as I can now appreciate!'

Jermain said dazedly, 'I can't get over it. And yet I knew we would meet again somewhere.' He shook his head. 'I wouldn't have missed this for anything.'

Her husband looked at his watch. "Well, this is it. I have to go now.'

Jermain saw the quick glance of private anguish pass between them.

She replied steadily, 'I know, John. Are you *sure* you've got everything?'

He winked at Jermain and patted his pockets. 'I guess so.' He picked up his cap, and as if at a prearranged signal a car squealed to a halt outside the house. He said, 'I'll be back in about ten weeks, honey. Just routine stuff.' He walked to the cot and touched his son. 'Take care of your Mom while I'm away.'

Then he kissed her, quickly and without emotion, much like an ordinary man on his way to the office or factory bench.

Jermain guessed that it was part of a careful routine which they had built up to protect themselves from constant heart-break.

'Well, that's it. I am now Commander John Hurtzig, United States Navy, again.' He grinned and gripped Jermain's hand. 'Next time it'll be longer, I hope. It's good to have you here, and I mean that.'

Then he was gone, and for several seconds they listened to the car's engine speeding down that straight road towards the base.

She poured another drink and said quickly, 'Tell me everything, David. Did you get my letters?' Her voice was husky, and Jermain knew she was still thinking of her husband.

He smiled, 'They haven't caught up with me yet. I am waiting for fresh orders. I don't really know what is going to happen.'

She sat down beside him, her dark eyes pensive. 'I was so worried about you. About what you might think. I knew how you felt about Ian marrying me, and what his friendship meant to you.' She shrugged. 'It's hard to expalin. It all seems so long ago.'

He said gently, 'You did what you wanted to do. After all, it was your life.'

She smiled sadly. 'Yes, it was. Now, what about this girl, Jill?' She smiled in spite of her inner anxiety. 'She really is quite a girl. Not a bit what I might have expected for a stick-in-the-mud like you!'

He bit his lip. 'It's nothing like that, Sarah. We met in Singapore. Her father was wounded when the *Malange* was sunk.' The casual words brought it all back like an old pain, and for several seconds he could only stare at the floor like a man coming out of some sick dream.

She said, 'Her mother was killed, too. Mercifully, she died while she was still asleep.' She smiled at Jermain's startled expression. 'Oh yes, she told me all about it.'

'Does she know about you? About your being my sister?'

She nodded. 'The lot. We girls had our heads together for quite a spell. I sat with her until the pills put her to sleep.' She glanced at her watch. 'You can take a peep at her later, if you like.'

Jermain said, 'I shall have to get back to the *Temeraire*. But I can come back if there's nothing fresh to attend to.'

He walked back through the hallway, his arm around her shoulders. At the door she asked suddenly, 'Did you see much of Ian in England? Do you know how he's getting on?'

Jermain swung round to face her, the realisation crowding in on him like a douche of cold water. 'My God, Sarah, I should have told you! He's *here*, as my number one!'

She looked away for a few moments, and when she faced him again her face was calm but resolved. 'Come back soon, David.' She studied his features sadly. 'But keep him away from me.'

He faltered by the door. 'But what happened, Sarah?'

She shook her head. 'Just keep him away.'

13

It Had to Happen One Day

A FULL week passed and still the *Temeraire* lay at her mooring alongside the U.S. depot ship. The first curiosity aroused by her arrival gave way to casual acceptance as the Americans became once more totally involved in their own affairs. Surface ships and submarines came and went with busy and unexplained purpose, and as the days dragged past the *Temeraire*'s crew became more and more aware of their own futility. When not employed on duties aboard the men found their way inland, each trip ashore adding to the problems of discipline and purpose. Even stable and reliable members of the crew became involved in fights and drunken brawls, either with the Americans or amongst themselves, and the trickle of mail from home only added to the general air of bitterness and discontent.

Then, on the seventh day, the weather broke to add its own weight to the *Temeraire*'s misery. The sky, which had up to now been clear and transparent, was hidden in low cloud, and as the humidity mounted like the interior of a steam bath the rain thundered down as if propelled from a dam. It drove the loungers from the depot ship's maindeck and turned the hills and roadways into rivers of yellow mud. Even inside the submarine's hull there seemed no escape, and the steady deluge battered on the toughened steel, making prisoners of the waiting men.

In his small cabin Jermain sat by the desk, an unlit pipe clamped between his teeth. Although he was dressed only in a pair of slacks his whole body felt stifled and damp with perspiration, and his mind seemed to take an age to deal with even the most routine problem.

Not that there was much to do any more. Several men had been brought before him as defaulters. A Lieutenant Trott had arrived as a hasty replacement for Victor. But otherwise he seemed bound to sit and watch his command falling apart before his eyes, like the hillsides washing away in the rain.

Time and time again he thought of Jill Conway. Nearly every day he had made his way to the bungalow to see her, only to come away feeling empty and discouraged. She seemed like a stranger. Like part of another life. Yet in some strange way he felt she was glad of his visits, if only to keep her own loneliness at bay. There was little news of her father, just the occasional communiqué to say he was 'as comfortable as could be expected'.

He stared round the cabin remembering the excitement when the *Temeraire* had first gone into commission. The speeches, the high hopes. Like the persistent rain they drummed at his mind like taunts.

Beyond the door the intercom intoned. 'Hands to tea. Duty part of the watch muster in the control room.'

The duty watch would probably be the only men aboard, he thought. It was as if they felt some sort of shame for the *Temeraire* and could no longer bear to be aboard for longer than necessary.

Propelled by some inner sense or urgency, Jermain stood up and began to throw on his clothes. He walked through the wardroom where Trott, the new officer, was sitting alone before a cup of tea, and on into the control room. Oxley was mustering the duty hands, a clipboard of papers under his arm.

Jermain said, 'I'll be ashore if I'm wanted. You have the phone number.'

Oxley nodded. 'Aye, aye, sir. No news about our going home, I suppose?'

Jermain caught sight of the assembled men watching him, their faces like strangers, and a flood of resentment made him suddenly angry. 'What's the matter? Isn't there enough work to do here?' He regretted his outburst immediately, but something made him turn on his heel leaving Oxley looking surprised and hurt.

The rain met him with savage glee, and within seconds it had soaked through his coat and made his shoes feel like paper. With luck there was a solitary car on the jetty and the driver headed away from the sodden base without a word. Jermain sat slumped in the rear seat, his eyes staring over the driver's shoulder at the streaming road.

What the hell was going to happen? If only there was a signal. Send the boat back to England; relieve him of command. *Anything* was better than this waiting!

The car squelched to a halt and the driver pushed open the door.

Jermain tugged his cap over his eyes and hurried the last few steps to the door. It opened before he could touch it and he saw Sarah framed in the yellow lamplight beyond. She closed the door behind him and waited until he had peeled off his dripping coat.

'Thank God you've come, David. Jill just got a message from the base.' She watched him steadily. 'Her father died this morning in hospital.'

'Is she all right?' Jermain felt suddenly calm. Perhaps this was what he had been expecting. Dreading.

'I'm not sure. I was going to telephone the *Temeraire* and send for you. I think she wants to see you.' She moved towards a door. 'I think it's better if you go in alone.' She shivered as the rain slashed at the shutters. 'I'll be with David if you need me.'

Jermain opened the door and stepped quietly inside. With all the shutters closed against the storm the room was deep in shadow. A single lamp burned beside the bed, and the girl was sitting on the window seat, her legs drawn up to her chin. She was wearing the slacks and shirt she had been given aboard the submarine, and she was very still.

Jermain said, 'I just heard. I don't have to tell you how sorry I am.' His voice seemed too loud in spite of the rain.

'I know.' Her eyes shone momentarily in the lamplight. 'But I think we expected it to happen.' Her shoulders moved slightly in what might have been either a shrug or a shudder. 'When I saw him on to the plane he was different. Changed. He didn't want to go on.'

Jermain moved closer. 'He was a good man.'

'I've been trying to prepare myself for this.' Her voice seemed to be coming from a long way off. 'But it's not possible, is it? One minute there's the family. You never think about it really. It's just there.' She moved one hand to her face. 'Then there's nothing. Nothing left.'

'What will you do, Jill? What do you *want* to do?' He felt the urge to hold her, the need to shut out the agony which was tearing her apart.

She did not seem to hear him. 'Do you remember Singapore? That night, that one night we had together?' She stood up and walked away from him. 'I wanted to tell you then, but I couldn't be sure. I thought I was lying to myself, as I lied to you.'

Jermain took a step towards her but she cried, 'No, David! Let me finish in my own way!' They both stood quite still, their shadows touching below the lamp.

Then she continued, 'I was afraid to let myself believe that it could happen so easily. I didn't even wait to find out what *you* thought.' She tried to laugh. 'But I watched you sail that morning and tried to let it die inside me. Then on that ship when your men came aboard. And one of them said, "We're from the *Temeraire*", I knew I couldn't go on without you.' Her voice shook. 'I wanted to tell you all this, here in this house. But I couldn't find the words. Not until now. And now maybe it's too late!' She faced him slowly, her body suddenly erect. 'I told my father about us, about everything.' Her head dropped. 'It seemed to please him.'

She did not resist as he pulled her gently against his body, nor did she look up as he said, 'I told you it couldn't end, Jill. I told you.' Her face felt hot and she was shaking. 'Everything will be all right, you see.' He held her tightly as she began to sob uncontrollably. 'After this things will be different. For both of us.'

The door opened quietly and Sarah said, 'I've got some brandy.' She studied them gravely. 'I'm glad you came, David.'

The girl released herself from his arms and brushed her hand across her face. 'Can you stay, David?'

Jermain looked at his sister. She said, 'I think it would be better. The base can call you if you're needed. I don't like being without a man either when the rain comes.'

They were both looking at him, and Jermain was conscious of the steady downpour across the metal roof. He thought of the submarine and of his earlier depression, but they no longer seemed important.

'I'd like to very much.'

The girl said quickly, 'I think I'll have a shower. It might make me feel better.'

Jermain followed his sister into the living room and waited as she poured him some brandy. Then she said, 'She wants to cry so let her do it in private. It will do her good. She's been going through hell.'

Jermain stared at the closed door. 'I liked her father. But I'm glad she stayed here instead of flying out with him. There was nothing she could do anyway.'

His sister smiled gently. 'You really are out of touch, David. She stayed to be near *you*. Now that her parents are dead you are all she has to hold on to.' She studied him evenly. 'How do you feel about that?'

Jermain downed the brandy. 'I think you know.'

'Well, that's settled then.' She sighed and looked at the clock. 'I'm going to bed. It's been a long day.' She touched his arm. 'Don't waste a minute of it, David. I nearly did once. You mustn't make the same mistake.' She brightened. 'Which reminds me, I must go and see if the offspring is alseep through all this!'

She led him to another room. 'Take this one. I don't like to use it while John's away.' She ran her eye around the familiar furniture. 'There's a shower through there.' She kissed him lightly. 'It'll all look better in the morning.'

Jermain stripped off his clothes and stood beneath the cold shower, his mind still dazed by the swift turn of events. She needed him. She had stayed to be near him. There was no mention of love, but it was enough. More than enough.

As he switched off the shower he realised with a start that the rain had stopped also. In the strange room the silence seemed suddenly deafening. Through the shutters he could see the pale bars of moonlight and the stark silhouette of dripping trees behind the house. Everything was motionless, like a dream sequence.

He towelled himself roughly and then threw himself on the bed. She would have to fly back to England. No doubt the flight was already being arranged. He found he could think about it without apprehension. As if he already felt part of her life. He switched off the light and smiled inwardly. Sarah had understood. The sister he had tried to protect and support had made him feel like some immature schoolboy.

He raised himself on his elbows as the door opened and closed in one swift movement. Without speaking the girl crossed the room her bare feet making no sound. She was wearing what appeared to be a man's bathrobe and her hair was tied back with a piece of ribbon, as if she had just stepped from the shower.

She sat on the edge of the bed and laid her hand on his chest. 'I had to come. You were too near.'

She sat motionless as he untied the bathrobe and let it fall to the floor. In the bright moonlight her naked body gleamed like silver.

He pulled her down beside him and kissed her throat and the shoulder were he had seen the scars. Her hair was damp and her skin felt cool beneath his touch.

Then she threw out her arms, her fingers gripping the sheets as he ran his hand gently over her breasts and down across her stomach. 'Make it last, David! Hurt me if you like, but make it last!'

His shadow blotted out the moonlight, and he felt her body rising to meet and enfold him with an urgency which made his respond with a fierceness he had never known.

Only when he was spent and they lay entwined together, each unwilling to release the other, did she speak again.

'I love you, David. Nothing else matters now.'

He propped himself up and stared down at her. It was complete. He could face everything and anything now.

Her hands moved up behind his neck, and he could feel her

breath warm against his chest as she pulled him towards her.

Outside the moon continued to shine on the trees, and beyond the dip in the hills it glittered briefly across the night sea.

The sea was quiet, and holding its secrets for the dawn.

• • •

Wolfe awoke with a violent start as his cabin was flooded with light. 'What the bloody hell!' His mouth felt raw from the gin he had consumed a few hours earlier and inside his head the hammers were busy with their relentless tattoo. He glared at his watch and then at Oxley who stood inside the doorway a jacket over his pyjamas. He added with a gasp of disbelief, 'Hell, it's only four o'clock!'

Oxley glanced quickly at the empty bottle on the deck and the pile of half-smoked cigarettes. He said, 'It's an emergency, Number One. The captain's wanted aboard the depot ship in the operations room.' He added, 'I'm still O.O.D., so I thought you'd better be told at once.'

Wolfe rubbed his eyes to clear away the mist. 'Well, where is the C.O.?'

'Ashore. I have the phone number, but it may take half an hour to get him back here.'

Wolfe rolled off his bunk, his mind working reluctantly. 'I'll bet he's with that bloody girl!' He stumbled to one side as he struggled into his trousers. 'The bitch!'

Oxley was watching him coldly. 'Did you say something?'

Wolfe glared at him. 'Who wants to see the captain anyway? Christ, it's one hell of an hour to call a conference!'

Oxley shrugged. 'It doesn't say on the flimsy, Number One. But there have been lights flashing all over the depot ship. Something big must be happening.'

Wolfe paused. 'What about our own W/T? Have we no signals coming in?'

'No. So it must be something to do with the Americans.'

Wolfe grinned. 'It would be. They get in a bloody flap at the drop of a hat! I expect their ice-cream supply has been buggered up by the Communists!'

Oxley sighed. He had had enough of Wolfe the previous evening. Sitting at dinner he had been speaking with Trott, the new assistant T.A.S. officer. Trott appeared to be an eager and willing addition, but he was undoubtedly very dull. He spoke nostalgically about spring in England. About the cricket score, and every other thing which, unbeknown to himself, was calculated to rub raw the brooding sores of the other officers.

Wolfe had shouted, 'Well, this isn't bloody Lord's, so for God's sake shut it! I wanted a replacement, not a flaming travel courier!'

Trott had retired red-faced and fuming from the table, and the mess had lapsed once more into its new state of gloom and inner deliberation.

Oxley said, 'Shall I call that number?'

Wolfe weighed the words in his mind. He had a clear picture of the girl sitting in the wardroom, her half-naked body smeared with oil and salt, her eyes wide from shock.

He replied coldy, 'No, I'll do it. You acknowledge the message and tell 'em the captain is on his way.' He waited until Oxley had gone and then made himself complete his dressing before he left the cabin.

He reached the radio room where the phone had been connected to the depot ship's switchboard, and after consulting the dutybook he began to dial the number.

In spite of his uncontrollable amusement at the idea of disturbing Jermain, Wolfe's mind kept returning to the other good piece of news he had received two days earlier. The signal had stated clearly that upon return to the United Kingdom Lieutenant-Commander Ian Wolfe would be relieved of his appointment and present himself forthwith for the final Commanding Officers Course. He had been thinking about it when that idiot Trott had started up about England again. What the hell did all that tripe count for? He was going to work. Real work, with a boat like the *Temeraire* at the end of it. A command of his own.

All the agitation and uncertainty was nearly behind him now. The cruel self-discipline he had exerted upon himself was over. But when he had shared his news with Jermain the latter had seemed caught off guard, even unhappy about it.

Looking back, Wolfe thought he knew why. Jermain stood a good chance of being beached after his affair with the *Malange*. If he left the *Temeraire*, Their Lordships would be hunting for a new, well-tried commanding officer. Wolfe's heart had given a jump at the sudden realisation that *he* might well be taking Jermain's command, and that Jermain had seen the writing on the wall in the signal's unemotional wording.

The telephone clicked and a voice said, 'Jermain speaking.'

Wolfe said, 'Recall, sir. You're wanted aboard the depot ship immediately.' He grinned at his reflection in the polished panel. The girl was probably stretched out beside him. Her father dead, yet she couldn't stay away.

Jermain replied, 'I'll come at once. Send a car for me, please.'

Wolfe heard the sound of a door creaking and a woman's voice in the background. His grin widened.

Jermain was covering the mouthpiece with his hand, but nevertheless Wolfe heard him say, 'It's all right, Sarah. It's only the base. You go back to bed.'

Wolfe felt pressure like a steel band tightening round his skull. He could not speak or think clearly. It was as if he had received some sort of seizure. Dimly he heard Jermain say, 'Give me fifteen minutes.' Then the phone went dead.

Oxley appeared by the door. He watched Wolfe curiously and then said, 'I've sent a car.' He frowned. 'Is everything all right, Number One?'

The phone dropped and swung at the end of its flex as Wolfe turned and pushed past the other man. Oxley replaced the instrument and pursed his lips. Another crisis was in the air. It was better than nothing, he decided.

• • •

The operations room was like a great steel cavern which ran the full width of the depot ship's hull. It was crammed with charts and plot tables, with complicated graphs and a barrage of telephones. But the perspex monitoring screens were unlit and unmanned, and all but one of the chart tables covered until the new day.

The air was stale with yesterday's tobacco smoke and the damp odour of condensation and sweat.

Admiral McKelway leaned on his hands across the one lighted table, his face made older by the grey stubble which showed so clearly in the glare. Several staff officers in various stages of undress were grouped around him, and in a far corner a yeoman was busy preparing coffee.

Jermain walked up to the table and waited in silence. He was immediately aware of the tension. As if it was pinned inside the steel room as part of the motionless figures around the table.

McKelway lifted his head and looked at Jermain. 'Sit down, Commander. Have some coffee.' His head moved sideways like a gun dog's as the teleprinter began its insane clatter behind him. An officer ripped away the message and handed it across to his chief.

Jermain saw the officer glance at the depot ship's captain and give a quick shake of the head.

McKelway's cold eyes flicked away from the paper and back to the chart. In a flat, unemotional tone he said, 'At 0100 this morning an American nuclear submarine failed to make her obligatory signal. I therefore have to assume that she is either in difficulties,' he paused and his eyes fastened on Jermain's face, 'or she has been destroyed!'

Every man in the room but Jermain was already aware of this information, yet the shock of the admiral's words seemed no less than if they were being uttered for the first time.

McKelway continued, 'The U.S.S. *Pyramus* should have discharged her radio-buoy at 0100 in this position.' His wizened finger moved along the chart. 'I know it's early to jump to conclusions, but we cannot afford to take one single chance.'

Jermain stared at the chart, only half his mind following McKelway's dry voice. The *Pyramus* was overdue on station. Somehow Jermain had known which submarine it would be as soon as McKelway had started to speak.

He thought of Sarah's anxious face in the doorway and his own casual words. 'It's only the base. You go back to bed.'

McKelway continued, 'I have the lines open with Washington. I have already been in contact with London.' They were all looking at Jermain. 'What I have to tell you, Jermain, is something which might surprise you, it may even sicken you.' He took a cigar out of his pocket and rolled it absently in his fingers. 'I want you to find that submarine, and I want it found quickly!'

The yeoman said quietly, 'Coffee, gentlemen?'

McKelway lowered himself into a steel chair. 'Might as well. There's a lot of work to be done.' He stared at Jermain. 'I will give you every piece of information I have available, Commander. I'll move heaven and earth to help you in any way I can.' He slammed his fist on the table. 'The *Pyramus* is carrying eighteen Polaris missiles! She has to be located!'

Jermain took a cup and drained the scalding coffee without even tasting it. He peered down at the coloured chart and said, 'This is the east coast of Korea, sir. What was a Polaris boat sent there for?'

He waited for the lash of McKelway's tongue, but instead the admiral replied evenly, 'That's right. Ask away.' He levered himself forward in his chair. 'It's been a regular patrol for two years.' The finger moved slowly up the Korean coastline. 'Now look at this. The sea is so deep in some parts it falls away to eighteen hundred fathoms. Ideal country for a deep-running nuclear boat.' The finger moved up and up the coast. 'If you look closely, Jermain, you'll see this valley. It's marked on the chart as the Wantsai Valley, and it runs south east away from the northern end of the Korean mainland. It really is a valley. Some of the surveys have been hazy, but it's a great natural crevasse in the sea bed, some three hundred miles long and never less than thirty miles wide.' He sounded tired. 'It was a natural right from the start. A Polaris submarine was given the Valley as a regular patrol area. Once a Red Alert was given the submarine patrolling the sector could reach her firing position within hours.' He swept his palm upwards across the land mass. 'There are three countries within a hundred miles of the firing point! It's unique. We have north Korea, Russia and China, all comfortably within a small arc of missle range!'

Jermain controlled his breathing with an effort. The admiral's words seemed vast in scale, like the scope of the operations he controlled. He stared at the chart and at the admiral's 'unique' situation. How unlike the other coast of Korea, he thought, where Conway's hopes had died with his wife in the *Malange*. This other coastline was certainly a temptation for any submarine strategist.

The operations officer said suddenly, 'The *Pyramus* may be damaged in some way.' He sounded doubtful. 'In which case there is a certain routine she will have followed. But if she has lost control, then she will have gone straight to the bottom of the Valley. Like the *Thresher*, she'll be scattered in minute fragments, beyond reach, beyond hope.'

McKelway tugged at his collar. 'Christ, it's hot in here!' He looked across at Jermain. 'If you accept this assignment, Commander, you'll be on your own the moment you get under way. Secrecy is our only hope.'

Jermain frowned. 'Do I have any choice, sir?'

'Your people in London have left the choice to you, Jermain. It will be your final responsibility.' He leaned back and watched him calmly.

Jermain said, 'My choice? Must I decide whether one hundred men are to be left trapped or not?' He nodded vehemently. 'Of course I'll go!'

McKelway held up his hand. 'Take it easy, son. There's more to come, a whole lot more!'

A phone buzzed and an officer said, 'Reconnaissance reports a zero, Admiral!'

McKelway did not even blink. 'If the Reds get one peep of what we're doing they'll be in there pitching, Jermain. The *Pyramus* is right on their front doorstep, miles beyond any aid which we can give her. If they guessed the *Pyramus* was crippled and within salvage possibilites they'd go into top gear! Can you imagine what it would mean to the Reds to capture a Polaris boat intact?' He slammed his palms together. 'They would have every goddamn secret in the book. Every detail of our target ability and all the computerised data that goes with it. There would be nothing, but *nothing*, to stop them overtaking our lead in Polaris and nuclear warfare!'

Jermain ran his fingers through his hair. 'When would you want me to sail, sir?'

McKelway glanced at his staff. 'I shall get the final go ahead from Washington in a few hours. You get your boat ready to leave within ten hours, okay?' He added slowly, 'There will be written orders for you by then. Everything legal and tied up!'

Jermain felt a sudden warmth for the small admiral with the weight of command on his slight shoulders.

'Just one more question, sir?' Jermain saw the flash of caution in McKelway's wintry eyes. 'Why me?'

McKelway stood up and took his arm. Together they walked out of the operations room and stood on the damp maindeck below the gaunt derricks.

Then the admiral said quietly, 'I was saving this for later,

Jermain.' He leaned on the rail and watched an aproned cook walking towards the galley rubbing the sleep from his eyes. 'I *could* tell you it's because your boat is the latest and best in nuclear submarines. Well, maybe it is at that, but I've got a dozen boats with captains who know that area a whole lot better than *you* do. I could also say it's because I was impressed by your unorthodox style, by the fact that you work things out for yourself as you feel your way. That's unusual nowdays.' He grinned in the grey dawn light. 'Seriously, I read your last report and I was impressed. You are a good man for this job. I sincerely believe that.' His tone hardened. 'But my main reason is this. If the *Pyramus* is still intact, but cannot be helped or prevented from falling into enemy hands,' he swung round to face Jermain, 'she must be destroyed.' He gripped Jermain's arms in a tight pincer-hold. 'I am afraid you will have to destroy her, Commander! I cannot and will not ask my own men to destroy their buddies in cold blood!'

Jermain felt the sweat running down his face in spite of the chill air. 'And you think I can, sir?'

McKelway rested his body on the rail and said bitterly, 'You don't know these boys. To you it will be a job. Just a job.' He looked sideways at Jermain's set face. 'It has to be this way, boy. We must always be ready with a final solution.'

Jermain straightened his back. 'I shall return to the *Temeraire,* sir. There's a lot to do.' His voice sounded hollow.

McKelway said quietly, 'This is one hell of an assignment, Commander. Both our governments are prepared to accept this final solution, but in the end it comes down to you and me.' He held out his hand. 'Then it comes down to you alone.'

He added, 'I know the *Pyramus*'s skipper well. He's a good boy.'

Jermain had a sudden glimpse of John Hurtzig bending over his son's cot and Sarah's anxious face watching him.

He replied, 'I'll do my best, sir.'

McKelway watched him go, hs face lined and sad. 'I never doubted it, boy,' he said quietly. 'Never for a minute!'

• • •

Jermain pulled the clean shirt over his head and ran a comb

carelessly through his hair. In his cabin mirror he could see Wolfe and Ross watching his every movement, their expressions masking their reactions to his words.

He swung round. 'You will both understand, of course, that this is all Top Secret. We may still hear that the submarine has been located and all is well. But the Americans are working on the opposite assumption, and so must we.'

Ross folded his notebook and thrust it into his white overalls. 'Well, the reactor is running smoothly, sir. I put my staff to work as soon as I got the word.' He shrugged. 'I would have argued with you over this, in view of the other troubles we've had with the boat, but what can I say now?' He met Jermain's eyes steadily. 'It might be us one day. I'd not like to think that we lack guts when it comes to helping another boat.'

Wolfe said, 'The boat is on stand-by, sir. Two men are still adrift, but I know where they are. The shore patrol is holding them for starting a brawl last night.'

Jermain pulled on his jacket and patted his pockets. He had to make sure that everything he needed was on his person. He might be confined to the clothes he stood up in for a very long time. 'Get them back aboard at once, Number One. I want a full complement.'

He was surprised that both Wolfe and Ross had taken his news so calmly and without argument. He wondered what their reactions might be when he told them of the admiral's 'final solution'. He forced the sickening possibility to the back of his mind. He had to find the *Pyramus* first.

A messenger tapped at the door. 'Pardon, Captain. But there's a Commander Martingale to see you.'

A thickset American officer was ushered into the cabin and Jermain said to his own officers, 'This is the other commanding officer of the *Pyramus*. He brought her in from the last patrol.'

The American shook hands, his face grave and lined with worry. He placed a thick folder on Jermain's desk and stared at it. 'This is all the intelligence stuff I've got, Commander. Aerial photographs from our high-fly reconnaissance boys, recognition and rendezvous procedure and so forth. You'll be sailing on the same route as we normally take.' He bit his lip. 'As Hurtzig took.'

He added impetuously, 'I asked the admiral if I could come

with you. I'd feel better to know what's happening.' He looked away. 'The old man refused. I guess he has no option.'

A sharp tremor ran through the deck and Ross said, 'Testing main propulsion. I'd better get aft and keep an eye on things.'

Jermain said slowly, 'Remember, this is secret until we sail. I'll tell the men myself. But until then it's a routine patrol.'

Martingale said, 'I hear you stayed with Hurtzig's wife? I had no idea she was your sister.'

He spoke quietly, but Jermain darted a quick glance at Wolfe's face as the man's unexpected words broke the silence like a bomb exploding. He was surprised at the calmness of his own reply. 'I'll take you on deck, Commander. There are a few points I'd like to discuss.'

Wolfe looked at him, his eyes completely steady and composed. 'I'll go round the boat and then check with the shore patrol, sir.'

Jermain nodded and walked through to the passageway. There was not a sign that Wolfe had heard the American's casual reference to Sarah. Not a blink of an eye.

They reached the upper deck and stood in the shadow of the depot ship's side to watch a frigate slipping seawards. Everything was businesslike but unruffled. No inkling of the feverish activity going on in the admiral's operations room or the flood of signals which might mean life or death to Hurtzig and his men.

Martingale said flatly, 'It's beyond me. The *Pyramus* is as safe as a house. I can't think what could have gone wrong.' He clasped Jermain's hand. 'I'll leave you in peace. But I'll be thinking of you.'

Jermain forced a smile. How would Martingale feel if he knew of his orders and the extent they might be carried out? He replied, 'It's nice to be of some use again.'

The American paused on the accommodation ladder and stared down at him. 'I think I know why McKelway wouldn't let me go with you. I guess that's why I wanted to meet you personally.' He looked along the *Temeraire*'s black hull towards the rounded bows and the hidden torpedo tubes. 'It had to happen one day. But that doesn't make it one bit easier for you.'

He hurried up the ladder as if he no longer trusted himself to speak.

Oxley walked briskly along the casing and saluted. He was properly dressed and freshly shaved, a different man from the one who had greeted Jermain in the dawn light.

He said, 'Signal, sir. Proceed to sea at 1500 in accordance with operational despatch.' He watched Jermain's face and added, 'Anything to add, sir?'

Jermain looked at his watch. Three hours. Perhaps the Americans were still hoping. He cursed himself for putting the empty faith in his mind.

'The first lieutenant will brief all officers. But once clear of the harbour limits I shall want the boat's number painted out.' They both stared up at the big S.191 on the side of the fin. There would be nothing to betray the *Temeraire*'s identity. She would be like a nameless pirate. An assassin. 'See to it, will you?'

Oxley watched Jermain walk towards the fin and waited as Mayo joined him on the casing. Mayo said, 'What do you make of it, Philip?'

Oxley shook his head. 'It's no bloody half-cock affair this time, Pilot. Did you see the captain's face?' He looked towards the lush hillsides. 'As our allies would say, "this is for real".'

Fifteen minutes after receiving the signal Jermain was summoned again to the depot ship where Admiral McKelway was waiting for him. There was little sign of the strain and anxiety he must be feeling and he was dressed in a fresh set of laundered khakis.

He snapped, 'I have a car waiting, Jermain. I thought you might like to say your farewells to Hurtzig's wife?' He studied him gravely. 'I've already been to see her. I think she deserves that at least.' He led the way to his big staff car and added, 'She'll be going through hell, but she's a navy wife now, and the wife of a commanding officer. If the worst happens it will fall to her to visit the other families.' He rapped on the driver's seat and finished, 'But I don't have to spell it out for you, do I?'

They drove in silence, the trees and white buildings flashing past without meaning. The road was rutted but as bone dry as if there had been no rain at all.

As they stopped outside the bungalow McKelway said

briefly, 'Ten minutes, Commander. I have radio contact with the base. I'll yell if I hear anything.'

Jermain stepped into the shaded living room, his body taut and heavy. The two women were standing together by the window watching his face. Sarah said, 'The admiral came here, David. He told me about John.'

Jermain replied, 'I'm sailing almost at once. I just wanted to see you first.' He could not find the words. 'You know I'm going to look for the *Pyramus*?'

She nodded. 'I'm glad it's you, David.' She walked to the door. 'I'll leave you two alone.' She was trying to smile. 'Just bring him back to me, David. To us!' Then she was gone, and the silence moved a step nearer.

When the staff car sounded its horn Jermain left the house like a man in a daze. Later his mind might be able to sort out the swift minutes, recall each precious word.

The girl had said, 'I'll take care of her, David.' Then she had looked up into his face, her eyes steady. 'But come back safely yourself. I need you, too.'

McKelway grunted, 'Let's get moving.' He sounded angry. 'There's been another development, Jermain. I just got it on the radio telephone.' He glared at the driver's back. 'Your top brass are sending a senior officer with you to take overall charge of the operations. I'm sorry, Jermain, I remember what it's like to have a goddamn admiral breathing down my neck!'

Jermain asked flatly, 'Sir John Colquhoun?'

'Exactly. But you don't seem surprised?' McKelway leaned back and lighted a cigar. 'Can you manage him okay?'

Jermain stared at his own reflection on the dusty window. They were all depending on him. Sarah, Jill and the *Pyramus*'s crew. Now Sir John Colquhoun was returning to the *Temeraire*, no doubt at his own insistence. Perhaps it was fitting, Jermain thought bitterly. In this way he was responsible for everything that had happened.

In a hard voice he replied, '*I* command the *Temeraire*, sir.'

The admiral blew out a thin stream of smoke and smiled grimly. 'I guess that answers a whole heap of questions!'

Two hours later McKelway stood alone on the depot ship's bridge and watched the British submarine slip her moorings. Without fuss or undue haste the black whale-shaped hull moved clear and glided towards the wider reaches of the inlet.

A line of blue-shirted seamen stood swaying on her casing, and as she passed the American flagship McKelway heard the shrill twitter of pipes as a last respect was paid.

The officers' white caps looked like small flowers at the tip of the *Temeraire*'s fin, and McKelway guessed that one of them was Jermain.

Across the anchorage a tug hooted. It was a mournful sound, and McKelway suddenly felt helpless and old as he watched the submarine turn slightly and head toward the lazy rollers of thc waiting sea. He lowered his glasses and walked back to the operations room. There was nothing he could do now, but wait.

14

Into the Valley

BALDWIN, the senior wardroom steward, whipped the breakfast tablecloth over his arm and took a quick glance around the assembled officers before vanishing into his pantry.

Without speaking, Jermain unrolled his chart and spread it on the empty table. He was conscious of the silent, watching officers and of Vice-Admiral Colquhoun who sat at the head of the table, his fingers interlaced across his stomach. For a moment longer he stood looking down at the chart as he assembled his words and listened to the muffled movements from the control room and the subdued murmur of fans.

The deck was quite motionless beneath his feet. There was nothing to betray the fact that the *Temeraire* was cruising at a depth of four hundred feet, her noiseless power thrusting her at a slow but steady ten knots. It would have been better if there was some sort of sensation, he thought vaguely. It had been four days since they had left the Nanlien Inlet, and for the last thirty-six hours they had been creeping slowly north west, listening and probing along the *Pyramus*'s ordered course, not knowing what to expect. Not even knowing if there was anything to find.

Sir John Colquhoun had seemed remarkably relaxed and affable when he had come aboard within minutes of sailing. Again he had insisted on taking a spare berth in the wardroom, and when not asleep could usually be found, as now, like a bemedalled buddha at the table.

When the *Temeraire* had dived for the first time and the complicated checks had been completed, he had joined Jermain in his cabin. He had come straight to the point. 'I've been attending a top-level SEATO conference, Jermain. Otherwise I would have flown down earlier. Much earlier.' He had tapped his fingertips together as he had watched Jermain from beneath lowered brows. 'When I heard about the *Malange* incident I was shocked, naturally. Not so much about Conway, although his death has obviously been a great loss.' His tone had hardened slightly. 'I think your own behaviour and general handling of the situation was lacking in many aspects. I'll go further, it was nothing short of madness.'

Jermain had not replied. But the effort of holding his words had cost him a good deal.

'You've a lot to learn. Such action would not have been tolerated in my time in submarines.' He had sighed. 'However, that part is now over. I can only thank God that we now have this opportunity to prove the *Temeraire*'s worth to the doubters and the critics!' He had added, as if to dismiss the matter, 'There are *some* senior officers who would have had you flown home immediately. It had even crossed my mind to do so. As you know, Jermain, the Board has selected Wolfe for command status. He would be quite capable of taking the boat back to the U.K. without you.'

There had fortunately been an interruption by way of Lieutenant Drew reporting that all tubes had been reloaded with homing torpedoes as instructed. The admiral had been content to keep his distance since that meeting. But his presence was constant, like a threat.

Jermain cleared his throat. 'Well, gentlemen, this is the picture. We will carry on along the Wantsai Valley, making a complete copy of the *Pyramus*'s usual procedure. As you can see from the chart, the Valley ends at a point some forty miles south of Linden Point, or Kokko Kutchi as it's shown here.'

They all craned forward to look at the coast's ragged outline which sprawled diagonally across the chart. All except the admiral, who continued to stare into space, as if his mind was on a higher plane.

'We are now passing through the area where the *Pyramus* should have made her safety signal.' He looked up as Kitson stirred uneasily. 'Do you want to say something?'

Kitson said awkwardly, 'I understood that no nuclear boats ever sent radio signals at sea, sir.'

'This is an exception. Due to the nature of the area and the complex grid layout of the patrol lines, the Polaris boats send up a radio-buoy at *this* point.' He rapped the chart with his pipe stem. 'It is timed to send a short, ten-second signal. After that it floods and sinks. The Americans have a series of high-flying reconnaissance aircraft which cover the whole area. They fly from Japan and to within sight of the North Korean coast before they turn and fly back. The schedules are timed so that these buoy signals can be recorded and reported immediately.' He pressed back the chart's folding edges.

Between his hands the Sea of Japan looked empty and impersonal. But in his mind's eye Jermain could picture it as a great submarine mountain range, with the Wantsai Valley running north west through the main part of it. Giant, unknown ridges and deep, plunging crevasses which hid their secrets in perpetual darkness. Maybe there was marine life which men's minds could never understand or discover. He pictured the submarine's slow-moving bulk gliding between the towering sides of the Valley, safely guided by her sensitive navigational systems. Below her keel the bottom dropped away for another ten thousand feet. It did not seem possible.

He continued, 'No such buoy was released or recorded, so we have to assume that the *Pyramus* was damaged in some way. She could have lost control, or the diving planes might have jammed. As you know, at these extreme depths, and at the boat's slow patrol speed, any such trouble might be too swift to rectify.' He looked around their faces. 'However, I am more inclined to believe otherwise. I know that this particular submarine was a well-tried boat. She was recently overhauled, and her crew are extremely competent.' He saw the admiral's eyes swing round and settle on him. 'My guess is that she made some sort of contact, either accidental or planned, with another vessel.'

The admiral wagged his finger and smiled. 'I'm not interrupting, but I should explain to your officers that this *is* only a guess.'

Jermain checked the anger which hovered at the back of his mind. 'Do you wish to add something, sir?'

'Just this. The *Pyramus* is probably sunk. She quite likely made a sudden and unavoidable dive straight to the bottom.' He spread his hands. 'If so, she's scattered for half a mile like so much scrap!' He looked at the shocked expression on Luard's face. 'If so, we can only locate her whereabouts and return to base. There's nothing anyone can do about it.' He looked at the chart. 'As for the theory that the *Pyramus* was intercepted in some way, well, of course, we must all be prepared for any eventualities. For that reason I suggested that the tubes were loaded with homing torpedoes.' He smiled innocently. 'We don't want any more *enemy* submarines to escape, do we?'

Jermain watched him, his mind suddenly calm. The admiral was actually enjoying it all. But at least he had shown his hand. He said abruptly, 'We shall continue the search until we find her. The American intelligence log suggests one further possibility.' He pointed at the end of the deep soundings on the chart. 'Just here, at the end of the area normally used by the *Pyramus*, the sea bottom is quite flat. From the coast itself the bottom deepens in steps, so that soundings change suddenly and at regular intervals.' He looked hard at each officer in turn as he spoke. 'Just try to picture it. It's like a small plateau, at the end of which the bottom drops away with a jump, down to eight thousand feet. The plateau is at a depth of only two hundred feet, and it was selected as a possible setting-down spot for any submarine in temporary trouble.'

His glance moved across Wolfe's face, but the first lieutenant immediately dropped his eyes to the chart, but not before Jermain had seen the bright intentness in them. 'So if the *Pyramus* has survived a disaster, she might well make for this place. Her captain could put her down on the bottom in comparative safety to effect minor repairs within the hull!' Again the inner pictures of his mind swept up to mock him like a clouded nightmare. Lying for ever, a rusting tomb for her crew, the *Pyramus* would be better to plunge over the edge into the Wantsai Valley. At least the end would be quick.

Drew said slowly, 'Suppose we locate her and we can't do anything to help her, sir?'

Jermain had been expecting it, yet it was still a shock. 'We have to find her first.'

Drew looked doubtful. 'Nasty. Wouldn't care to be in their shoes!'

Jermain felt drawn and tired. He had hardly found a moment to relax since leaving harbour. Yet he wanted to share his secret with these men. Or was it only to involve them and spread his own sense of shame at what he might have to do?

Oxley, sleek and alert. It would be his sonar which would find the missing *Pyramus*. The invisible waves which reached out from his sensitive devices would search her out, and decide her fate.

Drew, with his rugged Australian face deep in thought. His torpedoes would be the ones. His would be the final voice to urge them on their assassin's journey.

And Wolfe. What went on behind his strange, empty eyes? Was he still brooding over Sarah? Or worse still, was he deluding himself with the promise of his own command?

Jermain remembered his face when he had mentioned the signal from England. A boat of his own at last. And Sir John Colquhoun had mentioned it too, with something like pleasure. The cruel pleasure of a cat with a bird. The admiral at least must know the reality, Jermain thought savagely. That Wolfe could receive that final recommendation only from himself, his commanding officer. And that he could not do.

It was more than a cold-blooded report, and greater than any passing personal assessment.

Jermain had welcomed Wolfe's coming to the boat from the bottom of his heart. It had been like a link with that old past. Someone to share the words of friends and rise above the rigid codes of duty and routine.

But this Wolfe was a stranger. He seemed hard, yet brittle. And his attention to detail bordered on the small-minded rather than the trained and cheerful officer he had once been.

He looked again at the admiral, but he seemed intent on the chart. If it came to an open clash within the boat it would not be difficult for the admiral to drive a wedge between himself and Wolfe. Between captain and crew. He felt a chill on his spine as he recalled McKelway's words. 'You'll be on your own.' Now he knew that he had meant more than just the submarine's solitary search. The *Temeraire*'s captain would be quite alone. Whatever Sir John Colquhoun prescribed or suggested, whatever Wolfe and the others might think, *his* was the final decision.

Abruptly he folded the chart and said, 'That's all, gentlemen. I would like every officer to read and examine the American intelligence reports as soon as possible. I want each one of you to get a clear understanding of what we are doing, and of what we can expect.'

He walked out of the wardroom, and one by one the other officers returned to their duties.

Only Wolfe stayed in his chair, his eyes on the door.

The admiral stood up and stretched comfortably, 'Well, Number One, I don't suppose you've got any illusions about this job, eh?'

Wolfe stared fixedly at the door. 'Two birds with one stone.' Then he seemed to pull himself together, as if he had imagined he was talking to himself. He smiled and said, 'None at all, sir.' He walked from the wardroom, the smile still frozen on his face like a mask.

• • •

Lieutenant Oxley ducked his head through the watertight door and peered quickly around the sonar compartment. The operators looked welded to their seats, their heads hunched over the instrument controls as they had been since the weary search had begun. They worked round the clock, two hours on, four off, with hardly a break to ease the strain of watching and listening.

Colquhoun was sitting in his chair behind the operators, his eyes staring into space. He looked like death, Oxley thought. 'All right, Sub. You can lay aft for a bit.' Oxley saw the younger man stir stiffly in his seat.

Colquhoun said between his teeth. 'It's not time yet. There's another half hour still to run.' He turned his head, and Oxley was shocked to see the redness of his eyes, the deep lines around his mouth.

Oxley snapped, 'Take over the watch, Petty Officer.' Then to

Colquhoun he added quietly, 'Come outside.'

Colquhoun followed him obediently, his movements stiff and mechanical.

Oxley lit a cigarette and watched him thoughtfully. 'I've just been to the conference, Sub. The captain appears to think the American boat was interfered with by some sort of enemy action.'

Colquhoun said flatly, 'Is that so?'

Oxley tightened his lips. He might just as well have remarked on the Test-match score, or the state of his bank balance. He glanced quickly around to make sure they were undisturbed. Above his head through an oval hatch he could see the sick-bay entrance where Victor had died. Where Conway had laid in a deep coma awaiting his own fate. The white curtains shimmered in the fanned air and there was a gentle strain of dance music from Griffin's tape-recorder. It was hard to build up a sense of crisis. Harder still to believe that the submarine was in any sort of danger.

He said, 'Now look here, Max. I know you're still brooding about that seaman's death. Maybe you could have avoided it, and maybe you couldn't. It's not for me to say. But right now you've got a job to do. There's no room for self-pity or recriminations now!'

Colquhoun answered quietly, 'I'm surprised you allow me to take charge down here.' His tone was edged with bitterness.

Oxley said calmly, 'I don't have much option, do I?' He laid a hand on his arm and added wearily, 'Look, Max, we're all getting clapped out, but it can't be helped. Just try to think of all of *us*, trapped and waiting for outside help.' He gestured to the curved hull. 'Try and imagine it like that. It's easier to keep control that way.'

Colquhoun shrugged. 'I supppose so.'

'And another thing, Max.' Oxley's voice was cautious. 'Don't try and avoid your father all the time. When you're not actually on duty you scuttle off to your cabin like a hunted dog. You can't run away for ever.'

Colquhoun seemed to jerk himself out of his thoughts. 'Just stay out of my affairs, will you? How the hell can you know what it's been like for me? Do you know what he said to me when he came aboard?' He was starting to shout. 'Well, *do* you?'

Oxley eyed him coolly. 'Tell me, if it makes you feel better!'

'He said that he was surprised I had lasted so long without killing someone! He told me that he had let his judgement as a father overrule his duty for once and that he had managed to hush up any official enquiry!' He stared at Oxley's serious features. 'Can you imagine that? You'd think I killed Archer to spite him!' His eyes suddenly flooded with tears. 'My God, he wants to get his ounce of suffering out of me!'

Oxley looked away, unaccountably embarrassed. 'Pull yourself together! If it's any consolation, I don't hold much brief for the admiral either.' He shrugged. 'But, like God, he's always with us nowadays.' He became suddenly serious. 'And try to think of the men under you, Max. They're not bloody puppets. They're human beings! Right now most of them don't know if they're on their arse or their elbow. It only needs the officers to start bickering and the whole outfit will come apart at the seams!'

Colquhoun wiped his face with his sleeve. 'Well, that doesn't apply to me, thank God. Hardly anyone ever speaks to me now, let alone listens to what I have to say!'

Oxley said sharply, 'Well, go and have a lie down. I'm taking over the watch, so do as I say!'

He slammed through the door, and Colquhoun leaned back against the cool bulkhead, his eyes tightly closed. Why couldn't he be like Oxley? Never ruffled, always self-assured. He had tried so hard to be different from his father's mould, to believe that his own outlook could be transferred into a life he had been too timid to reject. Now, before his eyes, his whole personality seemed to be disintegrating into shame and failure.

By failing to conform to the old and tried codes of wardroom life he had built up a barrier between himself and his contemporaries which he seemed helpless to dislodge. Even Luard who shared his cabin had changed towards him. Whenever they were in the cabin together Luard was either asleep or quick to find an excuse for leaving.

He had tried to use understanding and friendship in his handling of the men, and that too had turned sour. It was as if they mistook friendship for weakness and incompetence.

It was strange that the one person he could talk to was now avoiding him, too. Lightfoot, the boy from the Battersea slums, must be too proud to be soiled by any sort of relationship with him!

Overhead the tannoy squawked, 'Senior hands of messes muster for rum. Damage-control parties will exercise at 1430.'

Colquhoun pounded his fist against the steel door. That's right, he groaned. Carry on as if nothing had ever happened. Routine and drill. Calm, stupid normality, no matter what disaster is waiting for us!

There was a step on the ladder and Lightfoot stood beside him, an enamel jug of tea in his hands. He stared fixedly at Colquhoun's face and then laid the jug carefully on the deck.

'Are you feeling all right, sir?'

Colquhoun could not speak, any more than he could control the stinging tears in his eyes which made Lightfoot swim like a mirage.

The boy fumbled in his pocket and brought out a watch. It was a large, old-fashioned one with a thick chain. He was speaking quickly and urgently, as if he could not control the flow of words. 'I forgot to give you this, sir.' He held it out. 'The mate of the *Malange* gave it to me when we fished him out of the water. It belonged to the ship's captain.' He clicked open the back of the watch and added breathlessly, 'It's got the ship's name and the date it was launched engraved on it!' He pushed it into Colquhoun's limp hands. 'The mate wanted you to have it, sir. He said you tried to save his ship. Tried to help.' He dropped his eyes and ended, 'So you did, too!'

Colquhoun stared blindly at the watch. When he spoke his voice was unsteady, like a stranger's. 'You're lying, Lightfoot.' He saw the boy looking at the watch, his eyes wretched. 'He gave it to you for looking after him when he was brought aboard. The doctor told me about it.' His arm moved again to wipe his face. 'Here, take it.'

Lightfoot stared at him with sudden defiance. 'Well, I want you to have it!' He looked around him with something like hatred. 'Christ, you deserve something after what you've been through!' He snatched up the jug and reached for the door. 'I *want* you to have it, see?'

Colquhoun walked slowly away, the watch grasped in his hand like a talisman.

Behind him in the open doorway, Lightfoot watched him go,

his lip trembling with anger and emotion. You poor bastard. It's not your fault. It's mine. You tried to help me, and I'm letting you suffer like this!

The petty officer called, 'Come on, lad. Chop, chop! Let's have the bloody tea then!'

From his seat at the rear of the compartment Oxley watched the boy's face, and wondered.

• • •

'I believe you wanted to see me, sir?' Jermain closed the wardroom door behind him and watched the admiral warily. Sir John Colquhoun was seated at the table, his jacket unbuttoned, as he pored over a collection of charts and written reports. He was wearing glasses, which gave him a deceptively human appearance.

'Ah yes, Jermain. Come and sit down.'

Jermain eased himself into a chair, the sudden immobility reminding him of his tiredness, of his complete disappointment. Another full day had dragged past since he had addressed his officers in this wardroom, a day of sudden hope and equally sudden despair. The sonar crew had obtained a solid contact during the night, and all the strain and concentration of the slow search had given way to something like excitement. But the contact had proved to be false. An old forgotten wreck, unmarked on the chart, probably a victim of the Second World War.

So the search had continued as before. A crawling examination of the Wantsai Valley, back and forth, with the mean course taking them slowly towards the end of the deep water. Towards the coast.

Sir John removed his glasses and pinched the bridge of his nose. 'It seems to me that our search will be in vain. Sooner or later we will have to turn and retrace our way back to base.' He sighed deeply. 'But I suppose that a negative search is just as final as reporting a few scraps of wreckage. In the end it might be better for all concerned.'

He leafed through a pile of aerial photographs. 'Now these were taken by the American reconnaisssance at regular intervals after the *Pyramus* was reported out of contact.' He grimaced.

'Of course they're not much use, the planes fly umpteen miles up to avoid interference. But they do show that the whole area was free of shipping. Apart from fishing boats and so forth.' He eyed Jermain with a slight smile. 'I suppose you still think that the fishing boats had something to do with all this?'

Jermain replied, 'I think it's very possible, sir. There's too much coincidence for comfort. When we were on the exercise off Hainan Island there were fishing boats present. Again where the *Malange* was sunk.' His jaw tightened defiantly. 'It's all we have to go on anyway.'

The admiral leaned back and regarded him calmly. 'I know how you feel, Jermain. You want to prove the boat, to make a place for her in the present situation.' He tapped the table. 'Well, so do I. I've been working for nothing else, in spite of government interference and the American efforts to squeeze us out of the Far East. But the facts of this missing submarine are more obvious. It seems hardly likely that a Polaris boat would be in danger from a lot of Chinese fishermen!'

'We still have to find the *Pyramus*, sir.' It was a stupid comment, but Jermain felt he had to say something if only to check himself. The admiral was goading him. Enjoying every aspect of this hopeless search.

Jermain wanted to ask him openly whether he had done anything to prevent Conway from sailing into an arena which he must have known to be potentially dangerous, or if he ever thought beyond the bounds of his own personal advancement.

The admiral wagged one finger. 'It's been over five days now. Even if the *Pyramus* survived one disaster, it is unlikely that the crew is in any shape to save itself.' He shook his head sadly. 'I know how you feel about it, Jermain. Just as we all feel.'

Jermain stood up, sick of the admiral's smooth words and thinly veiled hypocrisy. 'I must get back to the chart-room, sir.'

'Just one more thing, Jermain. It's not really my direct concern, of course, but I think your officers are beginning to doubt the necessity of all this care. You've done your best, *and* we've shown the Americans what that best can be.'

Jermain stared at him with sudden pity. That's all you care, he thought. Impress the Americans, and prove to the world that everything is as it was, and will always remain so.

Sir John continued, 'Now take Conway, for instance. He was

not only mistaken about the Far East situation, he was entirely *wrong*. But then you and I know that you can't make national leaders overnight, any more than you can expect a lower-deck rating to transform himself into a good officer.'

Jermain looked away. Don't answer him. Don't allow yourself to be drawn by his remarks.

He answered coldly, 'That is rather a generalisation, surely?' He cursed himself as the admiral gave a small smile.

'I think not. And if you had remembered this small fact I feel that things might have been different for you and the *Temeraire*.' He shrugged as if it was unimportant now. 'This commission has certainly done little for my son, or the two members of your crew who have died.'

Jermain felt the colour stinging his cheeks, but as he opened his mouth to reply the telephone buzzed at his side.

'Captain speaking!' His voice was unnecessarily sharp, and he heard Mayo say cautioulsy, 'Sonar have just reported some faint H.E. on green four five, sir. Sounds like several small fishing boats.'

Jermain felt suddenly calm. 'Why fishing boats?'

Mayo sounded vague. 'They heard that bleeping sound again, sir. You remember the fish-buoys off Hainan Island?'

Jermain dropped the handset. 'I must go to the control room, sir.'

The admiral stared at his impassive face. 'Well? What is it now?'

'The fish-buoys again, sir. I'm going up to periscope depth.'

The admiral looked uneasy. 'Aren't you taking a bit of a risk?'

'But you said you thought the fishing boats had nothing to do with all this, sir.' Jermain kept his features expressionless. 'I'll take full responsibility.'

The admiral watched him go. Aloud he said to the empty wardroom, 'You certainly will, Jermain. That I promise you!'

• • •

The atmosphere in the control room was tense. Only the men at the controls seemed normal and absorbed in their duties. The others stood in silence watching Jermain beside the periscope.

Mayo said quietly, 'The nearest vessels are about seven miles away, sir. Of course there may be some others just drifting without engines.'

A petty officer reported, 'No more fish-buoy transmissions, sir.'

They think I'm mad, Jermain thought. He could see several off-duty officers standing beyond the bulkhead door and the sick-berth attendant in his white smock like a watchful ghost.

'Sixty feet, sir.'

Jermain glanced at the clock. Both hands were overlapping and he screwed up his eyes to withstand the glare of the midday sun. 'Up periscope.' He gestured as the air hissed sharply. 'Slowly! Raise it *slowly*!'

He saw the lenses shimmering in distorted green light, and then with a quiet flurry the periscope broke surface. The water was like glass, flat and oily. The sun was hidden by haze-like clouds, so that the sea and sky were bright, yet without colour.

He swung the handles very slowly, his eyes becoming accustomed to the glare even as the first of the distant boats swam across the lenses. For a moment he felt another pang of disappointment. It was just a ragged fishing fleet. Like a thousand others which moved like hungry vagrants in search of food and life.

Jermain said, 'Seem to be about fifty or more. Moving slowly to the north.' He watched some black smoke billow down from one of the boats and hang above the sea like a stain.

He moved the handles to full power and swung the periscope a few more degrees. The boats were well scattered, like flotsam on the flat water. They were moving so slowly that only the occasional spash of foam beneath a stern gave any hint of motion.

Mayo asked, 'Shall I lay off an alteration of course to avoid them, sir?'

Jermain did not answer. The billowing black smoke had moved away slightly, caught in a hot down draught of air. He blinked his eyes rapidly and stared again. He made himself stay quite still, holding his breath, hardly daring to speak as one of the distant boats altered course and moved across his sights. Even at this range there was no mistaking that business-like hull and the high-raked stem.

He slammed back the handles. 'Down periscope. Take her

down to two hundred feet.' He walked quickly to the chart-room. 'Bring me the intelligence pack again!' Mayo followed him, mystified, but Jermain concentrated on his racing thoughts.

It had been right there all the time. He had guessed the most unlikely part, but the obvious facts had been staring him in the face.

He snatched the thick folio from the messenger and pulled the aerial photographs on to the table. 'Give me a pin!'

Nobody moved. They were all staring at him.

With a grunt Jermain snatched the brass dividers and bent over the blurred photographs. As his eyes moved carefully across the scattered shapes he said, 'Now, in nearly all these photographs we can see a collection of fishing boats, right?'

Mayo said, 'Is it the same lot, sir?'

'I think so.' He closed his eyes and tried to picture the scene as he had just seen it through the periscope. 'Roughly the same number anyway.' He pushed the sharp point of the dividers into one of the tiny shapes on the first photograph. 'It was here all the time.' He made another small hole in a second shape, and then a third.

Then he held up the photograph against the chart light, so that the small lamp cast a glow through his three minute holes. It was a perfect triangle.

Mayo said awkwardly, 'I still don't see . . .'

'Neither did I, Pilot!' He took another photograph. 'Look at this one. The same three boats, larger than all the other ones, and in the same position as before.' He squinted at the numbers across the margin. 'Yet this one was taken *one hour* after the first!' He stared round, aware for the first time that the place had filled with watching figures. He said, 'Check each picture, and I think you will find that in every one there appears to be a distinct pattern. Three larger boats of the type I have just seen through the periscope. Of the type which went out to meet the *Malange*.' He saw Wolfe standing silently in the doorway. 'Of the type which fired on us and killed Lieutenant Victor!'

Drew stood beside the chart, an electric razor still grasped in one hand. 'You think there's a connection, sir?'

Jermain watched Mayo's fingers prodding the dividers into another photograph. 'I've never been more sure. The fishing-buoys, everything, it all fits.'

Mayo straightened his back and nodded. 'The pattern is in all of them, sir. The same three boats are steering in a fixed triangle, and as far as I can make out they're about eight miles apart.'

Jermain said, 'The fish-buoys were a blind. It's my guess they are really some sort of variable depth sonar of an advanced type. By lowering them down through the isothermal barrier they are far more effective than any sort of detection device carried by surface craft. In a place like the Wantsai Valley they are doubly efficient. By relaying cross-bearings to one another, these ships could find and hold even a deep-running submarine.' He looked at Mayo. 'And in the confines of the Valley a damaged submarine would be incapable of avoiding them!'

'So we weren't so stupid after all, sir. The bastards must have been having a dummy-run off Hainan?'

'Something like that.' Jermain felt the excitement stirring his insides. 'The idea is not new, as you know. But out here, in these confined waters, it could be more than effective. It could be fatal!'

He glanced at his watch. 'But whatever they did to the *Pyramus*, they were only half successful. I think they are doing exactly what we are trying to do.' He looked around their faces. 'So it's up to us to find her before they do!'

Wolfe spoke for the first time. 'So what do you intend to do?'

'Take a chance, Number One. We have no other choice.' He leaned over the chart. 'We'll dive to maximum depth and then increase speed to by-pass this search party. Then we'll head direct to the plateau mentioned in the American folio. If the *Pyramus* is anywhere, she *has* to be there.'

Mayo was scribbling rapidly in his logbook. 'What depth, sir?'

Jermain looked directly at Wolfe's set face. 'Nine hundred feet, Pilot.' He continued looking at Wolfe. 'Inform the admiral, Number One. He will want to know what is happening.'

Mayo snapped his book shut. 'That's the deepest yet, sir.' He sounded calm enough, but his eyes were fixed to the chart. He added, 'At the school they said that at this sort of depth it was the same as having a fully loaded car on every square inch of the hull!'

Drew said dryly, 'Shouldn't think there are many cars down there, Pilot!'

Jermain glanced at the curving side to the chart-room and tried to imagine the black water beyond. Then he said sharply, 'Send the hands to action stations.'

As the alarm shattered the boat's silence Jermain walked slowly into the control room. On the strength of his own driving belief, and three pin holes in a blurred photograph, he was committing the *Temeraire* and ninety lives.

Throughout the hull these same men were running quietly to their stations, only half aware of what was happening.

Jermain thought suddenly of the only possible alternative, and dismissed the danger from his mind.

15

A Matter of Trust

WOLFE SAT bolt upright in his steel chair behind the helmsman, his eyes unwinking as he watched the depth gauges. How slowly they seemed to creep round, he thought. Down, down. Yet the slender needles appeared to have no connection with reality or the enfolding world outside the hull.

'Six hundred feet, sir.' The rating's voice was hushed, like a visitor in a church, but Wolfe hardly noticed him. His mind and brain were completely controlled and devoid of doubt or uncertainty. Everything around him was clear and crisp, like familiar objects on a bright winter's morning, and his whole body seemed to tingle with excitement.

He checked the slow smile as it spread across his face, and peered intently at the gyro repeater. The tranquilisers were having their effect. He felt like a different person. He thought momentarily of Griffin's earlier unwillingness to supply his needs, and the ease and simplicity with which he had obtained a large packet of pills from the American depot ship just prior to sailing. Like everything else about the Americans, he thought. Slapdash and careless. A bored pharmacist's mate had merely glanced at his uniform and muttered, 'Sign here,' and that was that.

'Seven hundred feet, sir.'

Wolfe took a glance around the control room. The cut-out figures of the men on watch, each wrapped in his own thoughts. The admiral's stocky shape beside the door, his pale eyes swivelling between Jermain and the gauges.

Wolfe allowed his gaze to rest on Jermain's tall figure. He was standing in the centre of the control room, his legs slightly apart, his shoulders hunched as if to test the weight of his command. His face was calm but watchful, and Wolfe could see a nerve jumping very slightly at the corner of his mouth. He's worried, he thought. Like all the rest of them.

'Eight hundred feet, sir.'

Twine, the coxswain, mouthed a silent curse as the metal frames above the control panel groaned as if from pain. Every foot of water added to the pressure, each agonising minute brought some new strain to the hull and men alike.

The intercom said briefly, 'No further contact with surface craft, sir.'

Jermain said quietly, 'Increase to fifteen knots. Steer three zero zero.'

Twine moved the horseshoe-shaped wheel very slightly in his hands, and at his side the planesman took a moment to dash the sweat from his eyes.

The air was damp and clammy, so that the atmosphere felt dank, like a tomb. Every unnecessary fan had been switched off to make the boat as silent as possible, yet Wolfe was unmoved and inwardly scornful of the shining faces around him.

There was a sharp crack, followed by a long-drawn-out humming which echoed along the hull structure like a tin roof shaking in a high wind. Over the open intercom Wolfe heard a man cry out, and behind him the young signalman whispered, 'Jesus Christ!'

'Nine hundred feet, sir.' The rating sounded dazed.

There was another long quiver, and a few flakes of paint floated down from the curved deckhead.

Jermain said, 'Check all compartments.'

The men at the voice-pipes and telephones stirred themselves unwillingly, as if afraid that their ears might miss something.

Mayo called, 'Next alteration, sir. Steer three one zero.'

Wolfe sat back in his chair and watched the controls. Not long now. In his brain he could hear the dull thuds as the torpedoes left the tubes. The distant searing explosions as they found the crippled submarine. He looked quickly at Jermain. He could hardly wait to see his face when the inevitable happened. The good, patient friend, David Jermain, who all this time, over the months of agony and suspense, had aided Sarah in her plans, had secretly sided with her and her bloody American!

He had almost given himself away when the officer from the *Pyramus* had let the cat out of the bag. Somehow he had managed to keep his face calm, perhaps because he already knew half of Jermain's secret.

Now it was almost a pleasure just to sit and watch each moment as it arrived. Two birds with one stone, and what could be more just, or more final? Sarah's lover destroyed by the man in whom she had confided against *him*.

He watched Jermain answering one of the telephones. All his cunning could not help him now. Sucking up to Conway and seducing his daughter had come to no purpose. In addition he had made a bad enemy of the admiral by sticking up for his useless son. The thought of Colquhoun brought back the memory of that night in his cabin with such suddenness that he felt a quiver of blind rage through him. The bloody insolence of it! And the incredible insult which followed when Jermain refused to take his part against that stupid, gutless little queer!

Jermain said to the admiral, 'The chief has reported some seepage aft, sir. But we're three hundred feet deeper than the last time. I think it'll be all right after all.'

The admiral grunted, 'It's a good time to remember it!'

Wolfe frowned. He remembered the admiral sitting at the table when he had gone to tell him of Jermain's intentions. The admiral had said, 'Well, if he's right about these ships it looks like putting a seal on the *Pyramus*'s fate.'

Then Wolfe had asked, 'My next appointment, sir.' He had tried to sound matter-of-fact. 'When will it be confirmed, do you think?'

The admiral had been evasive. 'It's not for me to say, Number One. Your commanding officer's personal report will carry a good deal of weight. If it's unfavourable,' he had fixed Wolfe with a flat stare, 'then of course that might well be the end of the matter for you. Of course, it can go either way. If a commanding officer is discredited in any manner,' he had shrugged, 'your case might be considered in a different light.'

Wolfe balled his hands into tight fists. The admiral had been passing him a warning. It was obvious. Jermain had not been content to deceive him and drive a wedge between himself and Sarah. No, he had to ruin his career, too! He gritted his teeth until his jaw ached. Well, nothing could help Jermain's plans any more. In a short while he would be discredited by his own eagerness.

Whatever the official report might say, Jermain would be remembered as the man who destroyed an American submarine. That, plus Conway's death and his conflict with the admiral, would finish the destruction.

He glared sideways at Mayo. You'll change your tune, too! He tried to picture the faces of the officers when they all knew what Jermain was going to do.

The navigating officer said, 'We shall be up to the plateau in seventy-five minutes, sir. If you raise her to one hundred feet we can commence the search immediately.' He looked worn out from his continued calculations.

The admiral muttered, 'I hope you're right about all this, Jermain. With those A/S ships coming up astern, I want to find the *Pyramus* quickly and get it over with.' He dropped his voice still further. 'Do you wish me to tell the ship's company what we have to do?'

Jermain gave a small smile. 'I think not, sir. After all, we don't yet know, do we?'

Wolfe moved restlessly in his seat. Go on, my friend. Try and wriggle off this one. There's no one to blame, and nobody to help you now. You are competely alone!

• • •

Jermain peered down across Mayo's shoulder at the criss-crossing pencilled lines on the chart. It was nearly two hours since the deep dive to avoid the bogus fishing boats, yet the searching sonar had recorded nothing. With the sureness of a whale the *Temeraire* had planed up from the incredible pressure of the deep valley, her hull seeming to quiver with relief as she crossed the steep-sided cliffs on to the plateau.

Suppose the *Pyramus* had limped further north, seeking escape in the futility of the shallow coastal waters? It was too late to try another area. The bleeping buoys would be swaying through the dark water, like the sticks of blind men in an enclosed room.

Mayo said gruffly, 'There's still a chance, sir.' His pencil made another small cross. 'But this is about our limit. We're within twenty miles of the coast right now.'

Jermain nodded. 'I know. Thank God it's pretty desolate hereabouts. Just a small town over there. All the same, I'll bet they've alerted all the local patrols.'

Mayo yawned. 'It's amazing to think we're here like this. With some useless strip of coast and a whole pile of people intent on killing us if we even show our little fingers above the surface. Why the hell don't we just declare war and be done with it?'

Griffin was standing just inside the door, his face deep in thought. He said, 'That's the stuff, Pilot. Us against the rest. The Good Guys against the Bad Ones!'

The admiral brushed past him, his features lined with irritation. 'Anything new, Jermain?'

'Not yet, sir.'

'For God's sake, there's not much time.' The admiral glared at the chart. 'We'll just have to clear the area if we can't make contact in the next hour.'

Mayo said, 'The A/S boats are coming straight up the Wantsai Valley, sir. Strung out like they are, they can flush out any submarine in their path, or so they seem to hope. The *Pyramus* could either try to avoid the sweep and risk running foul of the steep sides of the Valley. Or she could go ahead of them and get driven into shallow water. Either way, if she's damaged, her chances are pretty small.'

The admiral swung round. 'I'm quite aware of that, Mr. Mayo! Although why you or anyone else should imagine the *Pyramus* is still afloat is quite beyond me!' He looked at Jermain coldly. '*One* hour, Jermain.'

The intercom crackled, 'Contact, sir! Bearing green two zero, range four thousand yards!' A pause, and then Oxley added firmly, 'It's stationary, sir. Definitely the *Pyramus*!'

The admiral said, 'How can he be so damn sure?'

But Jermain was already in the control room, his voice crisp and urgent. 'Start plotting. Alter course and follow sonar. Slow ahead!'

He felt flushed, but his forehead when he wiped it was damp and cold. It must be the *Pyramus*. It had to be.

Mayo reported, 'Course three three zero, sir.' He glanced at the gauges. 'Depth now one hundred and fifty feet.'

'Keep her at that. I want to get as close as I can.' To the radio supervisor he said, 'Start calling her up on the acoustic radio. Keep calling her codename until I tell you otherwise.'

Harris's voice sounded heavy. 'Hello SUNRAY. Hello SUNRAY. This is BLUEBOY. Are you receiving me? Over!'

The minutes dragged by as the *Temeraire* moved slowly along the bearing.

Harris readjusted his headphones. 'No reply, sir.'

Jermain snapped, 'Keep trying! Just keep calling her!'

'Range now two thousand yards, sir.' Oxley cleared his throat, the sound rasping round the control room like a thunderclap.

Sir John Colquhoun played with the peak of his cap. 'Tell Oxley to keep a constant watch for the ships too, Jermain. They may have increased speed. I don't want to be caught napping!'

Jermain ignored him. The dim hope he had been feeling was slowly giving way to sick apprehension. Try as he might he could not blot out the mental picture of the American submarine with its crew members lying or lolling at their controls, dead even as they waited for help which could never come.

'Range one thousand yards, sir.'

Harris looked round, his face taut and pale. 'Maybe their set is smashed, sir?'

Wolfe eased himself in his chair. 'It's no use. They're finished!'

Jermain glanced at him. 'We'll do another circuit, Number One.'

Wolfe shrugged and said calmly, 'Give me a course, Pilot.'

'Hello SUNRAY, do you read me? This is BLUEBOY.' Harris's voice was getting hoarse, and his constant repetition sounded like an epitaph.

The admiral said sharply, 'It's hopeless, Jermain.' He

appeared to have difficulty in keeping his voice down. 'You're just putting off the inevitable. You must realise that.' He glanced at the clock. 'You must haul off and put some distance between us and the *Pyramus*. Even allowing for the missiles being set at safe, there will be one hell of an explosion.'

Jermain felt trapped. Around him he could see the waiting men watching him. Perhaps they guessed what was going to happen. He replied, 'Just a bit longer, sir. We must make sure!'

The admiral regarded him curiously. 'I believe that the skipper is your brother-in-law, Jermain? I know it's not easy for you.' He looked across at Wolfe. 'If you like, I could give the responsibility to the first lieutenant?'

Jermain turned away, sickened. 'Stand by to alter course to zero four five.' He forced himself to add, 'Tell Lieutenant Drew to prepare tubes One and Two for firing.'

Wolfe said quietly, 'I'll tell the hands to stand by for your announcement, sir. You'll want to tell them now, I expect?' His eyes shone like bright stones. 'It'll be something they'll remember!'

Oxley reported, 'We are now passing the *Pyramus*, sir. Abeam to port, one thousand yards. She's about eighty feet below our level of approach.'

Jermain felt the blood pumping through his veins, fogging his mind and vision, blotting out all else but the picture of the *Temeraire*'s smooth shape passing the other submarine. Her slow backwash would reach out and caress the other hull, like a final salute.

The admiral said, 'Carry on, Jermain. You can pull away and fire when you're ready. We can't wait any longer. These are British sailors. I'll not have them involved in more than this specific duty!'

Drew's voice said, 'Bows doors open, sir. One and Two ready!'

Jermain made himself walk to the chart-room where Wolfe had laid the public address handset on the table. He stared down blindly at the chart with its hopeful calculations and wasted efforts. But instead he saw Sarah's face and heard her last words, 'Bring him back to me, David!' And Jill, relaxed in sleep as he had leaned across her body to answer that telephone.

He picked up the handset. 'This is the captain speaking.' He saw the admiral's shoulders relax slightly and watched his quick interchange of glances with Wolfe.

'Hold it, sir!' Harris swung in his chair. 'For God's sake!' He turned his tuning dial, all else forgotten but the sudden wave of static on his speaker.

The voice seemed to come from a long way off. Very small and tired. 'This is SUNRAY. I am receiving you BLUEBOY.' There was a break and the voice continued, 'My God, I must be dreaming!'

Jermain said, 'Close the range, Pilot! Bring her round two points to port!' He strode to Harris's side. 'Here, give me the handset, Chief!'

He spoke very slowly. 'This is BLUEBOY. There is not much time. Just give me your exact position.'

This time it was a different voice, familiar in spite of the static. Jermain could picture him beside the cot looking down at the child, and wondered what sort of hell he had been suffering for these long, waiting days.

'We dived deep to avoid a fishing fleet. There was an explosion, maybe from a single depth-charge. Damage was sustained in the engine room when a salt-water inlet pipe was partially fractured.' He was speaking in sharp, staccato sentences. 'There was also some damage to the sail and the diving planes. Speed was reduced and we could not run deep to avoid further contact with the enemy.' He laughed bitterly. 'Whoever that was!'

Jermain said, 'Can you move?'

'We have been carrying out repairs lying here on the bottom. We had to shut down the reactor to repair the cooling system and the fractured inlet pipe. We will have to use our batteries to restart the reactor, and as you know we can't use our diesel generator submerged. It will take every drop of juice in every reserve battery to get it going. I've tried to cut down everything to save power. There's no ventilation, and every other bit of machinery is off, too. The engine-room crew have been working without a break. Before the reactor cooled they were in a temperature of over one hundred and forty degrees.' He added harshly, 'Six of them are dead.'

Jermain's mind was working like a precision drill. 'How long before you can start up?' He made his voice calmer. 'There is a strong force of anti-submarine craft sweeping up the Valley right now.'

'Christ! I'd have run slap into them!' He paused. 'Give me eight hours. I can probably get "airbone" by then. My speed will still be down to less than ten knots because of the outside damage. But when you've been fighting to stay alive, that seems a helluva lot!'

Jermain saw the admiral's quick shake of the head. He knew what he was thinking. Eight hours. Even half that time would have been too long. The sonar buoys would sniff the *Pyramus* out long before that.

Jermain said quickly, 'Harris, connect this microphone to the public address system. I want the whole crew to hear it!' He turned back to the microphone. 'You will have to blow right up to the surface, right?'

'That's it. I'll run up the snort and start my generators. That will see us back to base okay.' His voice became suddenly tired. 'Who are we kidding? The Reds'll be here before I can get away. You can't fight them all on your own. It was just a last crazy hope, but by God I won't let the bastards take us or our ship!'

His words came back from the *Temeraire*'s hull like an echo. In the torpedo space where the men waited beside the spare torpedoes, in the silent radio room, and amongst the gleaming machinery of the engine room, the men sat or stood listening to the American captain's voice.

Jermain made up his mind. 'I think I can give you those eight hours, John. Nobody knows about us yet. It's just you they're after.' He deliberately turned his back on the admiral's grim features. 'For the next eight hours I will become you. The bait. When I've led the search away from the area you must pull out all the stops and get the hell out of here. By the time they realise what's happened you should be clear enough from the patrol area to whistle up air cover. Now, have you got that?'

He waited, his heart pounding against his ribs.

Hurtzig's voice was muffled. 'Received it loud and clear. I wish you could see my boys, David. I wish I knew how to speak for all of us.'

Jermain said quickly, 'Later will do. Just you get cracking at your end and don't pay any attention to us. It'll be getting dark up top soon, so you should be able to finish your battery charging in safety once the sea's clear.'

The static was beginning to fade out the other man's voice. 'Until the next time, David. Maybe I'll have the right words by then. Over and out.'

The admiral seized his arm and whispered fiercely, 'What the devil do you think you're doing? Do you know what you're saying, man?'

Jermain handed the microphone to Harris and then paused as a ragged burst of cheering echoed over the intercom. He met the admiral's angry stare. 'As you remarked earlier, sir. These are British sailors. I didn't think they'd want to run away and leave men to die.' His tone hardened. 'Any more than they would want to kill them themselves!'

Sir John stared from his face to the microphone. 'So that's why you let the men listen! You deliberately invoked their sympathy!'

Jermain said evenly, 'If you will excuse me, sir.'

The intercom crackled to life. 'Faint hydrophone effect, bearing green one one zero, sir!'

The admiral's face went pale. 'You see! They're here already, you fool!'

Oxley continued, 'Single screw, sir. Maybe small diesel craft.'

Jermain nodded. 'We must take a look. Periscope depth, Number One. Starboard fifteen. Steer three zero zero.' He made himself take time to look at the admiral again. 'Look, sir, if I've done wrong I'll be ready to face the consequences. But my orders,' he paused, '*our* orders were to find and render assistance to the *Pyramus*. We've done the first bit. Now we can carry out the rest. Neither my orders nor the traditions of the Service allow for either cowardice or brutality, sir!'

The admiral followed him into the chart-room. 'How dare you speak to me like that!'

Jermain pulled out a fresh chart. 'Since we are alone, sir, I will just say this. I believe quite sincerely that you intended to destroy the *Pyramus* with or without waiting for her crew to make some effort to escape. She was too deep for her men to get to the surface, and in any case we might not have found them with a tide running. There was in your mind only the one alternative.' He stared hard at the admiral's stricken face. 'Well, I can't see it that way, sir. And if I'm required to answer to a court martial, I will be prepared to state these views.'

A voice called, 'Sixty feet, sir!'

Jermain continued relentlessly, 'No notice was taken of my earlier reports. They were shelved, in case we were "laughed at" by the Americans. No effort was made to understand the requirements and possible uses of my command in these waters, with the result we were operating in shallow water when the *Malange* was sunk.' His voice became scathing. 'My God, a frigate would have been better employed!' He strode away, suddenly aware what the strain and anxiety had cost him.

When he stooped beside the periscope he saw that the admiral was still standing beside the chart, like a man in a state of shock.

'Up periscope.' He sung it on to the bearing and waited for the lens to clear. The cloud was thicker and lower, and already the sea was patchy with dark shadows.

Oxley's voice called, 'The ship has stopped her engine, sir!'

Jermain stared at the small fishing boat which hovered in his cross-wires like a trapped insect. Even as Oxley finished speaking he saw the splash of white at her blunt bow as she dropped anchor and then swung easily on the calm water. Someone was hosting a riding light, its brightness telling Jermain how quickly the night was closing in.

'Down periscope.' He rubbed his chin. 'It's a small motor fishing boat. No more than fifty feet. Just dropped anchor about half a mile away.'

Mayo said, 'Well, she's not much danger.' He looked darkly at the admiral's motionless shape. 'Not the bloody Red Fleet after all!'

Jermain shook his head. 'I got a good look at her. She's anchored for the night, in my opinion, and she has a radio mast!' He looked at Wolfe's slumped shoulders. 'If *Pyramus* surfaces nearby, even for a second, that fisherman will scream it to the world!'

Mayo asked, 'What will we do, sir? Time's running out fast!'

Jermain smiled grimly. 'I'm aware of that, Pilot!' He stared at the sheathed periscopes. 'It will be dark within half an hour. Dark enough anyway.'

Mayo looked mystified. 'For what, sir?'

'We'll surface and board that fishing boat. We can launch the Gemini dinghy and have some men aboard before they've got their boiled fish on the plates!' He walked across to the plot table, speaking his thoughts aloud. 'She might come in handy. The boarding party can stay behind and make sure the *Pyramus* surfaces all right. If anything fouls up they can pick up survivors. And *we* can be getting on with our part of the operation!' The lines seemed to fade from his face and he appeared almost boyish. 'What do you think of that?'

Mayo's teeth shone through his black beard. 'I'll go across, sir. I'll make a good pirate.'

'Not on, Pilot. You're too valuable here.' He touched his arm. 'But thanks for the show of faith. It may come in handy at my court martial!'

Mayo frowned. 'With all respect, sir, that's a load of crap! If we pull this off, the admiral will be in there reaping the credit.' He shrugged. 'And if we don't, we'll be otherwise engaged and past caring!'

Jermain became serious again. 'Number One, I shall want the dinghy prepared for launching. Fall out the torpedo party and use them. I shall need two officers and four ratings. That should be enough. There won't be more than half a dozen fishermen aboard that tub.'

Wolfe turned and stared at him stonily. He seemed suddenly spent and exhausted, as if the fire was drained out of him. '*Two* officers?'

Jermain snapped, 'Up periscope.' As he took another quick look at the anchored boat he added, 'Yes, Number One. Just in case of accidents, I want someone in charge.'

There was a clatter from forward as the dinghy was manhandled below the main hatch.

He signalled for the periscope to be lowered and continued slowly, 'Colquhoun can take the boarders, but I want *you* in charge. If anything goes wrong when *Pyramus* bounces up it will need someone with real experience to make decisions on the spot.' He eyed him calmly. 'All right?'

Wolfe faced him without a flicker of emotion. 'Is that an order?'

'It's the obvious solution, Number One. When I have headed

off the submarine chasers I'll come back for you. If anything goes wrong you can find your own way south east and make contact with friendly forces. Everybody will be too busy looking for us to bother with just one more fishing boat.'

Wolfe glanced casually around the boat. 'And I'm to take Colquhoun. That makes it just about perfect!' He added, 'You're certainly quick to get rid of the bad apples!'

Lieutenant Drew clattered through the open hatch. 'Torpedo party fallen out, sir. Tubes secure.' He glanced quickly between them and added guardedly, 'What now?'

Wolfe picked up his cap. 'I'm leaving.'

He walked calmly away towards the petty officer who had been mustering the small boarding party.

Jermain said heavily, 'Take over from the first lieutenant in the control room. We will continue to circle the fisherman until it gets dark.'

The Australian lifted one eybrow. 'Number One seems a bit odd?'

'He's tired, that's all.' Jermain stared at Wolfe's shadow beyond the door. If only there was some way of regaining contact with him. Perhaps later there might be time.

Something Sarah had told him when he had tried to question her came into his mind. She had said, 'He seemed to change overnight. He never trusted me, and when I tried to share his problems he just shut himself off. Sometimes he frightened me, David.'

It was odd when you thought about it. Each submarine officer was trained and vetted from every possible angle. At each step in his career he was inspected and reported upon, checked for suitability until his seniority and usefulness put him beyond the reach of the training staff and the would-be medical experts.

Wolfe had been an excellent officer, and as far as his duty was concerned he still was. Yet his very soul was being gnawed away from within. One day it would destroy his outer shell, and when that happened he might well become unsafe, a real danger to those who depended on his judgment.

A perfectly normal officer had been known to crack under the demanding strain of submarine life, when nothing untoward might ever have occurred if he had stayed in conventional craft.

Drew was saying, 'My new cobber, Lieutenant Trott, can take over the tubes then.' He chuckled. 'He's eager enough anyway!'

They both turned as Colquhoun climbed over the coaming a Stirling dangling from one hand. He said urgently, 'Can I see you, sir?'

Jermain guided him into the chart-room. 'What is it?'

Mayo dropped his parallel rulers and left the compartment without a word. Then Colquhoun burst out, 'I can't do it, sir! Not again!'

Jermain waited, conscious of the ticking clock and the gentle tremble in the deck plates. 'Go on, Max. I'm still listening.'

Colquhoun swayed and then stammered, 'They don't trust me any more, sir. After what happened before. Archer's death. I'm finished, I don't even trust myself now!' He stared wretchedly at Jermain's grave face.

'*I* trust you, Max.' Jermain pointed at the chart. 'I wouldn't send you otherwise.' He remembered Wolfe's bitter 'quick to get rid of the bad apples!' He said, 'What happened to you might have happened to any of us. This new job will certainly help you later if there is any enquiry when we get home.'

Colquhoun sighed. 'I don't want to be helped. If I'm no good, I'd rather not risk any more lives!'

Jermain replied calmly, 'Everything is a risk. Right now, for instance. If I make some sort of error it will cost the lives of every man aboard, and the country will lose a twenty-million-pound boat.' He smiled quietly. 'Whereas you will be spared to tell the whole graphic account for the annals of naval history.'

Colquhoun's jaw dropped. 'But it's different for you, sir.' He struggled to find the words. 'You're the Captain. You know what to do!'

'Do I? What experience do you imagine I've had for this sort of thing, Max? The attack-table at the school, full of little models? Or exercising with a lot of friendly ships and men I've known for most of my life? No, there's no precedent for this. I am trained to use my judgement. The problems I have to face are of other men's making.' He gestured towards the deckhead. 'Like now, for instance. This submarine and the *Pyramus* are tied down by a helpless unarmed fishing boat. We can neither move nor escape without neutralising her first! Ironic, isn't it?'

Colquhoun asked quietly, 'Why are you telling me this, sir?'

'Because I want you to make an effort. Because I rely on you and every other man aboard. I'm like a fighter pilot, Max. I have to do the job I've been selected for. I must never have to ask myself about the parts of the aircraft, the accuracy of the controls. I have to rely on what I have!'

A messenger looked in. 'Mr. Drew says it's dark enough now, Captain!'

'Very good.' Jermain looked at Colquhoun's pale face. 'Forget all the old troubles for the moment. And back up the first lieutenant. He's experienced at this sort of thing, but he can't do it all alone.'

Colquhoun turned on his heel and walked back through the control room. He was only half aware of the watching eyes, the quick pat of encouragement from Drew, and Mayo's, 'You lucky bastard, Max! Yachting while we're playing tag with a lot of gooks!'

Beneath the forward hatch a group of men were checking over the bulbous inflatable dinghy with its paddles and neat outboard motor. Jeffers, the second coxswain, blocked his path, his face creased into a grin. 'I'm not coming this time, sir. Can't be spared.' He pointed at the tall leading seaman with a Stirling under his arm. 'Ted Haley will be with you though, 'e's a good 'and.' He glanced at the other three ratings with a practised eye. 'Cowley's the signalman, and Stoker Mechanic Nettle will be able to cope with the fishing boat's engine.' He darted him a quick glance. 'The other seaman is Lightfoot, sir. 'E volunteered.'

The intercom intoned. 'Stand by to surface! Bridge party close up!'

Colquhoun looked away. 'I don't want him, Jeffers! Get someone else!'

Jeffers shrugged. 'Too late now, sir. Anyway, 'e insisted like. 'E swapped over with another bloke for it!'

Colquhoun turned and made himself meet Lightfoot's gaze. The boy looked weighed down with cross-belt and ammunition, but he was smiling. He said emptily, 'Very well.' He added, 'And thanks, Jeffers, for all you've done for me. For all you've tried to do.'

Jeffers shifted uncomfortably. 'You'll be okay, sir. You see! Anyway, you was right to take this job. You're always better after the second go!'

He stepped back as Wolfe pushed amongst the group, his eyes searching over the dinghy.

He snapped, 'All ready? Grenades and Stirlings?' He tightened his belt. 'Right then. No mistakes, just do as I tell you.' He let his gaze drop on Colquhoun and he added quietly, 'And no shooting. This has to be quiet, see?' Then he smiled. 'You can't live for ever, you know!'

A bell clanged, and Jermain peered through the open door. He was wearing an oilskin and his glasses were slung round his neck.

'I'm going to move in a bit so that you can paddle over. It'll be about five minutes.' He looked at Wolfe searchingly. 'Good luck, Number One.'

Wolfe yawned. 'Thanks.' As Jermain moved back towards the ladder he called gently, 'Give my love to Sarah, will you?'

Jermain stared at him and then climbed slowly up the ladder.

The waiting men stiffened as the admiral's stocky figure filled the doorway. Without pausing he said, 'Can I speak to you a minute?'

Colquhoun looked at Wolfe. The latter said, 'Two minutes. No more!'

The admiral was waiting beyond the heavy steel door, his face in shadows.

Colquhoun asked flatly, 'Well, what is it?' His father did not reply and he added bitterly, 'I suppose you asked that I should be sent on this boarding party? Kill or cure, is that it?'

The admiral said quietly, 'I didn't know about it, Max. I really didn't.' He seemed at a loss for words. 'I just wanted to wish you luck.'

Colquhoun took a grip on himself. 'You what? Are you serious? After all the things you've said about me!' He laughed shortly. 'I'd have thought you'd have been more afraid of my tarnishing the family's name!'

The intercom droned, 'Surfacing!' And the deck gave a sudden lurch.

The admiral stepped forward and gripped his hands. The

words were tumbling out of his mouth as if he could no longer control them. 'I've been wrong, Max! I'm out of touch, I can see that now. I wanted it my way, but it was all for you, you must believe that!'

Colquhoun stared at him. His father seemed to be ageing before his eyes.

Wolfe called harshly, 'Come on, Sub! Jump about!'

He replied heavily, 'It's a bit late now.' Then he released his hands from his father's grip and stepped back to the hatch.

16

The Bait

COLQUHOUN GRIPPED the sides of the dinghy and stared fixedly at the distant riding light. In spite of the steady thrust of paddles and the heavy breathing of the four ratings behind him, the dinghy's progress seemed maddeningly slow.

It had been merely minutes since the *Temeraire* had eased herself carefully to the surface and the main hatch had been flung open. Before the spray had finished cascading on their heads the handling party had heaved the small boat up and over the side of the hull, and urgent hands had pushed Colquhoun and the others after it.

Somehow they had paddled clear, and as they steadied on a course towards the anchored fishing boat the *Temeraire*'s black shape had sidled beneath the water in a frothing welter of white spray.

Alone on the surface they had all felt suddenly unprotected and lost. It had been too quick, too violent for consideration. One minute they had been hemmed in by familiar faces, and the next instant the submarine had vanished, as if it had never been.

Wolfe wiped the spray from his face. 'Must be bloody deaf aboard that boat!'

Colquhoun did not reply. The splash and slice of each paddle sounded deafening. The slap of water against the rounded hull even louder. But aboard the fishing boat there was little sign of life, but for the swaying lantern and a thin column of smoke from her galley funnel which rose vertically across the darkening sky, like a stain on an old and faded painting.

Wolfe said, 'Right then. You know what to do. No shooting unless you have to.' His eyes gleamed in the darkness. 'Use your knives, anything, but make it quick!'

Colquhoun swallowed hard and tried to hold back the nausea. When he looked up the fishing boat was almost above him. It was no longer just a threat. It was real.

Leading Seaman Haley hurled his grapnel across the gunwale and pulled the line tight. Then with a few muffled gasps they were all up and on the deserted deck, their weapons ready and cocked.

Wolfe snapped, 'Nettle, take the wheelhouse and guard the radio. Cowley, guard the engine hatch aft!' He gestured at the others. 'Follow me!'

There was a curved hatchway just forward of the tiny wheelhouse, and as their feet thudded across the deck it was flung open and a shaft of lamplight glittered on the levelled weapons.

Wolfe barked, 'Stand still! We will shoot if we have to!' To Colquhoun he added sharply, 'Down you go with Haley. We'll cover you from here!'

Dumbly Colquhoun lowered himself down the steep ladder, his stomach retching uncontrollably. It was a small, box-like cabin, lined with crude bunks, and unbearably hot from a tall charcoal stove which glowed like a furnace. Four roughly dressed men stood in attitudes of fear and shock, and by the stove, a black pot poised in mid-air, was a plump, round-faced woman.

Colquhoun said, 'Does anyone speak English?'

Nobody answered, but as Colquhoun stared at their watching faces he was almost unnerved by a high-pitched wail from one of the bunks.

Haley said gruffly, 'Hell, it's a baby, sir. They look a pretty harmless bunch to me.'

Wolfe called down, 'Nobody's asking you! Just search them for weapons and make sure there's no other exit to this bloody pigsty!'

Haley slung his Stirling and said softly, '*I'll* do it, sir. You just keep a weather eye open.'

Colquhoun watched as the big seaman moved slowly and purposefully around the mesmerised fishermen. All the time he kept talking, empty, casual sentences, like a man with a fretful horse. Not one of the men flinched or objected as Haley ran his hands over their rough smocks and quilted jackets, and even the baby fell silent as he lifted each piece of bedding and peered underneath.

'Pongs a bit,' he remarked. 'Still, I don't suppose they notice it.' He looked at the woman. 'I think you're all right, my love.' He grinned encouragingly. 'You just get on with the cooking and forget about us!'

There was a sudden stamp of feet as Wolfe threw himself down the ladder. He pushed Haley roughly aside and barked, 'What the hell is the matter with you?' He glared accusingly at Colquhoun. 'Can't you do *anything*?'

Haley said, 'They're only ordinary fishermen, sir.'

Wolfe eyed him bleakly. 'Did you never hear about the *ordinary* peasants in Viet Nam, Haley? Or in Malaysia, and all the other tinpot places where they can manoeuvre the sympathies of soft-hearted fools like you!' He pushed the woman away from the stove and jerked open her coat. 'She might have a bloody arsenal here for all you care!'

The tallest of the fishermen, obviously the skipper of the boat, began to speak excitedly in a high-pitched twittering tone. He pulled at Wolfe's arm and tried to haul him away from the woman.

Colquhoun's eye was not quick enough to see the blow. In a split second Wolfe had drawn the pistol from his belt and brought the barrel hard across the fisherman's temple. He fell without a further sound, his blood making red diamonds on the deck planking.

Wolfe holstered his gun and snapped, 'They're clean. We'll

get back on deck and secure the hatch over this little lot.' He glanced casually at the unconscious fisherman and the woman who was trying to staunch the blood with her apron. 'Next time we'll have a little respect around here!'

Colquhoun reached the gunwale and leaned his hands on the worn woodwork. For several seconds he drew in deep breaths and allowed his taut body to relax. It was even worse than the last time. He could not forget the look on the woman's face, the dark hurt in her eyes as she had stared up at Wolfe. Why did he behave like that? What the hell was the point?

Wolfe's voice seemed to be right in his ear. 'Wake up, Sub, there's still a lot to do before the Yank tries to surface.' His breathing sounded unsteady. 'We'll form into two watches. I'll take Nettle and Lightfoot. We'll keep anchored until daylight and then move off as arranged. We don't want to excite attention. We'll probably be in sight of land if it's a clear day tomorrow.'

'What about the rendezvous?' Colquhoun could feel the other man watching him. 'Will the captain be able to find us again?'

Wolfe replied coolly, 'You really are a windy character, Sub! Tell me, seriously, what does it feel like to be afraid? I can see from here what it *looks* like!'

Haley coughed discreetly. 'I've put Nettle as lookout, sir. And I've had the dinghy hoisted inboard.'

Wolfe grunted. 'Good. Now check the weapons and grenades. Then we'll open the rations and have a bit to eat.' He added to Colquhoun, 'Should be quite pleasant really. She's a seaworthy little craft!' Then he walked aft towards the wheelhouse.

Haley said quietly, 'All right, sir? Not too rough on you, was he?'

Colquhoun sighed. 'I just don't understand him. He changes like the weather.'

Haley frowned. 'No call for poking that bloke with his pistol. I think the woman was his wife. I'd act the same way if some bloody matelot dropped out of the sky and started pawing her about!'

Wolfe's voice echoed along the deck, 'Come on then! Stop

chattering like a pack of old crows and search this boat. Any weapons can be dumped overboard.' He adjusted his belt. 'I'll be in the wheelhouse if you need me, Sub.'

They heard the wheelhouse door slam shut, and then Haley said, 'I'm a bit worried, sir. Suppose the *Temeraire* doesn't come back for us?' He added quickly, 'But what am I spouting about? The admiral will have something to say about that, eh? He'll not want his own son left to find his way home in *this* scow!'

Colquhoun turned his face away. 'That's a great comfort, Haley.'

The tall leading seaman tapped his pipe in his palm and chuckled. 'Well, I'd better arrange the watches, sir. Must have things done navy-style!'

Cowley, a big, square-jawed stoker, came up rubbing his hands. 'She's got an old diesel engine, sir.' He stared dourly at the black water. 'Vintage nineteen 'undred, I should think. Still, it seems to go fair enough.'

Having searched the boat and found nothing more warlike than a rusty shotgun, the *Temeraire*'s boarding party settled down for the night. After a hasty sandwich and a cup of lukewarm tea from a leaking Thermos, Colquhoun made himself comfortable inside the submarine's dinghy abaft the wheelhouse. For a long while he lay staring at the unmoving clouds and listening to each strange and unexplained sound. He heard Nettle, the signalman, whistling softly, and from below decks the sound of a woman's voice. She was either crooning a strange song or sobbing. Colquhoun could not be sure. He kept seeing her face in his thoughts, and the look of fury on Wolfe's features as he had stormed below to search her.

He fell asleep, his head lolling in time to the boat's gentle roll.

Then he felt a hand shaking his arm and he sat bolt upright, his eyes trying to pierce the darkness. Lightfoot was bending over him. 'Time to get up, sir.' The boy sounded nervous. 'The first lieutenant's been yelling for you.'

Colquhoun threw his legs on to the deck and winced. 'For God's sake, what time is it?'

'Nearly one o'clock, sir.' He gestured towards the sea. 'Number One says it's time for the American to come up.'

Together they walked towards the bows. The others were

already there, staring at the unbroken water, each apparently wrapped in thought.

Wolfe was hatless and leaning against the stumpy foremast. 'Ah, Sub! Slept well, I hope? Sorry I couldn't arrange tea and toast!' He laughed loudly. 'Well, it won't be long now!'

Haley asked cautiously, 'Do you reckon they'll make it, sir?'

'Not very likely.' Wolfe grinned in the darkness. 'You know what the Yanks are like! It's funny when you think of it. Us stuck up here, and the *Pyramus* somewhere down there. While our own boat is God knows where, getting the hell out of it!'

Colquhoun sensed the apprehension as it transmitted itself amongst the other men, and said quietly, 'They'll be back for us, Number One.'

Wolfe sighed. 'Oh well, if you want to believe in fairy tales!'

There was a sullen rumble deep down in the water and a dull, metallic clatter. It was a feeling more than a sound, and the fishing boat seemed to quiver as if caught in a whirlpool.

Someone shouted, 'There she is! She's blowing to the top now!'

They all stood transfixed as the dark water changed into a beaten maelstrom of seething foam and bursting air bubbles. Then with a mighty roar the streaming bulk of the submarine lifted itself into view. This was no gentle or stealthy surfacing, this was a final desperate lunge to life and freedom. Even in the poor light they could see the jagged outline of the fin with its great gaping holes and shattered plates. Part of the casing was twisted like soft lead, and one of the diving planes looked as if it had been gnawed by some giant shark.

They heard the clang of hatches, and imagined the sick and gasping crew sucking in the air and listening to the sea's noises like men back from the grave. A generator kicked over, and the sour smell of diesel floated between the two craft.

Colquhoun took a deep breath and felt strangely moved. Then he asked, 'Shall we signal them, Number One?'

Wolfe had been staring at the submarine's dark outline as if he was too shocked to move. Colquhoun's question seemed to break the trance, and he answered thickly, 'Do what the hell you like!' Then he marched back towards the wheelhouse.

Haley looked after him and then muttered, 'We could go back home in the *Pyramus*, sir. It might be easier.'

Colquhoun shook his head. 'Our orders are to stay here until we're picked up. If some warships turn up here after all, we might still be able to call up help on the boat's radio.'

Cowley said, 'She's goin' ahead, sir! Look, she's under way again!'

Very slowly, like a wounded whale, the *Pyramus* nudged her bows into the lapping water, and as they strained their eyes to watch, her outline became more indistinct and merged with the night sky.

Haley insisted, 'I'm not questioning the orders, sir.' He seemed to make a decision. 'But I didn't join the Service just to die out here, in a place nobody's ever heard of!'

Colquhoun felt very tired. 'You must make your complaints to the first lieutenant. You should know that, Haley!'

'That's just it, sir.' Haley sounded desperate. 'With all due respect, I think the first lieutenant's past caring.'

'What the hell do you mean, Haley?'

The man stared down at the deck. 'When I went to get him from the wheelhouse just now he was halfway down a bottle of hooch, sir. In my opinion he's hitting it pretty hard!'

Colquhoun felt the fear moving through him like a cold wind. He stared quickly over the bulwark, but the damaged submarine had already vanished. It should have been a moment of triumph for all of them. They had found *Pyramus*, and with any luck, and *Temeraire* acting as bait, she should limp back to base and safety.

But all Colquhoun could feel was despair and the unfairness which had left him once more with impossible decisions to face. He thought of Haley's words and what they must have cost this disciplined seaman's pride to make. 'I didn't join the Service just to die out here!'

Just thinking about the words made him sick with apprehension. In daylight they would see the hostile coastline and the completeness of their own isolation.

He stammered some vague reply and walked quickly to the opposite side of the deck.

Cowley spat over the side. ''E'll be a lot of 'elp, I *must* say!'

'That's enough of that!' Haley's voice was sharp, if only to try and restore his own confidence. 'When the time comes he'll do well enough!'

The stoker laughed bitterly. 'Like 'e did for Archer? *That* I can live without, mate!'

Neither of them saw Lightfoot move away to stand silently beside Colquhoun. Not even Colquhoun noticed or saw the misery on his face, as like the others he stared at the empty sea.

• • •

'Down periscope! Dive to two hundred feet!'

Jermain stepped back, rubbing his eyes as the men around him relaxed and waited for fresh orders.

Drew's face split into a broad grin. 'I take it that our side has successfully captured the fishing boat?'

'Yes.' Jermain moved his shoulders to ease away the stiffness. 'It's up to us now.'

He stared thoughtfully at the chart and said, 'Alter course to one three zero. That should bring us into contact with the enemy so that we can draw them away from the *Pyramus*.'

'You still believe that she'll make it to the surface, sir?' Mayo looked up from his calculations.

'I'm sure of it.' Jermain still thinking about the probing search party with which he intended to make contact. He had openly referred to them as the *enemy*. So, in spite of everything, he was already dropping into the part he had been trained for. He added quickly, 'When you've got as far as Commander Hurtzig and his crew towards the edge of the grave you don't allow a few more risks to get in your way.'

Twine called, 'Steady on one three zero, Captain. Depth two hundred feet.'

'Very good. You can fall out from action stations. Get the men fed as soon as possible. Whatever they have to face now will be better if they've a full belly per man!" Jermain saw some of the men grinning. Just simple, meaningless words, yet they hung to them like liferafts.

A few minutes later Lieutenant Oxley emerged from his cramped compartment stretching and yawning hugely.

Jermain said, 'Although you should be taking over from Number One, I want you to continue with the sonar. Right now you're just about the most vital member of the crew.'

Oxley spread his hands. 'I never doubted it, sir.'

'Your conceit does you credit!' Jermain felt better in spite of his nagging worries. Oxley's casual acceptance of everything was like a tonic.

'I hope Number One is managing all right, sir.' Oxley looked dubious. 'Not a very comfortable job for anyone.'

'I know.' Jermain turned it over again in his mind. He kept thinking of Sarah's words, of his own attitude towards Wolfe. Maybe he had allowed himself to become biased after all. It should be enough to take a man at face value without becoming personally involved.

He said abruptly, 'I'm going to see the admiral. I suggest you have a quick meal.'

Oxley looked at Mayo. 'Shall we dine, Pilot? Nothing like a few overripe kippers to strengthen the soul!'

Mayo groaned. 'Not Spithead Pheasants again surely! Does Luard get everything out of tins for God's sake?'

Jermain found the admiral standing alone in the wardroom staring at the picture of the *Fighting Temeraire*. He said slowly, 'We've altered course, sir. All being well we can draw the A/S boats off without too much danger.'

When Sir John Colquhoun turned Jermain was shocked to see the change which had come over him. He looked shrunken, a mere caricature of the brisk, confident man who had stepped aboard.

The admiral nodded. 'I see. Well, I suppose we can only wait now.'

Jermain waited for the outburst, or some fresh criticism. When nothing happened he added, 'The first lieutenant will be able to keep an eye on the *Pyramus* when she surfaces, sir. Then if other hostile craft show up in spite of our own efforts he can flash a signal for air cover. It might be of little use, but it is a last resort.'

'You've known Wolfe a long time.' The admiral seemed unsure, and it showed in the restlessness of his pale eyes. 'I—I hope he keeps his head.'

'He's been in a lot of domestic trouble, sir. But then you know all about that. But when the chips are down he has always been a very level-headed officer.'

'Yes. I see.' The admiral toyed with the buttons of his jacket. 'I hope he's not worried about this promotion business.'

Jermain shook his head. 'We must just think of this one job now, sir.' He stopped as the chill of realisation crept over him. 'You didn't say anything to him about it, did you, sir?'

The admiral looked away and made a quick, angry gesture with his hand. 'Not exactly! Naturally when he asked me point-blank I had to say something.' He met Jermain's steady eyes with a flash of his old vigour. 'Yes, I *may* have mentioned something of the sort!'

Jermain eyed him coldly. 'Look, sir, I must know. There are men aboard that fishing boat who are relying on his judgment. It may even go further than that.'

'Do you think I don't know that, Jermain?' His face was lined with anxiety. 'My son is back there too, remember that! And you sent him, Jermain! *You* sent him!'

A steward entered the wardroom, faltered at the sound of the raised voices and hurriedly withdrew.

'Yes, I did, sir. Because he is a good officer in many ways. But he has to regain his confidence.' His tone hardened. 'You were his age when you first went into submarines. You must have known this could happen.'

'It was different then.' The admiral moved round the wardroom, his steps slow and unsteady. 'There was a war on. They were a different sort of men then.'

Jermain pushed the pity to the back of his mind. 'I expect your senior officers said that about you, sir. But men don't change. Only the situations and the methods become more complex!'

He wanted to get away, to find the privacy of his cabin for just a few moments. He had to think, to drag upon his inner resources to combat this new danger. But was he really worried about what Wolfe might do? Or was he just concerned because the admiral had revealed what he should have told Wofle himself?

He said flatly, 'We shall just have to hope for the best, sir.' He made to leave the wardroom but the admiral blocked his path.

'I spoke to my son. He treated me like a stranger!' There was stark misery in his eyes.

'Perhaps he had his own reasons.' Jermain checked the condemnation which nearly slipped from his mouth.

The admiral stared at him wildly and then shouted, 'What the *hell* do you know about it? You don't understand a thing about tradition and continuity! You're like all the rest of the new breed of naval officer! It's just a job to you!'

Jermain replied quietly, 'That's not true. I happen to believe that we can no longer abide by the old standards. It's not only a question of nationality and insular pride. Surely these last few weeks would convince anyone of that fact?' He added calmly, 'I know that I do not have your experience, but it doesn't alter my sense of duty, sir.'

The admiral did not seem to have heard him. He muttered vaguely, 'It was all different before. Then there was a code, even an understanding between enemies. You fought by the rules. It all had some *meaning*!'

Jermain turned to leave. 'It still has meaning, sir. But it isn't just a game. There's too much at stake to lose this fight.'

He walked quickly to his cabin and sat down heavily on the bunk. For several minutes he stared emptily at the opposite bulkhead, his mind awhirl with words and meaningless thoughts.

He tried to picture Wolfe aboard the captured boat, and wondered if his sense of purpose and possible danger had changed him towards young Colquhoun. He remembered too the expression on Wolfe's face as the submarine had made ready to surface. 'Give my love to Sarah.' It had been like a taunt. Like an insult.

Jermain found himself on his feet, his fists clenched at his sides. What was the point of worrying about it now? He could no longer afford the luxury of doubt. He had made the decisions. It was up to him how he played the next move.

The intercom barked, 'Captain in the control room!'

He snatched his unlit pipe from the desk and ran swiftly along the passageway. As he approached the oval door he slowed his pace, and by the time he reached the familiar compartment his face was again calm, his voice steady and even, as he forced himself back into his set role.

Drew said, 'Faint H.E. on green three zero, sir. Fourteen

thousand yards. Confused but regular. Must be the fishing fleet.' He sounded breathless, as if he had been running.

Jermain looked at the plot and said quietly, 'Action stations. Bring her up to sixty feet and reduce speed to ten knots.'

Drew swallowed hard. 'That's a bit slow for manoeuvering, sir.'

Jermain made his voice patient. 'We have to act out the whole part. They must think that we are crippled, otherwise they'll soon guess there's another submarine in their pond!'

The alarm screamed through the hull, and Drew dragged his eyes from the scampering seamen. 'Fourteen thousand yards. That's one hell of a range, sir. Maybe their sonar won't reach us yet!'

Mayo called, 'Boat at Action Stations, sir!'

He looked jumpy and Jermain said quickly, 'How were the kippers, Pilot? Up to your expectations?'

Mayo looked blank and then grinned. 'Not like Mother used to give me!'

Jermain relaxed slightly. This was the time. The waiting game. If there was open battle, or even a known danger, he could rely on all of them. But right now each man was as brittle as glass.

'Sixty feet, sir.'

He waited until the periscope had hissed from its well and then peered quickly through the lens. Just a few stars between the low clouds. It was very still, and strangely menacing.

'Down periscope.' He walked back to the plot table where a petty officer was staring fixedly at the winking lights. An empty cup stood on the table, and a small dog manufactured from pipe cleaners. Normal, familiar objects left by the watchkeepers.

He glanced across at Drew. It was strange not to see Wolfe's erect figure behind the helmsman. But then nothing was the same any more.

'H.E. closing, sir. Range twelve thousand yards.' Oxley's voice sounded tense.

The admiral entered the control room but seemed unable to find anywhere to stand. Jermain watched him with sudden compassion. He must feel like a piece of extra cargo, he thought briefly. He had allowed his guard to drop in front of Jermain, and was no doubt still brooding about it.

A messenger dropped a torch on the deck plates and Jeffers snarled, 'For Chrissake watch what yer doin', you useless bastard!'

'Range eleven thousand yards, sir.'

Twine stared at the ticking gyro and moved his wheel very slightly. Through his teeth he muttered, 'Can't hear anything yet!'

Jeffers replied with a tight grin, 'You wait, Swain. It'll be like Piccadilly in the rush hour in a minute or two!'

Mayo whispered, 'Maybe they've called it off, sir?'

Oxley's voice came once more. 'Faint sonar transmissions on same bearing, sir!' A pause. 'Range ten thousand yards. Bearing moving to green three five.'

Mayo opened his mouth to speak but stopped with his jaw hanging down as the sound suddenly penetrated the stillness.

It was very faint, but regular, a stealthy, gentle tapping along the hull.

Jermain made himself stare down at the plot table, but his ears strained towards the threatening sound. He was reminded of his childhood and reading *Treasure Island* for the first time. Of old Blind Pew's stick tapping up the dark street towards the inn and the frightened boy inside.

The petty officer adjusted his headphones and shifted in his seat. 'Bloody hell!'

Jermain glanced at him. 'Worried, P.O.?'

The man grimaced. 'Just the thought of all them torpedoes up in the bow, sir. We could blow this lot of rubbish to kingdom come and hardly notice the difference!'

Jermain smiled. 'I know how you feel. But we have to let them think they're the hunters. Otherwise we'll bring the whole fleet down on our ears!'

The petty officer grinned ruefully. 'Next time I go to the dogs back home I'll be rooting for the poor bloody hare, sir!'

'Nine thousand yards, sir.' Oxley seemed entirely absorbed. 'Mixed transmissions from green two five to green six zero.'

The plot table began to vibrate as the information was fed into it. May said, 'It's a pattern, sir. It looks like the same little group as before.'

The tapping along the hull was louder now, and without a break. It preyed on the eardrums and seemed to blot out everything else. Yet still the unseen hunters retained their course and speed, as if the *Temeraire* was merely part of the imagination.

Drew looked over his shoulder anxiously. 'They're going to pass us, sir. Maybe they're not fooled after all!'

Jermain did not answer him. He was waiting for the next move.

It was almost a relief when Oxley called, 'Ships have altered course, sir! Bearings coming in now!'

The lights on the plot winked malevolently as the approaching ships swung lightly towards the *Temeraire*'s line of approach. They were still in perfect formation, the three leading vessels about six miles apart.

Mayo breathed, 'Come into my parlour...'

'H.E. is speeding up, sir! Range closing! All vessels have increased revolutions!'

Jermain wiped his forehead. The game had started. 'Alter course. Steer one zero zero.'

Mayo cocked his head. 'I can hear 'em now!'

Heads tilted. Eyes stared at the curved steel overhead. *'Schoo... schoo... schoo...'* Like the beat of powerful locomotives. It mingled with the tapping, driving down into the hull, remorseless and without pity for the listening men.

A signalman clasped his hands across his ears, his mouth quivering with fear. The messenger who had earlier incurred Jeffers' anger began to polish the torch on his trousers as if it was the most important thing in the whole world.

'Increase to fifteen knots. Alter course to zero nine zero.' Jermain watched the gyro and then snapped, 'What is the estimated range of the nearest ship?'

Mayo said, 'Six thousand yards, sir. That's the centre ship at bearing green nine zero.'

'Well, keep me informed. I'm not a mind reader!' Jermain peered at the table. The three ships had retained their pattern, but were swinging outwards from the central craft like the arms of a trap. *Temeraire*'s sudden alteration of course had brought their well-rehearsed drill into full swing, like troops on a parade ground.

'Estimated speed is twenty knots, sir. Still closing.'

Jermain bit his lower lip. 'Increase to eighteen knots. Alter course to zero eight zero!'

Oxley reported, 'All ships are reducing speed, sir!'

Jermain gestured towards the plot. 'Keep checking. I think they're settling down to follow us in comfort.'

Mayo said, 'They'll wait for us to turn south away from the side of the deep channel, sir. Or they can just let us run into the shallows.'

'Faint H.E. bearing red one one zero, sir. Range twelve thousand yards!'

Jermain rubbed his chin. 'That follows. They must have had another single patrol to the north. Just in case.' He listened to the steady flow of bearings and watched the pattern closing in around him. Three ships blocking the southern escape route, and a fourth content to tag along on a parallel course to northwest.

Drew scratched his hair noisily. 'All roads lead to Rome! God, I'm as dry as a boot!'

Jermain stared at the clock. The *Pyramus* must be under way by now. Every minute was vital for her safety. 'Right, we'll dive to two hundred feet. That'll give them something to think about. They'll have to use their sonar buoys again, so their speed will be reduced for a while.'

The needles crept round obediently, and Oxley called, 'Still in contact, sir. Slight reduction of revolutions!'

Then Oxley said, 'Ship at red one one zero has increased speed, sir! Range now nine thousand yards!'

Jermain nodded. 'This is it. He's going to make a run over us if he can while the others keep us plotted.'

Mayo sounded hoarse. 'Can't we run deep, sir?'

He shook his head. 'It's too early, Pilot. They'd guess immediately that we are only shamming.'

They all fell silent as the fourth ship's propellers cut through the other sounds. *'Schoo... schoo... schoo...'* Louder and nearer with each steady beat.

'Range now seven thousand yards, sir!'

Jermain did not reply. From the corner of his eye he saw the admiral running a finger around his collar and staring at the deckhead. Of all the people aboard he knows what to expect,

Jermain thought coldly. He must be living again all the horrors, all the nerve-stretching agonies of that other war. But this time he was older, and was powerless to retaliate.

'Watch the range, Pilot.' He saw Mayo's eyes gleam in the reflected lights. 'Let this one close to four thousand yards and then increase speed to give us a slight lead on her. We must hang it out as long as possible.'

Mayo grmiaced. 'We've only got another three-quarters of an hour, sir. Then we'll have to lift over the edge of the Valley.' He paused. 'Or turn and face this little lot.'

Jermain made himself walk the full length of the control room and back to ease the tension in his limbs. It was like some terrible dream. The powerful little ships above, goading and herding the submarine across the channel like dogs and a wounded bear. Except that *Temeraire* was the wrong target for their efforts. He could well imagine what would have happened once these same craft had found the *Pyramus*. She would have been hunted and finally bracketed by depth-charges. Her captain would have had the choice of being pounded to fragments or surfacing to face surrender and worse. Jermain had little doubt which decision Hurtzig would have taken.

The admiral joined him beside the plot table, his face white in the lamplight. Jermain asked, 'Are you feeling all right, sir?'

'I was just thinking back. All this seems like yesterday, Jermain.' He waved a limp hand. 'Except that we used to have little more than our wits to combat the enemy!' He shuddered slightly. 'I used to hate the depth-charging. We all did. My little S-boat used to operate off the Danish coast and through into the Baltic. Shallow water, and not too much of that either. I had a good first hand at the time. Young chap like Oxley, a real tower of strength. I remember when we were being hunted for a full day after tin-fishing a freighter off Flensburg, he said that it was like being chased by a blind maniac in a pitch-dark room. You never knew what or where he was going to strike next.' He stared at the impassive dials. 'Even now it seems much the same. All this complex gear, and it still comes down to the man in command. Matching his brains against those of the fellow above.'

Jermain frowned. The admiral seemed incapable of remaining silent. He appeared unwilling to face the endless waiting alone.

Jermain said gently, 'I shall be looking to you later on, sir. My experience has all been learned in the training grounds. I'm not much of a judge when it comes down to the time to duck and run.'

The admiral shook his head. 'Not me, Jermain. I feel as old as the sea. It's a new feeling for me.' He looked round startled as Mayo said, 'Range coming down to four thousand, sir.'

Then Jermain ordered, 'Increase to twenty knots.'

Drew swayed about in his seat like an organist as he adjusted his controls and checked the gauges. Then he remarked harshly, 'Much more of this caper and the bastard'll be able to drop rocks on us!'

Jermain walked into the chart-room and picked up the tannoy handset. 'This is the captain speaking. So far we've made a very good job of drawing the hunt away from the *Pyramus*. In a short while now we shall make a sharp turn and head back to the centre of the channel.' He tried not to think of the last time he had used this method of address. Of his men listening to the trapped and desperate Americans. And of the admiral's cold eagerness to fire the torpedoes. He continued quietly, 'There will almost certainly be some sort of depth-charging, but the Black Pig is built for this kind of game, and I have no doubt that she is as eager as we are to get back home, to England.'

He replaced the handset and stood listening to the silence. No cheers, not even a too-bright comment to break the tension.

Mayo said 'They're closing in for the kill, sir. They've probably signalled for reinforcements to cover the shallows towards the coast by now.'

Jermain nodded. 'Most likely. The more the merrier. It will leave *Pyramus* a nice clear run.'

Mayo pulled at his beard. 'Suppose the American was too far gone to surface, sir? All this danger will be for nothing!' He looked around the compartment. 'It could mean two boats sunk instead of just one!'

Jermain retained a smile on his lips for the benefit of the men watching his face, but his reply was like ice. 'I don't expect to hear that sort of thing from you, Pilot. Just keep those thoughts to yourself!'

He stared hard at the clock and then at the plot table, and the small, glittering lights which represented the eager hunters above. He could wait no longer. The *Temeraire* had been built to withstand a great deal of punishment, but his men were untried. The human mind could take just so much.

He thrust one hand into his pocket and gripped the familiar shape of his pipe. 'Very well, Pilot. Stand by to go about.' He nodded to a watching petty officer who barked into the intercom, 'Shut off for depth-charging! Damage-control parties stand by!'

One last look round. There was no further chance. It had to be right.

Then he said, 'Hard a-starboard! Steer one seven zero!'

The deck tilted steeply as the hull swam round obediently like a whale.

'Take her down to three hundred feet!' Throughout the hull he could feel the thud of watertight doors, the metallic click of hatches. This was the worst part. When men were shut off from their companions and friends. When the world was confined to the walls of a steel cell and the remorseless tap of the enemy's transmissions.

'Ship closing to starboard, sir! Green four five!' The propellers thrashed nearer and nearer, drowning every other sound with their awful symphony.

Jermain looked at the deckhead. 'Hard a-port! Steer one one zero!'

He tried to picture the depth-charges. Three hundred feet at fifty feet a second.

The waiting was over. The time was now.

17

'I Am Not God!'

THE TWO DEPTH-CHARGES, fired from deck mortars, exploded beneath and well ahead of the submerged *Temeraire*. Their twin detonations came as one loud crack which lifted the submarine's bows like a tidal wave and smashed against the toughened steel with a nerve-shattering roar.

Lieutenant Oxley clung to the arms of his seat and held his breath as the sonar compartment tilted sideways and seemed to fall away beneath him. Signal pads and loose fittings slithered from shelves and tables, and from the deckhead the paint chippings floated down like confetti on to the heads of the crouching men around him. He felt the seat pressing into his buttocks as the boat heaved upwards against the enormous pressure of water, and then as his mind grappled to retain control of his shocked senses it slipped away again in a further sickening sweep.

He vaguely remembered the harsh warning across the intercom and his own quick order to his companions. 'Open your mouths wide!' It was said to help withstand these underwater shocks, yet even at the realisation of what was about to happen he found himself considering the futility of his words.

Petty Officer Irons pulled himself upright in his seat and groped for his controls. Aloud he muttered, 'Jesus, I *felt* that!'

Oxley stared down at the bright droplets of blood on his lap and realised with sudden anger that his nose was bleeding. As he felt for his handkerchief he heard the captain's voice over the intercom. 'Starboard fifteen. Steer one nine zero.' Then in the same calm tone, 'Not too close that time.'

There was a sudden jangle of chains from above and Jermain added sharply, 'Keep silent in the torpedo space! They can hear that row up top!'

Oxley let his eyes move to the deck above. The whole forward space over the sonar compartment was given to the two torpedo sections. Right in the bows, behind the six torpedo tubes, was the loading bay and tube space. Astern of that, long and barren like a garage, was the stowage compartment where racks of spare torpedos lined the sides of the hull in shining readiness. Now, as the submarine manoeuvred hastily to avoid a further attack, the two sections were separated by a closed bulkhead door, connected only by phone and the chattering intercom.

Irons glanced at Oxley. 'I'll bet P.O. Mason is havin' a time up there, sir!'

Oxley twisted his mouth in a smile as he watched the flickering dials on the control panel. Mason was the petty officer in charge of torpedoes. It was a complicated task at the best of times. Now, under sudden attack, and with Lieutenant Trott as his immeidate superior instead of the unflappable Drew, he must be suffering, Oxley thought.

One of the operators called, 'H.E. closing from red nine zero, sir!' He craned his head forward intently. 'Bearing steady!'

Oxley watched the information being fed back to the plot in the control room and found time to marvel at the speed with which the attacking ship had gone about. Like a maddened dog after a rabbit, he thought angrily.

He jerked himself out of his brooding thoughts and looked quickly around his men. Their faces were moist with sweat, their movements jerky and only half under control. He barked, 'Stand by for the next attack, lads! Just stay in your positions, no matter what happens! I want to know exactly what everyone is doing!'

Again without warning the depth-charges exploded on either side of the hull. This time the sound was even louder, and the men gasped with pain or rolled drunkenly in their seats. The lights flickered and died, but as the gasps changed to cries of fear they came on again, their bulbs dulled by the splintered paintwork and the humid breaths in the sealed compartment.

The hoisting chains clanged once more through the deck plating and Oxley heard the quick stampede of feet as the torpedomen ran to quell the noise.

Oxley placed his hands palms downwards on his knees and stared at them with fixed attention. He felt strained and physically sick, and he knew he had to draw on resources as yet unknown to control the shaking in his limbs. His own men were near breaking point. He knew each one of them well enough to realise what this strain was doing to them.

Another pair of explosions rocked the hull sideways and threw two of the men into a yelling heap against the unyielding steel. Oxley could feel the boat sliding away in a downward sweep, and as his eyes sought the depth gauge he saw that the submarine had already dived to four hundred feet. He stared at the needle, mesmerised. In his reeling thoughts he could picture the hull spiralling through the dark water like a falling leaf, out of control, already lost.

Jermain's voice penetrated his shocked mind, as if from another world. 'Hold her at four hundred. Steer one seven zero!' Then, 'Report damage!'

Through the intercom Oxley could hear the squeak of telephones and the murmured replies from the control room. Jermain said, 'Not bad at all, Pilot. Just a few more minutes and we'll be through the worst.'

Then a strange voice came across the intercom, and Oxley had to force his mind to clear completely before he realised that it was Lieutenant Trott, the new officer.

'Captain, sir? If possible I would like permission to open up the rear door to the stowage space.' He sounded nervous but tightly determined. Oxley could hear the petty officer's gruff voice muttering in the background but could not make out what he was saying.

Jermain's voice was sharp. 'You know the orders, Trott. We are still under attack, you know!'

Trott tried again. 'Number Three tube has sprung a leak in

the bow door, sir. It must have been after the last attack. There is a definite seepage."

Jermain's voice was calmer, as if he was using his last reserve of patience to still Trott's worries. 'Just keep the breech closed. We can write off Number Three until we get back to base!'

Oxley gritted his teeth. Jermain must be run off his feet without Trott bleating his stupid head off!

Trott said weakly, 'The breech is open, sir. I discovered the seepage when I was checking for damage. I ordered the men to withdraw the torpedo ready for unloading, but I must have the rear door opened!'

He sounded almost frantic, and for the first time Oxley realised the seriousness of his broken words. Each torpedo was too long to be unloaded without first opening up the two complete sections. Trott had half withdrawn this one, but the bulkhead door prevented its moving any further.

Jermain said, 'Repeat, please! Did you say you've withdrawn the torpedo?'

Trott replied, 'Yes, sir. And it's jammed! I can't get it back.'

Petty Officer Mason's voice took over the intercom. 'It's me, sir, the T.I.' He sounded anxious. 'It's jammed like he says. The tube seepage is exerting some pressure in the bow. The pumps are coping with it for now, but we have to get the breech shut somehow!'

Trott yelled, 'Get away from there, Mason! It's my decision! You stay out of it!'

Irons looked at Oxley and grimaced. 'Christ! He's getting in a panic!'

'Keep trying to replace that torpedo, Trott.' Jermain sounded too calm, Oxley thought. 'There is another ship closing from starboard. You must get that tube sealed! I can't afford to open the whole space. If it flooded the boat would dive for good!' His voice hardened. 'Now take it step at a time!'

A sonar operator snapped, 'Ship closing fast from green one one zero! Bearing steady!'

Oxley breathed out slowly. 'God, we're right amongst them!'

Vaguely he heard Jermain order another increase of speed. The *Temeraire* was now logging about twenty-five knots! That would give the bastards up there something to ponder over! Just a while longer and the deception could be finished. *Temeraire* would dive deep, and the attackers could think what they liked. They could either carry on with a fruitless search, or claim the boat sunk with all hands! He found that he was smiling openly like an idiot.

Irons stared up at him. 'Sir, I've just realised something. We can't dive deep! Not with that tube unsealed!'

Even as their eyes met, the thrashing screws of the attacking ship sluiced over the deckhead. It was more muffled by the distance, but none the less deadly.

The charges exploded together near the port beam, so that Oxley felt the pain in his lungs as if he had received the blow himself. The lights faded away, and the men cried out in terror as lamps and gauges shattered overhead and showered them with fragments of glass.

Obediently the emergency lighting came into force, and Oxley stared aghast at the littered compartment, the shocked and bleeding men around him. He gazed blankly at the buckled depth gauge and realised that the boat was porpoising towards the surface. He could feel himself falling backwards in his seat, could sense the sudden change of pressure on his breathing.

Irons croaked, 'Two ships closing fast, sir! Bearing red four five!'

Oxley closed his eyes for a few seconds to search for his inner control. A double attack, with the submarine already shooting towards the surface. It was nearly over. They were finished.

Then he heard Jermain again, level and precise above the roar of the approaching ships. 'Emergency dive! Take her down to eight hundred feet! Steer one six zero!'

The depth gauge quivered uncertainly and then began to move slowly forwards. Oxley stared at the needle, willing it to move faster. Praying that Jermain would be in time.

The roar of depth-charges rolled around the hull and shook the compartment with murderous contempt. More lights shattered, and in the semi-darkness the men clung to any fixed object to stop themselves from being hurled against the treacherous steel.

From far away someone reported, 'Diving correctly, sir! Seven hundred feet!'

Oxley swung round and stared at the intercom speaker as Trott's voice cut through the other sounds and reached out to every quarter of the hull.

'Sir! I can't close the tube! The water's pouring in! *For God's sake, stop the dive!*'

From the control room Jermain sounded empty of emotion. 'How bad is it?'

'It—it's pouring in!' Trott was gabbling, the words mixed up and confused in sudden terror. In the background Oxley could hear the mounting hiss of pressurised water as it ripped past the torpedo and scythed into the small space beyond. He pressed his hand to his forehead and brushed the clammy sweat from his eyes. Once past this depth the water would force into the circular space at the rate of one hundred thousand pounds per minute!

As if in a dream he heard Jermain say, 'Watch the trim!' Just three words, but Oxley knew he was telling the men at the diving controls to make allowance for the tube space filling with water. It was a matter of slide-rule precision. Cold and without feeling. Trott and his six men were already written off, like so much extra ballast in the bows!

Oxley made himself look at the depth gauge. Already the planesman was levelling out towards eight hundred feet. He felt suddenly and uncontrollably sick.

A young sonarman stared at a voice-pipe and croaked, 'Sir! He's calling you!'

Even from his seat behind the panel Oxley could hear Trott sobbing and pleading through the emergency voice-pipe which connected him with the sonar compartment.

Then over the intercom he heard Mason's voice again. Devoid of emotion, it sounded calm and quite controlled. 'Now then, lads! Stand fast! You know we can't get the door open!'

Oxley looked away. Dear God! He could picture Mason with his back to the oval door which led aft, away from the spurting water. Mason, the ordinary, run-of-the-mill petty officer who was now calming his handful of men to stand still and wait for death without panic.

Oxley remembered with sudden clarity that Mason had been the witness to the argument between Colquhoun and the first lieutenant. He recalled too how embarrassed he had been when his small son had been christened in the depot ship's bell back in the Gareloch. He had made an awkward, clumsy speech, after which he had been happy to sink back into the obscurity of his companions.

The sonarman beside the pipe clasped his hands together and said, 'My Christ! *Look!*'

Oxley stared at the water which already seeped through the open voice-pipe, gathering force and power with each dragging second.

In a harsh, strangled tone which he did not recognise he said, 'Close the vent! Shut it, man!'

Irons pushed the man aside and clamped the tube with one savage movement.

For a long moment they all stared at the voice-pipe and listened to a strange hollow clanging overhead. With no hands to still them, the hoisting chains swung gratingly against the projecting torpedo, the sound carrying through the trapped water like the tolling of a funeral bell.

Far away, booming and dull like distant thunder, the baffled depth-charges kept up their steady accompaniment. But throughout the *Temeraire* there was complete silence, but for the steady clanging condemnation from the torpedo space.

• • •

'Eight hundred feet, sir.' Petty Officer Jeffers managed to keep his voice calm, but his eyes stayed fixed on the hydroplane telltales, and the knuckles of his hands shone white above his brass wheel.

Jermain took a pace away from the plot table and then stared down at his feet. His shoes crunched on a thick layer of broken glass and metallic dust, and he realised dully that he had hardly moved throughout the whole nerve-racking attack.

Drew cleared his throat and reported, 'I've compensated for the extra weight forrard, sir.' He faltered then continued, 'I think we should retain these revolutions for the moment to give better control.'

Then he turned his head, and Jermain saw the naked misery in his eyes.

'It was my fault, sir!' He could not hold it back any longer. 'I should have told Trott what to expect!'

'You can't allow for everything.' Jermain felt empty and drained. 'He should have known.'

A telephone buzzed and Mayo stood with the handset cradled against his jacket. 'It's the chief, sir.' He watched Jermain's face with a mixture of anxiety and pity. 'He wants a word with you.'

Jermain took the receiver and tried not to listen to the hollow echo from the chains. 'Yes, Chief?'

'That last pattern, sir.' Ross was crisp and normal. 'I think it must have damaged the screw. Nothing vital, but when I went aft I did notice a new sound.' He seemed to be considering the matter. 'It's either a chip out of one of the blades, or maybe one of them is buckled. It will add quite considerably to the noise factor. If you intend to maintain speed I would suggest you run deeper for a while. That is, until the chase is well clear.'

Jermain found that he was weighing each word, dragging every syllable across his aching mind for painful examination. It was difficult to think any more.

He answered slowly, 'Any more trouble with that seepage, Chief?'

Ross said reluctantly, 'No, sir. Nothing to write home about now.'

Jermain bit his lip and stared fixedly at Drew's bent shoulders. How typical, he thought. The one thing which had nagged him since coming out here, yet it had been the unforseen which had struck without warning. Maybe the bow door on the torpedo tube had been faulty all the time, an overlooked detail from the hasty trials. Now they might never know.

Ross continued quietly, 'I'm sorry about Trott and the others. No one should have to make the decision you did.'

'Keep checking on the screw, Chief.' Jermain dropped the handset and stared emptily at the depth gauges.

The *Temeraire* had pulled it off. By now the American boat would be well clear of the Valley and on her way to safety. He tried to hold on to that fact and ease the pain of the cost to the back of his mind.

The *Temeraire* had suffered with her crew, but her faults could be rectified.

Mayo said, 'Shall we run deep, sir?'

Jermain turned on him. 'Yes, we'll dive to nine hundred feet until we're clear of the area. Then we'll go up to periscope depth and start the high-power pumps in the tube space. We have a damaged screw, and the sound will attract attention unless we are very careful.'

Mayo continued, 'At the periscope depth we'll be more vulnerable, sir.'

'God, I know that, Pilot!' His voice seemed to affect Mayo like a blow. 'But I want the tube space pumped dry and inspected for damage, do you understnad? If we are challenged again I intend to have something with which to hit back!'

He swung on his heel and looked at the admiral. 'With your permission, sir, I would like to discuss the next phase of this operation.'

The admiral followed him into the chart-room without a word. Once inside Jermain slid the door into place and then said, 'I have carried out the text of my orders, sir. But the damaged screw makes any sort of silent approach extremely difficult.' He made himself speak in a clipped, almost matter-of-fact tone, and he saw the look of stunned disbelief in the admiral's pale eyes.

The latter quickly said thickly. 'What do you want me to say, Jermain? You've had it your way, and it can be said that the whole operation was a success.' He looked away. 'Your decision to dive the boat was the right one. If you had been in the tube space at the time you would have expected nothing different!'

Jermain clenched his fists. Don't say any more, for God's sake! One more piece of consolation, one further word of alleged understanding and *I will break!*

Coldly he answered, 'You are in charge of the operation, sir. You must decide if you think the *Temeraire* should make straight back to base.'

The admiral gasped. 'But the fishing boat, Jermain! My son and the others are still back there!'

Jermain's voice was relentless. 'The decision is the same as mine, sir. Are you prepared to risk the safety of this boat for the sake of a few more men? If it was not your son back there, would you still want to risk disaster?'

'That is unfair!' The admiral began to pace back and forth, his arms swinging in time with his words. 'What are you asking me to do?'

'I am in command of the *Temeraire*, sir. I am not God! The

area will be alive with ships by now, and the noise of the damaged screw might well attract attention. I can't even fight back until I've pumped out the tube space.' He leaned against the chart table and felt the weariness spreading through him like a drug.

The admiral replied quietly, 'You once implied that I was old fashioned in my thinking, Jermain. Perhaps you were right.' He looked up, his eyes suddenly bright. 'You stuck out to save the *Pyramus* because they were depending on you. On your faith in your men and in your own judgement. I can see now that their faith was well-founded!'

Jermain dropped his eyes. 'You are telling me to go back, is that it?'

'No, I am not, Jermain. I am telling you that this is still a decision which only you can make. *Must* make!' He shook his head sadly. 'Don't worry, I will promise you my support either way. This time there will be no recriminations from me!'

'Thank you, sir.' Jermain saw the admiral's hands trembling. 'In that case I would like to return for the others immediately.'

The admiral thrust his hands beneath his jacket and nodded firmly. 'I pray that it is what I would have done in your position.' He sat down heavily on the chart locker and stared fixedly at the deck. Then with something of his former strength he barked, 'Now just leave me alone for a few moments, will you!'

Jermain glanced at the chart and then opened the door. In a firm voice he said, 'Bring her round to two eight zero. Fall out Action Stations!'

Behind him he heard the admiral whisper, 'Thank God! *Thank God!*'

Griffin appeared in the control room as the men on watch were relieved. He looked around at the litter of shattered gauges and splintered paint, and then said evenly, 'I'll be standing by when you need me, sir.' He gestured forward. 'We'll take the bodies below once we've got them out.'

Jermain faced him savagely, his nerves screaming. What the hell did Griffin think they were? So much dead meat to be hidden away for later disposal?

Then he saw the deep concern on the young doctor's face, and all he could bring himself to say was, 'Take care of them, will you?'

Without another word he walked quickly to his cabin and shut the door behind him.

• • •

'Time to get up, sir. The sky's getting brighter already.' Leading Seaman Haley placed a metal mug on the deck and rubbed his hands noisily. 'I got the woman to heat some tea for us.'

Colquhoun threw his legs over the edge of the dinghy and staggered to his feet. His body felt bitterly cold, and he realised that his clothing was wet through to his skin.

He took the mug and cradled it gratefully in his hands. 'God, it's cold, Haley! I never thought it would be like this!'

The seaman grimaced. 'If this is the Sea of Japan, you can keep it!'

Colquhoun took a few steps to the low bulwark and stared around him. He could already see the boat taking definite shape and outline, as well as the flat, lapping water around it. The sky was much clearer, and there was a hint of the brightness to come along the vague horizon line.

'Are the fishermen all right?' The memories of the previous night came crowding back, and he added, 'How is the injured one?'

Haley shrugged. 'Seems okay, sir. Probably got a head like a cannon ball.' He peered at the uneasy water. 'We'll be getting the hook up shortly, I suppose. Then we can get under way and meet the old Black Pig. I'll never complain about anything after this!'

Colquhoun tried to stop his teeth from chattering. 'Yes, I'll go and find the first lieutenant.'

Wolfe was sitting in one corner of the minute wheelhouse his feet propped up on the wheel. He was red-eyed and unshaven, and hardly looked up at Colquhoun's entrance.

'It's getting light, Number One.' Colquhoun noticed that there was a half-filled tumbler of pale spirit at Wolfe's elbow, and his heavy automatic pistol lay cocked beside it.

Wolfe glanced at him indifferently. 'So I've noticed.' His eye fastened on the metal mug. 'I see you've been crawling to those bloody gooks again!'

'I thought we could do with something hot. I told Haley to fix it.' Colquhoun did not know why he bothered to lie. Nothing he said seemed to make any difference to Wolfe's animosity. 'Shall I get Nettle to start the engine?'

'When I say so.' Wolfe reached beneath his seat and produced a full bottle. He slopped some of the bitter-smelling drink into his glass and held it up to the grey light. 'Rice wine. Not too bad, provided you don't inhale!' He chuckled and took a deep swallow. 'Better than your bloody tea, I can tell you!'

Colquhoun said wearily, 'When are we supposed to rendezvous?'

'All in good time.' Wolfe's eyes flashed with sudden irritation. Then he added, 'You worry too much, did you know that?' He wagged his glass towards him and some of the drink spilled over his chest. 'What you need is a good woman!' He grinned broadly. 'That's *exactly* what you want.'

'Look, Number One, if you don't want to tell me...'

Wolfe leaned forward and studied him intently. 'Now, did I say something to offend you, Sub? I certainly wouldn't want that. You might feel bound to put me under arrest, eh?' He leaned back again and laughed loudly. 'Yes, I think you should find yourself a nice, ambitious woman and settle down! Like me!'

Colquhoun turned to go, but Wolfe shouted, 'You dismiss when I tell you, got it?' Then he became calmer. 'Did you know I was married once, Sub?'

Colquhoun leaned against the stained window and shook his head. 'No.' In spite of Wolfe's even tone he was obviously drunk. Colquhoun was surprised to find that it hardly seemed to matter any more. It was just one more impossible obstacle.

'Oh yes. I never wanted a girl so much in my whole life. I'd have done anything for her. Anything at all.' His head lolled, but he pulled himself together with a jerk. 'Just because I made certain rules, certain definite standards, she started playing around!' He glared at Colquhoun, searching his face. 'The little bitch! She thought I didn't know! But I used to keep a check on her, watched her every move! Of course, I never actually caught her at it, but that was because of her brother, you see.'

Colquhoun tried to follow Wolfe's line of reasoning. 'Whose brother?'

Wolfe heaved himself to his feet, sending the pistol spinning to the deck. 'Don't you get cheeky with me, *Mister* Colquhoun! Just you pay attention!' He was breathing heavier. '*Her* brother, the high and mighty Commander Jermain!'

Colquhoun stared at him. 'I—I didn't know . . .'

'Oh, you didn't know, eh?' Wolfe slumped back on the seat. 'I find that hard to believe.' He took another long swallow and coughed uncontrollably. 'Oh yes, they had it all set up between them. He was jealous of me. Always was, in fact. They thought I'd fight to keep the marriage going by contesting a divorce, knowing that it would ruin me in the Service.' He was quite calm again. 'So I played it by ear. I let them put their story of mental cruelty and all that rubbish across without a murmur!' He smiled at some inner thought. 'I've waited all this time. All this bloody time!'

'Did the captain actually say all this?' Colquhoun tried to gauge Wolfe's reaction to each word. 'I mean, what did he have to gain?'

'I told you! Are you *deaf*?' Wolfe stood up and pressed his hands on the wheel. 'He was jealous! Even after smashing my marriage he was not satisfied. Do you know he actually tried to ruin my chances of getting a command?' He stared at Colquhoun's shocked face and added grimly, 'You may well look surprised, my lad! But after this little lot is over I think we shall see a change for the better!'

'I still don't see what you mean. What made you think the captain could act like that?'

Wolfe seized him by the front of his jacket. 'Who the hell cares what you see? And what the devil do you mean by asking all these questions?' He shook him slowly in time with his words. 'Just you keep a civil tongue in your head in future!' He released his grip and added vaguely, 'Call the hands and prepare to get under way!'

Colquhoun staggered back against the door. 'The rendezvous, Number One! Have you worked it out yet?'

Surprisingly, Wolfe remained unprovoked by his question. 'Oh, *that*, well as a matter of fact, I've made other arrangements.' He picked up his pistol and clicked the safety catch back and forth in deep concentration. 'Jermain has no intention of coming back for us. No intention at all. He thinks he can sneak back to base and get all the glory. Oh yes, I've got his measure all right!'

Colquhoun felt the wheelhouse spinning round, and said desperately, 'He will come back! You're wrong!'

'Wrong, am I?' Wolfe watched him pityingly. 'I've been thinking about it all night. He wants to get rid of me, you see.' He grinned widely. 'Don't look so shocked, Sub. He wants to do the same for you, too! He knows the admiral is against him, so this is one clear way to get even with him, too!' He frowned. 'But we're wasting time. We must get under way immediately. I have no intention of letting that bastard get away with it!' He bent down, and Colquhoun heard the clink of glass. Over his shoulder he said sharply, 'Now attend to your duties. I've had just about a bellyful of you!'

Colquhoun climbed blindly down to the deck, his mind awhirl. Wolfe's outburst was all the more terrible because he had tried to make it sound so reasonable. But drunk or mad, it made little difference to the immediate outcome. It was plain that he had no intention of making any rendezvous, just as it was equally obvious that Jermain would not leave them to fend for themselves.

Once during the night he had heard the distant rumble of explosions rolling across the calm water like thunder, and he guessed it was the *Temeraire* under attack as she led the enemy away from the channel. But soon the searching ships would be reinforced, and every extra hour in these waters would bring new danger to the submarine. Jermain would return, but the fishing boat would have gone. He might go on searching until it was too late, and be caught in the shallows like the *Pyramus* had so nearly been.

Haley greeted him eagerly. 'We going now, sir? Are we off to meet the Pig?'

Colquhoun screwed up his mind in an effort to think clearly. 'Soon, Haley. Right now you'd better tell Nettle to start the engine. I'll go forrard and help winch up the anchor.' He was only putting it off. Shelving what had to be done.

A shaft of watery sunlight reflected against the wheelhouse windows, and even as he looked round Colquhoun realised that the little ship had regained her personality and seemed suddenly vulnerable.

The engine coughed twice and then grumbled into life. Fumes lifted above the stern and the deck began to vibrate impatiently.

Cowley, the signalman, spat on his hands and leaned on the winch handle. 'Right! 'Ere we go then!'

Lightfoot watched Colquhoun's worried face and asked quietly, 'Anything wrong, sir?'

Colquhoun looked away. 'Of course not! What the hell should be wrong?' He knew then that he had decided to do nothing. He was already a failure, there was no point in adding to it. If he clashed again with Wolfe everyone would say it was for personal reasons. Because of what had happened before, because of Lightfoot, because of... He gritted his teeth and threw his own weight on the winch.

Anyway, he told himself desperately, he was only guessing. Maybe Wolfe was right about the submarine not returning. He was the senior officer, it was his responsibility.

But when he looked quickly at Lightfoot and saw the hurt in his eyes, he felt nothing but shame.

There was a flurry of foam beneath the boat's counter, and as the anchor broke surface Colquhoun saw the water parting across the blunt bows as the small vessel gathered way. Immediately, there was a protesting chorus of shouts and wails from the sealed cabin, which brought an instant response from the wheelhouse.

Wolfe yelled hoarsely, 'Keep those bastards quiet, Sub! One more peep out of them and I'll lob a grenade amongst 'em!'

The wheelhouse window slammed shut, and Haley said, 'That's laying it on a bit thick, isn't it?'

Cowley grinned. 'Serve 'em right!' He glanced nervously over the bow. 'They'll have somethin' to cag about after this!'

The boat settled down to a steady speed, and as the sun lifted above the sharp horizon line the dampened decks gave off a curtain of steam as a warning of the heat to come.

Haley was the first to notice that something was wrong. He touched Colquhoun's arm and beckoned him away from the others.

'Look, sir, I'm not one to question my officers, but I'm not blind!' In the growing light his face looked crumpled and tired. 'I've been watching the shadows along the deck.' He dropped his voice to a whisper. 'The sun's over the port quarter.' He watched Colquhoun's expression anxiously and then added urgently, 'Well, is it or not, sir?'

'What if it is?' Colquhoun could not meet his stare.

'Hell, sir, that means we're running level with the coast, to the south west!' He glanced nervously at the other men. 'That's away from the channel!'

Colquhoun stared across the bulwark. Just faintly, like a darker patch of low cloud, he could see the line of the coast. Wolfe was keeping his word. Quickly he looked up at the wheelhouse and saw Wolfe's head and shoulders framed in the centre of the window behind the spokes.

Colwley interrupted his thoughts with a wild shout. 'Look, sir! I can see some boats on the starboard bow!'

Colquhoun replied flatly, 'There's a small inlet over there. It'll be the usual coastal traffic!'

Haley stared at him with sudden anger. 'Don't you see what's happening, sir? We're going in the wrong bloody direction! The skipper'll never find us if we stay on this course!'

His words carried to the others, and Nettle, the stoker, who had just emerged from the engine hatch, muttered, 'What's it all mean, Ted?' He tried to laugh. ''As Number One got himself lost?'

'Listen to me, lads!' Haley's voice shook with emotion. 'I think we're going the wrong way!' He pointed accusingly at Colquhoun. 'If you don't believe it, ask *him*!'

Colquhoun saw their faces changing to tight hostility. 'What's the good of acting like this?' He looked around him helplessly. 'I'm not in charge! There's nothing I can do!'

Haley exploded, 'For God's sake, sir! Are you going to let this happen? We'll be captured or killed if we keep like this!'

The window above their heads jerked back, and Wolfe snapped, 'I heard that, Leading Hand! I shan't forget this insubordination!' He glared at Colquhoun. 'So you're still trying to make trouble, are you?' He spun the wheel angrily. 'Well, just you listen to me! This boat does what *I* want it to!'

Haley fell back a pace, his eyes shocked. 'My God, he's off his head!'

Wolfe continued calmly, 'Just for the record, I have all your weapons up here, so don't try to do anything foolish!' He closed the window and resumed his study of the horizon.

Haley removed his cap and wiped his forehead. 'For God's sake, what'll we do?' He stared at the others.

Cowley said quietly, ''E's an officer. What *can* we do?' He looked accusingly at Colquhoun. 'It's not just us, is it, sir? The lads aboard the *Temeraire*'ll catch it too if they 'ang around lookin' for us.' He tore his eyes away. 'You do what you like. I'm goin' to force me way into the wheelhouse!'

Lightfoot put up his hand. 'Don't do that, Bert! We'll think of something.' He looked imploringly at Colquhoun. 'You'll get us out of it, won't you, sir?'

Haley snarled, '*Him?* He couldn't knock the skin off a rice pudding!' Then he stared wretchedly over the bows towards the distant, slow-moving shapes of two junks. 'It can't happen! Not out here like this!'

Cowley said, 'What about you, Stokes? Could you bust up the engine or somethin'?'

Nettle shook his head. 'No. 'E told me to put the thing full ahead and then clear out.'

Wolfe suddenly yelled, 'Get down behind the bulwark! We'll be passing near these junks soon, and I don't want your stupid faces all over the place!' He brandished his pistol. 'And stay up forward where I can see you!'

Haley slumped down beside the worn woodwork. 'Jesus! He's grinning! He's actually enjoying himself!'

Lightfoot sat on the deck with his knees drawn up to his chin. He was staring very hard at the wheelhouse, his brow creased in a frown.

'You'll have to help us, sir.' His voice was pitched so low that Colquhoun could hardly hear it. 'Maybe if you speak to the first lieutenant?'

'It's no use!' Colquhoun stared fixedly at a slow moving shadow as it glided across the wheelhouse. The junk's tall sail must be less than twenty yards clear. He added, 'He's mad. He'll do anything now!'

Cowley muttered, 'If the Reds catch us, you know what they'll do to us?' He shuddered. 'I 'ope they kill the officers first, so I can bloody cheer!'

Colquhoun looked round startled as Haley rasped, 'Get down, you young fool!' Then he saw Lightfoot walking very slowly aft towards the wheelhouse, his hands in his pockets, his head sunk forward as if in deep thought.

Wolfe opened the window an called, 'Get back! Keep under cover, you idiot!' When the boy continued to advance he lifted his pistol above the sill. 'Go back, or I'll shoot!'

Lightfoot halted and stared up at Wolfe's livid face. The others, crouching like statues in the bows, heard his voice, clear and steady. 'We want to go back, sir! It's only fair you should think about the rest of us!'

He put his hands behind his back and twined his fingers into a tight knot. Colquhoun could see his wrists shaking with suppressed fear, but somehow he was keeping his voice under control.

Wolfe snarled, 'How dare you speak to me like that? I'm telling you just once more. *Get back!*'

Lightfoot shrugged and then began to advance.

The noise of the shot was like a thunderclap, and for one split second no one really understood what had happened.

Lightfoot seemed to swing round in his stride, as if he had at last decided to obey Wolfe's order. Then, very slowly, he buckled on his knees, his fingers interlaced across his stomach. Without a sound he pitched forward on to his face and lay quite still.

Colquhoun staggered to his feet, his mind collapsing with shock and sudden madness. Before he realised what he was doing he found himself at the wheelhouse door, tugging at the handle and screaming like a maniac.

He tore it open, his body braced for the bullet's impact, his mind blank to everything but the sight of Lightfoot's form on the sunlit deck.

Wolfe still stood behind the wheel, the gun grasped in one hand. He turned and stared at Colquhoun, his eyes entirely devoid of recognition or knowledge. He said vaguely, 'I didn't want to shoot him. I had to make him understand!'

Blindly Colquhoun wrenched the pistol from his grip, feeling the metal warm against his fingers. He stepped back and raised the gun level with Wolfe's face.

'You bastard! You rotten, lousy bastard!' He was sobbing with each word, so that Wolfe's face was misty above the shaking foresight.

Wolfe opened his eyes very wide. 'My God, Sub, I can't think what's got into you these days!' Then he giggled, a long-drawn, inhuman sound. 'Still, if you must carry on like this, I suppose we'll just have to tolerate it, eh?' . . . Cowley pushed into the small space and snatched up a Stirling from the deck.

Colquhoun lowered the pistol and stared at it with sick horror. 'I nearly killed him!' He saw Cowley watching him like an unwinking bird. 'Another second and I would have blown his head off!'

Nettle was waiting below the ladder, and Colquhoun said thickly, 'Tie the first lieutenant's hands, Nettle. Then help Cowley to bring the helm round to the south-east.' He did not wait for a reply, but hurried across the deck and dropped to his knees beside Lightfoot's body.

Haley had opened the boy's shirt and was trying to control the stream of blood which seemed to be pouring continuously across the deck planks in a living flood.

Colquhoun lifted Lightfoot's head on to his knees and said, 'Why did you do it, John? For God's sake, why? It was my job. I should have been the one!'

Lightfoot opened his eyes and stared straight up at the empty sky. His face was deathly pale, and there were bright flecks of blood on his lips. He said, 'I had to. *Had* to!' His breathing was very slow. 'You were good to me. You understood. I couldn't let you go on thinking you was no use.'

Haley said tightly, 'Hold on, lad! Just lie quiet!'

But Lightfoot lifted himself on his elbows his voice desperate. 'You never killed Archer, sir! He was already dead when he was put behind the door! It was nothing to do with you!'

Haley gasped and looked across at Colquhoun. 'So that was how it happened!'

Colquhoun whispered, 'Never mind that! It doesn't matter any more!'

Lightfoot's head fell back on his lap. 'No, it don't matter any more.' He was smiling, but his eyes did not seem to focus properly. 'You'll be all right now, sir! You see!'

He coughed, and this time the blood did not stop.

Colquhoun wiped the boy's face with his handkerchief and leaned forward to keep the sun from his eyes.

Haley said gently, 'It's no use, sir. He's gone.' Then he stood up and walked slowly to the bulwark.

Colquhoun stayed where he was, quite motionless. Only his shadow moved, as the boat turned and swung on to her new course.

18

Someone Should Talk About It!

'DOWN PERISCOPE! Dive to two hundred feet!' Jermain stepped back and said sharply. 'There is a seaplane of some sort bearing green one three five.'

He waited until the deck steadied at the new depth and added, 'The sea's empty. Like a sheet of bloody glass!'

Mayo watched him worriedly. 'What do you think, sir?'

'We'll try another sweep, Pilot. Bring her round two points to port, and tell Oxley to keep a sharp watch. The fishing boat is very small. She might even have some sort of engine trouble.'

He swung on his heel and strode to the chart-room. It gave him the delusion of privacy. A place where he could be alone with his thoughts.

But how much longer could he go on searching? There was no sign of the fishing boat, and every passing minute added to the submarine's own danger. At each furtive search through the periscope there had been some new hint or sign that more ships were coming into the area. Twice he had seen smoke on the burnished horizon. Low, fast-moving smoke, like that of warships. Now there was an aircraft. The enemy had been fooled by the deception, but was still taking no chances.

He swung round as a foot grated on the deck. 'What do you want?' Then he saw that it was the imperturbable Baldwin with a fresh mug of black coffee. 'Thank you. I'm sorry if I sounded rough!'

Baldwin put the mug carefully on the chart table and wiped his hands across his white jacket. "'S'all, right, sir. Reckon you've quite a bit on yer mind just now!'

Jermain watched him leave with something like affection. Baldwin, whose duties were so unwarlike, yet were essential to all of them. His world was confined to wardroom cutlery, the proper routine of meals and the collection of mess bills. In all his service he had learned little of the ships which carried him from one end of the world to the other. He had to rely on trust.

The coffee was hot and bitter. Jermain leaned his arms on the table and stared moodily at the straggling outline of the Korean coast.

It was all unreal and fantastic. They had been attacked and had suffered sudden death, yet to the outside world the crisis hardly existed. He thought back to the day they had left the Gareloch, and knew he had felt the same way. The Korean War had ended nearly twenty years ago. Surely nothing more could happen there?

In the control room he heard two ratings removing the last of the broken glass, the sound scraping at his ears like a drill on the nerve of a bad tooth.

From the moment the *Temeraire* had made her stealthy escape from the searching ships overhead the work of putting right the damage had continued without a pause. The men seemed almost glad to do it, only to keep their minds occupied and away from the unknown dangers.

They had planed up to periscope depth, and Jermain had taken his first look around. After the threatening darkness the blinding daylight came wth the shock of an iced shower. The sun so bright that the sea's burnished glare was almost unbearable, and he imagined he could feel its heat through the periscope. And as he stared and searched the empty horizons he was at the same time conscious of the noises inside the hull. The staccato beat of the power pumps, the clatter of feet on the deck below as hatches were thrown open and men waited for the worst job of all.

It should all have been over and finished with. They should have been running deep with the damaged screw whining at full pitch to carry them all to safety. Instead they were still searching, still tied to this damned and mocking Wantsai Valley with all its horrors and nightmare memories.

Jermain had crossed the control room to speak with Mayo who was standing above the open hatch at the far end. He had been staring down the shining ladder, his face set like a mask. Jermain had been about to speak, but had suddenly looked down to follow his glance.

At the foot of the ladder Griffin's first-aid party were just passing aft with a stretcher. Jermain knew that their sodden, lolling burden had once been Lieuteant Trott. He knew this fact from the uniform. Otherwise there had been no sort of resemblance. No sense of belonging, no part of something once familiar. Just a thing. A staring, open-mouthed remnant.

Now the last of the corpses had been removed from the pumped-out tube space, and there was a smell of disinfectant on the damp air.

Drew had gone forward with Lieutenant Kitson to check the damage to the delicate firing mechanisms and to repair any faults in the circuits. He could hear their tools and hammers rattling through the hull at top speed. At least it was an improvement on the clanging chains, although even now he seemed to hear them, mocking him . . . rebuking him. . . .

He realised that his head had fallen almost on to the chart, and he stood up angrily, shaking himself awake like a dog.

If he gave up the search for Wolfe and the others now he knew he could never forgive himself. The cost was already too high. He had to hold on a little longer.

Even if he was praised for getting the *Pyramus* clear, he would not be able to accept the satisfaction for himself. Sarah's happiness, even the longed for unity with Jill, would be clouded by his own knowledge that he had left his own men to die without reason.

Drew appeared in the doorway. 'Kitson is still working on the circuits, sir. The inrush of water must have cut through some of them like a saw!' He shook his head heavily. 'I'll never forget it!'

Jermain walked past him. It was if he could no longer stand personal contact. Not yet. Not until the search was over.

'Periscope depth again!' His voice was hard. 'Anything from sonar?'

Mayo shook his head. 'Do you think the seaplane will still be there?'

'How the hell do I know?' Jermain ignored the look on Mayo's face.

'Up periscope!' He leaned on the handles and squinted as his eyes received the full glare of the waiting sun.

The sea was once more clear. Only a few gulls swooped angrily above the periscope, outraged by its intrusion. Jermain watched their grimacing protests as he swung the handles to full power. Tonight these gulls will sleep safely in their nests and crannies ashore. Where will he be? He ground his teeth together with sudden despair. What had happened to the fishing boat? Sunk or captured? Or had Wolfe decided to act independently after all?

He snapped, 'Raise the radio mast! See if you can hear anything.' He thought of the boat's powerful radar, unused and impotent. With that he might find the small boat within minutes. It was tempting, but he knew it was an empty thought. Any such transmission might be instantly detected, then any chance of saving Wolfe and his companions, if there still was one, would be lost for good.

Mayo reported, 'Nothing on sonar, sir.'

'Well, *keep trying*!' He kept his eyes to the periscope and did not see Mayo's face as he looked at Drew. The latter shook his head very slightly. But the gesture seemed to sum up his understanding and his pity for what Jermain was trying to do.

The big lenses moved slowly around the glittering seascape as Jermain searched horizon and sky alike. If an aircraft dived suddenly from the sun there might be precious little time to act. With the sea so clear and calm the *Temeraire*'s bulk would stand out as sharply as if they had been basking on the surface.

Harris burst from the radio room, his lined face alight with excitement. 'Captain, sir! Signal from Flag!' His voice was shattering in the stillness. '*Pyramus* has made her contact! She's out of danger!' He held out the signal pad as if he had to remind himself it was not a dream. 'Flag must have been calling us regularly, sir. This is our recall!'

'Down periscope! Two hundred feet!' Jermain looked coldly at Harris and then moved to the chart table. 'Thank you. You may lower the mast now.'

Harris looked lost. 'I'm sorry, sir, I just thought...' His voice trailed away as Mayo shot him a warning frown and, still mystified, he returned to the radio room.

Jermain said, 'Alter course, Pilot. Bring her round to three three zero. Reduce speed to ten knots.' His tone was clipped and final. 'Periscope depth again in fifteen minutes.'

He walked slowly back to the chart-room. The sudden signal had only added to his sense of urgency and despair. Now the whole boat would know that officially the mission was over. The only thing which kept the crew and the *Temeraire* in pressing danger was his own personal stubbornness. Or was it only pride?

The intercom broke into his thoughts. 'Very faint hydrophone effect bearing red four five. Range twenty thousand yards.' Oxley added after a few seconds, 'Could be a small diesel engine, sir!'

Jermain took one quick glance at the chart. It was well away from the area slected for rendezvous but it could be the fishing boat. He felt suddenly sick from the controlled tension. It *had* to be!

'Course to intercept, Pilot!' He pushed past Mayo and snatched up the engine-room handset.

'Captain here! How is the propeller noise, Chief?'

'About the same, sir. But at this speed it's not too bad. More like a whistling than anything.'

He heard Mayo murmur, 'Port twenty. Steady. Steer two eight five!'

Ross added doubtfully, 'If you have to clap on power you'll need to run deep again, sir. The noise would certainly be detectable at present depths.'

'Yes, thank you.' Jermain replaced the handset. So, if this was a false contact he might have to break off the search. Even the admiral, who remained sitting in the deserted wardroom like an old man, would never allow him to risk the boat further.

Mayo said, 'On new course, sir.'

'Very good.' Jermain turned his back on the looming possibility of failure. 'Find out if Kitson has completed his work and then clear for action. There is nothing wrong with the boat's hearing.' He looked around their grim faces. 'I want her teeth ready, too!'

• • •

Leading Seaman Haley climbed up the short ladder and eased his body into the wheelhouse. In spite of the fact that every window was fully lowered it was quite airless and as hot as an oven. Colquhoun was standing at the wheel, his slim body stripped to the waist, his skin gleaming with sweat.

Haley said, 'There's some more smoke on the port beam, sir.'

Colquhoun replied, 'Take the wheel.' He picked up the long, battered telescope which he had found in a locker and rested it on the sill of a window. After a few moments he said, 'It's one of those ships.'

Haley knew what he meant well enough, but took the telescope as Colquhoun thrust it into his hands. The dark smudge on the horizon sprung alive in the big glass, and he saw the raked bow slicing through the calm water, the low plume of smoke from her funnel. Like a fast trawler. Like the ones which had hounded the *Temeraire* and had been responsible for Lieutenant Victor's death.

He said slowly, 'The hunt's still going on then. Let's hope she doesn't come over to take a look at *us*!'

Colquhoun answered briefly, 'They'll have us spotted on the radar. They're obviously not bothered.'

Haley moved his legs uneasily. 'Not *yet*!'

Colquhoun ignored him. It was strange how calm he felt. Empty, and completely composed. Like another person.

He said sharply, 'Have you let the fishermen out of their cabin?'

Haley nodded. 'Yes, sir.' The released Koreans were directly below the front of the wheelhouse, watched over by Cowley with his Stirling. Yet Colquhoun had apparently not even seen them. His eyes stayed either on the ancient compass or the harsh light of the horizon. He added cautiously, 'The sun's getting damned high, sir. Do you think we've missed the rendezvous?'

Colquhoun shrugged. 'The compass is well adrift, and the only chart available looks home made. It's got a few crayoned areas for fishing, and not much else. But allowing for the alteration of course and the drift, we're just about on the right track.'

Haley persisted, 'We could be miles off course, as I see it. Even if the skipper does come back for us he'll not find it easy to spot us.' He watched the fast-moving smoke. 'And there's not much time left!'

He stiffened as the black-haired Korean woman left the small group by the hatch and moved quietly to the bulwark. Ignoring Cowley, she unwrapped an old blanket and laid it carefully across Lightfoot's body which had been moved into the shade of the boat's side. Haley shot a glance at Colquhoun's stiff face, but apart from a quick blink of his pale eyes there was nothing to give away his inner feelings.

Colquhoun saw Haley's apprehensive stare and kept his own gaze fixed on the open sea beyond the gently corkscrewing bows. He had carried Lightfoot's body to the bulwark himself. He had been surprised how light it had been. Now, as he let his eyes move to the blanketed shape, the shock seemed to affect him more deeply, and he was again reminded of his sense of loss. Before, as he had made himself stand rigidly behind the wheel staring at the mocking horizon, he had been able to glance at Lightfoot's body, to deceive himself for just a few more seconds. In the shade of the bulwark the boy had appeared to be asleep, or sheltering from the sun. The blanket made a stark difference. It was final.

He realised that he was gripping the spokes so tightly his hands were throbbing with pain.

Lightfoot had made him act. Had forced him to accept a role he had so long avoided. It was as if he had been betrayed and deceived by so many others in his short life that he was unable to see Colquhoun become another fallen idol. Even if it cost him his blood. He was suddenly conscious of the heavy watch in his trouser pocket, and he remembered Lightfoot's determined and angry face as he had thrust it into his hands. *'I want you to have it, see?'*

He felt the pain rising again to prick at his eyes and he said sharply, 'Take the wheel, Haley. I'm going to walk around for a bit.' He stepped down from the wheelhouse and immediately felt the sun across his bare shoulders like the cut of a whip.

Wolfe was sitting in the shade of the wheelhouse, his bound hands hidden behind his back. He looked up at Colquhoun's taut features and said, 'You'll see that I was right! He'll not come back for us now!' When Colquhoun failed to reply he shouted loudly, 'You'll regret this, Mr. Colquhoun!'

Colquhoun stopped and stared down at him. He still felt strangely calm, like a man under drugs, and he said, 'The only thing I regret is that I did not shoot you! But I intend to meet the *Temeraire*.' He looked away. 'If only to see you court-martialled!'

He walked slowly towards the bows where it had all started. As he passed the Koreans they bowed their heads, as if they too sensed his new and dangerous strength.

The little boat steamed on steadily, each turn of the screw piling the distance between them and the distant shoreline. Only the jagged mountains were visible now, detached from the horizon by a low bank of haze. Soon they would be too far out. They would be seen and singled out for closer inspection. If he had allowed Wolfe to have his way they might still be sneaking down the coastline itself, lost and safe amongst countless similar craft. And Lightfoot would still be alive.

He stamped his foot with sudden anger. No! It was not like that. Just this once he had to be right!

Haley called from the wheelhouse. 'Would you come up here, sir? I think there's a small boat coming up astern!'

Colquhoun ran up the ladder and groped for the telescope as Haley added, 'Can't make it out myself. The haze is too thick back there.'

Colquhoun moved the telescope slowly and watched the glittering reflections playing across the water. A small boat might come too close for comfort. It might be as well to keep the Koreans in sight and let them know that they must behave quite normally, no matter what.

Haley started as Colquhoun snapped the telescope shut and threw it on the locker. 'What is it, sir?'

Colquhoun stared past him. 'Submarine! Dead astern! That was the conning tower you saw!' He watched the compass. 'Alter course slightly to port.' He waited a few moments and then trained the telescope once again.

This time he found it immediately. The submarine was moving fast, her hull trimmed down so low that it was lost in a welter of spray thrown back from the bows. Only the conning tower seemed real. It cruised above the water like some strange war-machine, the white hats of the men on watch like tiny flowers on a sea-washed rock. As he studied the submarine Colquhoun saw the conning tower changing shape and becoming wafer-thin as when he had first seen it.

He said, 'She's altered course. She's coming after us.' There was neither surprise nor panic in his voice. Just a plain statement of fact.

Haley swallowed. 'I could go and tell the Koreans to act dumb, sir. I could make 'em understand!'

Colquhoun turned and studied him calmly. There was almost a wistful look in his eyes as he said, 'You really don't understand, do you, Haley?'

Haley shook his head. 'We could bluff it out, sir!'

'No. This is the same submarine which attacked the *Malange*.'

Haley stared at him. 'How can you be sure, sir?'

'Do you think I'm ever likely to forget, Haley?' Colquhoun looked emptily at Lightfoot's blanketed body and then said crisply, 'She must have been at the shallow end of the Wantsai Valley waiting for the trawlers to drive the *Pyramus* or the *Temeraire* across her sights!' He gripped the seaman's arm fiercely. 'God, man, don't you understand? The *Temeraire* will come straight into her! She'll surface to take us aboard, and she'll be a sitting target!'

Haley's face was drained of colour. 'What'll we do, sir?' He looked around the wheelhouse like a trapped animal. 'We can't do *anything*!'

Colquhoun picked up his Stirling and cocked it deliberately. 'There is a dinghy lashed forrard, Haley. It belongs to the fishermen. Get it ready for launching.'

Haley seemed dazed. 'Launching, sir?'

'I shall want the Koreans to leave the boat at once. We'll put them over the side before the submarine gets up to us.' He looked straight into Haley's eyes. 'You know what I'm asking, don't you, Haley?'

The man licked his lips and tried to grin. 'It had to be us, didn't it, sir?' He straightened his cap and added, 'I'll tell the others.' He turned to go and then said, 'The *Temeraire* wouldn't stand a chance, sir. We can't let these bastards use us as the bait!'

Colquhoun lifted the telescope and watched the submarine growing larger in the lens. It would be so easy to 'bluff it out' as Haley had suggested. *Temeraire* might not be able to make the rendezvous, and their deaths would be for nothing. Even if they delayed the approaching submarine, there was still the possibility that Jermain might not detect her presence in time. Again, their deaths would be in vain.

He picked up the Stirling and stared at it savagely. Then he shouted, 'Slow ahead, Nettle!' As the engine's roar subsided he added, 'Now get that boat over the rail, and be quick about it!'

He got a vague impression of the protesting fishermen and the stolid-faced woman with the baby hugged to her side as they were helped down into the tethered dinghy alongside. Then as a knife slashed away the line it grated down the side of the hull and curtsied astern on the fishing boat's wake. Colquhoun watched them drop further and further astern. Small, lost people caught up in someone else's struggle.

'Full ahead, Nettle! I don't care if you burst the engine apart now!'

Then he yelled through the window, 'The submarine will come up on our port quarter, Haley! You and Cowley keep in the bows out of sight. When I give the signal I want you to open fire on her conning tower with everything you've got!' He looked down at Nettle who sat perched on the edge of the engine hatch swinging his legs. 'You, too. Just concentrate on her bridge and keep her crew away from the deck gun!'

He turned back to watch the submarine again. It had increased speed, the wash from the lean hull brushing aside the bobbing dinghy like a leaf. He clamped his jaws tightly together. Soon now. The submarine was moving so fast that she would be overhauling the fishing boat as if she had been stationary.

Haley yelled, 'Smoke on the horizon, sir! Bearing green four five! It'll be that A/S trawler again, I expect!'

Colquhoun lifted his hand in acknowledgement. It made little difference now. If he could lure the submarine close enough to attack her, he could make her submerge. It was unlikely that her commander would want to risk unnecessary damage to his periscopes, quite apart from possible casualties.

Colquhoun felt the sweat running free down his spine. No, the submarine's skipper would dive and finish off this irritating attacker with a single torpedo.

He raised his Stirling very slowly and held it against the side of the window. He watched the low bows and then the front edge of the conning tower moving into his vision, but he made himself wait just a bit longer, counting the seconds like a runner under the starting gun.

No matter how far from the rendezvous she was, *Temeraire*'s sensitive ears would detect the torpedo's explosion. He had a sudden picture of the cramped sonar compartment alongside Oxley and with Lightfoot just below him at the controls.

He rested his forehead on his wrist and wiped the mist from his eyes. When he looked up the submarine was drawing abeam, barely fifty yards away. He heard the squawk of a loud-hailer, saw the glint of sunlight on raised binoculars. There was no mistaking her now. She was the same boat.

His despair gave way to sudden fury, and as his finger tightened on the trigger he yelled, 'Open fire! Sweep her bridge!'

He heard himself yelling as the gun vibrated against his armpit, and through the drifting smoke he saw the figures crumple away from the conning tower like discarded puppets as the four Stirlings poured a deadly fire amongst them.

Colquhoun swung the wheel and sent the boat careering towards the grey hull, which even now was pulling away, the surprise giving way to trained reaction. The conning tower was already tilting, and across the gap he could hear the water roaring into her tanks as she started to dive. Two or three bodies floated free from the empty bridge, and as the sea cascaded over the periscope standards they twirled and pirouetted in a macabre dance before being sucked down to oblivion.

Colquhoun reloaded his gun and stared at the disturbed water. The submerged submarine would either move clear to fire her *coup de grâce*, or she might wait for the smokecloud on the horizon to come to her aid. Either way, there was nothing more to be done. He rested his chin on his forearm and watched the place where the enemy had dived.

• • •

The atmosphere in the *Temeraire*'s control room was so charged with suppressed tension that it was almost unbearable. Beside the chart table the navigator's yeoman busied himself aimlessly sharpening a pencil, until Mayo's glare quelled him too into silence. Jermain stood with his fists deep in his jacket pockets, his eyes on the clock. It seemed as if the hands were welded to the face, and he had to stop himself from checking with his own watch.

Oxley reported, 'Stronger diesel H.E. on same bearing, sir. Closing.'

Mayo let out a slow breath. 'Damn!' He glanced at Jermain's impassive features. 'A patrol boat, do you think?'

Jermain said, 'Check the range again!'

'Ten thousand yards, sir. The second vessel is moving fast. Around twenty knots. Still closing.'

Jermain felt the admiral at his side. He said quietly, 'It seems as if we might have to act fast, sir.'

Sir John Colquhoun stared at the plot table. 'This second ship. Do you think it's after the fishing boat?' He sounded strained to breaking point.

'We don't know for sure that the other one is *our* fishing boat, sir.' Jermain added gently, 'I'm going up to take a look round.'

Oxley's voice came like a slap in the face. 'More H.E. bearing green one six zero, sir! Range fourteen thousand yards! Fast diesel engines. Closing!'

The plot table hummed into life, its lights winking malevolently.

Jermain said slowly, 'One ahead and one astern. This second one might be the A/S boat we sighted earlier. She seems to be coming back for something.'

As if to confirm this Oxley snapped, 'Second H.E. sounds like the other A/S craft, sir. Still closing.'

Jermain made up his mind. 'Take her up to sixty feet! Make it as slow as possible.' He lifted his arm as the deck titled very slightly. 'Up periscope!' He crouched down with his head against the pad, his eyes staring into the churning panorama of sunlit water as the lens glided towards the surface. Hardly daring to breathe he swung the handles on to the given bearing and waited for the spray to clear from the glass. The others around him saw his mouth tighten with satisfaction.

'It *is* our boat!' He watched the little vessel move slowly into the cross-wires, her bows throwing up a tremendous moustache of white foam. The periscope was at full power, but with the heavy surface heat haze to contend with it was still difficult to obtain a hard picture. But it was the same boat. There was no doubt about it.

He swung the periscope round in another half circle and stared fixedly at the new menace astern. Here there was no haze, nothing to hide or soften the outline of the fast-moving ship. But she still had a long way to come. There was still time.

He turned back to watch the fishing boat. From the corner of his mouth he said, 'Where's the other ship now, I can't see anything!'

Oxley said, 'On the same bearing, sir. Closing fast!' He sounded unusually edgy. 'She's there all right!'

Jermain blinked his eyes and pressed his head harder against the rubber pad. Even allowing for the haze he should be able to see something. The sun was behind him, and the water was as calm as a millpond.

He cursed inwardly as spray twisted the little picture into interminglings of blue and silver. He could imagine Wolfe and the others watching each horizon, hanging on to hope, and yet not daring to take it for granted.

Then he tensed as the fishing boat's deck was further distorted by a drifting cloud of smoke. There were sudden, vicious pin-pricks of light too, matching the sunlight with their brilliance. Even as his mind grappled with this unexpected turn of events he saw the submarine. She had been in a direct line with the fishing boat, but now as the latter swung on some crazy collision course he could see the conning tower, the shine of spray on the smooth steel.

He straightened his back. 'Down periscope! There is a submarine on the surface. Bearing red one zero. Same range as the fishing boat!'

There was a momentary shocked silence, and then Mayo snapped, 'Start the attack!'

Jermain gave him a quiet nod. 'Stand by tubes One and Two!' To the control room at large he said harshly, 'It's the same sub. Right now she's attacking the fishing boat, and it's my guess she's called up assistance.'

He stood quietly as the ranges and bearings rattled through the intercom. Then he said, 'Up periscope!'

'One and Two ready, sir. Bow doors open!'

He swung the handles very slightly from the previous bearing. The fishing boat was still afloat and unharmed, but the submarine seemed to have turned end on.

Oxley shouted, 'Diesels have stopped, sir! She's diving!'

'Down periscope!' He watched the flickering lights on the plot table. 'He's either running away from Wolfe's Stirlings, or he'll haul off to fire a torpedo.'

Mayo said, 'More likely he'll wait for the A/S ship to arrive. He'll not want to waste a torpedo!'

Jermain nodded. 'That's what I think.' He rubbed his chin. 'In that case we must rescue Wolfe's party first. By the time we caught the submarine the surface ship would be here. Stirlings would be useless against *her*!'

'Submarine has dived, sir.' Oxley was in control again. 'Bearing green two five. Her course is zero nine zero. Depth steady at about one hundred feet.'

Jermain rested his hand lightly on Mayo's shoulder. 'Take over as Number One in the control room, Pilot.' To Drew he added, 'You get forrard. I want the torpedo department to run like clockwork if I give the order!'

Drew slipped from his seat. 'It will be a pleasure, Skipper!'

Another glance at the clock. 'Stand by to surface!'

The admiral said urgently, 'What can I do, Jermain? I can't just stand here. I'll go mad!'

Jermain picked up his glasses and checked their lenses. Quietly he said, 'I would like you to stay right here in the control room, sir. When we get started in a few minutes I want my men to be able to see you.' He let his eyes drop to the admiral's bright rectangle of decorations. 'They are all trained men, sir. But yours is the experience which will hold them together in a real emergency!' He turned away from the admiral's silent stare. He was not sure if the expression was one of pride or whether he was just grateful for being needed.

Jermain let his eyes move slowly over the assembled men. Lookouts, handling party below the main hatch, and the attack team around the plot table.

Then he knocked the clips off the lower hatch and started up the ladder. Over his shoulder he yelled, 'Surface!' He noticed that his voice sounded hollow inside the steel tower, and he tried not to picture what would have happened if he had not seen the gunfire aboard the fishing boat. He would have surfaced right on top of the submarine's sights. It would have been over very quickly, if they were lucky.

He forgot everything else as he knocked off the second lot of clips and ducked his head as the spray splashed down over his cap. His hands and feet moved automatically, his voice too was crisp and expressionless as he climbed the last few rungs to the cockpit with the lookouts and messengers panting behind him.

He swung his glasses to his eyes, searching astern for the approaching enemy. She seemed much closer, her bows high above a tremendous crescent of foam, upperworks glinting in the harsh sunlight. By comparison the little fishing boat still seemed a long way off.

'Full ahead!' He kept his glasses trained on her bows, and then breathed out with satisfaction as they began to swing towards him. 'They've seen us at last!'

He peered quickly over the screen as the *Temeraire* rose to her full buoyancy, her black flanks streaming with spray as she gathered speed and pushed harder into the clear water. There was weed on her plates too, and he could see a few bright scars left by the depth-charges. In spite of his inner anxiety the sight seemed to reassure him, and some of the watching lookouts saw him smile and run his hand along the top of the screen like a man stroking a great beast.

Never before, even on trials, had the *Temeraire* mounted such a surface speed. The great bow waves creamed back from her rounded stem, high sided and steep like ocean rollers. The whole fin vibrated wildly, and long streamers of spray floated above their heads in ragged arrows.

A messenger shouted, 'Sonar still in contact, sir! Submarine now bearing green four five! Range four thousand yards! Her present course is still zero nine zero!'

Jermain banged his fist on the wet metal. The enemy commander must have heard the *Temeraire* by now. With all stops pulled and the damaged screw whining like a bandsaw, she would be hard *not* to hear!

He found himself smiling again. No wonder the other commander was clearing out of the area. For all he knew, the *Temeraire* might be after him!

He shouted, 'Continue tracking! He may decide to have a go!'

There was a high-pitched whistle and he ducked his head as a tall waterspout rose lazily midway between the submarine and the fishing boat. 'Port twenty!' He craned his head to watch the orange flash from the pursuing ship astern. Again the sharp, abbreviated whistle close overhead. He could almost feel the rush of air, taste the foul bite of cordite as the shell exploded on the water beyond the swinging bows.

'Steady! Steer two seven zero!' He lifted his glasses to watch the other ship. If only they could fire one torpedo at her. But there were too many in the game for that now. There was no time. No time left.

He snapped, 'Signal the fishing boat to lower their dinghy! We'll pick them straight out of the water!' He heard the clatter of the Aldis, and marvelled that the nineteen years old signalman was keeping his head.

He ducked his head again as another shell shrieked past the fin and ricocheted across the flat water before exploding with a sullen bang.

Through his glasses he could see the fishing boat's deck very clearly now. He could make out Haley's tall figure struggling with the *Temeraire*'s dinghy abaft the wheelhouse, assisted by Nettle and Cowley. Colquhoun appeared to be at the helm, and he could see Wolfe sitting on the deck below the ladder. He was the only one not employed, and Jermain said aloud, 'I think Number One must be wounded!'

The gap narrowed rapidly. It was far enough. With half a mile still between them Jermain rapped, 'Open the forehatch! Stand by deck party to take on dinghy!' He saw one of the lookouts trembling uncontrollably and added calmly, 'No point in leaving anything lying about, eh?'

The man nodded and dragged his eyes from the last fall of shot. 'That's right, sir. We might as well keep the bastards guessin'!'

Jermain leaned forward to watch the big hatch being jacked open. Now the submarine was really vulnerable. She could not dive. She was a sitting duck.

'Watch out for aircraft!' Then he cupped his hands. 'I shall not stop the engine, so get ready to grab the dinghy!' He saw the huddled deck party watching him anxiously, their bodies frail and vulnerable to the screaming shellfire. Jermain made himself speak slowly, 'Remember all the practice you had with the C.N.D. dinghy! You should be able to do it blindfolded!' Mercifully, someone grinned and waved up at him. He snapped, 'Signal the fishing boat to bale out!'

He watched Colquhoun lean from his wheelhouse and raise his arm in reply to the brief message. There was a splash, and he saw Haley leap down into the dinghy, his hands already groping for the outboard motor.

There was a sharp crack astern, and the air was filled with screaming splinters. Jermain ducked his head as they clanged against the steel or thudded into the fin's fibreglass covering. He heard a sharp cry and turned to see the young signalman slipping down the side of the cockpit, his eyes wide and frightened as he stared at the blood which poured from his shoulder.

A lookout seized the boy and yelled, 'First-aid party on the bridge!'

The signalman looked dazedly at Jermain and said, 'It's okay, sir! I'm all right really!' Then he fainted.

Lieutenant Kitson struggled past the stretcher party and joined Jermain in the cockpit. He was carrying some glasses and peered quickly at the fishing boat. Between explosions he yelled, 'All electrical circuits are working well, sir!'

Jermain smiled. 'You already told me! But you might as well stay if you want to!'

Then he forgot Kitson's excited face as one of the deck party called, 'They haven't left the boat yet, sir!'

Jermain swore savagely. The shell fire was getting more accurate. It only needed one true hit to prevent them from diving. He levelled his glasses as Kitson said thickly, 'It's the first lieutenant, sir! He's fighting with Colquhoun!'

Jermain watched the little drama and felt his elation changing to dread. He could see Wolfe's mouth opening in a wild grin as he pushed Colquhoun back on the bulwark while the other sailors swayed helplessly in the dinghy.

One of the seamen was holding a limp body on the side of the dinghy, and Jermain gussed it was Lightfoot. It was strange he had not seen him earlier. But perhaps he had died when the submarine had made her first attack.

He felt the spray slashing over the bridge as another shell exploded astern. 'Starboard fifteen! Steer two nine zero!' When he looked up from the gyro repeater Wolfe had vanished, and then Jermain saw him slamming the wheelhouse door to seal himself inside. Colquhoun seemed to falter, and then as another shell filled the air with jagged splinters he leapt over the rail and cut the dinghy's line.

A messenger said urgently, 'Sonar reports submarine contact is turning, sir! Now bearing green six zero! *Closing*!'

Jermain gripped the screen with all his strength and concentrated on the small, gleaming dinghy. 'Come on! For God's sake, come *on*!'

Kitson said, 'Number One's steering the fishing boat, sir! What the hell has got into him?' Then he saw Jermain's face and added quietly, 'Poor bastard. It must have been too much for him.'

Jermain lifted his glasses and watched the dinghy as it scudded towards the onrushing submarine. The faces of the men leapt into focus, so that he could see each line of suffering and fear. Colquhoun crouched by the bow, with one hand on the dead sailor beside him. Haley was sitting upright, with his fingers round the tiller, his eyes already gauging the approach.

The other two were staring back at the fishing boat, which was still steaming on the same course, her diesel sending a steady plume of blue smoke over her wake.

Jermain said heavily, 'Slow ahead! Stand by on the forecasing!'

He felt the tension sapping his remaining strength as the first grapnel missed its target. But the next fell beside Colquhoun, and as the line jerked taut the waiting seamen dashed forward to haul the dinghy up and over the curved hull.

A messenger, who had been stooped intently over his microphone, rolled his eyes and yelled, 'Sonar reports torpedoes approaching from starboard, sir!'

Jermain dragged his eyes from the gaping hatch and the dinghy which was still being manhandled below. 'Full ahead! Hard astarboard!'

It would not be in time. He could feel the urgent thrust of the screw and the sluggish swing of the bows.

Kitson seemed unable to take the glasses away from his eyes. 'I can see them, sir! Two torpedoes running just below the surface! Jesus! They're coming right at us!'

There was a dull clang from the casing, and a messenger said in a broken voice, 'Fore hatch shut, sir!'

Jermain raised his own glasses and watched the twin parallel lines streaking through the glittering water towards him. So it had all been in vain. He had brought the *Temeraire* and every man aboard to this.

He blinked as the left lens of his glasses hardened into a white, thrusting bow wave. Like a man in a trance he heard Kitson screaming, 'It's Number One! Oh Christ Jesus, *look at him*!' He was sobbing uncontrollably as the little fishing boat steamed purposefully across the *Temeraire*'s swing bows, her blunt outline blotting out the twin white lines as she passed.

Jermain shouted, 'Clear the bridge! Stand by One and Two!' With his eyes still on the little fishing boat he pressed the diving button and heard the klaxon screaming below him.

Once, as the sunlight glanced off the boat's wheelhouse, he imagined that he could see Wolfe looking at him. He was standing quite still and relaxed, even as the two torpedoes bit into the frail hull and exploded in one deafening roar.

As the *Temeraire* filled her tanks and plunged into a steep dive, Jermain threw himself through the hatch. Above, patterned against the bright sky, he could see the remains of the shattered boat falling like so much matchwood. They seemed to fall very slowly, as if unwilling to return to the sea.

His feet thudded into the control room as the lower hatch was slammed shut. Colquhoun was standing beside his father, his eyes dull with fatigue.

Jermain snapped, 'Hold her at sixty feet! The submarine is at periscope depth!' He waited, counting the seconds as the lights kept up their merry dance.

The intercom barked, 'Ready to fire, sir!'

Jermain dropped his hand and the speaker intoned, 'Fire One!' He felt the slight thud as the torpedo left the tube. 'Fire Two!' Then the voice said, 'Both torpedoes running, sir!'

'Up periscope!' He hardly recognised his own voice.

The sea was calm again, but for a few scattered pieces of bobbing flotsam. He moved the handles briefly to watch for the other ship. It had altered course, baffled by the *Temeraire*'s sudden dive.

He remembered Colquhoun's stricken face as he had clambered aboard with Lightfoot's body. There was a story there, he thought. But it could keep. Colquhoun had done well. They had all done well.

He tensed as a double explosion rumbled through the sea and battered against the *Temeraire*'s hull. Then there were other, disjointed sounds, terrible noises of tearing metal, accompanied by the jubilant inrush of water.

Then he saw it. Just briefly. Like the ending of a nightmare. The sticken submarine's stern was rising straight up out of the sea, her twin screws still turning, burnished in the sunlight.

Around him, excluded from what he could see through the periscope, the others watched his face and waited.

Jermain saw the grey hull begin to slide under a welter of giant air bubbles and a thick, spreading blanket of black oil. It was like blood, he thought.

Then with sudden force the submarine gave up the fight and went into a steep dive. For many minutes they all heard her falling, down and down, the toughened steel screaming through the water as if in torment.

Jermain stepped back from the periscope and said, 'Bring her round to one seven zero. Dive to six hundred feet.'

When he looked again through the periscope he could see the water already closing over the upper lens to blot out the nodding flotsam and the spreading stain of oil.

Mayo asked quietly, 'Shall we attack the A/S trawler, sir?'

Jermain shook his head. It was almost an effort to reply. 'No, Pilot, We'll leave them to talk about it.' He looked around at the tired, watching faces. 'I think someone should talk about it!'

The *Temeraire* lifted her rudder and dived deep into the embracing darkness, and set course for home.

THE END